Unnatural Selection

Ryan Stark

Also by the Author:

Killing by the Book
The Farm

ISBN: 9781793919908

To my late father, Austin, who never saw my writing.
Hopefully somewhere out there he is smiling.

ACKNOWLEDGMENTS

As I have remarked upon before, writing is a lonely occupation – just me, a screen and twenty or so people who don't exist.

Again, I need to salute the forbearance of my family. Val had become somewhat of a writing widow, as I spent much of my free time in a small box room carving out words. However, now I am semi-retired and can put in a day shift, so we spend more time together. As always, my eldest daughter Emma has provided her proofreading expertise.

I would also like to acknowledge the assistance given to me by Apple Support. Whilst writing Unnatural Selection, my computer was stolen. With one free call – via the Philippines, US and Ireland, they emailed me with receipts dating back many years, allowing me to submit my insurance claim and replace the equipment within two weeks.

Most of all, I would like to thank those readers and fellow authors who have taken the time and trouble to exchange a few words with me. It's always good to hear from you.

Chapter 1

Alton Road Retail Park, Northolt, 2:00am, 5th June

Dean Hewell rubbed the cramp from his knees and attempted to stretch his legs in the confines of the front seat. They were late. If there was one thing that irked him it was tardiness; the knowing theft of a few minutes of someone else's life. Every day there were more reasons to quit this bloody job, even if that meant driving a desk. Lighting another cigarette, picking a fragment of tobacco from his tongue, he testily wiped it off on his trouser leg. He really needed to pee.

Beyond the windscreen and the orange of the dash, the car park was black and still. Hewell's Range Rover stuck out like a spot on a teenager's forehead, too damn obvious, even in the shadow of the loading bay.

In his pocket, his phone buzzed. A text.

Are you there as arranged?

He texted back—*I'm here.*

Opening the door, Hewell circled the Range Rover and relieved himself in the shadows. Above him, a caterpillar of truck roofs rumbled along the North Circular as Wednesday night yielded to Thursday morning. Information or not, he couldn't hang around forever. He was where he shouldn't be meeting people he shouldn't and that rarely came out good. But information on Azeri was hard to come by so he had to believe it was worth the risk.

Checking his watch, only the second hand had moved, slower than a constipated tortoise. They had better appear soon or he was off. Why did these guys keep such odd hours, anyway?

Hewell was sick of the job. Unsociable hours, spending more time away from the office than in it. He rarely told the truth, spent most of his time remembering his cover story and a name that belonged to someone else. There were times when he believed he had become his cover, become Colin Standish, become the snivelling, street corner dealer. Times when Dean Hewell, Detective Sergeant, seemed a distant memory. The glamour of undercover operations had definitely worn off.

Glamour? That was a joke. Six months of reeking stairwells, seedy hotel rooms and sordid flats, seeking out Urdin Azeri. Incremental steps. Hewell wanted out and after tonight he would have the means to engineer that.

A dart of fear shot through him. He opened the centre console and pulled out the other phone. One number in its memory. For emergencies only, Dean. Don't spoil my evenings. Ringing at 2:00am would really piss off the Inspector, especially as he wasn't meant to be there in the first place.

Returning the phone, he picked up his own and texted Janine.

Thinking of you, Babe

Lonely without you need you to keep me warm xx

Hewell felt his stomach flutter, his crutch tighten.

There was a rap on the glass and Hewell's heart leapt to his throat. A black shadow filled the side window.

Back soon. Promise.

Frustrated and annoyed, Hewell returned the phone to his pocket and wound down the window, assaulted by bad breath, patchouli and stale body odour. Potter wore army surplus, a grimy cap pulled tight over wiry ginger hair.

"Col, glad it's you. You got anything?"

He was crap with names and even after all this time, it took a beat to realise it was his.

In front, the faint silhouette of a vehicle parked up a hundred yards away, a flash of lights. Four round halo eyes briefly opened, a cat biding its time. They had arrived and Potter needed to leave. Digging behind the speaker grille, he dangled a small Ziploc bag in front of Potter, whose eyes grew large as pennies. A greedy hand, dirty, broken nails eagerly reached for the bag. Hewell pulled back.

"Ah-ah, Potter. Payment before product."

A pained expression crossed Potter's face, a kid denied sweets. Reluctantly, he reached into his pocket and handed over a folded, scruffy twenty.

"You're a bloody life-saver, Col."

"Piss off, Potter." Transaction done, he turned away and wound up the window. It had taken a week to broker this meeting. He wasn't going to sacrifice it for a junkie. The tune on the radio had changed; more sentimental garbage. Again the BMW flashed its lights, four lids flicked more urgently. He flashed his own headlights. Hopefully, the junkie's presence had not spooked them.

Hewell started. There was a pop, a sound like someone spilling porridge and the window peppered red. Then, it occurred to him. The car, Potter's sudden appearance. Col, glad it's you. Had he been set up?

He swung around as the muzzle of the silencer eyed him through the gore and he felt the merest tap on his brow.

Chapter 2

Alton Road Retail Park, 8:00am, 5th June.

Screwing up his nose at the stench, PC Keith *The Uniform* Parrish staved off the nausea and leaned in to the microphone on his chest. Blow flies had already begun to gather.

By the time he and Rob Briggs had arrived, the Range Rover was already alight, sending a tower of noxious clouds bubbling skywards. Now blackened and skeletal, the steaming wreck had disappeared under a forensic tent along with the driver and the charred bundle of rags on the ground beside it.

There was always an extra edge to a shout where death was involved. The image of the corpse burned into the mental album that he would leaf through when sleep wouldn't come. Then there were protocols to remember, procedures to follow, an ever-growing crowd of ghoulish onlookers to manage. Control had informed him that the owner details for the Range Rover were withheld, adding an extra layer of intrigue.

But none of those were Keith Parrish's main concern.

Detective Sergeant Deborah Whetstone of the North West London Homicide Unit scanned the scene from the open door of her VW Golf. He saw her shoulders drop as she spotted him. Compared to the tall stocky traffic cop, Whetstone was tiny. Her hair was short, blonde, a tousled style like the swirls on top of coffee. Dressed in a T shirt and jeans underneath a maroon blazer, she drew the lapels together and strode over. Detective Constable Mike Corby, a tall, mop-haired man with a rather blushful face, left the passenger side and trudged off to take statements. A pretty good detective, he had picked up on Whetstone's mood and decided to leave them to it. After all, he was looking towards his stripes.

"Deb. Morning."

"PC Parrish." Whetstone forced a brief, practised smile, the rank to emphasise that this was an official call. "What have we got?"

After six months, their relationship had ceased to be station gossip. In fact, it had all but ceased to be anything. Parrish was in two minds which was his biggest problem - the two charred bodies or Deb Whetstone.

He shuffled self-consciously. "Gov. Passers-by reported the fire and a crew attended at around 3:45am. Range Rover. One occupant, front driver's seat, a second body outside by the driver's door."

"Do we have IDs?"

"No, gov. Len Ganlow and Harry Ramesh are in there now."

"What about the car?"

"Details withheld."

Parrish puffed hard and cast his eyes about. In amongst the hordes of ghouls and onlookers, maybe the firebug was still there, admiring his handiwork.

"Have a word with Briggs." Whetstone threw a finger towards the other uniformed officer. "Keep it amongst ourselves for now. Send any details through to Detective Sergeant Monaghan when you have them. I have a nasty feeling about this."

Chapter 3

Hanover Road, Wembley, 8:00am

The Renault van was the only vehicle on the petrol station forecourt. Conspicuous, white, a sitting duck. Above, a tube train clattered across the viaduct which made the street a dead-end. One way in and one out.

Mick Bullard cursed his bladder as he trotted around to the kiosk for a key to the lavatory. This was a young man's game - a younger man with a bigger bladder. They should not have stopped. Not for coffee. Not for a slash. Behind him, Tony Mason drummed on the steering wheel, anxious to get shot of the load and back home.

Returning the key, Bullard's mouth watered at the smell of warm pies. He had never been a cook. Peg had raised the kids and kept house while he had been off getting his face rearranged for a few quid. Now he looked like a bulldog in a fairground mirror. Searching for change, he heard a bell as a BMW pulled onto a pump. Alert, no longer hungry, he watched the girl in the kiosk turn to eye it lazily, waiting for the light on her console. From the window, an object arced towards a bin, the car drove off and was gone. The girl returned to her phone. Bullard breathed again.

It had been almost a month since masked raiders had looted the Westsiders van, stolen ten kilos and left a man maimed for life. They used BMWs, or so Mick had heard. Picking up his pace back to the van, he looked around warily but the car had pissed off. Good riddance.

The girl in the kiosk was on her mobile, twisting the ponytail around her finger, her face a warm, lascivious grin. He imagined the boy at the other end jerking himself off. He felt suddenly heavy, wrinkled and old. Then he stopped. A squeal of tyres, a punch of adrenaline as he caught the flash of lights in the garage windows.

Shit!

Chapter 4

Easing back the tent flap, Whetstone gagged briefly at the smell of roast pork and burnt fuel. Four years in homicide hadn't annealed her to it. The humidity was rising, the white paper suit cloyed and the flies buzzed incessantly.

The car was a shell, skeletal and black, barely recognisable. Through the hole where the windscreen had been, a head was visible, a charred shop-window mannequin, gaping mouth, white teeth. A second charred mass lay beside the gutted hulk with the on-call Pathologist kneeling beside it.

Len Ganlow, a small matter-of-fact man with the air of a Trade Union Convenor, had stepped in following the untimely death of the previous pathologist, Professor Patrick Gascoigne. Irreverent and avuncular, preferring first names to surnames or ranks, Whetstone still missed his graveyard humour. Even now, she half expected him to come wheezing around the corner carrying his ever-present black bag and a fresh folded white overall, complaining about traffic and blustering in to command the scene.

"Len? You have a cause of death?"

"Sergeant. Preliminary cause for both bodies seems to be a gunshot wound to the head. At this stage I cannot definitively say whether the driver was shot pre or post mortem but there are no signs of a struggle. The rear of the skull may have exploded due to thermal pressure in the cranium but fires don't often leave a round hole in the forehead. If the bullet is in the car, we'll find it.

"I have taken blood samples for a carboxyhaemoglobin test but there is no soot in the upper airway suggesting he was deceased before the fire started."

"And the other one?"

"Some desiccation and scorching due to proximity but death was almost certainly as a result of a shot to the head. The fire hasn't made the muscles contract and there is no rigor so death would be in the very early hours, say midnight to 3:00am. I suspect they were both killed at the same time."

"The weapon?" Whetstone frowned as Ganlow shook his head.

She crouched down. Though blackened by soot, dampened by water and bearing a fixed rictus grin, the face was familiar.

"This is Danny Potter."

Ganlow paused. "If you say so."

"Local low-life. Crack addict." Whetstone considered the coincidence; glass lying next to a dead junkie, a burnt-out car with a broken side window. "So what? One shot for the junkie, one shot through the window, then torch the car?"

Ganlow cocked his head. "If I were to make a completely unprofessional, educated guess—I'm told you like them—I would say yes."

Whetstone stood and edged around the tent to where Ramesh was busy with the corpse of the driver.

"Sergeant Whetstone. We meet again so soon. Seems like only...oh, yes, nine hours." His face was only partly visible, tired and drawn, but Harry Ramesh's eyes were smiling.

"Ramesh, tell me."

"Twenty minutes, sergeant. I have barely got the overall on! Body's in the driver's seat. Looks like the fire was started in the rear footwell, using an accelerant. Judging by the smell, I would say, petrol but I will need further analysis. The driver's window is broken. In a fire, windows usually blow out but most of the glass is inside, over the driver, suggesting it was broken before the fire. I will need to sift through the contents of the car to locate the bullet, though."

Waving a thank you and goodbye, Whetstone left the tent, and dragged the mask from her mouth. The sweat cooled on her forehead and her lungs ached for the dry fresh June air to replace the stench of death. Around her, the crowd had hushed to an expectant hubbub, like the pauses between events on a school sports day. Parrish was leaning against a fence post, speaking into his chest radio. Stripping off the overalls, disposing of the gloves and plastic bootees, she ambled over.

"Deb." Parrish smiled broad and business-like but he was looking elsewhere. "You OK?"

"Yeah," she lied and turned towards the blackened shell of the Range Rover, once powerful, moody and desirable, now a memory, dead and cold. "Yeah, long night over in Brent, murdered teenager, then the funeral later. Lucky to get anything done today."

Parrish fidgeted. "Look, Deb. We have to talk."

"Seriously? You spend all day cooped up in that patrol car, listening to Radio 2 and you choose now?"

"When then? You tell me. For Christ's sake, Deb."

Saved by the bell, Whetstone drew her mobile from her pocket and glanced at the screen.

"Look, I have to be somewhere. Later, yeah?

Chapter 5

Hanover Road, Wembley, 8:12am

The van was only fifteen feet away, the car thirty. Bullard needed to get the boy away from here. He willed Tony to turn to catch a glimpse of his terrified expression. To reach for the sawn-off behind the seat.

What the Hell was he playing at? He was too old for this sort of caper. Fifty-eight and still sparring with kids a third of his age. Vicious bastards too. Paisley John had taken his pound of flesh over the years and, God knows, Bullard had repaid him in service and protection.

Then he froze as a second set of headlights, wide and angry, screeched around the corner. Rooted to the spot, he shouted to Tony, watching the boy's eyes widen as he fumbled with the keys. Doors slammed and shouts rang as three balaclavas jumped out and raced across to the van. Bullard felt a hand from behind and he was down on the floor wheezing like a broken accordion. A baseball bat was raised and he shied back.

"Not your lucky day, is it mate?" The accent was local, Middlesex, which puzzled him. The Cjevovod were *Polacks*.

In a sudden and inexplicable fit of bravado, Bullard cast the ski mask a look of contempt. "Piss off you wank-stain."

"Well, that's not very polite." The man's head bobbed and Bullard could tell he was chuckling. He wanted to leap up and punch that smile right through his spine. Twenty years ago he would have eaten guys like these for breakfast and still had room for elevenses. But as the man spoke Bullard's legs turned to lead.

"Urdin Azeri says *Hi*. Sorry, mate."

As the bat swung, blue and yellow stars filled the world. Through the fireworks, he remembered his training. Stay down and curl up. He heard the van windscreen explode and

Tony yelp as the young lad fell onto his face amid repeated blows. *Be gentle. He's only a nipper.* Then their attention returned to Bullard. Rolling onto his back, he tensed his stomach muscles against the boots and the bats, feeling every strike. He gritted his teeth as his leg exploded.

Then it stopped.

Opening his eyes, the blue skies were tinted red. A metallic taste filled his mouth. The pain in his legs gnawed up towards his groin consuming him like a savage beast. Somewhere Tony sobbed and coughed. At least the boy was still able to sob.

The three men were at the van. Muffled conversations through balaclavas, incoherent through the ringing in his ears. Middlesex? Definitely not foreign. He heard the metallic clank of the doors; the boxes being transferred. Twelve kilos. A huge amount of money when cut. Paisley John would be pissed.

One of the balaclavas bent down. His heavy breath had moistened the material around his mouth. A smell of stale tobacco on his breath.

"Thanks, mate. Urdin Azeri owes you one. You twat."

Yeah. Definitely Middlesex. A bat swung and the world flashed yellow then black before drifting away forever.

Chapter 6

St. Peter's Church, Iver, 11:00am

A meagre family group gathered around the grave, three generations, tearful and solemn, as the committal was read. Behind, a throng of immaculately uniformed colleagues from the Metropolitan Police Service, and minor dignitaries gathered. Some to show their respect for a man who moved in many circles, others to be seen doing so, some probably just for a day out in the sunshine.

Detective Inspector Scott Daley crouched under the shade of a sycamore, maintaining a respectful distance. Given the amount of top brass here today, that was probably the best place for him. His superior, Detective Superintendent Bilko Bob Allenby, of the North West London Homicide Unit, was in deep conversation with Assistant Chief Constable Diane Browning, probably involving some new strategy to emphasise Daley's inadequacies.

Ruefully, Daley mused on how few would muster at his graveside. Few of his colleagues. Certainly not Detective Superintendent Allenby, the mood he was in.

Ashes to ashes, dust to dust.

Tall and lanky, with a habitual stoop, Daley ducked below the low-hanging branches to get a good view of the show. A weak mid-morning sun, incongruous with the solemn occasion was flooding the graveyard, warm against his skin. The black suit was sticky and uncomfortable, not to mention the tie a noose. Eerily, the warmth of the sun was momentarily shrouded in cloud and he felt a shudder down his spine. Catching the moisture in the corner of his eye, Daley squeezed Theresa Somerville's hand. Petite and slight, with hazel eyes to match her short bobbed hair, she cast him a sympathetic smile. Too many people had been lost in the last few years but, as Daley smiled down at her, he knew one had been gained.

Occasions like this reinforced how lucky he had been to find her, by accident, in a cold, damp car park. They had been two pieces of a puzzle, separately incomprehensible and unfathomable but together suddenly lucid and logical. At a time when his life was spiralling into a toilet of post-traumatic depression and dependency on prescription drugs, it had been Terri who caught him when he fell. She held him when he woke to the demons in his head and she made it right.

Being the partner of a police officer was a solitary existence but paradoxically, what had destroyed his previous marriage now brought him and Terri closer together. As an Inspector at Harrow, keeping equally odd hours, each time they met was like the first time.

And she did look good in a uniform.

Professor Patrick Gascoigne, late Senior Home Office Pathologist, had died when his beloved black Jaguar S-type had careered off the road on his way home to Iver. The coroner had ruled accidental death. A stroke or a heart attack, maybe swerving to avoid wildlife. Igniting on impact, the body destroyed, investigations had been inconclusive.

Christened *the Dark Lord*, the Professor had been a rather curmudgeonly individual, with a reputational mystique stretching back some thirty years. However, since his death, he had relinquished most of his secrets. Much to Daley's surprise, he had a wife, children and grandchildren, and a private life he had never discussed. Much to Daley's disappointment, they were quite normal, with no proclivity for hanging upside down from the rafters, shying from crosses nor drinking the blood of virgins. Judith Gascoigne was a retired magistrate and the two daughters had gone into medicine, neither of them phlebotomists. Though, the granddaughters did look a little like the twins from *The Shining*.

The George Medal was a surprise. Characteristically, Gascoigne had never spoken of it. Daley had noticed a pronounced limp, especially when there was rain in the air, but had put this down to old age or arthritis. The truth turned out to be less prosaic. Called to a fatal shooting, and ignoring the attending officers, Gascoigne had waded in to save an injured boy. He had received a bullet to the leg as repayment.

If the man were here today, he would have quipped that, as a pathologist, letting one specimen get away was an oversight but, with the bullet narrowly missing the femoral artery, two was downright careless.

To Daley, however, Patrick Gascoigne had been simply *Prof.* Portly and well-spoken with thinning grey hair, imposing spectacles and an ability to be scrupulous in his work and light in his wit.

"Back in five." Daley planted a peck on Terri's cheek and reluctantly released her hand, instantly feeling the loss. Beyond the grave, beyond the mourners, Detective Sergeant Deborah Whetstone lifted a hand and nodded. Beside her, Detective Sergeant Dave Monaghan, a dour Irishman, at fifty-eight was some twenty years Daley's senior. Dependable. Safe as houses. Perhaps more so than Daley's own house in Alperton. Certainly, more than his seat in their Lambourne Road office.

"Sir." Predictably, Whetstone was in floods of tears. Beneath her black coat, she was wearing a modest skirt and patent leather shoes with a small heel. Daley thought back to the last time he had seen her legs and couldn't remember. Formal and smart, five years younger than he, Daley was concerned how tired she looked. With a spate of drug-related murders, the last three months had been busy ones. Monaghan, as constant as the stream of paperwork which flowed across his desk, wore a black overcoat, as long as his face, over his run-of-the-mill work suit. He nodded as the senior approached.

"Nice day for it. Good crowd and all that."

Daley smiled ruefully. "Yeah, Dave. Even managed to drag the ACC out from behind her desk."

"Sure, she'd be at your funeral too, Scott. Unscrew the coffin to make sure you were actually in it." The long Irish face cracked briefly, the bushy moustache wriggling like a furry caterpillar. Following Daley's meltdown, Monaghan had also leant a steadying hand.

Whetstone dried her eyes and squinted into a small mirror dabbing powder over puffy cheeks. "Sir, you know a Danny Potter?"

"Stringy fellow, smack-head. Ginger. Scabs." Daley pursed his lips and considered. That description could fit half the people he knew, many of whom were fellow policemen.

"'S' the one. Double shooting in a car park in Northolt. Unidentified corpse in a burnt-out car. Potter dead beside it. Medium calibre automatic. From the entry wound, Ganlow thinks they used a silencer." Whetstone sighed. It felt disingenuous speaking of a case in front of Patrick Gascoigne when the great man was barely cold.

Daley raised an eyebrow. "Silencer? A hit? Little extreme. Why would anyone order a hit on a junkie?"

"That was what I asked. Middle of a secluded car park. Could have just run him down."

"Could have just dealt him some full-strength smack and made a few bob on the side." Daley pictured Potter. Always one hit away from an overdose. Seems he got a hit of an entirely different kind.

"Len Ganlow thinks between midnight and 3:00am. There was a bag of blow by the body, so our best guess is Potter went to score. Then someone took him and his dealer out."

"Bit risky taking out a drug dealer. Someone's got more trouble than they asked for."

Chapter 7

Wembley, West London, 12:00pm

Paisley John McKaig let loose a guttural roar and hurled the pot across the kitchen, barely noticing the explosion of glass and coffee over the wall.

"You just tell him, not on my bloody watch, Dougie. You had better sort it out now or I will sort you out. Understand?"

The voice on the phone made to speak but was scythed down by the broad Glaswegian bark.

"And you can shut your fat pie-hole too. I don't employ you to give me excuses. I employ you to keep my manor in order. Now you get out there and find out who is stealing my stock, and do it quickly 'cos I want to rip them a new fuckin' arse."

Slamming the phone down, McKaig paused as the brown stain drizzled down the paintwork and the explosion of red lights disappeared from his retinas. It had been a mistake to throw the pot before pouring some out but somehow, the need for coffee had abated. Bullard wasn't the sharpest knife in the box but he wasn't employed for his intellect. He was there to protect the stock. So why had he and Mason driven *off-piste*?

Lately the van raids were becoming all too common. Everyone seemed to know McKaig's business. Stock movements, routes, and just when he would be at his most vulnerable. Since the last time, the drivers had been tooled up and ordered to remain with their vehicles yet still it was happening. Still, someone was stealing his gear right from under his nose. But it was not just the gear. McKaig realised how impotent all of this made him look.

Coming down from Glasgow with nothing but the nickname they gave him in Barlinnie, he had dragged himself up by the bootstraps and fought to the top of the firm. He was damned if he was going to bend over now. Of course, he knew who was responsible. For years there had been tensions between McKaig's firm the Westsiders and the Cjevovod. The Bosnian firm, ruled by Danilo Bašić, were vying for territory in West London that the Westsiders were not willing to relinquish. It had taken twenty years to build this territory. He was not going to hand it all to some *Polack* scum who had breezed in from Europe. If he didn't deal with these cabbage eating bastards quickly, it would be the Chinese, the Asians. For Christ's sake! What was this? A bloody charity?

The beast inside McKaig bellowed a roar and he hammered a fist on the work surface. They would all need to be taught a lesson and lessons from him were hard taught.

No-one messes with Paisley John McKaig.

Chapter 8

North West London Homicide Team, Lambourne Road

In March 2013, the Mayor's Office for Policing and Crime (MOPAC) released its first Police and Crime Plan. Receiving a mixed reception, it proclaimed its vision of policing to meet the needs of modern Londoners and to please the swathes of politicians riding on its back. Many saw the document as a paradox, declaring the need for economies whilst still demanding increases in effectiveness. The euphemistic *20:20:20 Challenge*, aimed to reduce key neighbourhood crimes by 20%, boost public confidence by 20%, and cut costs by 20%. Whilst the ninety-two pages espoused many initiatives, in the view of D/Supt Bob Allenby, it was short on practicalities. In a moment of poor judgement, somewhat recklessly in hindsight, he had shared his views with Assistant Chief Constable Browning at Patrick Gascoigne's graveside.

"Make sense, don't you think, ma'am? Streamlining the line of command. A greater presence on the streets. Fewer chiefs, more Indians."

"More Indians, very apt," she had countered. "It'll be like the bloody Wild West. Seasoned officers put out to pasture in favour of inexperienced juniors running around with no idea." It was widely known the ACC was vehemently against MOPAC.

Close to retirement with the prospect of a decent pension, Allenby himself may be side-lined. Still, he understood ACC Browning's nervousness. Since the release of MOPAC, everyone was looking over their shoulder, fearing an unseen axe.

"Yes, but the losses can be achieved by attrition. Surely, increasing bodies on the ground," - a phrase that, as leader of a homicide team, Allenby had smirked at when he first read it - "means a greater visible presence on the streets."

"Don't be so naïve, Bob, burglary rates, car crime, violent crime, offences are plummeting. Take it from me, MOPAC is a blunt instrument."

As the coffin lowered into the grave, she expanded upon her concerns.

"Times have changed. Counter-terrorism is the golden child nowadays. These days we need specialist skills, cyber-intelligence and new technologies. That's where the money is being directed now, Bob. Detecting and dismantling terrorist operations before they can take hold. Your average *bobby* as about as likely to come across a terrorist crime as they are a winning lottery ticket and by then it is often too late. Traditional policing is now the poor relation. We are dinosaurs."

"I take the point, ma'am, but that's progress. Surely it's just survival of the fittest, Natural selection?"

"There's nothing natural about it. Transfer our funding to Cyber-crime and you reduce our effectiveness. In turn, organised crime increases as does funding to terrorism. Where do you think terrorist finance in mainland Britain comes from? Drugs, prostitution, extortion, organised crime, all of which fall under the purview of Major Crime."

And I would lose half my budget mused Allenby. Bored with the argument, Browning diverted it.

"Bob, there are five Drugs Intelligence Units and three Homicide Units across my Command. I am planning to amalgamate some of them and streamline the middle tiers in the process. If the Commissioner wishes us to follow MOPAC recommendations, I need to give him something."

Even before the report, the Lambourne Road offices had been scheduled for disposal. Some bright spark with a degree in sociology had supposed that competing teams from Harrow, Hillingdon and Ealing would all play nicely together. Another Machiavellian toss-pot with a degree in human resources had probably worked out this was the best chance of binning a few on the way.

So move they all would—eventually. The impending relocation of Scotland Yard to the Curtis Green building signified that everyone was doing their bit, even the top brass.

As Scott Daley entered, he pulled himself from his reverie, and reread the initial report into the Northolt shootings. The murder of a police officer promised a painful investigation. The murder of two did not bear thinking about.

Chapter 9

Lambourne Road, 2:00pm

Relieved to be away from the church, DS Monaghan loosened his black tie and top button. He was not one for the maudlin reminiscences and rueful smiles, After Daley and Whetstone left the wake, he thanked Gascoigne's wife for a lovely spread, banked a few handshakes with the great and good and returned to work.

"How was it, sir?" DC Steve Taylor was hunched down, focussing on his monitor. Several decades Monaghan's junior, a few stone slimmer and an entirely different hue, Monaghan wondered what the young constable would have expected from a funeral.

"Well, you know, Stevie. Loads of crying, lots of fond memories and tributes which should have been paid while he was alive. You would have liked the buffet."

Taylor nodded dispassionately without turning from his screen. "I have never liked burials. Seems untidy. Lying in your own soup for all eternity. Every time the family walk past that cemetery, they will know he is there, rotting and cold, dressed in his best suit. At least with cremation, it's neat and tidy. Anyway, after the fire, he was half cremated anyway."

Monaghan grimaced. "Sure, you're a bundle of laughs today. Perhaps you should go and cheer up his widow?"

Behind him, cresting the top step, heaving open the double doors, Scott Daley glanced around the room. "Nice send-off, eh Dave?" he beamed.

There had been something irrepressibly upbeat about Daley since he had met Terri Somerville. Monaghan found it unnerving, given the state he had been in before.

"Sure, yes, he had a good innings and all that. I was just telling Stevie here, he would have enjoyed the buffet."

Daley frowned. "Not sure that is the point of the exercise, though, is it?"

"Dunno, sir. Most of the top brass hardly knew him. What else would they be there for if not the free lunch?"

"Jeez, Dave. Show a little respect. Did you know he had a George Medal?"

"Oh, yes. He showed it to me once, over a glass or two of Irish when I was over at his place."

"You've been to his house?" Daley was flabbergasted just how little he knew about Patrick Gascoigne, believing for many years that the professor had come with the lease on Loughton Street Forensic Laboratory and occupied a small dark attic room.

"Patrick and I were good mates. Had a lot in common." Smiling enigmatically, Monaghan let the inference hang and turned back to his desk.

Daley hung up his coat and lowered himself into his chair. "I will miss this place."

Taylor again stopped typing and considered. "I won't, sir. It's a shit-hole."

Of course, mused Daley, Taylor's summation was accurate. Around fifty feet square, with battleship grey walls and a meagre glimmer of daylight lazily edging through the strip of windows, the room didn't carry its age well. It was a haphazard archipelago of desks, arranged in islands of four, subsumed by a flora of beige and white stationery and singing to the calls of twenty desk phones. Every morning, when one entered, it felt like putting on someone else's dirty underwear, yet after ten years, one had grown used to it. Fond even. Or was it Stockholm syndrome?

Monaghan, not one for change, ran a hand over the pock-marked teak veneer of his desk. He would miss its history and character.

Earlier, Daley had kissed Terri goodbye as she returned to Harrow and he travelled in the opposite direction to Ealing. It was still three months until her maternity leave. She had decided that she wouldn't be returning, at least not to a front-line role. A vacancy would be opening up for an Inspector.

Which left Daley with a dilemma.

Whetstone was studying for her Inspector's exam. Allenby had made enquiries on the QT and she had a more than even chance of success in getting the post. Despite their sometimes rather too public differences, Daley felt he had knocked Deborah Whetstone into shape and she would make a fine Detective Inspector in a Homicide unit. However, the Harrow posting was not homicide and Daley would have to trawl the pond for someone half as decent.

Making himself a brew, he took a moment to browse the details of the Northolt shooting. Potter was thirty-five, though he looked much older than he would ever become even if the bullet had missed. Once a familiar face in the custody suite, the council had found him a bed and the custody sergeant had decided the magistrate had better things to worry about. Meaningless and utterly invisible, he earned his money from information. Tiny fragments of data which he gleaned from conversations, strung together and fed back to the right people. Had he learned one nugget too many?

Accessing the Fleet Management portal, Daley entered the VIN from the Range Rover. Frowning as the screen refused him entry, he pondered on the shooting as vague bells rang but he could not place the tune.

Behind him, he heard the soft metallic catch of the Goldfish bowl and felt the presence of his superior hovering in the doorway.

"Inspector. Do you have a minute?"

Chapter 10

The Goldfish Bowl, Lambourne Road

Housed in a corner of the Team Room, with a window onto Lambourne Road, the Goldfish Bowl was comfortable and warm. It was Allenby's inner sanctum, akin to a study or den, a plethora of golfing and angling memorabilia occupying the wall behind the mammoth desk. Daley settled himself into the *Throne of Doom,* an uncomfortable chrome and fabric chair with which D/Supt Bob Allenby tortured his visitors. To be seated in it meant trouble; a one-way torrent of guano, either self-inflicted or dropped from a great height.

The revelations that Patrick Gascoigne, behind the lab coat and odour of formaldehyde, was a perfectly normal family man, had unnerved Daley. He had known Bob Allenby for a similar length of time, yet in some ways, he hardly knew him at all. The Robert Allenby who took off the uniform, laid down the warrant card each night, was a complete mystery. Daley glanced at the photographs of Allenby's wife, of his children or grandchildren, yet he had never met them nor learnt their names.

Hearing a knock, Daley turned as Whetstone entered self-consciously, a chronic weariness painted across her face. Everyone seemed so pre-occupied at the moment. Everyone except him. What had he missed?

As Whetstone sat, Allenby leaned forwards and rested his chin on steepled fingers. "That burned-out Range Rover, Scott. Who have you spoken to about it?"

Daley raised an eyebrow, scouring the last few hours for any minor transgression which could have bounded the flights of stairs faster than he had. "No-one yet, sir. Briggs and Parrish attended and secured the site. DS Whetstone and DC Corby were on the ground."

"Er, yes," added Whetstone, cautiously. "Len Ganlow examined the victims and Harry Ramesh removed the vehicle.

DS Monaghan ran the VIN, but it came back with a Restriction Order. We were hoping to consult with you."

"Good, and the body on the ground?"

"Local druggie called Potter, after a fix and got more than he bargained for. Both were shot at close range. No firearms or shell cases recovered. We are waiting for full forensic reports. In the meantime, DC Corby is securing the CCTV from the rear of the superstore."

Allenby nodded. The Range Rover is assigned to a Detective Sergeant Dean Hewell of the Drugs Squad in Hillingdon, part of Organised Crime Command. He was operating undercover. Bells rung right up to the 7th Floor of Scotland Yard and Assistant Chief Constable Browning has requested a D Notice for the Press.

"Brown-nose?" remarked Daley. *"*Unusual for her to come down to the factory floor."

Allenby tutted and glanced sideways at Whetstone who quickly stifled a smirk. "Everyone knows your opinion of ACC Browning but like it or not, she's the boss."

Assistant Chief Constable Diane Browning and Scott Daley were a similar age, entering service at the same time. Gelling as friends, Daley soon realised the difference between *what you know* and *who you know* as Browning drove a desk to the top. Similar age, similar aspirations, entirely different trajectory. Whilst the friendship had waned as paths diverged, in a rare act of good judgement, Daley had felt it wise not to piss off this particular senior officer unlike virtually every other he had met since.

"Sorry, sir."

Why was this all so familiar? A Restriction Order usually meant a public figure or an undercover operation. Alongside the D Notice, or as they were now called Defence and Security Media Advisories—DSMAs—that meant it was serious. "Must be someone important to go to all this trouble."

Allenby nodded." This is the second undercover officer from the North West London Covert Drugs Intelligence Unit to be killed in as many months." He flourished a report sheet, with a photo of a young man, shaved head, mean attitude.

Then, like the lens of a camera being adjusted, the pieces slotted into place inside Daley's head. "CDIU? Joe Gordon. April. Burned-out car in Holborn. The same gun?"

"Potentially. The rounds are at the lab being compared."

"So what? Someone blew their cover?"

"That's a hypothesis but the ACC and I are not convinced."

"How so?" asked Whetstone.

"It's the manner of the killings. Drugs deaths are usually less clinical. Gordon and Hewell were killed by a professional. Unregistered weapon. Point-blank range and the bodies burnt. Shell cases retrieved. No clues left. Anyway, we have a meeting with ACC Browning at 9:00 sharp tomorrow. Until then, enquiries ongoing, bodies unidentified awaiting forensic reports. Need to know basis."

As the pair rose, Allenby called Daley back.

"How's it going, Scott?" Allenby's face cracked a paternal smile, which did not fool Daley for a moment.

"OK, sir. A twinge or two from my shoulder." Psychosomatically, he grabbed his shoulder and rotated it somewhat theatrically.

"That's not what I meant and you know it."

After a locomotive nearly killed him, Daley had suffered significantly. Whilst the physical wounds had gone, mental scars remained. There were nights he woke to screaming brakes and thudding engines, yet the man he saved came out unscathed, remembering nothing. Now all that remained were his pet gremlins, lurking in the depths of his soul, muttering to themselves. He was not worthy. His career was failing like his marriage had, his judgement slipping away.

And he needed to look over his shoulder because everyone knew.

"Oh, I almost forgot. Judith Gascoigne gave me this earlier at the funeral. It was behind the clock in his study at home.

Addressed to you." Allenby lifted a small *Jiffy* bag and passed it across.

As Daley closed the door behind him, Allenby rubbed the ache in his left arm and assumed his favourite position by the window. Outside, traffic was building along Lambourne Road forecasting a slow drive home. With a slot on the driving range booked for the evening, he hoped ACC Browning would either be quick in her deliberations or delay it until the morning.

Chapter 11

Central Middlesex Hospital, 3:00pm

When McKaig arrived at the hospital, he found Tony Mason dozing in a side ward. Quietly, he popped inside, fastened the door and closed the blinds.

"Tony. My man. How're you going?" McKaig cracked the broadest smile he could muster considering he wanted to tear Mason's head off. Twelve kilos.

Immediately alert, Mason tried to heave himself up in the bed but the pain made him slump down defeated. "Paisley John. Look, I'm sorry. We had only stopped a minute or two. They jumped us."

McKaig laid a hand on the boy's arm, warm and clammy. "I know that." The clammy hand squeezed slightly harder. "But you thought it was a good idea to disobey my orders?"

"Mick needed a piss. What was I supposed to do?"

McKaig felt the blood rising. He squeezed Mason's cheek until he thought his eyes would explode. "You should tell him to piss in a bottle. And the guys who jumped you? Who were they?"

"Polacks," Mason lied. "They had hoods but I am sure the shit they spoke was Polack. They jumped me in the cab and pulled me out. They had bats. One had a shotgun. I am sure I saw a shotgun."

"And *your* shotgun?"

"The van, Mr McKaig. Mick left it in the van. It was behind the passenger seat."

McKaig threw his arms in the air. "So not content with thieving my bloody gear, Bašić now wants my firearms. I'm surprised he didn't take the bloody van and have done with it."

"Azeri."

McKaig swung round, his eyes blazing. "What did you say?"

"It was Azeri's men who attacked us, not Bašić."

"Don't talk bollocks, you wee shite!" McKaig took a pace, raised a hand. Mason cowered and pain ripped through his chest like shards of steel.

"Honestly. I'm telling you. Before they laid into me, I distinctly remember the name. *Urdin Azeri sends his compliments.*"

McKaig stopped. The hand still raised. The name Urdin Azeri was becoming a thorn in his very considerable side. For a year or so, the trouble on his turf had been escalating. Violent beatings, intimidation, raids on shipments. It was becoming tiresome. Always the same message—*Urdin Azeri sends his compliments.* At first, he had assumed there was a new player in town. Someone tooled up with foreign money and an eye on the immense profits to be made from the manor. Nowadays, he wasn't so convinced. Turning, he lifted the blind and peered out. The uniformed officer was still leaning against the nurse's reception desk chancing his arm.

"So, you're in the van. You've just parked up. Tell me and make it good."

Mason steadied his breathing, waited for the weight on his chest to lift. "Mick said he was bursting. I pulled into the garage and stopped in the van."

"Commendable. Then what?"

"Well, suddenly the street was full of Beemers. The driver's door opened and some guy in a ski mask grabbed my arm. Next thing I know, I'm on the tarmac and they are laying into me. All I heard was *Urdin Azeri sends his compliments* and then I must have passed out. Woke up on a trolley here."

"Did they say where they were taking the gear?"

Mason shook his head solemnly.

"Urdin Azeri sends his compliments? I thought you said they spoke Polack?"

"Well, they must have said that in English otherwise I wouldn't understand but the rest sounded like *Polack*."

"Not Spanish?"

Tony Mason eyed McKaig quizzically and shrugged. "Sounded like *Polack* but I don't know. Foreign is foreign."

McKaig pondered for a moment. What had Mason to gain by lying to the most sadistic bastard he would ever come across, especially in a quiet room where no-one would hear his screams?

On balance, he believed him.

Patting Mason on the shoulder, McKaig pulled a magazine from his coat and threw it on the bed. "I bought you a comic from *The League of Friends. Top Gear.* It's about some dickheads who think they can drive around doing stupid things and get away with it. The young one keeps ending up in hospital. There is a lesson there, laddie. Learn it, and quick."

Chapter 12

When Deborah Whetstone had found out Keith *the Uniform* Parrish was the attending officer at Hewell's murder, the dread of meeting him made her feel sick. Then the awkwardness when they met, the lack of even the slightest arousal, the squall which blew up from nowhere. But most of all the eyes, darting this way and that but never at her. Keith had stopped calling her *Babe* and *Hun* months ago but today for the first time, it registered.

Now, as she sat heavily in her chair and turned on the ancient, steam driven computer, she knew it was over.

She called his number, in her mind a trite rehearsal of what she needed to say but yet again the words evaporated as the ringtone changed to voicemail and a third pointless *call me* message was all she could manage. Maybe he would call back. Something simple yet final. *I think we both know this is going nowhere. Still friends?* She glanced at her watch. Keith would still be on duty. Maybe he was unable to call.

And a million and one other excuses.

Of course, there had been break-ups before. Monumental, cataclysmic disintegrations where the world seemed irreparably fractured. Impossible to endure at the time, seemingly endless days of regret and self-recrimination, those were the easiest. There was a finality about them that made even the slenderest hope of a reconciliation inconceivable.

Then there were the gradual ones. Scorching flames of animal desire cooling to a permafrost of disinterest. Insidious and unacknowledged, a cancer choking the life from a relationship, until so little remained that one wondered if it ever existed at all. On reflection, that's where she was with Keith. He was always busy, an extra shift here, helping a mate there, his phone unanswered. In a relationship for just over a year and she couldn't remember the last time they had slept together.

Most painful were the rumours; office tittle-tattle which, had they been about someone else she would have revelled in. Oblique references to his infidelity, glossed over in matey backslaps and laddish banter. Keith had been assigned as her driver during a different investigation. In the frenetic weeks that followed, he unceremoniously discarded WPC Jane Morris, yet never devoted himself fully to her. Now, the talk was he had taken up with Morris again and she herself was to be unceremoniously discarded.

Was it some flaw of her personality that frightened men off? Did she wear an invisible cloak of enmity or antipathy that made her unattractive or formidable, or just cold? Or maybe it was this bloody job? Long, unsocial hours, wallowing in the misery and decay of other peoples' existences and dragging some of it away. Or was it her poor choice in men? There was no doubt she had a type. Men for whom a relationship was an adjunct, rather than a goal, the woman an accessory rather than a part of the whole. Keith was tall and stocky, every inch the image of a uniformed traffic cop. Solid, muscular, square jawed. From the start, she was punching above her weight but in those first few months she had believed miracles could happen.

She looked about the Team Room. Dave Monaghan and Margaret; married so long they were indistinguishable. Mike Corby bouncing from one girl to the next without a care and Steve Taylor, she suspected, was waiting for the right man. Then there was Scott Daley. Divorced and bitterly single, he had somehow validated her sorry state. As her relationship with Keith stuttered and slowed, at least she could believe Daley was still worse off than she. Now, even he was settling down.

Six months into the relationship, Daley and Terri Somerville, the petite Scottish Inspector from whom he had stolen a Missing Persons case, were moving in together. Before Terri, Daley had been a broken man dragging himself through each day, chained to the trauma of a year that nearly killed him. Whetstone was pleased for them but she envied them in equal measure.

Perhaps she should reinvent herself? Maybe now was a time for change? Blonde since she had met Keith, an unconscious attempt to live up to the type of girl she pictured him with; an attempt to measure up to Jane Morris, from whom she had stolen him. Perhaps, she should try auburn or even red? Should she take a lead from Scott Daley and sell the house in Ealing? Cast herself off from the anchor of memories it contained, reinvent herself in a new place, a new job, a new town?

Chapter 13

The Sonata Cafe, Egmont Street, Wembley

After leaving the hospital, Paisley John McKaig detoured past Hanover Road to make sure there had been a thorough clean-up after the raid. Apart from a few rhinestone flashes of glass on the forecourt, there was nothing. Someone had spoken to the girl in the garage about what she had not seen. Such was her amnesia, she even forgotten being paid to forget. For good measure, they would follow the girl home to ensure her memory did not return.

On Wednesdays, McKaig held court in the Sonata cafe, when a steady stream of individuals came to hand over his cut of their takings. Tucked away in a side street in a quiet corner of Wembley, the run-down establishment relied heavily on the patronage of McKaig's firm, the Westsiders, to stay afloat. Little had changed in half a century, with mock Tudor beams and check thermoplastic floor tiles, the walls carried faded pictures of the Italian Riviera, vying for space above the scuffed Norwegian wood panelling. There was a vague undertone of tarry tobacco and congealed lard beneath the aroma of fried bacon and cheap coffee. Big band music played loud enough to be heard but quiet enough to be annoying. No self-respecting citizen would venture there, unless they needed a loan at extortionate rates along with more trouble than they could handle. Or they owed McKaig.

For private affairs, he kept an office in the less than salubrious living quarters behind the cafe. By the time Dougie Murdoch arrived, McKaig had poured a scotch and propped his feet up on the desk. Dressing smart yet casual in a black T-shirt, leather jacket and jeans, Murdoch drew up a chair.

To the casual observer, McKaig and his second in command were polar opposites. What McKaig lacked in intellect and tact, Murdoch had in spades. Stubbled and overweight, McKaig had the appearance of a rutting walrus and the temperament to match. Conversely, Murdoch was small and wiry, with searching eyes. He also supplied patience, restraint and the voice of reason when McKaig tried to think for himself. During a three stretch at Barlinnie, the two men had become friends, or at least not enemies. McKaig considered himself a hard man but time inside is tough without a compatriot. He had seen Murdoch take the complete works of Lord Byron into a confinement cell. He had also seen him disembowel a man with a toothbrush and barely a splash of blood. That was real class.

More importantly, Murdoch was the only person McKaig could fully trust.

Dispensing with pleasantries, McKaig began. "I have decided. I have reached my limit with Danilo Bašić. I cannot allow him to get away with this."

Murdoch frowned and brushed lint from his trousers. McKaig was thinking for himself again. Never a good sign. "So, what do you want to happen here, John?"

"That place in Neasden? The meat processing factory?"

"What of it?"

"Round up some men and torch the place. Burn the bastards alive and all of his gear. Let's see how he likes it."

"What will that prove? He has more than one warehouse. He has spread his risk like we spread ours."

"Bollocks. We can just blame it on Azeri, like Bašić does."

"Azeri?" Murdoch sighed. It was a familiar name heralding a familiar conversation.

"Yes, Dougie, Urdin Azeri. That's all I bloody hear these days. When a shipment gets boosted, it's Azeri. Tony Mason today, again Azeri. Blue tits peck the top off the milk, it's bloody Azeri. *Urdin Azeri sends his compliments to Paisley Bloody John.* Well, let's see how Bašić like it. I think Urdin *bloody* Azeri needs to burn down a warehouse."

"I would advise against a knee-jerk reaction. That would only invite more trouble." McKaig's head turned and the eyes flared but Murdoch held up a hand. "Hang on, hear me out before you start breaking stuff."

McKaig furrowed his brow and disconsolately turned back to his phone.

"We need to get our own house in order before burning down someone else's." Murdoch pulled a handwritten list from the pocket of his jacket. "There are ten names on this list. Me and you, Fat Leon, Aidan and Eddie," Murdoch pointed at McKaig's personal bodyguard and the two knuckleheads beyond the door in the cafe. "The rest are street bosses and managers. When we make plans, we involve only the names on the list. If the plans leak, we know it was one of us who leaked them. Also, let's spread some misinformation, see if we can wheedle out the mole in our organisation."

"And what about the bastard who is jerking me about?"

"All in good time, John. Right now, it's about damage limitation. We need to stop the raids, stop the rot. Then our patience will be rewarded. Trust me on this."

"And Bašić?"

"Nothing. We do nothing." Murdoch locked eyes with McKaig, as one would with an angry bull.

"Dougie. That bastard is costing me a fortune and making me look like a pussy. He is laughing his fat, ugly Polack head off at my bloody expense. I want his head on a stick."

"Look, John. You agree Bašić has a mole in our camp?"

"Yes...?"

"And he uses Urdin Azeri and the Encubierto as a cover. Plausible deniability?"

The words were getting longer and McKaig was struggling. "If you say so..."

"So, once we catch the mole, the raids will stop and Bašić will pick on someone else. Urdin Azeri will fade into legend and we can all get on with our lives."

"Just like that?"

"Just like that."

"And if he doesn't?"

"I will help you sharpen the stick."

Chapter 14

Ivan Terzić unnecessarily flashed the lights of his Ford as the whirls of dust caught the warm breeze. Through the clouds, the head of Danilo Bašić, leader of the Cjevovod, slowly appeared from the ancient Mercedes, warily looking left and right. As his boss sat in the passenger seat, Terzić passed across a takeout cup and breathed a sigh of relief.

"Boss, you got to get rid of the Mercedes. It's like a wart on a whore's face. You could not advertise your presence better if you employed dancing girls and a big band."

Bašić sniggered. "Since when do I take orders from you, Ivan? Anyway, I like that car. She is like a sister to me. Better than this shit-heap."

"Maybe you could borrow this shit heap and travel incognito now and again? However much you want to be inside your sister, perhaps sometimes a change is as good as a rest." Terzić's shoulders raised and lowered spasmodically as he chuckled at his own wit.

Bašić harrumphed. He was in no mood to take instruction from his second in command though he knew the diminutive balding Bosnian only had his best interest at heart. The Westsiders' men would probably have the number of the Mercedes tattooed on their genitals, so they would remember it even when taking a pee. But that Mercedes was a classic. It imbued its owner with style and taste... even if the Greeks used them as taxis. He sipped at the coffee and winced.

"Decaf skinny, idiot. This tastes like half a cow is in there."

Terzić curled his mouth sheepishly, wiped coffee stains from the lid of his own, then swapped the cups.

"So, are we ready for tonight?" Bašić half turned and locked eyes with Terzić. Down to business. Terzić nodded.

"And the shipment? Will it fit in the Mercedes?"

"Easily, boss." Terzić pulled out a pack of *Gitane*, squeezing the sides and flipping a couple out. After the pair had filled the car with pungent smoke, Bašić picked a fragment of tobacco from his lip and continued.

"So what are the plans?"

"Bruno and Alva will take the van. They will follow the pre-arranged route. We will have a car behind just in case."

"And the Mercedes?"

Terzić tapped the side of his nose, cascading ash into his lap. "No, boss. If the Westsiders have a mole in our camp, I need to keep that to myself. I reckon Bojan and Daris would be the best ones. Daris can drive. Bojan is better with guns. I will tell them the route before they leave."

"What? I am to trust that little shit with my car? He will tear the engine out."

"Really, boss. You gotta have a little faith. Anyway, you can tear his lungs out in return, if he so much as scratches it." Once more Terzić's shoulders danced spasmodically. "You know he is sniffing about your niece, Sonia?"

"Like I said, little shit. Perhaps, I tear his balls off instead. He better look after my car, that's all." Bašić risked the coffee and pondered. "I need you to arrange something else."

Terzić turned. "Anything boss."

Earlier, news of the raid in Wembley had ruined his lunch. The word on the street was that the Cjevovod had mounted a deliberate raid on the Westsiders. An encroachment. The Westsiders had lost twelve kilos and no-one knew where it was. More the point, Anatoly, his sector boss in the old country was asking questions. The Cjevovod was losing face.

It was so easy for Anatoly. He spoke, it happened. Thousands of miles away, insulated from the minutiae, the detail. For Bašić, at the sharp end, it was more complicated. There were routes to run, houses, whores, street firms, not to mention the legitimate businesses. Now, Bašić's nerves were on edge. He knew he was running out of opportunities to put things right. He had to regain the trust of the Cjevovod before they lost faith in him.

"Ivan. We need to hit the Westsiders hard."

Chapter 15

Loughton Street Forensic Laboratory

Daley had never become accustomed to post-mortems. The point in time where a living, breathing person with a lifetime of experiences, forebears and antecedents, jobs, responsibilities and cares, is reduced to a slowly decaying bag of evidence, to be pawed, sliced and dismantled. Len Ganlow's approach always seemed to Daley to be more agricultural than Patrick Gascoigne's, as if the latter had yet to accept life was extinct was doing everything he could to keep his patient comfortable.

Providing a running commentary into an overhead microphone, Len Ganlow eased the roasted corpse of Dean Hewell from the black plastic bag, stiff and posed, like a victim of Pompeii, fixed in time by Vesuvius. Then Daley felt his stomach roll as the pathologist set about the thorax and sawed off a rack of ribs. Beneath the surface, the blackened flesh and the smell of Sunday dinners had given way to a raw pinkness and the odour of an abattoir. Ganlow and his assistant carefully removed and weighed the vital organs, writing up details on a whiteboard. Taking a scalpel, he ran it over one lobe of the right lung, stripping it back to reveal glistening salmon pink flesh.

"No sign of smoke inhalation. Subject to toxicology, he died before the fire."

Turning his attention to the head, Ganlow called over Harry Ramesh. The two craned nearer as he scored a line around the roughened head with a scalpel. The flesh, stiffened by the fire separated like the rubbery rind beneath crackling, folding forwards like peeling off a swimming cap, over the face to reveal the skull. It reminded Daley of jam mixed into yoghurt, uneven, purple, red, grey. With the heart stopped and sitting in a tray on the side counter, barely a trace of blood flowed.

"There you go." Ganlow pointed a blue latex finger at the pinkness of the forehead. There was a neat, almost perfectly round hole.

"Cause of death?" asked Daley.

"Maybe." Reaching over for a small handheld saw, Ganlow traced an arc around the line of his previous incision. With a surreal sound, like a large ladle taking a spoonful of blancmange, the dome came free.

"Yes, Inspector. Cause of death. Extensive brain trauma caused by a gunshot wound to the front of the head." This time Daley could see. The grey pinkness of the brain could have a weird beauty, like the undulating landscape of coral viewed from above, wave patterns in the bed of a tropical sea. The rear of Dean Hewell's brain resembled chopped meat, tracked with wormholes and smashed by the bullet, distorted and flattened, as it rattled around inside the skull.

Behind Daley, Ramesh craned for a better look.

Ganlow sensed his impatience and smiled. "I'll let you have the bullet when I find it, Ramesh." Ganlow turned to Daley. "I will examine stomach contents and toxicology but a brain like Eton mess is a bit of a slam-dunk."

Two hours later, with the smell of the charnel house lingering in his nostrils, the disquiet that Daley felt earlier had multiplied. Serious though the cold-blooded murder of a police officer was, he could not understand why the investigation had not already started. Maybe in the morning, he would find out what was going on.

Chapter 16

Neasden, 1:13am, 6th June

"All clear."

Bojan kept his eyes peeled as the Mercedes headed out towards the North Circular. His hands were shaking on the stock of the shotgun. Fortunately, Daris was driving.

Earlier, Danilo Bašić himself had visited the warehouse, an event so rare Bojan could not remember another occasion. Christened *the Mad Bear*, Bašić was a man to be feared. When he turned up, one either made oneself busy or scarce. Gathering the men together in the centre of the warehouse, Bašić had gone ballistic. There had been five raids, two on Cjevovod shipments. The word was that the Cjevovod was losing face, unable to manage its own operations. Unable to manage its own people.

Then Ivan Terzić had chosen Bojan and Daris for the night's transport. They were to turn up at the meat processing plant in Neasden and drive a van to the Brent Cross lockup, stopping for no-one. But just before they were about to leave, everything changed. The shipment was transferred to the Mercedes and Terzić gave them a new route. He explained that the van would follow the original route as a decoy.

Now, as they turned Eastbound onto the North Circular, the dark, early morning streets were quiet.

"So, Daris. Sonia in the office. Have you asked her out yet?"

"Not now Bojan. I need to concentrate."

"Come on. I saw you and her behind the vans yesterday. Your tongue was so far down her throat I could see the end of it coming out of her skirt."

"Shit, Bojan. Do you have to be so bloody disgusting? Anyway, I have seen the way you look at Hana Kovač. Like a big lost puppy wanting its mommy. She is forty if she is a day.

Anyway, don't you know she shares a lift with *The Bear*? She is marked goods. I would steer clear."

"I don't know. Maybe older women are attracted to me."

Daris looked briefly across. "Like flies are attracted to shit. Get me a cigarette."

"Bašić would kill you if he caught you smoking in his car."

"Just get me the damn cigarette. After all, without me you would be driving this wreck."

"Wreck? This is a classic Mercedes 500E, 1992. Nought to 100ks in 6 seconds, max speed 260ks. Left-hand drive. Sportline trim." Bojan ran an appreciative finger across the wood dash, clicking down the cigarette lighter. "Do you know this car was engineered by Porsche?"

Daris took the cigarette and filled his lungs, exhaling through a slit in the driver's window. "I don't care if NASA engineered it. It's a pile of crap and I look like a pimp."

Bojan laughed as he drew on a second cigarette. "Don't worry, Daris. No-one will confuse you with a pimp. A pimp's little gay brother, maybe."

Daris smiled. Then the smile drained away as the half-moon eyes of the BMW flashed in the door mirror.

"We have a tail, Bojan."

"Don't shit me, Daris. I am nervous as it is." Bojan peered between the seats. The half-moon eyes were fifty metres behind.

"It picked us up about a kilometre ago. I was waiting for it to turn off or overtake."

Bojan had to think quickly. They had altered the route before leaving. How could anyone know? Across his lap, the sawn-off felt heavy. Their junction was still three kilometres away. The road was straight and clear. They were sitting ducks.

"Take the next slip road, then go right. We will go through the houses. We can lose them in the maze of streets."

"But *the Bear* said stick to the route..." Daris gripped the steering wheel, the sinews forming ridges on his hands.

"Just do it, OK?"

Puffing noisily, Daris hammered the throttle and swung down the slip road. The rear-view mirror went dark but then the half-moon eyes reappeared. Daris took a left down a residential street and again they followed.

"We have to get back to the main road, Bojan. We are an easy target in these side streets."

"Take a right at the end of the road. I am sure we can get out that way." Was his mental map right? Bojan was doubting himself. "Once we get back onto the North Circular, you can floor this thing and see how fast their Beemer is." He fiddled with the sawn-off shotgun, felt the grip, ran a finger across the trigger guard, checked the safety off and on. Who had betrayed them? Only he, Daris, Bašić and Terzić knew the route. Surely not Terzić?

The half-moon eyes were keeping their distance as the Mercedes turned onto Conduit Way, tree-lined, residential, quiet as the grave, then onto Meadow Garth, the strip of tarmac straight and true. Soon Daris could see the end of the road. A left at the roundabout then less than a kilometre back to the North Circular. The traffic was heavier but still only a few vehicles and a double-decker night bus. He could see the traffic lights ahead changing to green.

Bojan reached out and laid a hand on Daris's shoulder. "Slow down, man. Take the lights as they change." In front, green turned to amber and Daris eased off the gas. He moved the selector from auto to first gear and waited. Then red and he floored it. The Mercedes screeched across the yellow cross-hatching and, amidst blaring horns, screamed through the startled traffic. The half-moon eyes remained at the lights as the scant night traffic crossed the junction behind. Bojan craned his neck and peered through the rear window, pleased at his own skill. As the traffic lights grew smaller and Daris opened up the engine, he breathed a sigh and eased his grip on the sawn-off.

"*Jebati!* They are still there." Daris glanced nervously in the rear-view mirror. Now there were two sets of eyes roaring up behind straddling the carriageway. "What are we going to do,

Bojan?" Daris was flicking from mirror to windscreen. His eyes were wide, his mouth dry.

"Just drive." Bojan dialled Terzić's number, seconds like hours as the eyes growled closer, then fell back.

"Bojan? What's up?" The voice was weary.

"Šef, we are being followed. A BMW. Two BMWs. We tried to shake them off but they're still there."

"Don't be an imbecile. How could that be? No-one knows the route. No-one knows the car. You are getting jumpy, Bojan. Pull yourself together."

Bojan studied the half-moon eyes, two predators, side by side, awaiting their opportunity. "Jumpy or not Šef, they are following us."

"Where are you?"

Bojan squinted at the map on the sat-nav and read out their position.

"Sit tight. I am sending help."

Just then one of the BMW's peeled off and with a throaty roar edged alongside the Mercedes. Bojan saw the masked face, the finger extended, the mock trigger pulled. Daris swung the wheel and with a thud, Bojan felt the door beside him give.

"Daris, the car! The Bear will kill us."

"Fuck the car and fuck the Bear." Daris pulled again at the wheel, another thud, a squealing of metal against metal. The Mercedes slewed violently. Bojan heard a crack beneath him and the world began to tilt. Suddenly, the phone leapt from his hand as the car's roof impacted heavily and slid along the road. His lap peppered with sparkling fragments and he grabbed around him, unsure which way was up and which was down. Then the movement stopped. Briefly stunned, Bojan looked across at Daris, hanging in his belt, his face crimson and raw, blood dripping from his forehead. He could feel the warmth trickling down his own face as his breath howled in his ears. Outside were shouts and footsteps.

The gun.

It had leapt from his hands in the crash. Stretching out an arm, groping in the well of the roof, he patted with the palms of his hand, feeling only the fabric roof and crystals of glass. Something smooth, varnished. The butt of the gun. His fingers grasped but could not gain a purchase and all the time the shouts outside became more urgent, ever closer. Then the door yawed wide, and they dragged him out onto the road, the hard tarmac against his head, the street lights sending red and green flashes across his eyes.

"Urdin Azeri sends his best wishes to the Bear."

Above him the arm swung, the bat tracked across the light, then nothing.

Chapter 17

New Scotland Yard, 10 Broadway, 9:00am, 6th June

Assistant Chief Constable Diane Browning's office was on the seventh floor. It was plain and straightforward with beige walls and an ink blue carpet. A framed set of insignia badges were the only wall decoration. Unfortunately, the view was of the City rather than St. James's Park but one can't have everything. Hopefully, the move to Curtis Green may afford a better vista but that lottery was down to politics rather than chance. With the prospect of mergers and consolidation as part of the MOPAC changes, many in 10 Broadway worried there might not even be an office.

Seated self-consciously at a short meeting table Detective Superintendent Bob Allenby was fiddling with a pen, as a sixth-former awaiting a carpeting. Browning, in the slightly more comfortable chair behind the desk, was asserting her superiority by ignoring him and busying herself with some paperwork.

Daley and Whetstone thanked the PA and extended hands as the two senior officers stood. Diane Browning was tall and slender with tightly styled auburn hair filigreed silver, and an immaculate though strict uniform. It gave her the air of a schoolteacher. She had been a fast track entrant into the force, clinging onto the greasy pole high enough to avoid real policing and to exploit the gradual fracturing of the glass ceiling. Her handshake was firm and Daley made a note to check later that his watch was still there.

"Scott. Seems like forever." Browning smiled, her slit of a mouth barely moving except at the corners.

"You too, ma'am." Daley dutifully reciprocated the smile. He neglected to mention that she had been front and centre at the presentation of his Police Medal not three months prior. However, with the Chief Constable by her side, her attention was probably elsewhere. It was she who had approved the award, for his actions on a fast track of an entirely different kind. A year ago, he had faced an oncoming locomotive to save a man incapable on Rohypnol. Then, before Christmas, a bullet had almost parted his hair as he faced down a terrified refugee. Allenby had read him the *riot* act. His *act first and think later* attitude had won him few friends amongst the higher ranks, even earning the epithet *Suicide Scott Daley* and would not be tolerated any longer. Now that Terri was in his life, Daley hoped, when it came to a choice, he would choose wisely.

Pleasantries over, Browning nodded and retreated to the sanctuary of her desk. "Thanks for coming over at such short notice. Let's make this quick. I have a 10 o'clock with the Deputy Assistant Commissioner."

Daley's eyebrows raised as the rank dropped hard enough to splinter a floorboard.

Browning continued: "Gordon and Hewell were both working undercover. They were part of *Operation Deep Shadow,* a multi-agency initiative working to infiltrate drugs operations, discover trafficking routes and ultimately dismantle them. To date, *Deep Shadow* has cost a lot and yielded little. It is important to the Home Secretary to protect that investment. Inspector. I want you to take a lead on this. Investigate the two deaths. Report directly to Superintendent Allenby. For now, the CDIU will offer their full co-operation but must be allowed to continue their work. Remember, two police officers. You will be under the scrutiny of Professional Standards."

Daley was confused. "Why not leave it to the Drugs Intelligence Unit? Surely, they have all the intel on Gordon and Hewell's operations." Snooping on one's fellow officers was not a great way to make friends and Daley had precious few of those without shitting on his own doorstep.

ACC Browning leaned forwards resting her elbows on the desk. "The CDIU are involved in some highly complex operations. The level of activity across West London is unusually high. They need to retain their focus. They will be in no mood for Homicide tramping all over their patch so I am trusting you to act sensitively and independently. I have already spoken to the commanding officer, and he has grudgingly accepted my view. Arrange time with him. See if you can wheedle out a few more details of the operation, about Gordon and Hewell's involvement."

As they left the ACC's office, a thought occurred to Daley, a wry smile appearing as he turned to Allenby. "Hang on, Hillingdon CDIU? Isn't that where Ray Kramer ended up?"

As Whetstone pursed her lips and turned purposefully away, Allenby stopped and eyed Daley. "This has all the hallmarks of being a messy one. You'll be investigating your own, including DCI Kramer, so you need to be on your best behaviour. Oh, and play nicely with the ACC. I know she can be a little, er, difficult at times but remember, I'm in the middle and it's because of me you still have your badge."

"Sir." Daley donned what he hoped would be a sufficiently contrite expression. Assigned to an investigation which was barely hours old and already he felt under scrutiny. With both Browning and Allenby breathing down his neck he would need to be on his guard or resourceful enough to work round them. He realised sentences were forming in his head he needed to stop from reaching his mouth.

"Anyway," continued Allenby, "Kramer is still gunning for you after that fiasco before Christmas with the cosmetic clinic, so tread carefully."

"I seem to remember it was him and his DI leaving with their arses in a sling."

"Yes, well, you only just squeaked through yourself. Remember that."

Chapter 18

North West London Covert Drugs Intelligence Unit (CDIU), Hillingdon.

The young woman who showed Daley and Whetstone into the boardroom said DCI Kramer and DI Dodds would only be a few minutes. She offered tea or coffee and left them to it.

Daley puffed. "Typical Kramer. Late for his own funeral."

"Cut him some slack. Someone killed one of his officers last night."

"The only thing I'll cut him is a new arsehole. Twat!"

"Look, sir, Inspector or not, if you don't behave, I will walk out." The enmity between DI Daley and DCI Kramer stretched back a long way.

Daley harrumphed and folded his arms. "Yes, mom."

DCI Ray Kramer was the sort of person who carried a chip on his shoulder when the world didn't deliver. Since the top brass had seen fit to move him from a cushy office in New Scotland Yard to the backwater of Hillingdon Road and a team nobody wanted to manage, the chip had grown somewhat.

The story of his altercation with Scott Daley was part of Met. folklore, embellished with each retelling depending upon the narrator's viewpoint or rank. Or gender. It had begun when Ray Kramer, Scott Daley, and Daley's then wife Lynne, sat together at a Federation dinner in 2008. Neither had been up for an award forcing them to applaud a significant number of desk jockeys who had. As the night drew to a close, probably because the bar had run dry, Lynne Daley expressed her desire to leave. She had spent most of the evening between Daley and Kramer, refereeing the bouts of juvenile one-upmanship that alcohol begets in the male of the species. She was at the end of a short and fiery tether and suggested it was time to leave.

Then accounts vary.

According to the Kramer camp, Kramer had risen too, chivalrously drawing back her chair. In the process, the flat of a palm had accidentally and entirely innocently impacted a buttock. Daley, being three sheets to the wind and obviously irrational, had become leery and aggressive, needlessly continuing the verbal sparring out into the warm August air. With Lynne Daley now in floods of tears at her partner's boorish behaviour, Ray Kramer had selflessly attempted to comfort her. Daley, brute that he was, then assaulted Ray Kramer, a right hook sending him sprawling into a flower bed, followed by a barrage of blows until several more sober colleagues had arrived to drag him off.

If you happened to sit in the Scott Daley camp, however, the story was a little different.

Ray Kramer had arrived with a girl on his arm. At first, everyone assumed that the girl was a daughter, or a niece or a dubious choice on Tinder, as Kramer seemed to be punching well above his weight. As the alcohol removed what little inhibition he had, the DCI then spent the entire evening being an absolute boor, making improper advances towards his date. Sometime between the desserts and the coffee, the date had risen and slapped Kramer across the face, shouting "What sort of dancer do you think I am?" before storming out. Kramer had shrugged the event away, maintaining that it had *all been a misunderstanding*. Then, he had moved across to occupy the seat next to Lynne Daley. His hands became a little freer in their roaming. Scott Daley, nigh-on a teetotaller like many in the Met, gave Kramer the benefit of the doubt. Eventually, though, Kramer crossed the Rubicon and the eight inches of space between their chairs and groped Lynne Daley's thigh. She asked to leave, at which point Kramer had risen too and continued his impropriety. Violence is a complete anathema to Scott Daley, or so he tells people. So he had shown strength of character and restraint up to the point where Kramer's freely roaming hands had helped Lynne Daley's perfectly formed backside into the taxi. Daley had gently and accidentally nudged Kramer, with the latter losing his balance and tottering into the ornamental shrubbery.

Neither camp disputes what happened next. Nursing their respective hangovers, Daley his bruised hand and Kramer a crooked and bloodied nose, both were brought before the Chief Superintendent. Subsequently, everyone who attended the Federation dinner apparently succumbed to a sudden onset of amnesia. They dropped the case through lack of evidence, an act which frequently drove Ray Kramer to the point of incandescence. Even though the waters had stilled between Kramer and Daley, beneath a dangerous current still flowed.

"If you ask me, you're all a bunch of twats. You, Kramer, Keith - the lot of you."

"Keith?"

It was Whetstone's turn to puff. "Yeah. Twat!"

Daley smiled wryly. "Love us or loathe us, Deb, we are all the bloody same." Folding his arms, he watched as a young officer placed a tray on the polished teak table. Kramer would regret keeping him waiting.

Chapter 19

DCI Ray Kramer's eyes were slits, cautious and scanning as he entered the room as if fearing an ambush, or a toad calculating the distance between flicked tongue and fly. He was stocky, balding, somewhat gone to seed. As he sat back in a chair opposite Scott Daley, his head seemed to rest on the roll of neck fat which obscured his chin and prevented the top button of his shirt from fastening.

"So, they sent a boy to do a man's job again."

Daley's mind formed a retort but a stiletto glance from Whetstone killed it before it reached his mouth. "Good morning, *sir*," he said. "Thanks for agreeing to see us. I can understand it may be difficult right now."

"The only reason you're here at all is because of ACC Browning. Everything I do for you, I do under bloody sufferance, don't you forget that."

They had offered Kramer the chance to lead the North West London CDIU three years ago. More an order than an offer. He and Detective Inspector Phil Dodds had been given charge of an ailing team in an anonymous office building in Hillingdon, thankfully away from Daley. As fate would have it, they would soon be thrust back together, thanks to MOPAC.

As DI Dodds blustered noisily through the doors, he appraised the landscape, the theatre of war and, skirting the table, chose the home side.

"Sorry I'm late, guys." He smiled effusively and totally disingenuously. "You haven't been winding up the DCI again, have you? Bad form before elevenses." He flashed a smile, ignoring the slit eyes, amused by his own banal wittiness.

Dodds was a stark contrast to his superior. Leaner, restive, his eyes darted about the room. If previous encounters had been anything to go by, Dodds would do all the heavy lifting, whilst Kramer would listen on.

Daley leaned forwards. "Right, let's get started. As you know, Sergeant Whetstone and I are investigating the deaths of Sergeant Joe Gordon and Sergeant Dean Hewell. The ACC has initially asked us to come in as independents. No-one is under caution. They require us to document the facts for her to make a submission to the IPCC if necessary."

Daley watched as Kramer's eyes rolled. Was it the word *independents* or *facts* that had caused consternation? He nodded to Whetstone, who opened a transparent binder on the desk and skim-read the first page. The previous evening, she had demolished a deep-pan four seasons pizza and ensconced herself in the chair next to her mother's, flicking through the file that DS Monaghan had pulled out of the Drugs Intelligence servers. Gordon's notes were a carbon copy of Dean Hewell's. Times, dates and names were different, but the story was the same.

"Tell me about the operation that Gordon and Hewell were involved in, sir?"

Kramer settled back into his chair. As Whetstone suspected, Dodds took up the running. "You know about *Deep Shadow*?"

Whetstone nodded.

"Well, officially, the Met's policy is to staunch the supply of Class A drugs but the problem is overwhelming. It doesn't help having the river and an international airport nearby. There are initiatives in place to control trafficking into the Capital and intelligence-led operations to monitor its source. West London has been divided into several fiefdoms. Bosnian, Czech, British, Polish and Chinese firms, each controlling their pitch, and broadly, they are self-policing. Anybody puts a foot over the line, geographically or metaphorically, and they are likely to lose it. Our job is to control the amount percolating down to the streets. Starve them of that and they will go elsewhere. Occasionally, we pitch in to put manners on them, they throw a hissy fit and the *status quo* is restored."

"So what part did Gordon and Hewell play?" Prior to Homicide, Daley had been seconded to Drugs in Essex. He understood how the drugs market operated. Today, he was more concerned with how two coppers had their heads blown off.

"The last major trouble was four years ago when Danilo *The Bear* Bašić rocked up. The Bosnians had already infiltrated the Neasden manor. They sent in Bašić to make the takeover permanent. Once the kneecapping and neck shots had ceased, he met with the fellow bosses and agreed a reluctant detente."

"When Superintendent Dick Bartlett retired, things became somewhat lax, shall we say," added Kramer. "DI Dodds and I were parachuted in reorganise the squad and improve the clear-up rate. Since Christmas we have increased our own numbers and embedded officers in the various local firms."

"Gordon and Hewell?" Impatience getting the better of him, Daley cajoled Dodds back to the point.

"Yes, amongst others," continued Dodds. "Gordon was sent into the Westsiders based out of Wembley and Greenford. Hewell was embedded into the Cjevovod, the Bosnian outfit headed by Danilo Bašić, in Neasden, Dollis Green and Monks Park. The two firms appear to be the main protagonists. Gordon was an experienced undercover officer, he had worked before with the Westsiders and their boss, Paisley John McKaig. He knew the firm and had an established cover. They knew and trusted him. Gordon had been embedded for six months. Ironically, we were lining up his replacement." Dodds sighed ruefully and sipped at his coffee. "Lousy timing."

"So what exactly was Gordon working on?"

"The usual. Dates, times, amounts. Run-of-the-mill stuff mainly. Shipments in and out, meetings and personnel."

Daley frowned. "Doesn't seem like a great deal. Surely a snout would have been sufficient?"

Dodds considered. "Depends what you're hoping for, I suppose. We have intercepted shipments, probably five, six hundred kilos over time. When cut, that's a lot of product off the streets. Narcotics is a business. Day to day, it's as humdrum as running a supermarket. Gordon's job was to keep an eye open for that one piece of information that could indicate a big job, something exceptional. Like mining for gold, you chip away."

"And he found it?"

"Maybe."

"What's that supposed to mean?" retorted Daley, sharply.

Dodds paused and shared a glance with Kramer, then eyed the pair cautiously. "There have been unsubstantiated rumours of a new player in town. Someone who wanted to muscle in and annex part of West London for himself." Daley glanced at Whetstone and they hunkered down for the story. Even fairy-tales carry a crumb of truth, however deeply ingrained.

Six months ago, we would be lucky to hear of an incident once a month. Then, there was a marked upsurge in activity across the patch. Now there may be two a week. Intimidation and violence, attacks by street gangs, van hold-ups. In late March, early April, a new name pops up - Urdin Azeri and an organisation called the *Encubierto*, intent on establishing themselves in West London, plying a new West African route through Portugal, Spain and France. We instructed Gordon to keep his ear to the ground. All he found was a growing feud between McKaig and Bašić, the Westsiders and the Cjevovod, each laying the blame fairly and squarely on the other."

Daley huffed "Tit-for-tat? All this sounds like something from the 1950s."

Kramer glanced at Dodds and smiled disparagingly. "What would you know, Inspector? Little has changed in the old British firms since then. The faces may be different, even the language they speak, but it's the same old businesses - gambling, prostitution, drugs, extortion - you name it."

"Why not pull the firms off the street? Mark their cards? The in-fighting alone would be enough to charge them. With them out of the equation, surely, all this would just cease?"

Kramer snorted contemptuously. "You really have no idea do you. These are not sad housewives knifing their husbands. They are vicious bastards. We go in heavy-handed and the

West side of London would implode as everyone and his brother piles in to fill the vacuum."

"With all due respect, sir," sighed Daley, "someone has to step in and bang their bloody heads together. Only last night another of the Westsiders' vans was ambushed. How long before another of your guys gets a bullet? It has to stop."

Resenting the less than veiled criticism, Kramer leaned across the desk, a fire burning behind his eyes. "Look, Daley. If you think you can come in here and question the way my team operates, you've another thing coming."

"Chrissakes, sir. That's exactly what they sent me here to do!"

"If we go in all guns blazing, we will all be up in front of a tribunal."

"Seriously? A police officer dead, no leads after two months and now another? I am surprised you can't hear the alarm bells ringing in Professional Standards from here."

"Enough—*sirs*." As Whetstone's command echoed off the walls, the pair stopped, eyes still locked. "DI Dodds and I are not here to referee your infantile squabbles. Two fellow officers have been killed. At least show them some bloody respect."

Daley and Kramer settled back onto their haunches, eyes still locked, boiling tempers reduced to a bubbling simmer.

Whetstone continued. "So, where does this..." She referred to her notes, "...*Urdin Azeri* come in?"

Dodds nodded. "Every time there is an incident, the names Azeri, the *Encubierto* are on everyone's lips. Even McKaig and Bašić become pre-occupied with trying to track them down but everything points back to the Westsiders and the Cjevovod."

"But surely if this is all a fabrication of either McKaig or Bašić...? And Joe Gordon found nothing?"

"Nothing." Dodds shook his head. "In each case, either the Westsiders or the Cjevovod were the victims of the violence. In each case the other denied involvement. In each case they blame the Encubierto. Then, two days before he died, Gordon claimed he had made a breakthrough. He claimed had discovered Azeri's identity and just needed to confirm his facts. That was the last we heard from him."

Whetstone continued. "Why was he in Holborn alone at 3:00am?"

Dodds shrugged. "No idea. Nothing in his reports. I've had the team check his digs, his computer, his phones, transcripts of conversations. Nothing."

"And Dean Hewell?"

"Hewell was undercover with the Cjevovod. When Gordon was killed, we ordered him to keep his head down and ride out this storm. We would not waste the months of work we had put in. In hindsight, Gordon and Hewell must have been sharing intel."

"And no reason why Hewell was in Northolt yesterday?"

Dodds shook his head.

"We've pulled our other embedded officers out, at least until this all blows over." added Kramer. "It's going to put our operation back by months, years even, but we can't risk any more officers."

"So, Gordon and Hewell. Do you think someone had blown their covers?"

"That's all we can think."

Kramer leaned forwards, arching his fingers beneath his chin. There was still a fire burning. "There's nothing abnormal about any of this. Embedded officers must tread carefully. There are strict protocols about communications. We have a daily report. If either of them can't make that, they drop a coded text to a monitored line. If they can't phone, there are several other ways they can get a message through."

"But they didn't," countered Daley. "Surely, being on the verge of a breakthrough was significant. If it were any of my officers, I would insist on more frequent reports, more detail."

"Now look, Daley. It's all right for you to run around playing *Keystone Kops* but these two firms were already at each other's throats. We have to trust our operatives. It's their necks on the line, not ours."

"Six separate van raids. Fifteen people hospitalised and one dead. Outpatients at the Central are laying on an extra ward and having a sweepstake for days off. And still you didn't think it wise to bring Hewell out? We might be the *Keystone Kops*, Detective Chief Inspector, but at least our guys have half a chance of surviving their shift."

Dodds made to speak but Kramer stretched out a hand, silencing him. "Meaning?"

"Meaning whatever Sergeant Gordon discovered was probably linked to the rise in violence and the all-out-war between these two gangs. And three months down the line, with another officer dead, you have no clue what that is." Daley threw Kramer another scornful look and revelled as his dander rose a few more millimetres.

"Don't you think I lie awake at night thinking about Eileen Gordon and their little girl? About Janine, Hewell's fiancée?"

As Kramer's last words resounded off the walls. Phil Dodds rose and stretched out a hand towards Whetstone. "This has gone far enough for today." He handed her a card. "Ask your guys to call me. If I can help. I will but for now..."

Chapter 20

"You two really have to sort out your differences."

DI Dodds was leaning forward, hammering a password through his keyboard, springs creaking as he bounced his foot.

Daley envied Dodds' cubicle, three sides of acoustic screens; privacy. Also, a place to call one's own in a sea of grey. "The man's a twat, Phil. I know he's your boss, and you have to show loyalty but you have to admit he's a twat."

Dodds chuckled wryly. "You don't have to work with him."

"Thank God."

"That's not what I meant and you know it. OK, so you two might have had your differences but Ray Kramer is a good copper. He's a safe pair of hands. What's more he can handle the politics so me and the team don't have to."

"Yeah but..."

"No buts, Scott. Play nicely with him or bugger off. Morale is low enough around here at the moment, what with Joe and Dean, then the rumours of redundancies and mergers. We don't need a slanging match between you and Kramer. Anyway, he says the same of you and, judging by your performance in there, I am inclined to agree."

Daley held up his hands in apology and huffed. "Fair enough Phil. Message received. I'll have a word with him. Try to smooth things over."

"Best thing you can do is keep a wide berth."

Daley mused on the embarrassing debacle between himself and Kramer. There was a part of him that enjoyed a good scrap and no amount of work by his therapist or admonishment from Bilko Allenby had curbed that. Still, he needed to mend bridges, not least with Dodds so he set about a charm offensive. He pointed to a small photo of a football team pinned behind Dodds monitor.

"So, football's your thing?"

Dodds slowly turned, dragging his mind from one hundred miles away. "Uh? Er, no, not really. Friendly rivalry between me and the DCI. He was born in the Midlands too. Wanderers fan. I'm from Leicester."

"Leicester? Weren't they in the play-off? Watford?"

For years, Saturday nights involved the company of several beers and the ethereal voice of Gary Lineker as Daley dozed through Match of the Day. This year he had missed most of the season because of Terri's influence but felt drawn to the back pages nonetheless. "I used to have a season ticket at Fulham a few years ago." Since a case the previous year, a young Fulham fan missing after a Saturday match, Daley had promised himself he would buy a ticket. Try to revive the passion and anguish he remembered. Something else to focus on. "The Cottagers - although that has connotations so I prefer the Whites. Always there or thereabouts in the Premiership. Never stellar, never rubbish." The parallels with his own career were astonishing.

"Yeah. Narrowly missed out on promotion. Ninety-seventh minute, can you believe it? Knockaert's penalty saved by Almunia and Watford break to score at the other end. Three-two on aggregate."

"Sickener."

Dodds nodded resignedly. "Yep. Wanderers are going down, so it's the only stick the DCI has to beat me with."

"You at the match?"

"Uh, No. I was abroad. Bilbao. Wife's family has a place there."

It was so long since Daley had been abroad, his passport was in Latin. After the move, once he and Terri were settled and before the baby bump became too large, he needed to rectify that. A week on the Algarve, maybe, but for now, there were more urgent matters. Then a thought occurred. Allenby's plea for him to play nicely with the Drugs Unit.

"I used to have a season ticket at Fulham. Years ago. I was thinking of catching a few games. You fancy coming along?"

Dodds turned to Daley, surprised. "Really? And betray my birthright?"

"You could always watch Wolverhampton Wanderers play in League One and keep the boss happy."

"Take more than that. Why don't you invite him along to Craven Cottage? Share a Bovril and a pie?"

"I might just do that!" Daley considered the potential for disaster and filed it under *bad ideas*. "I'll let you know and you can decide..."

"Sounds good, Scott." Dodds smiled, distractedly.

Pleased with his successful schmoozing, Daley steered a course back to business. "So Azeri, the Encubierto..."

"Forget it. We have used all the resources at our disposal. The CDIU at Hillingdon, the combined resources of Operation *Deep Shadow*, the National Drugs Agency. We could discover nothing to substantiate the existence of Azeri or his organisation beyond the Cjevovod and the Westsiders. We even widened our search to the UNODC, the INCB, even the CIA and FBI. Nothing. There is not a single piece of tangible evidence outside the feud between these two parochial drugs firms that leads us to believe Urdin Azeri exists."

"Yet still the name keeps surfacing."

Dodds lowered his head, exasperated. "Believe me, this is just a pissing contest between McKaig and Bašić."

"And you? What do you think?"

"Danilo Bašić. McKaig's a thug but he wouldn't risk his empire. Bašić has a massive European network to call on. He could easily demolish McKaig if he wished."

"So why hasn't he?"

"$64,000 question, Scott."

Chapter 21

Lambourne Road

Major Incident Room A, on the third floor was light, airy and sterile. The room comprised banks of identical workstations in groups of five. There were no personal mementos attached to screens or on desks. Teams mingled organically, promoting collaboration and communication. Around the plain white walls, the only decorations were posters adorned with mnemonics and procedures, aide-memoires and contact numbers. The room screamed professionalism and dedication, a mind to the job. At one end, Daley and Whetstone sat in front of a massive flat screen and a whiteboard that would become the incident board. Around them, bristling and expectant, a meagre collection of uniformed and plain clothes support watched as Allenby asked everyone to gather round and started proceedings.

"It's Thursday 6th June at 5:38pm. This is the first briefing for *Operation Nightjar*." At the start of an investigation, a computer randomly assigned a code name. At the Assistant Chief Constable's request, and based on the similarities between the two murders, Allenby had consented to a joint investigation into the deaths of Gordon and Hewell. Operation Sandpiper, the investigation into Gordon's murder, was to be assimilated into the new investigation.

"OK, ladies and gentlemen. This will be a short briefing, just to kick things off." He paused as a sigh murmured through the audience. "Before we start, I need to impress upon you the sensitivity of the investigation. We are investigating the death of two police officers, two of our own. Please bear that in mind. There will be a great deal of media interest, which should be directed to me. Any issues, report to Detective Inspector Daley at once. Is that understood?"

A weak Mexican wave of less than enthusiastic agreement rippled around the room.

"Inspector Daley."

Daley cleared his throat. Since the meeting with ACC Browning, the butterflies of anxiety had been fluttering through his stomach. To Daley, every case was a reset, a wipe clean. It felt as though everything he knew meant nothing.

It didn't help that Allenby had already received a call from Ray Kramer.

"Right. Detective Sergeant Joe Gordon was found dead in his car on 12th April." Daley attached a gruesome photo to the board with a magnetic pin. "A single fatal gunshot to the head before the car was set alight. At 5:00am yesterday morning, Detective Sergeant Dean Hewell was found dead. Again, a single fatal gunshot and the car torched." He pinned up a second photo, equally gruesome. "Both officers were working undercover on *Operation Deep Shadow,* a joint forces initiative aimed at reducing the supply of Class A drugs into the country and onto the streets. The likely scenario is that they had each arranged a meeting which ended badly."

"Given the similarities, sir, are we looking for one killer or more than one?" It was DC Smollett, a short, rather rotund man in his twenties with an unruly mop of dark hair, which he was continually sweeping from his face. Whenever there was a briefing, Smollett was always the first to ask a question.

"We can't rule anything in or out at this stage. Preliminary examination suggests that the same gun fired both rounds. A single gun suggests a single killer. Investigate each death separately until we have a positive link." Daley knew which option he favoured and it sent a chill down his spine. He also knew any evidence from the Gordon killing, not already collected, was gone. The Hewell crime scene was still fresh but would deteriorate quickly.

"Detective Sergeant Monaghan. Gather any CCTV evidence. There must be cameras around the truck bay where Hewell was found but widen the perimeter. See if we can catch anyone entering or leaving. Also, pull the CCTV from the Gordon shooting. Detective Constable Taylor. Examine the phone records for these two officers. According to the Drugs Unit, they each had three phones; a personal phone, a

Met phone and a burner for use undercover. Find out who they talked to, how often and whether they spoke to each other."

Daley referred to his notes. "Detective Constable Corby. Interview the partners of the dead officers. Visit Hewell's girlfriend first. Let's see if she can give us a fresh perspective on what her fiancé was doing in that car park. Then Eileen Gordon. Maybe she has recalled something more after two months."

"Detective Constable Smollett. I need you to concentrate on these two drugs firms, the Cjevovod and the Westsiders. We need to understand the feud between them. Oh, and any mention of a third firm, African or Iberian: see if the name Urdin Azeri or the Encubierto appears anywhere."

Behind him, as if by magic, more photos appeared on the whiteboard; a spider trails of lines annotated with names and times which began the web of facts that would sooner or later hold the key.

"Detective Sergeant Whetstone and I will concentrate on the cases Hewell and Gordon were working on. Smollett, keep us informed of anything you find which may assist us in that. OK, guys. Until tomorrow. Same time, same place. Let's get to it but remember, if anything comes to light, don't wait until the next briefing."

Chapter 22

The Monarch View Hotel, Greenford

Hotel was a grandiose description of the Monarch View. Nowadays, it was little more than a discrete bordello. With tariffs paid by the half-day or the hour, rooms were basic and expectations more so. However, it went about its business quietly and efficiently; it turned a tidy profit and Danilo Bašić's cut was healthy. Of the six houses under his control, this was the least problematic.

The tiny windowless office behind the reception, held the ranks of video monitors connected to the hotel's CCTV. Tiny square monochrome images of the corridors, the kitchens and, most interestingly, the first-floor rooms. There were twelve rooms, twelve girls and twelve recorders. Right now the images were still and the recorders idle. Evenings and weekends would see the most activity; more tapes to add to the burgeoning stack in the old Chubb safe behind the door.

Bašić tutted again as his thoughts wandered and he lost count of the banknotes in his hand. Last night, news of the raid on Bojan and Daris had interrupted his sleep. The total loss of his beloved E-class coupe, not to mention five more kilos of powder and ten thousand in accumulated takings. McKaig and the Westsiders were becoming a distraction. He began again from the top. To his right, Dimitri Minolev, the house manager nervously chewed a nail.

Bašić had put the first heist down to misfortune. The second, despite changes to the route, a different van, and a passenger riding shotgun, made him suspicious. Last night, he sent a crew and van off as a decoy, not knowing their load was bogus. For God's sake, he had even seen off the van himself before throwing the keys to his beloved Mercedes to Bojan and Daris and giving them an entirely different route and destination.

Yet still somehow, somebody knew.

After the ambush, Ivan Terzić had torched the Mercedes and brought Bojan and Daris back to the warehouse. Daris was in a bad way, his face smashed to jam and unable to talk. Bojan, whilst shit scared, could recount everything. The BMWs appearing from nowhere, attempts to shake them off, the sideswipe and collision with the lamppost. Four masked assailants grabbing him before he could wield the shotgun.

Bojan had sworn on his mother's life there was nothing he could do to protect the consignment. Bašić knew Bojan's mother. He was offering nothing Bašić had not taken many times before. As a precaution, he gave Bojan and Daris a bullet to the head. Then he had turned his attentions to Terzić. The only other person present who knew the true route, it would have taken moments to give the raiders a different target, a different location. He too had protested his innocence, despite the gun against his head, right up to the point when the cocked trigger had fired on an empty chamber and Terzić had pissed himself.

Ironically, the decoy van had arrived unmolested.

Urdin Azeri sends his best wishes to The Bear. Did McKaig really consider him that naïve? Typical British.

Still, McKaig must get his intelligence from somewhere. Amongst the Cjevovod, loyalty was an obligation. The informant must be someone close to the warehouse, close to Bašić. Hell, for a moment, Bašić even suspected himself. Did he talk in his sleep?

"So what would you do?" The words inadvertently spoken aloud.

Dimitri Minolev started and shuffled on the uncomfortable chair, feeling the legs twist and creak beneath him and an aroma of musty sweat which he knew was his own. His major concern was the pile of twenties and tens which he had handed to Bašić. There was always the nagging doubt he might have inadvertently counted short.

"I don't know, *Bear*. About what?"

Bašić raised his eyes and glowered. Dimitri knew how to run a whorehouse but he was as thick as pig shit. The money had never been short. A further recount would seem incompetent, so Bašić slid the wad of notes into his bag.

If it wasn't Terzić then who was it?

Chapter 23

Leaving Whetstone to brief the team, Daley drove across to the outskirts of Harrow. As he steered into the small sparse cul-de-sac, Terri Somerville's head turned as her eyes left the rear-view mirror of her Insignia.

The sun was slowly descending but the warmth of the day lingered. There was an aroma of new-mown grass lifting from neat lawns and a heady scent, sending the bees and insects into a frenzy around tidied, burgeoning borders. It brought an inner peace he had not known for many years. Ahead two bikes haphazard on the pavements, playful shouts echoed from backyards and the waning sun turned everything a golden amber.

And they *had* erected the Sold board at Number 6.

Life had altered beyond all recognition since he had met Theresa Somerville. Her joyous bon vivant had pulled him from the abyss into which he was spiralling. At last he felt his life was back on the rails, which was ironic considering what had pushed it off in the first place. Less than a year ago, he was a career copper, married to the job and divorced from life, rarely giving the future, or the consequences of his actions, a second thought. *Suicide Scott Daley.*

They had met the previous November. Two Inspectors comparing notes on a muddy, cold footpath. A missing jogger, a dead dog and everything that tumbled from it. From the moment he had seen her, it was as if a separate part of his soul, closed and cold, had opened to the heat of the sun, grey to green. By Christmas of that year, the real magic had begun to happen, the rehabilitation of Scott Daley from lonely, divorced policeman to Scott Daley the man, the partner. Now the job, the be-all and end-all of his existence not twelve months ago, became his occupation rather than his life. As Sophie Jennings, his trauma counsellor had said: "Life's about who you are, not what you do."

Now Daley was to embark on a whole new journey. That of money-starved homeowner in an expensive part of West London.

The visit to ACC Browning's office had been a surprise. For her to become involved made Daley uneasy. Diane Browning had risen to an echelon where politics were more important, above the glass ceiling where the nuts and bolts of policing were rarely considered. It suggested that another wheel was turning, one he knew nothing about. After they had left, Allenby had read a riot act of sorts. Various bollocks about houses being in order and mud sticking. It was common for higher ranks to have the conversation, so later they could deliver the line-crossing lecture. Also, they could claim they had done everything in their powers but, well, coppers will be coppers. Daley had barely listened. To be fair, his mind was comparing floral to chintz, wooden poles to plastic rails; his excitement more domestic than vocational. As long as Daley and his team continued to yield results and as long as the lines were crossed delicately and not trampled into the sands.

Which was probably the reason for the continuing animosity between himself and Ray Kramer. The DCI wore his procedures on his sleeve and lived by the book. Daley used it to wedge the interview room door shut whilst he harassed a witness.

The feud with Kramer was over now, wasn't it? The trauma counselling had re-oriented his mind and with Lynne no longer in the picture, he could let bygones be bygones. Of course he could, but that didn't mean he couldn't have a little fun along the way. He smiled as he recalled Kramer's bewildered face gazing up from the rhododendrons still reeling from the punch.

So Allenby had marked his card. Investigate the Drugs Unit, limit your fun to finding the killer of the two junior officers but don't wind up the DCI.

Which would be no fun at all.

He opened the car door and let the early evening sun wash over his face. Terri's legs were silhouetted through her light, summery dress, her arms folded. Shadow veiled her face, but he knew she was smiling. She was always smiling.

Walking around to the boot, he retrieved a tape measure, a pencil and a pad. Even six months ago, he could not conceive of a time when he would help a beautiful woman size up curtains, let alone move into a house with her. Life was slowly but surely resuming its course.

Scott Daley, don't cock it up now.

Chapter 24

DI Dodds had emailed to say the paper files on Gordon and Hewell were ready for Whetstone to collect, so she detoured via the Hillingdon offices on her way home. Leaving Dodds a *Post-it* with a smiley face and hoping it would annoy him sufficiently. Parking up, the house was dark and cold. Her sister, Louise, had stayed in Sheffield where she was studying. Summer work and new friends were more of an allure than a cold empty house in Ealing. Avoiding the situation. Maybe she should invest in one of those gizmos that turns on a light, makes it look like someone was in but what was there to steal?

Latching the front door, she peered into the lounge, dim and quiet. On a similar evening two months ago, the TV had lit the room, her mother's hand rested on the arm of the chair, clutching the half-full glass but Maureen Whetstone's open eyes were not watching. There followed a procession of sympathetic handshakes from people she hardly knew. Relatives, friends, people just there for the show, dressed in black, waiting for the next one to pass. Then Patrick Gascoigne had died. Whilst she loved her mother, she felt closer to the professor. His friendly, paternal manner filled the void that her father had left, the wastelands which Keith created. She put all her efforts into grieving him and not her mother.

Blinking as the neon flashes filled the kitchen, she opened the fridge. Empty. The air echoed with silence. The space echoed with her mother. Opening a bottle of red, she adjourned to the lounge and opened the first folder. An almost indecipherable scrawl on familiar yellow notepaper and a few photographs.

A little bedtime reading to take her mind off Keith but still she was drawn back to him.

Less of this maudlin self-pity, Deb. Time to move on.

Rubbing the stinging salt tears from her cheeks, she grabbed her phone.

I've had enough Keith. We both know it's over. I need to move on.

Then with barely a hesitation, she clicked send.

Chapter 25

Danilo Bašić's meat packing plant, an anonymous prefabricated building, lay on the Eastern edge of Neasden. In the car park, throwing a spent cigarette through the open window of his Vauxhall, the night patrol man welcomed the cool breeze and decided he could relax his grip on the rifle. Earlier, Bašić himself had been round and read them all the riot act. Tensions were running high.

He watched lazily as the taillights of the last articulated lorry turned the corner out on to the road. With collections finished for the day, he could relax. Lulled by the gentle hum of the building's heat exchangers, he loosened his tie and closed his eyes. Just for a while. Behind the huge roller shutter door, the despatch manager lolled in his chair. A radio echoed through the busy space, barely audible above the somnolent buzz of the machinery. The peaceful early hours made for an easy shift.

With barely a sound of tyres on concrete, the three BMWs 520is doused their halo eyes and rolled into the empty car park. The night patrol man's eyes were wide as a hand pushed his head back, gurgling as the knife scored his throat and the white of his shirt turned crimson.

Suddenly, in a roar, two blinding headlights careered around the corner. Turning sharply, the beams formed targets on the roller door, growing larger until the front of the van tore the aluminium from its frame, sending the seated manager sprawling to the floor. Dazed, shaking away the surprise, he scrabbled to his feet, then froze as a black mask stared down the muzzle of a shotgun pointed directly at his face. Raising his hands above his head, stifling the urge to urinate, he fell back onto the concrete and watched three more black-clad figures climb through the shattered door, brace their firearms and hold station.

To his left, the van had stopped, steam venting from the smashed radiator. Two more men leapt out and raced around to the rear of the van. Soon, the manager was coughing as a pungent petrochemical stench prickled his nostrils and he fought to swallow back the nausea. Then, the blast of warmth singed his eyebrows and the inside of the warehouse blazed orange behind the silhouetted van.

Briefly distracted, all eyes were now on the flames. The manager considered his options. The shotgun barrel was wavering. He could grab the gun, turn the tables but what were the odds? He was a warehouseman not a soldier. Easy night-work in a factory that packed meat, not a bullion store. A family to go home to, a cooked breakfast in less than four hours.

But what would Bašić think if he did not at least try?

So he leapt at the legs of the black mask and tackled him to the ground. There was a shot, and he smelt the acrid odour of the discharge, waiting for the pain to start but it did not. Grasping the barrel, he wrestled with the intruder as the gun bobbed perilously between them. Then a blow impacted the side of his head and his vision sparked red and yellow. He found himself against the cold concrete floor, his heart pumping and his breath heavy in his ears.

"Urdin Azeri sends his best wishes. Now be a good boy and stay down."

Then, mere seconds after the door had caved in around him, he shuddered as the van exploded in a ball of flame and he finally let the darkness consume him.

Chapter 26

I've had enough Keith. We both know it's over. I need to move on.

Keith Parrish tutted and deleted the text.

Knowing when it was over should be an instinct though for Parrish it never had been. Deborah Whetstone had never been more than a diversion; something to relieve the boredom of the job. He had a natural yen for something younger. Much younger.

Outside the Monarch View hotel, the air was warm and underneath a star-strewn sky, the early hours hummed with the undercurrent of the city. From the shadow of the alley, Parrish watched a punter furtively glance left and right before descending the front steps. Nowadays, Parrish used the side exit. Knowing who owned the place, he had to be on his guard.

For Parrish, there was something deeply satisfying about the contract of paid sex. No expectation beyond the act and the price. Glassy, cold eyes, submitting her body for nothing more than his money. It was clandestine, a little dangerous, the grunts and moans were little more than window dressing. Knowing he gained more from the liaison than she did.

Irina had been his first and was still his favourite. Still, it had been a shock when she was pulled in for possession, seeing the charge sheet and learning her age. He knew she was young; that's how he liked them. Not pre-pubescent but with that precocious balance of teenage rebelliousness and childish innocence. That first time, when his hankering had gotten the better of him in the kitchen at the back of the hotel, she had been fourteen. If they're big enough, they're old enough the guys used to say and, damn, some they brought in were hot, mature beyond their years. It was just a number anyway.

It was a thin line between the upholders of the law and those who broke it; a line he straddled all too often.

When the coast was clear, Parrish made his way to where he had left the squad car. Going off-grid during his shift was risky, still more leaving the marked car unattended. Changing into his regulation shirt and black stab vest, turning on the radio, a wave of panic coursed through him as he heard the urgent chatter. Surely not? He checked the time and huffed. He had only been away an hour and all manner of hell had kicked off. Surely they could spare him that long?

Pulling away, he listened to the exchange between Dispatch and the mobile units. Something big was going down. Reporting in, he headed for Neasden. Soon the walls ahead flashed blue with converging mobile units. The car lurched forwards as instinct pushed down his foot. Out of a side street, a dark shape pitched across the road into the headlights of his patrol car. What was it? Mondeo? Vectra? Then he was turning, flicking on the sound and vision and keeping his eyes firmly on the black unlit car as it sped away. He pressed the button on his chest.

"Sierra Alpha one-one. In pursuit of suspects, Eastbound Ben Hill, junction with Sillins Road."

"Roger, Sierra Alpha one-one."

Ahead the shape grew large as the squad car complained. BMW, definitely a BMW. Dark against the streetlights. Four heads, a masked face strobed blue as it peered around at him, two round white eyes. Then the car slewed into a side street.

"Multiple suspects, dark BMW 5 series. Index MG05 AGU. Left into Welby Road."

"Roger, Sierra Alpha one-one."

Parrish's car yawed, and he saw the BMWs tyre impact the kerb in a shower of sparks. Wounded, the vehicle fish-tailed as the driver wrestled with the wheel. Then the BMW was sideways. A parked car yawed as the rear quarter folded and a lamppost topple, bouncing onto the BMW which skidded to a stop in a cloud of steam. As the doors opened, Parrish was on foot and racing towards it.

"Sierra Alpha one-one. BMW decamped. In pursuit. Four suspects on foot. Welby road. Request assistance."

"Roger, Sierra Alpha one-one. All units. Welby Road. Suspects on foot."

"Sierra X-ray three-four responding. On route, Welby Road."

"Roger, Sierra X-ray three-four."

As the fleeing shapes separated, Parrish weighed up the odds. He had to make a call. A lanky, wiry man pushed open a twisted door and fell to the pavement, clumsily hauling himself to his feet and limping off. Carrying extra weight, Parrish was not one for athletics nor heroics, so he chose the easy pickings.

With footsteps resounding from the sodium-lit terraced fronts, he pursued the man over the road and down another shadowed street, feeling his lungs ache, driven by adrenaline. The man was hobbling. He was gaining. A howl broke the quiet as a car horn sounded to Parrish's left and a screech of brakes. Stalling, he felt his heart leap and lifted his hand in apology, cursing beneath his laboured breath. Up in front, the space between him and the black shadow had lengthened. Then the man dodged sideways and disappeared.

There was an alley, unlit and treacherous, which led to the allotments. Once in there, the guy was away. He should wait for back-up. His mouth parched and his breath pumped. Measuring his steps, rolling his shoes to reduce the sound, Parrish headed into the darkness, through a corridor of fences into an open sea of black, a featureless horizon, prickling green and white as his eyes adjusted. Then a movement against the horizon; a shadow up ahead. His pulse pounded in his ears, he strained to still his breath, creeping towards the shadow but then it vanished. His radio crackled, a gunshot against the silence. Cursing, he turned down the volume and dropped to his haunches, feeling the sounds of the night across the earthy damp of the ground. The sky glowed amber above the horizon then plunged into a void. looking left, a rustle, right a creak.

Where was he?

A rush of air. And another. The distinct sound of breathing. Parrish rotated his head to pinpoint the sound and carefully edged towards it, cursing the crush of gravel. Soon he was on top of the sounds, his eyes straining to see anything but the deep black in front of him. Beside him, a movement, a shadow loomed. Instinctively, arms outstretched, Parrish pushed aside the fear which gripped him and leapt. Then he impacted the solid trunk of the rising body. With a splintering of bamboo canes, the two men hit the ground, flailing arms, grasping hands. Parrish felt boots ripping the skin from his shins, hands grabbing his hair. He swung a fist and felt his knuckles burn as they hit the wool of the balaclava and the solid jaw beneath. Then another and another and the man lay on his back his chest heaving rasps of pain through the mask.

Then Parrish felt his groin explode and pain shot through his body. Gasping for breath, he rolled onto the damp grass, his vision filled with a sea of stars. Forcing himself to his knees, he saw his assailant dark against the sky, he heard the wheezing as the man made his escape.

Not tonight, sonny. You're mine.

Climbing unsteadily to his feet, he chased footsteps on gravel then paving, as the dark shape strobed beneath streetlights, Left, right, down alleys, panicking as the shape disappeared, relief as he caught up. Then at last, a chain-link fence topped with razor wire rattled, as the fleeing man turned, trapped.

Parrish jerked to a halt. Between rasping breaths, he wheezed "Give it up, mate. Nowhere to go. You're under arrest." The beam from his torch arced across the balaclava and the man flinched. Slowly, as the red flashes dissipated from his eyes, he made for his radio.

"You don't want to do that, Keith."

Parrish paused, catching his breath at the sound of his name. "Take off the mask—slowly." He pressed the call button. "Sierra Alpha one-one to Control."

"Roger, Sierra Alpha one-one. Go ahead."

"Seriously mate, that's not a good idea." A gloved hand rose to remove the mask, squinting, a blur of red smearing a cheek. And someone Parrish could not believe he was seeing.

He felt the nausea rise as the eyes locked with his and a smile broke the bloodied face.

"Sierra Alpha one-one to Control. Stand by."

"Roger, Sierra Alpha one-one."

Time slowed as Parrish stood, confused. In front of him, the mask dropped to the floor. Slowly, a pistol rose until he could see the black hole of the muzzle.

"Put the gun down. There's nowhere you can go. There are cars homing in on this location as we speak." Around, the sounds of London chorused to faint sirens. Parrish just hoped some of them were singing to him.

"So, we had better be quick then, don't you think?" As the man stared back, Parrish could feel the ice in the veins. "The way I see it, Keith, there are two ways this could go. You can act the hero, just like Joe and Dean. I get away and you're dead. Or, you can overpower me and take me in but I'd say that's a bit risky, wouldn't you? OK, so if you're lucky you get your collar, I spend a night in the cells and my brief makes you look stupid. Oh, where were you this evening? You know, when you should have been on shift? Partial to tender meat, aren't you Keith? Then there's Danilo Bašić's factory."

"What of it? What of the factory?"

"Well, we only have your word you were with your teenage whore, don't we? Maybe you were in Neasden with us, watching the flames? Maybe... it was all your idea?"

That explained the shout earlier. "Don't talk stupid. No-one would ever believe that."

"Maybe. Maybe not. Oh, I suppose there is another option. You could let me go, say I got away, in the struggle. In return, I could keep quiet about your... habits?"

"And how far do you think you'd get? There are police crawling all over the area. They've probably picked half your guys up already. Let's face it you're on your own."

"So are you, Keith. So are you." The man strode purposefully forward until Parrish felt the cold metal of the muzzle against his head. Gripped by terror, he froze and heard his torch clatter to the pavement. The eyes were cold and hard and full of evil. "Anyway, not sure that's true, mate."

Suddenly, Keith felt his arms grabbed from behind, a warm panting breath on his neck as his shoulders threatened to pop. Exhausted and defeated, he yielded to the inevitable. The sirens were louder. A voice behind said "We've got to go—now."

"Seems it's your lucky day. You had better keep your mouth shut about tonight or better still have a sudden loss of memory. You keep quiet and so will I. This'll be our little secret, eh?" Behind the muzzle, the safety catch clicked and Parrish closed his eyes, as the voice, condescending and superior, whispered: "I'll be watching."

Then the arm swung. The gun impacted Parrish's jaw sending yellow and white stars through his brain. His breath swam away, and the ground loomed closer. He wondered if the whole evening was a dream and he would wake in the arms of Irina.

Chapter 27

Neasden, 8:30am, 7th June

The odour would never leave Scott Daley. A sickening, sweet, acrid stench of roasted flesh and burnt petroleum that assaulted the nostrils and coated the tongue. For weeks, it would cling to clothing, clouding the air each time he took off his overcoat. It would lurk around the coat stand next to his desk and inside his car. Even in retirement, he knew the smell would be there, waiting for his mind to dredge up some half-forgotten memory, some gruesome, grinning black mannequin, taut-skinned, sunken-eyed.

His mobile had jolted him upright at 3:30am. Deb Whetstone made the call. For the second morning that week, she was dragged early from her beauty sleep and, in Daley's view, it was showing. Racing around to the outskirts of Neasden, the factory was easy to find, stubborn flames still turning the sky orange, fogged by water jets and boiling, leaden smoke. Five appliances, thirty men. The ubiquitous white tent and four twisted, blackened corpses. Crews were still damping down what remained of the building. A viperous mass of hoses corralled fast-flowing streams of ash-blackened water across the car park. Blue flashes strobed off the puddles and high-vis tabards as firefighters dashed hither and thither, expediently clearing rubble under the harsh light of the hastily erected floodlights. Like a fallen soufflé, the roof had cascaded into the belly of the factory leaving a skeletal frame black against the clouded sky.

And the all-consuming smell brought bile to his throat.

Sleeping fitfully, his brain inevitably dwelt on the meetings with ACC Browning, with Kramer and Dodds. How could Gordon and Hewell be operating in different organisations, yet meet identical ends? What was the breakthrough? Why had Kramer not exerted more control over his operatives and, perhaps, saved a life?

In Daley's mind, middle-ranking officers fitted into three distinct types. There were the ones who preferred to steer the ship from the safety of an office, only venturing out when the proverbial hit the fan. Career coppers riding the waves to the harbour of a handsome pension and comfortable retirement. Like *Bilko* Bob Allenby.

And there were the Ray Kramers. The ones who seemed to know something or someone he didn't. Who managed to cosy up to the right people. Whose way always seemed to prevail. Daley tried to recall a single piece of work, a single collar that he could attribute solely to Kramer but he could not. *It's not what you know, it's who you know.*

Then there were those like Daley himself. Living and breathing the job, consumed by it. Immersed to the point of obsession. *Suicide Scott Daley* on the rail tracks to save a life, staring down the barrel of a gun to protect a serial killer.

DI Phil Dodds was much like Daley. They could have been hewn from the same rock. Now the blond-haired Inspector was striding across the sodden tarmac holding a cardboard tray of coffees. A crisp white shirt and primrose silk tie complemented an immaculate three-piece suit. Perhaps another area where the two differed. With a limited selection of shirts and ties in Terri's wardrobe, the choice owed more to Hobson than haute couture and Daley felt distinctly underdressed.

"Anyone inside, Scott?" Dodds glanced at the tent, in no rush to peer in.

Daley took a coffee and gestured his thanks. He had been hoping for a leisurely breakfast and a stroll through the St. George's Shopping Mall with Terri. Instead, it was carry-out and the reek of death. "Four in the tent. One of them was a night guard from the car outside. Throat slit. They want to bring in a specialist team later today once the building is safe. We are trying to contact the manager for a shift roster."

"Any witnesses?"

"Night security next door, heard a crash. Seems three cars arrived and took out the guard. Then, while they stayed outside, someone ram-raided the doors and torched the place.

Then he said the whole place lit up like a christmas tree. The cars reversed out and disappeared. Clinical. Corby is contacting the security firm for CCTV. Anything from those probably went up with the rest." He waved an arm at the devices attached to the front of the building. "The sprinklers were off and the Chief Fire Officer reckons they used an accelerant."

"Insurance job, maybe?" Dodds screwed up his face at the smell.

"No. No-one torches an occupied building for insurance. What is this place? Deb says it's one of Bašić's warehouses?"

"Yeah. He has three operations which he uses as a front. There are the *Cash and Carries* over at Dollis Hill and Wembley. This is his meat-packing plant. He has managers in and runs them all as legitimate businesses. Occasionally, we get wind of drugs or booze being stored but on the whole these places are the least of our problems. We are too busy focusing on the people further up the chain."

"So why torch it?"

"Who knows, Scott. Maybe smashing up vans is no longer enough. Maybe the lesson hasn't been learned."

"So you are connecting this to the van raids?" It puzzled Daley. The violence between the Westsiders and the Cjevovod had been going on for some time. Why suddenly escalate it?

"Stands to reason."

"What reason? What lesson?" Daley remained unconvinced. Too many assumptions.

"Well, respect, or lack of it. Bašić and McKaig have been at each other's throats for months. Maybe McKaig has made a decisive move?"

"Seems a little excessive." Daley gestured at the smouldering carcass. "Any idea what has sparked this escalation?"

Dodds shrugged, this time a little too casually for Daley's liking and he felt his hackles rise. "There must be something.

Christ, Phil. You're the specialist here. New shipments, payment problems. Changes to the routes, something."

"Seriously, Scott. Don't you think we've been over this? All we know is that Bašić is taking it out on McKaig and McKaig is returning the favour."

"Taking what out? Someone been stealing lunch money, knocking on doors and running away? What?" This was like blood from a stone. "Come on, Phil, two officers dead, four people in the tent, probably more in the factory."

"What do you want me to say, Scott? Revenge, tit-for-tat, my dad's bigger than your dad. Does it have to be more than that?"

"Seriously? That's the best you've got for half the villains in West London knocking seven shades of shit out of each other? You could have stepped in weeks ago. Made a few key arrests, put down a marker. Hell, you could even have saved Dean Hewell's life." Daley knew there was more. He had been around liars too long not to realise when someone, even a fellow officer, was being economical with the truth. "So are you happy now you have your massacre?" Daley swung an arm at the white tent. "What kind of outfit are you and Ray Kramer running here?"

"Just because you and Kramer don't see eye to eye..."

"Look, this is not about me and Ray *bloody* Kramer. This is about Joe Gordon and Dean Hewell, about those four corpses and all the others. How many more have to die before you and Kramer realise you can't just let things meander on? You have to stop these people." Exasperated, he turned away from Dodds and headed for his car.

Suddenly, Daley felt himself submerging in the anger he felt for those who could perpetrate such atrocities in his city but more, he was enraged no-one had sought to stop it. Good men were doing nothing and evil was prevailing. He needed to be away from this carnage and destruction, away from the ash-laden air sticking to his skin. He needed to feel cool, clear air in his lungs. He needed to look into Terri's eyes, feel her hand in his and know this wasn't his entire world. As he unlocked his Audi, he felt a vibration in his pocket. It was DS Monaghan.

"Gov. We have a problem."

"Shoot."

"Keith *the Uniform* Parrish. He answered a shout last night following your factory raid. They found his squad car burnt out just off the North Circular at his last known location - Welby Road."

Daley sighed and asked the inevitable, not wanting to hear. "And Parrish?"

"No sign, sir. Car was empty."

"Get on to Whetstone. See if she can track him down. And keep me informed. I have other business to attend to."

Chapter 28

Neither Hillingdon nor Lambourne Road had enough space to accommodate a press conference so Detective Superintendent Allenby sequestered the largest meeting room in a nearby hotel. To be fair, the gutter press would sniff out a story wherever they held it if there was a chance of a free sandwich and a cup of coffee. He requested forty seats be set out, so that the MPS, BBC and Sky camera crews could rearrange them when they arrived. Forty feet long, navy blue drapes made the room appear windowless. Air conditioning whirred but it still felt stifling. To Daley's right the front wall, fringed by a bridge of disco lights, hinted at parties and dancing, raucous congas and drunken declarations of undying love before the fight in the car park. Today though, the lights were off, except for a few piercing spots which lit the top table and curved white backdrop carrying the Met logo and the strap-line *Working together for a safer London.* Two or three technicians checked microphones and adjusted cameras. There was an air of expectancy, or was it trepidation?

A handful of early bird reporters had arrived by the time Daley sidled in. He recognised Karina Montague, the crime and community correspondent from one of the cable channels. Around thirty, pencil thin, wearing a maroon two-piece and a functional yet flattering cream blouse, her heels were low enough to walk in but high enough to pierce the jugular. Daley had learned not to relate looks to intelligence; her beautiful green eyes were lasers and her tongue barbed and razor sharp.

The BBC had sent their usual man, Jared Waseem, suited and booted but somehow invisible. He was the guy that stood outside Downing Street when the regular chap thought it too wet or cold. Around him, like tramps expecting a handout, four or five reporters from the local rags hoped that a broadcasting contract would rub off on them.

They had spared Daley the top table. In a room further along the corridor, Allenby, Kramer and Diane Browning were discussing tactics involving the relative positioning of feet and mouths. As they entered the room, the strobe flash of cameras temporarily blinded Daley. Diane Browning took the central seat with Bob Allenby to her right and Ray Kramer to her left. Tamping her sheaf of papers, she surveyed the room, scrutinising faces, assessing the trouble makers. Karina Montague was already sharpening her scythe, Waseem honing his righteous indignation. Clearing her throat, Browning began.

"First, thanks for coming at such short notice." She flashed a business-like, polite smile, paused and then read from the page.

"In the early hours of Wednesday morning, Detective Sergeant Dean Hewell, of the North West London Drugs Intelligence Unit, was found dead in Northolt. We are treating the death as suspicious and have launched a murder investigation. We are appealing for witnesses who may have been in the vicinity of the Alton Retail Park, at the time of the incident. Also, we ask that if anyone has any information, however insignificant it may at first seem, they should phone the Incident Room on the number being shown on screen now.

"Dean Hewell was a dedicated officer who gave his life serving the community—his community. He has an outstanding record of service and we are all deeply saddened by his death. I would like to extend our sympathies to his family and his fiancée. Now, we have," Browning twisted her wrist, "ten minutes for questions. Bob?"

Allenby scanned the mass of hands, shooting skywards like lances at a military re-enactment. "Jared?"

As one, the hands fell disconsolately and Waseem checked the arrangement of words on his pad. No open question that would allow the catch to wriggle off the hook.

"Jared Waseem, BBC News. Superintendent, are you connecting this latest incident with the death of Sergeant Joe Gordon, almost two months ago?"

Allenby checked sideways but met a deadpan face. "At the moment, we are keeping an open mind but we will re-evaluate based on the evidence."

"Can you tell us what Sergeant Gordon and Sergeant Hewell were working on?"

"Both officers were involved in a multi-agency initiative aimed at reducing the availability of Class A substances on our streets. Other than that, I cannot comment for operational reasons."

Or, thought Daley, because Kramer and his team have given us bugger all to work on.

"Do you believe the same killer is involved?"

"Again, at this stage we are not linking the deaths. It would be wrong to speculate." Allenby broke eye contact with Waseem and flicked over to Karina Montague, a short nod for her to assume the mantle. Montague leaned forwards in her seat, her skirt riding above her knees, intentionally in Daley's view. She aimed her question at Ray Kramer, at whom she had been staring since the conference had begun.

"Karina Montague, Sky News. Detective Chief Inspector. Could you confirm that these murders are linked to the recent upsurge in gang- and drug-related violence in the Neasden and Wembley areas and will you be making any arrests?"

Kramer seemed genuinely shocked that anyone had spoken to him. "We are, er, pursuing several lines of enquiry and arrests will follow."

Daley closed his eyes and puffed. Currently, there was no sign of an arrest. No wonder Wolverhampton Wanderers were going down if even their supporters left an open goal.

Montague sensed blood. "Given that Sergeant Gordon was killed nearly two months ago and there have been no arrests to date, are you able to explain the lack of progress made so far in bringing the killer to justice?"

"Investigations of this kind are complex and require dedicated manpower. Timing of arrests is crucial in securing a conviction." Kramer shuffled papers as he quoted from the textbook. "Due to the tragic death of Dean Hewell, investigations have been stepped up and we have drafted in a specialist team."

"So, Detective Chief Inspector, it takes the death of a second officer to warrant Joe Gordon's murder important enough to draft in a specialist team?"

Even at twenty feet, Daley could see the beads of sweat on Kramer's brow. Browning had her head down, but she was a seething cauldron. Montague drove the knife a little deeper.

"Do you think Gordon's wife and child are happy that you treat their husband and father as second best?"

"Both cases receive equal priority. We value all of our officers..." Kramer's mouth was a tent flap in a force ten gale. "Sergeant Gordon's wife and family are at the top of our thoughts every day..."

"Chief Inspector. Given your lack of progress, do you still believe you are the right man for the job?"

"I, er, we ..." Kramer paled as the room erupted in camera flashes. His eyes were wide. Allenby anxiously looked across the table and took over.

"Karina," Daley noted the use of a first name, disarming. "Sergeant Gordon's death was callous and meticulously planned. The investigation has been painstaking and thorough. I can assure you, we have spared no resources over the last two months..." *Bollocks*, thought Daley. *Kramer and Dodds have had their thumbs up their arses.*

"But you are no nearer to finding out who killed these officers?"

"We are working on several significant leads and are confident we can bring the killer to justice." In the darkness of the wall, Daley had to admire Bilko Bob's calmness under fire. Allenby asked for questions and spears shot skywards.

"John Whiting, ITV London News. Given the two months since Sergeant Gordon's death, and now another police officer has been brutally killed, can you reassure the citizens of these boroughs they are safe to walk to work, to let their children play in the street?"

"Well, John, the recent upsurge in violence is largely drug-related. The public should not be concerned for their personal safety. However, I would again urge anyone who feels they have information that may be helpful, however insignificant it may seem, to come forward. We will treat all information as confidential."

"Assistant Chief Constable. Andy Snow, Daily Mail." A whippet of a man, sharp-eyed and cynical, as befitted his role of a reporter on one of the country's most right-wing tabloids. "Where does that leave the Mayor's Office proposals for cutting police numbers across the city? In the light of this upsurge in violence, will you be recommending to the Mayor that the proposals are unworkable?"

Browning shared a glance with Allenby. The discussions had moved on to the politics of MOPAC quicker than expected.

"The fight against crime cannot be fought with statistics and plans, Andy. I—we—fully support the Mayor's proposals and we will offer him every assistance in achieving his goals."

"...at the expense of officers like Sergeant Gordon and Sergeant Hewell. Surely, we need more police on the streets not fewer? We need to be opening police stations not closing them."

"The deployment of officers on the street is a small, though significant, part of the Service. MOPAC considers police numbers across the entire Metropolitan Police Service estate. To achieve its aim of a twenty percent reduction in overall numbers, consideration will be given to many factors, including existing numbers and areas of focus. Inevitably, some areas will see a reduction but others, where a positive benefit can be realised, may see an increase."

Again Daley felt relieved that he was not on the top table as he would invariably have told several of these reporters to sod off. His respect for Browning grew infinitely as she answered Snow's question with a huge number of words which meant nothing.

"In terms of MPS estate, I see it as a proactive step to close under-utilised facilities and refocus our personnel where they can be of most use. One last question. Bob?"

Allenby surveyed the sea of raised arms and chose a woman in the second row. Slender and blonde, she reminded him of his elder daughter. Less likely to go for the jugular. How wrong could a man be?

"Melissa Roan, Herald Tribune. Assistant Chief Constable. With the death of two police officers, an unprecedented rise in gang-related violence, guns increasingly being used on the streets of the Capital, Londoners do not feel safe in their homes. Do you not think it is time you stepped aside and let someone else take over?"

"Far from it, Ms Roan." Browning spat the title like an insult. "The Chief Constable has expressed every confidence in our approach and that of the North West London Drugs Unit. Over the last year, they removed over six hundred kilos of Class A drugs from the streets, saving countless lives. That work will continue alongside the investigation into these officers' deaths. In the last forty-eight hours we have combined the resources of the Drugs Unit and the North West London Homicide Unit under the command of Superintendent Allenby. Both teams have an excellent track record on cases of this type. However, as I stated earlier, there is a need to refocus our personnel where they can be of most use, so I am asking the Chief Constable to sanction the redeployment of more officers to assist in the investigation. I am confident that the efforts of Superintendent Allenby and his team will soon yield results."

Behind her eyes, Daley could see that Browning was fuming. Surely she must have understood that the media care little for two dead officers. Their page inches prefer to focus on what went wrong, on responsibility and culpability. People in power being brought down to size sold newspapers. As reporters filed their copy and crews packed up their gear Daley could not help but muse on the paradox. At a time of increasing austerity in the Metropolitan Police Service, Browning had doubled the combined resources of the Drugs and Homicide Units. It was up to Bilko Allenby to make good on her promises now, especially given the rumour regarding Chief Constable Roger Summerhill's tenure.

Chapter 29

Moscow Court Mansions, Ealing. 10:00am

"Is that his?" DC Mike Corby peered through the windscreen at the dated Lexus IS200. Lowered and tinted, mean and black, a typical phallic statement.

"Yep."

Reversing the Golf down the alley, Whetstone parked next to the Lexus. Above, a curtain flapped at an open window. A cat stretched on a flat roof in the stifling heat and an anger boiled and frothed inside her. Keith would probably saunter in for his shift, having spent the night on some bloke's floor sleeping off a skinful, blissfully unaware someone had torched his patrol car.

Yet a sixth sense told her something was wrong.

Parrish's bedsit was a pokey medley of rooms at the rear of a mansion block. The once smart set of 1930s mock Georgian apartments, were past their best. Over-painted sashes and unweeded verges behind a squat peeling fence. Though the building seemed to have existed forever, convenient for the University of West London, there was a sense of impermanence as students came and went. Now, as her eyes adjusted to the gloom, the oppressive must and rancid food smells hung in her nostrils.

Why did Keith prefer this to her house? Several times she had suggested he move in. Maybe he was hanging on to his youth, a commitment thing? Maybe he was just being awkward?

Squinting in the gloom, she led Corby up the dark flight of stairs, down a corridor and around a dogleg. She heard a distant arrhythmic thump, as the door knocked against the latch. Thin slivers of light pulsed around the doorway to Keith's apartment and a chill coursed down her spine.

Gingerly, Corby edged open the door. The room beyond, a small, unloved sitting room, was empty. There was a layer of dust across every surface, the detritus of a single man lying everywhere. In the kitchenette, the kettle was cold, a scum stuck to the dishes in the sink. Whetstone eased open the bedroom door. The bed was drawn back, sheets crumpled but cold to the touch. A dark, musky odour hinting at vague frantic memories which now seemed absurd. Had the flat always been this untidy or had someone ransacked it? It was hard to tell.

"God, this place is a mess." With his fingertips, Corby raised a shirt draped over a dining room chair. "My girlfriend would throw an eppy if I was this untidy. TV on standby. Jeez!"

The open window, the flapping curtain, caught Whetstone's eyes. Why would Keith leave and not close the window? *Was someone in here when we arrived?* Her heart quickened as she felt the pressure of unseen eyes watching her every move.

"We need to get Forensics over here."

In the bathroom, a razor and toothbrush still lay on the glass shelf but the cabinet was open. The sink was dry. The fear balled in her stomach. Where was he?

"Sarge. We've got company." Corby edged a curtain aside. "I noticed them driving over but thought nothing of it."

Whetstone followed Corby's finger.

"Dark blue BMW. Two occupants." Parked at the end of the alley, the half-moon eyes were ablaze, the engine idling. "We picked them up at by the viaduct in Hanwell."

"Did you get a number?"

"No, couldn't see the plate. They were two cars back."

"Let's find a better vantage point without them seeing us."

Whetstone locked Parrish's apartment as she closed the door. Together, the pair edged back along the corridor. Whetstone recalled a window in an alcove, a cul-de-sac between apartments. Outside an engine revved, a roar resounding off the brickwork. Pressing her face against the grubby pane, she could see the BMW as it reversed up the alley and skidded onto the road.

"Shit!"

"What's this about, sarge?" said Corby, nervously.

"Don't know, Mike."

"There were BMWs in the reports of the van ambushes."

"Lots of BMWs in London."

"Still..."

"Yeah, I know."

Chapter 30

Despite the humidity, a distinct chill had descended on the streets of Ealing as Browning and Allenby left the hotel. A storm was brewing. Close, electric. Soon car doors closed against the ever-present rumble of London and the Mercedes glided out into the fractious Friday afternoon traffic.

"Jesus Christ, Bob. What the hell is wrong with DCI Kramer? I thought I told you to have a word. Get him on the same page." Browning charged into the conversation, not sparing the horses.

"Two men down, ma'am. He feels their loss deeply like the rest of us. For that woman to be inferring he cares more about Hewell than Gordon... I can understand how he feels."

"He made us look like bloody idiots. Either he smartens up his act, or he goes. Next time, I want Scott Daley there. He may not be the most politically correct person in the force but at least he can give that bitch from Sky a run for her money."

Allenby pursed his lips and nodded. Press conferences were a game, and they all played by the rules. The panel sat behind their microphones with a prepared agenda and an aim to stick to it. The audience, the interrogators, also had an agenda, aimed at derailing the panel. Allenby had never been a fan of the media; their scathing black-and-white analyses usually ignored the infinite shades of grey between. Their questions concealed accusations. Kramer was no stranger to press conferences either but he was not a natural.

"Then that guy from the *Daily Mail* brings up bloody MOPAC. For Christ's Sake, put on another record!"

"Flavour of the month, ma'am. By Sunday, it will be some aristocrat screwing his wife's gym instructor in a Nissan Micra."

"Maybe, Bob, but you have no idea how much I am laying on the line here. Roger Summerhill pretty-well blew a fuse when I asked for more resources. If Dean Hewell hadn't been killed, he would have sent me away with a flea in my ear. You know Summerhill and Hewell are related? Cousins or something."

Allenby rolled his eyes undiplomatically. Nepotism over ability. Not something he had enjoyed himself.

"Soon, you'll have thirty people in your division, Bob. The Hillingdon Drugs Unit is completely ineffective. If it wasn't for DI Dodds, they would be roaming around clueless. Your own team isn't much better. I need you to bring focus to the team. Make them play nicely together, carve out some results. If we are lucky, we can keep most of them, regardless of MOPAC, but it's down to you." Browning's tone tautened. "I—the Chief Constable—will need results and fast. And for God's sake, put a boot up Ray Kramer's arse. He's making us all look like bloody amateurs."

Allenby could feel his blood rising and checked the need to defend himself. It was always easy to criticise from the comfort of a desk at Scotland Yard. Salvation was six short minutes away and he could restrain himself that long.

Not that she wasn't right.

As he crested the steps outside Lambourne Road, Allenby could feel his heart pumping. He watched the Mercedes thread into the afternoon traffic and stifled the urge to throw an uncomplimentary finger after it. With twenty years' experience before Diane Browning had even been born, he felt he knew a thing or two about team dynamics and despite appearing, as Browning had often described them, *a bunch of mavericks*, they achieved results. Their clean-up rate was in the upper quartile. Maybe a well-oiled machine is important when you are pushing out press releases and drawing organisational charts, but when dealing with murder, one had to think like a murderer, not a bureaucrat.

If only he could say the same about the Drugs Unit. He had skim-read their records, case summaries and arrest rates and it alarmed him. Already under siege and over-stretched when Ray Kramer had joined, little had improved. In fact, despite an influx of resources, things had only gotten worse.

Now the brouhaha between rival firms had escalated beyond a squabble, it had been Dodds who had stepped up to the plate.

Competent and supremely confident, a natural leader, Phil Dodds carried the bulk of the load. He led case conferences and team meetings. He managed the workload and determined their priorities. Within six months of the pair taking over the team, Ray Kramer appeared to have given up. He simply did not seem dialled in.

However, it concerned Allenby that Dodds was content to cover for Kramer's inadequacies. Maybe Dodds had taken the line of least resistance with a view to ousting him sooner or later?

As Allenby pressed the button for the fourth floor, his arm gave him gyp once again. A dull aching numbness down behind his elbow had extended behind his shoulder, urging him to rotate his arm, to squeeze away the pain. Checking his watch, he resolved that he may just catch the GP's surgery if he could find a minute before the afternoon briefing.

Chapter 31

Bašić's Cash and Carry, Dollis Hill, 12:00pm

Against his better judgement, Daley knew he needed to strike while the iron, or brickwork, was hot. Before Bašić organised his thoughts. So reluctantly he agreed to accompany Phil Dodds across to Dollis Hill. On the drive over, Dodds left Daley in no doubt about three things. First, the Cash and Carry, like Bašić's other public facing businesses was straight-up, legit, legal. Second, Bašić would already know everything there was to know about the factory fire. And third, in between the bouts of rage and wanton destruction, regardless of how calm they themselves kept, he would say absolutely nothing of interest. For Daley, that was par for the course, even with Kramer and Dodds. Even so, he assumed that if his mind was on the fire, it may not be fully on other matters.

Of course, the fire was important but the conflict between Bašić and McKaig intrigued Daley more. Almost overnight, quarrelsome neighbours had become the worst of enemies. Five van raids, violent and public, had set the two overlords at each other's throats. Now two drugs officers had been executed and a factory destroyed.

As they left the car, two enormous goons without a neck between them, ambled across the car park and shadowed them through the warehouse and up to the office. Bašić himself was fashionably late. Flanked by the two minders, he arrived five minutes later, stretching out a hand, his face lit by a wide, business-like smile.

"Mr Dodds. To what do I owe this enormous pleasure?" Danilo Bašić, was a short man, shaved salt and pepper grey with a square jaw and rough fashionable stubble. His English bore only the slightest hint of an accent. The image of urbane, European cool, dressed in a check lumberjack shirt and jeans and a casual tweed blazer, his sunglasses raised like a visor to rest on top of his head. He seemed incongruous amongst the paraphernalia of the untidy makeshift office.

"Mr Bašić. Thanks for seeing us at such short notice. This is my colleague from Homicide, Detective Inspector Scott Daley."

Bašić made the most imperceptible of nods as he shook Daley's hand so hard as to crush his fingers. His eyes were dark, sharp and calculating. Right now, they were summing up Daley. Considering his presence. Perhaps, defining the word *homicide*.

"The fire in Neasden?" asked Dodds.

"Yes. Four, maybe five people? That is a tragedy." Bašić rested his chin on a hand and gazed ruefully sideways. "My manager says a total loss."

"Ivan Terzić? Yes, we have spoken to him. Do you have any idea who would want to do such a thing?"

Bašić hunched his shoulders and smiled. "I am a legitimate businessman, Mr Dodds. All of my employees are happy or they are not my employees. I pay them well and the food in their bellies makes them loyal. You would need to speak to Terzić. He has said nothing to me."

Factories like Bašić's had sprung up all over London, catering for the influx of foreigners into the Capital, to satisfy their tastes for familiar foods from home. Many of them also served as a cover for illegal workers and people trafficking. Workers were often zero-hours, casual staff, off-payroll and invisible. There was a risk that the bodies in the ruins may never be identified, if they were found at all.

"Still, looks like you pissed off someone big-time, sir." Daley watched Bašić's eyes. "Someone owed money? Employee with a grudge maybe? Or was it something else?"

Bašić shrugged noncommittally. "I have plenty of enemies. I arrived in the UK ten years ago and I have been very successful. Plenty of people are jealous. Maybe they think my success is unfair?"

"But you think one particular person?"

Bašić ignored the question. Daley continued: "So you think one of these *enemies* might have taken it upon themselves to commit arson to spite you?"

"Who knows what these people think?" Bašić replied dismissively.

"These people?"

Bašić cracked a derisory half-smile. "We are all grown-ups here. You know as well as I do what is happening. This is McKaig, the Westsiders obviously. They have been causing trouble for weeks. They ambush my vans, steal my stock. They put my men into hospital."

"That's not what I am hearing, though, is it? Word is that this is not a war between the Cjevovod and the Westsiders. Word is that you are staging the attacks on your own people to draw attention away from the Cjevovod, then casting the blame at McKaig and the Westsiders."

"These are very serious allegations, Inspector. Do you have any evidence to back them up?"

"Merely what I've heard, Mr Bašić."

"Well, you have heard wrong. We all know who is behind this, Inspector. John McKaig. For fuck's sake, he destroyed my Mercedes. That Scottish bastard can burn down my property, kill my men yet I am the first person you come to? Is it not about time you stopped him?"

Daley watched as Dodds smiled. It was a game.

Dodds continued: "Forensics teams are scouring the factory. If there is anything that links to McKaig—or anyone else—we will know."

"This has been going on for months," snapped Bašić, "and all I hear from the police is that they are investigating. Why am I not surprised that you throw the blame at me?"

"Joe Gordon. Killed in April," interrupted Daley. "Dean Hewell. Killed last Wednesday. Both undercover police officers. Both shot through the head. What can you tell me about that?"

"Nothing, Inspector. Hewell was one of our street bosses. He called himself Colin Standish. I did not hear of him until yesterday when I was told they had found a body. It is a great shame because everyone says he was hardworking. Given his divided loyalties, I am not surprised someone took a dislike to him. As for this other officer—Gordon?" Bašić shrugged his shoulders.

"Did *you* take a dislike to him? Did *you* blow his cover? Maybe you got sick of him disclosing your business to us?"

"No, Inspector. For one, you discovered the body. If the Cjevovod had killed him, there would be no body." Bašić grinned patronisingly.

"Urdin Azeri. What do you know of him?" Daley stuck a metaphorical foot out in front of Bašić who stopped momentarily, confused. His eyes flicked briefly down and to the right, then were back on Daley, who could almost feel the sigh of desperation from Dodds. Then, back in character, Bašić smiled wryly, almost pityingly.

"There is no such person, Inspector. If there was, he would be dead. His men would be dead and you *plods* would know nothing. He is a concoction of John McKaig. To divert attention away from what he is doing." He shared a glance with Dodds. *The Inspector is out of his depth.* "Seems like he is doing a good job."

"Or a concoction of yours, Mr Bašić," responded Daley.

"Look, Inspector. You and I both know what business I am in. For years the Cjevovod and the Westsiders have lived together in relative peace. Then, suddenly, we have Urdin Azeri. Suddenly, I am losing stock and vans. My *workers* cannot go about their business without the look over a shoulder. And where is this happening? On my ground and only my ground. Not to the West and the North. My ground. Gang wars are expensive and bad for business. Why risk my livelihood?"

Daley was unsympathetic to the Bosnian's mewling. "But it's not just your ground, is it? It's not just the Cjevovod. The Westsiders are suffering attacks, losing vans and stock."

"Of course they are. A few self-inflicted wounds to divert attention. Plausible deniability, I think the Americans call it."

"That argument could work both ways, Mr Bašić. You must agree, it's convenient that we hear the name Urdin Azeri every time someone attacks your property. Then when the Westsiders get hit, it's the same. Yet nowhere can we find any evidence that anyone, other than the Cjevovod and the Westsiders are involved."

Returning to Hillingdon Road, Daley fished out his car keys. Dodds had been right. They had learned nothing. Almost as if on script, Bašić had blamed his opposite number Paisley John McKaig. It troubled Daley that in the space of a few hours, the mysterious Azeri had been mentioned twice, each time dismissed as a ghost. But as the embers of the stricken factory cooled, and the smoke dwindled, there could still be a fire somewhere.

Chapter 32

"Ivan Terzić."

"Ivan. The police have been here. What did you tell them?" Bašić cradled the phone receiver on his shoulder, lit a cigarette and exhaled a fog of cigarette smoke.

"Only what they needed to know. The manager has given them access to the staff rosters. Apart from that..."

"What about the storeroom?" Whilst the meat packing factory was a legitimate business, many of Bašić's affairs were not. The men had used a small storeroom behind the factory's offices as a temporary cache for shipments.

"Empty, boss. We cleared it out yesterday after the attack on your car. Dogs might smell the powder but I doubt they will bring dogs."

"This is all getting out of hand, Ivan, and the police don't seem to give a damn. I had that Inspector from Drugs around. He was only going through the motions, how do they say, *putting the manners onto us*. But there was another policeman too. I think he may be trouble."

"What do you mean, boss?"

"He says I have burnt down my own factory."

"Come on, boss. What evidence does he have? You and I know there is none. Nothing links you to any of this."

"Still, I am worried. I can handle the Drugs Squad but this other guy... I think he will keep on digging."

"You want us to sort him out?"

"No, not for the time being. Keep an eye on him. If he becomes too big a problem, then we will act." Bašić took another deep draw on the cigarette, staring at the slug of ash teetering on the tip, then mashed it out into his cup. This spat between the Cjevovod and the Westsiders was getting out of hand. Only a decisive move would end it. McKaig had tried, and he had hurt Bašić. Now it was up to Bašić to kill McKaig.

"I need you to gather the men. Burn down *the Sonata Cafe*. That should give McKaig something to think about. Something to take his mind away from my affairs."

The Sonata Cafe was Paisley John McKaig's field headquarters. A small, insignificant business where his managers and bosses came to settle their accounts. It also did a mean cooked breakfast. Torching the building would send McKaig stratospheric.

The line lapsed into silence, then Terzić said: "Seriously, boss. Surely that will just anger him more?" Bašić could sense the nervousness in his voice, an attempt to distance himself, maybe?

"So what do you propose? We throw him a tea party?"

"No, boss but maybe we could wait a day or so. With two runs, clearing up the factory, we are stretching resources too thinly. There is more scope for something to go wrong. If McKaig attacks either of our runs, I will personally pour the petrol in the bottles and light the rags."

Bašić pondered. He was on a knife-edge with Anatoly and, for the first time since he took over the London operation, he was racked with indecision.

"OK. Two days. Then burn the place down and make sure McKaig is inside."

Chapter 33

Major Incident Suite, Lambourne Road

Allenby had asked Daley to take the briefing on his own. On Friday afternoon, with another raid and the potential for the weekend to be cancelled, there was an undercurrent of resentment that *Bilko Bob* was already on the driving range. Putting down his coffee, Daley began.

"It's Friday 7th June at 5:32pm. This is the second briefing for Operation Nightjar." There was a round-robin as the key players identified themselves. "Sergeant Monaghan, the video evidence?"

Monaghan had located two cameras so far; one of each shooting. Others were probably available, but they were on Council property and it was POETS day - *Piss Off Early, Tomorrow's Saturday.* The first was a night vision camera in the loading bay in Northolt. A distorted green haze over the car park with Hewell's Range Rover along the top right of the frame, grainy and indistinct. The time stamp rolled as a stooped figure shuffled across the void to the driver's door and there was an exchange. As he stood beside the car, another figure strode in, a stilted gait, almost comical, like frames from a silent Mack Sennett short. The second man raised an arm. A tiny flash and the stooped figure fell. Then another and the car window became a black void. After a cursory search, presumably for the ejected shell cases, the man disappeared as a glow began inside the car, ebbing and flowing, increasing by degrees until it overloaded the frame with orange.

"This is Holborn, April 12th."

Monaghan ran similar footage of Joe Gordon's car. This time facing the camera. Again, silhouetted against the dimness of night. Once more the arm raised. The window exploding. Again, the ground searched and the ball of orange consuming the frame.

To Daley, the events were identical. A single killer. "Can we identify the gunman?"

"No, sir. Estimate five-nine or five-ten but he has a ski mask and a boiler suit." Taylor flicked the display to show his own screen, a series of grainy images, a vague figure, pacing across the front of Hewell's car, a wary glance at the camera. Taylor stilled the frame, zooming in. The face now filled the screen.

"Cocky bastard." Daley felt the chill. A challenge in the eyes. Catch me if you can. Was there a smile beneath the mask?

"Any evidence left by the killer?"

Taylor shook his head. "No, sir."

"Potter?"

Taylor shrugged. "Looks like he *did* simply get in the way."

"Anyone else on the CCTV?"

"No, sir."

"So, Mike?"

Corby's head bobbed up from his pad. "I went to see Janine Riley first. They have put her on medication so I didn't get much. She said Hewell never talked about his job but that recently he had become preoccupied, though with what she didn't know. I asked if he had a computer but the Drugs Unit had already taken it. I will visit again in a couple of days. Eileen Gordon said the same. Neither woman could recall hearing anything unusual. Seems both Gordon and Hewell took their calls in the garden out of earshot."

Daley had hoped for more. "DC Smollett, what do we know about the war between the Westsiders and the Cjevovod?"

Smollett turned over a page. "25th April. Bašić's van is held up in Dollis Hill. Witnesses claim two cars intercept the van. Four masked men armed with baseball bats or pick-axe handles attack the driver and steal the load. Roughly two weeks later, McKaig's van is held up in Wembley Park. Same MO. Then another one-and-a-half weeks and Bašić's new van, in the meat packing plant livery, held up in Neasden. Another two weeks. McKaig's transport, a white Renault Kangoo, held up in Hanover Road Wembley. Then, Wednesday night. Another raid, this time on Bašić's Mercedes saloon. Witnesses report masks and baseball bats, loads transferred from the Mercedes to some saloon cars, dark coloured, model indeterminate. Each time, whatever the van or car is carrying is spirited away, probably drugs, maybe cash, along with the victims. By the time plod arrives, the mess is cleared up."

"I spoke to an associate at Organised Crime," added Monaghan "He reckons they have all the hallmarks of a message being sent."

"Message? What sort of message?"

"No idea. Stop stealing my punters. Don't piss on my chips. Whatever. To have it prolonged over almost two months sounds more serious than that. A turf war, maybe."

"Maybe Joe Gordon's death was the catalyst?" interjected Whetstone. "Maybe he asked one question too many? Revealed too many of McKaig's secrets?"

"But the feud continued. Surely, if it were about Gordon, that would be the end of it?"

Whetstone shrugged. "Who knows? Maybe Gordon discovered something about Bašić's operation and it was Bašić who had him killed?"

"Then in June, Hewell is killed." Monaghan considered. "Perhaps it took that long for Hewell to make the same mistake as Gordon."

"Occam's razor. Maybe they got careless and let something slip?" Daley sipped at the canteen coffee and grimaced. Most covers were blown in the first weeks. Yet criminals were innately suspicious. Fart in the wrong place and one could have one's throat cut.

"Maybe, but it wouldn't take much of a slip."

Corby wasn't convinced. "Both of them? By different firms? Surely one or the other. Not both."

Monaghan sat up straight and opened the file in front of him. "Tend to agree. As a matter of protocol they had little direct contact. With the two gangs at each other's throats, even if they met, Gordon and Hewell would probably lamp each other to keep up appearances."

"The only point of convergence," remarked Whetstone, "apart from the Drugs Unit, was that both reported a breakthrough."

"And the way they died," added Corby.

Daley had the feeling they were wearing a circle in the carpet. "Any more on the drugs gangs?"

"Nothing we don't know already, sir. Reading through the files from Hillingdon, they were regularly busting street dealers from each of the firms. No patterns, nothing that might constitute a breakthrough."

"And Urdin Azeri and the Encubierto?"

Smollett shook his head. "Again, sir, only what we know. Files are full of reports. Seems this new organisation is blamed for everything but keeps so low a profile as to be horizontal."

"Keep at it, Rob. If Urdin Azeri is real, then we need to know. If not, we need to find out which of these two is pulling our plonker."

"You know what worries me," pondered Whetstone. "This is all too elaborate for a drugs killing. This is clinical and planned. You step on a cockroach. You don't plan its death."

Monaghan nodded. "I agree, Deb. This all points to assassination. How likely is it that two rival gangs would hire the same assassin to commit two separate murders?"

"Unless they happened to do it independently...," interjected Whetstone. "If they hired the same killer, odds on it was the same person or persons doing the hiring. The point of convergence. The breakthrough."

"OK. We need to get as much footage as possible. Even stills. Other cameras, entrance to the car parks, neighbouring properties. We need to identify who else was there. If possible, we need to discover how the killer arrived, whether he was already suited up or whether he changed nearer the scene. Dave, Steve, concentrate on that."

"Rob." Daley turned to Smollett. "Extend your net. Look for similar crimes being committed elsewhere. Signs that other gangs in the area may be masquerading as the *Encubierto*."

As the team dispersed, Daley held back Whetstone.

"Deb. You OK?"

Whetstone sighed and placed her bundle of papers on the table. "Yes, sir. Just a lot on at the moment, then there's Keith."

"He'll turn up. You know Keith." But somehow, Daley knew it would not be that simple. Units had been on the lookout for Parrish but there had been no sightings. Whetstone had reported the Lexus parked outside the apartment. Corby had found the keys in a draw but had neglected to remove them. Now the car was gone.

As Whetstone dropped behind her monitor, Daley remembered the *Jiffy Bag* that had come from Judith Gascoigne. Tearing away the corner, tipping out the contents, he stared at the key for a long moment. Cut from a single piece of aluminium, it was from a simple padlock or bicycle lock; a deterrent rather than security. In his mind's eye, he pictured a ramshackle rural garage, peeling paint and dry rot where a vintage Aston Martin languished, just waiting for a new owner, such as Daley, to take good care of it. After all, he had no idea what Gascoigne got up to in his spare time. It might as well be vintage car restoration, or boats, or vintage planes. But not locomotives. Definitely not locomotives.

Tied to the key, a label bore the numerals 1, 2, 5, 13, 34, 89. Bemused, Daley peered expectantly inside the *Jiffy Bag*. Maybe there was a note. Alas, it was empty.

"What good is a key if you don't know what it's for?"

"Eh?" Whetstone's head bobbed up briefly.

"Nothing." Not realising he had spoken out loud, Daley quickly pocketed the key. With two murdered policemen, it would need to wait for another day.

Chapter 34

Alperton, 7:00pm

Two days in and Daley was already weary. He had made an enemy out of Kramer and he sensed Dodds' patience was wearing thin. To investigate one's colleagues was uncomfortable enough, but to scrutinise the conduct of a fellow officer was tantamount to treason. He resolved that there was no easy way out of the situation other than head-long through it.

The house in Alperton was already partially boxed up and had been since Christmas two years ago. With uncharacteristic naivety, Daley assumed that the divorce would be amicable; that, differences aside, they could apportion the assets fairly and bid farewell. However, Lynne's smartly dressed yet overly ambitious divorce lawyer thought differently. He drew up a list containing everything Daley owned, and a few things he didn't—including the house. Subsequently, Daley's own more experienced lawyer, sourced via the Met, became involved. He informed his opposite number of how the divorce would work, broadly involving fair settlement, a rolled-up decree absolute and a place where the sun don't shine.

After that, the boxes languished unemptied along the hall and landing, compelling him to shimmy his way through, cursing each time he stubbed his toe or grazed his thigh. For the life of him he couldn't remember what they contained.

Terri lay in ambush, arms folded, as he latched the front door. "If you think I am having all this crap in our new house, Scott Daley, then think again."

"I'll sort it, honestly." He watched as she sidled along the corridor of boxes, into the living room, then recoiled as her head bobbed back around the door frame.

"You better had. Now, away and bring me my supper."

With paperwork signed, the three respective house sales would complete in a couple of weeks. Many metaphorical sets of buttocks were clenched as chains held and deposits were banked.

Which left Daley with a few problems.

The Gordon and Hewell murders were likely to dominate his life, leaving little time to organise the move, let alone sort the boxes. A removals firm had been engaged but, in Daley's opinion, most tradesmen were charlatans so would need to be closely supervised. As would Terri. Her idea of tidying up was akin to slash and burn, especially when it involved anything Lynne had brought into the house. Terri's own house in Harrow was a typical single woman's abode, all soft furnishings, colour-sense and flowery fragrances. Alperton, in contrast, was a man-pad; hard and plain with a vague smell of dust, sweat and cold takeaway. He could only hope that the new house would be an amalgam of both, minus the smells.

Then there was Terri's condition. At four months, the bump was showing; she was craving pickles and Daley's heart was full of dread. Centuries ago, he and Lynne had planned their family; two parents, two children, two window seats in the back of the car, a bedroom each in the house. However, the first attempt became the last, the baby became a miscarriage, and the relationship foundered. He and Terri had known each other for three months when fate conspired. The blink of an eye. Still getting used to being a couple, they would soon be a family.

Finally, there was his career. Something in the back of his mind was unnerving him, something basal and raw. Two officers murdered. Why not a third?

Why not him?

Was it right to put himself in harm's way again? His responsibilities were changing. Where there was one, there would soon be three.

As he brought a tray through to the living room, Terri was reclining in the corner of the sofa, her legs brought up, shoes kicked off. The television was playing an early evening soap. Usually an immense sense of peace came over Daley when he came home and she was there. Today, though, as she picked from the tray he was filled with self-doubt.

"Terri. You are happy, aren't you?"

Mouth full of bread, she turned her head and stared, puzzled. "What's brought this on?"

"Me, you, the baby, the house. Things have changed so fast."

"Thank God for that, eh? You were a right mess when I picked you up."

"I'm just scared that it's all an illusion. That I will wake one morning and it will all be gone."

"I say that every day about those boxes."

"This weekend, I promise."

The look of scorn said everything. She moved his hand onto the tiniest of bumps. "This isn't going to be like before. Things are different. You are different. You've finally grown up."

Daley was not sure he liked the notion it had taken him until thirty-eight to grow up but he understood what she meant.

But maybe the dramatic changes in his life were a smoke screen? Maybe it was the case? At the start of an enquiry, a huge abyss that opened up between himself and the truth he would inevitably need to find. The bottomless chasm that moaned and wailed the failings of the past, the insecurities he tried to conceal, the feelings that deep down, he was not good enough.

Leaning over, he kissed on the cheek.

"Right now. There is nowhere else I would rather be."

"Well, that's a shame then because you forgot the ketchup."

Chapter 35

The Goldfish Bowl, Lambourne Road

Allenby glanced up at the clock. 7:00pm. If he were quick, he might just make his slot on the driving range. Testily, he cast the manilla folder across his desk. If there was one trait he found irritating it was incompetence and, to his mind, there was plenty of that at Hillingdon. Already failing, this latest upsurge in activity had stretched DCI Kramer beyond the level of his incompetence. The Drugs Unit ship sinking but Kramer was whistling *Dixie* while Dodds paddled like crazy, both of them staring at the water spouts as they gushed through the hull. With DI Dodds, holding the wheel from the passenger seat, there was a need for a stronger captain. Now a new appointment seemed doubtful in light of the MOPAC.

To Allenby's mind, they should have monitored Gordon and Hewell more closely. All the records, the reports, telephone transcripts amounted to data with no analysis. Much of it was meaningless. Reports of events after they had happened with no attempt to prevent, or at least, predict another occurrence. Why were Kramer and Dodds not asking questions as he had of his team? Now it seemed that pleasure lay with him. His PA had finally found a slot that Kramer could not wheedle out of but that was not for a couple of days. Until then he had to rely on Daley and Whetstone.

Allenby started as a sonorous beep disturbed his musing.

"ACC Browning for you, sir."

"Put her through, Pat. Would you ring the golf club and tell them I won't be there tonight? Oh, and could you rustle up some coffee please? This could be a long 'un."

Sitting upright in his chair, jarring his already sore arm, Allenby imagined what catastrophes were so important that they had percolated to the 7th floor of 10 Broadway.

"Ma'am?"

"Bob, how's it going?"

"OK. I was just about to leave," he added hopefully. "You received my email?"

"Yes. To tell you the truth, it worried me."

"Sorry, ma'am but that was the intention. I am sure Ray Kramer is doing his best but perhaps that is not enough. Given the recent spate of incidents, maybe he has a resource issue?"

"Bollocks, Bob. I am sure he would appreciate your loyalty but it's misplaced. DCI Kramer has a Detective Inspector, a team of three Sergeants and five Constables. Then there are the collators and civilian support. At a rough guess that's fifteen individuals plus Kramer himself, yet their work rate is poor. All I ever get from him is that Dodds and the team are busy and it should not be long before they produce results. Candidly, what do you really think?"

In Allenby's experience, when someone, especially a senior officer, asked what one *really* thought, that was the last thing she wanted to know. He genuinely believed Kramer was a waste of rank, that they should make Dodds up and that both should fall under the purview of an experienced Superintendent who could whip them into shape. However, if he said that, Browning might think he was touting for the job which he definitely was not.

"I don't know, ma'am," he lied. "Perhaps Kramer is just temporarily overwhelmed."

"Seriously, Bob? What do you have? A Detective Inspector, two Sergeants, three Detectives Constables, a couple of uniformed Constables and two civilian support officers. Your clean-up rate is exemplary and the number of cases on your books is far higher than DCI Kramer's."

"I have an excellent team around me." He neglected to point out how many of those cases had stalled.

"Exactly my point. Look, two officers down, mayhem on the streets. It's like the Wild West out there. I'm just waiting for the Gunfight at the OK Corral then we will all be up in front of the IPCC, or worse the Commissioner. It's clear that things cannot carry on the way they are at Hillingdon. I need to show the Roger Summerhill some results. Right now, they all appear to be chasing their tails."

"So maybe he needs an experienced Superintendent?" Allenby felt the magnetic draw of the conversation in his direction.

"We all need to be seen to be making progress, positive inroads. Including your lot."

"Ma'am, I assure you that my team..."

"Bob, again, I admire your loyalty but it's not me you have to impress. You know that. If we are going to amalgamate Drugs and Homicide anyway, I see no harm in doing it sooner rather than later. We need to mix things up a little."

Allenby rose and gazed down on the steady stream of mid-afternoon traffic. An unsavoury juxtaposition between what his ears heard and his eyes saw.

"These teams have very different ways of working, different styles of leadership. I am not so sure that's a good idea, ma'am."

"And that's why I want you to step in and provide guidance. DCI Kramer and DI Daley need to work more closely together. If the changes go through, soon they will have to. Ask Inspector Daley and Sergeant Whetstone to transfer over to Hillingdon. I want Kramer to report to you in future. I have every confidence you can sort the Drugs Unit out. On the QT, if Daley and Dodds can take up the reins, we can decide what to do about Kramer as we go along."

Exasperated, Allenby's shoulders dropped. The aim was to take on less responsibility rather than more. He stretched out his left arm and flexed his fingers. He blamed the new number two wood and some overzealous midweek practice. Of late, he had been concentrating on distance rather than accuracy and the club stretched the tendons a little. Peeling two Ibuprofen capsules from a blister pack, he gulped them down with what remained of his coffee. Maybe he was a little too old even for golf? Was that all he had to look forward to when work had released his shackles? Enforced retirement due to restructuring, only to languish in a floral armchair watching *Countdown*. Or mouth agape, dribbling and dreaming of the fairways?

"Ma'am, drugs is a whole different discipline. This is not an overnight process."

"I know that, Bob, and I have assured the Chief Constable that you are the man to pull these teams together. In return he has authorised a further five civilian support officers based at Lambourne Road with Sergeant Monaghan. That will give you command of around thirty staff."

"With all due respect, ma'am, I have my team investigating the death of two of their officers. Even now they are struggling to maintain their impartiality."

"All the more reason for them to work together. Division of labour, Superintendent. I need your Homicide Unit to concentrate on the murdered officers and I need Kramer to pull his socks up. Look, Bob, there's an opportunity here for both of us if we play our cards right. If we can show that our services are in demand, maybe someone else will draw the Chief Constable's fire. Outside of domestic violence, there is a huge correlation between drugs and violent crime, especially murder. I believe a combined Drugs and Homicide Unit will prove itself invaluable to the MPS, even in the light of the priorities being given to Cyber-intelligence."

"Ma'am." Allenby's tone was conciliatory. Perhaps the amalgamation of Drugs and Homicide under one roof would be beneficial? Maybe the bean counters were right after all. Economies of scale, a leaner team, a meaner one. Once Daley and Kramer had finally knocked the living shite out of each other and were playing nicely, that is. But he didn't relish the extra responsibility the sudden increase in workload would bring.

Roger Summerhill, the Chief Constable, had mentioned a trip up to Scotland, fly-fishing on the Tay. When this was all over, when the dust had settled a little, he would call him.

Chapter 36

For the umpteenth time since arriving home, Deborah Whetstone cast a wary eye through the curtains. The road was still and empty. Earlier an ice-cream van had lured a gaggle of small children with the promise of ices. A delivery man on a Lambretta had delivered a pizza and for the first time in over a year she had waved to the neighbours. For the life of her, she could not remember their names. Now it was growing dark and the street-lamps were illuminating the dusk.

Arriving home earlier, she had half expected to see Keith sitting in the kitchen, stealing her beer and grinning that inane grin which, in the early days, had made her horny beyond belief, but the house was still.

Then she checked the street again. But no dark blue BMWs.

Round at Keith's, a SOCO had taken samples from the window frame and the doorjamb, confirming that someone had forced the window but little else. Only Keith could tell if anything was missing, such was the state of the place. Corby had spent the afternoon performing a fingertip search, establishing that, if it were a burglary, the thief was not interested in jewellery or watches nor the obscenely large flat screen television. More concerning, there was nothing to indicate what could have happened to Parrish.

Walking through to the kitchen, she poured a *Cup-a-Soup* into a cup. There was little else of any calorific value in the house and she really didn't want pizza again. Earlier, Corby had found copies of Parrish's recent bank statements; a little bedtime reading to help her drift off. Lazily casting an eye down the columns, she smiled wryly. Things were bad when even bank statements could not send one to sleep.

Then she noticed something strange. Puzzled she reached for her phone and found Corby's number.

"Corby?"

"Hi, Mike. It's Deb Whetstone. Not disturbing you, am I?"

"Well, actually, yes. Melanie has me cleaning the bathroom tiles. Yellow marigolds and everything. I'd appreciate it if you could keep it to yourself as my street cred will be shot."

"Already shot, Mike. We had you down as a mommy's boy."

"Harsh. Anyway, what can I do for you?"

"When you searched Keith's apartment, did you find anything out of the ordinary?"

"Like what?"

"Drugs, alcohol. Anything that might point to addiction." Was she clutching at straws? Anything to explain his erratic behaviour, the cooling of their relationship.

"He had a small bag of weed hidden behind the bathroom cabinet, a few tins of Carling in the fridge but no. Why?"

"These bank statements. There are regular cash withdrawals from the same ATM every Sunday evening. Two hundred pounds."

"Shopping money for the week?"

"Come on, Mike. Did you see two hundred pounds worth of shopping? And anyway, there are lots of other small card transactions at supermarkets."

"There were a few decent shirts but now you mention it, no. Where was the ATM?"

"Fisher's Gate. That's Greenford."

"What would he be doing there on a Sunday evening?"

"Dunno, Mike." Whetstone tried to picture the area, seedy and grubby, nothing but a few tired terraced houses. She thought back to a time when she and Keith used to go out together. To her knowledge there were no friends in Greenford. "Anyway, who's Melanie? I thought it was Claudine?"

"Well, you know..."

Closing the call, Whetstone poured water into her cup and walked through to the living room, stirring as she went. There was an old film on TV. A platinum blonde, helpless and fawning, panting over a musclebound square-jaw. She imagined herself and Keith six months before. Huffing she switched it off and burnt her tongue on the piping hot soup.

Was this the extent of her existence? Maybe she should get some cats?

Chapter 37

The Sonata Cafe, Wembley. 8:30 am, 8th June

As the door slammed and the sprung bell chimed furiously, Daley cast an eye around the Sonata Cafe. The air hung heavy with the odour of frying bacon and burnt grease and there was a vibrant murmur as punters clogged their arteries. At one end, a middle-aged bottle blonde was studying her phone, casting but a short glance at the two police officers. Kramer gave her a short nod and, opening the hinged flap in the counter, he and Daley passed through to the back.

"To what do I owe this enormous pleasure, Mr Kramer?"

Paisley John McKaig lowered the broadsheet he was reading for effect. Dressed in a navy-blue shell suit and upmarket trainers, his face beamed a broad, if disingenuous smile. Beside him Dougie Murdoch, arms folded, was cautiously eying Scott Daley and Ray Kramer, as they screeched out chairs and sat uninvited. Two sentries stood outside the door, ready to re-educate anyone foolish enough to enter.

Despite his own misgivings, Daley had taken Bob Allenby's advice, agreeing that the only sensible approach would be a direct one. Sensible for whom, he was unsure. Still, cards needed to be marked and damn quickly. So, the previous evening, he had contacted Dodds and asked him to arrange the meet. Dodds himself had cried off, jokingly suggesting that Kramer was more than man enough for the job, once he had become accustomed to the light outside his office.

Ray Kramer adjusted his sharp but ill-fitting suit and cleared his throat. The nerves were already beginning to show, thought Daley. His eyes were skipping between Murdoch and McKaig as if one or the other was about to shout *Boo!*

"Alex Jordan?" The question carried little authority.

Paisley John stroked his chin theatrically and leaned over to Murdoch. "Oh, Jordan. No, I don't know a Jordan. Do you, Dougie? Alex - Jordan?" He laboured the name, in case Murdoch hadn't caught it, knowing he had.

Murdoch unwavering, expressionless, was tight-lipped. Arms still folded.

"No, me neither. However, I think I met a Joe Gordon once. Bald, kinda ugly looking. Weegie like me and Dougie here. Used to work for me. Yes, he called himself Jordan. Fooled no one. I wonder what happened tae him?"

"I think you already know, John. Holborn. Someone put a gun to his head and then torched his car."

"Oh, well, there you go. That's what comes of secrets, Chief Inspector." McKaig grinned broadly. Assured he had said enough, he flapped the broadsheet and pretended to read.

"So, Jordan, Gordon, whatever. Tell me. Do you know if he was in any kind of trouble? Whether he had pissed off anyone enough to want to kill him?"

Daley inwardly sank. A police officer working undercover in a drugs firm. Most people wanted to kill him. Kramer was as much use as a van full of chimps.

Feigning slight irritation, McKaig once more lowered the broadsheet. "Mr Kramer, as soon as he rocked up, we could tell he was polis. If me and my boys weren't such law-abiding citizens, church people and all, we'd have sent him packing months ago with a boot up his arse but as we have nothing to hide..."

"What about Mick Bullard? Now I am certain you know him." Ray Kramer's face had hardened. Lacing his hands, placing his elbows on the table he leaned forward. Through the determination, Daley could see the fear in his eyes.

"Now there's a name that takes me back, Mr Kramer. Aye, I know him. Short guy. Ex-boxer. Part of Frank Warren's stable back in the day. Used to be handy with his fists but rumour was he had a glass jaw. Whatever happened tae him?"

"Enough of this convenient amnesia. We know Mick Bullard worked for you up until last Wednesday. We know he was riding shotgun in one of your vans when it was attacked in the early hours. Now he's dead."

"I heard a heart attack. So sad. I must arrange flowers for his wee grandchildren."

"What was he doing in Wembley that early in the morning?"

"How should I know? Walking the dog? Buying chocolates for his tart?"

"I think he was taking a new shipment of cocaine over to Dollis Hill where it could be cut and distributed."

"Well, you know more than me, Mr Kramer. I don't deal in drugs. Nasty, filthy stuff. Dollis Hill is a legitimate business. Fancy Goods. If Bullard was out at that time of night, he was doing a foreigner. Nothing to do with me or my men."

Murdoch's eyes flicked towards McKaig. The first movement since they entered apart from breathing, and Daley suspected he controlled that. He decided to intervene.

"So how is it we have you on CCTV entering and leaving the Middlesex Central, on the same day that Mick Bullard dies there? Bit of a coincidence, wouldn't you say?"

"Not really. If you must know, I visited Tony Mason. He was pretty banged up by those bastards, no thanks to your guys who were nowhere to be seen. There's nothing wrong with showing a bit of compassion. You should try it yersel, sometime."

"So, Bullard. What did he do, John?" asked Daley. "Did he go off piste, grass on you to Bašić? Tell him where and when the van would be parked up?"

McKaig leaned over the table and growled. "You know he bloody did. I changed that route ten minutes before the bloody van left. No-one knew where it was going. No-one! Still, that bloody Polack bastard found it. Bullard conveniently stops for a waz. A bloody waz! And lo and behold, Bašić and his men turn up and knock ten colours of crap out of them."

"What about Jordan? Was he grassing on you to Bašić too? Is that why he had to go?"

"Who's your poodle, Mr Kramer? Is he house-trained?" Once more a smirk from McKaig. Kramer's head swivelled sideways, acknowledging Daley, then swivelled back.

"Inspector." Murdoch kept his arms folded as he spoke. Daley sensed the power behind the throne. "We had nothing to do with the murder of your officer, nor of the other one— Sergeant Hewell? Unless you have more concrete evidence to the contrary, I suggest this meeting is at an end. Gentlemen?"

"Look, Mr McKaig. We know what that van was carrying and where it was going. We have you entering and leaving the hospital..." Kramer was now floundering, scattering disconnected suppositions like corn feed.

McKaig bolted upright, clattering the chair to the floor and leaned over the table. The veins in his neck throbbed. "You come into my manor, threatening me with all kinds of shite while Danilo bloody Bašić is making me look like a pooftah and pissing himself laughing. They have beaten nearly a dozen of my best men to minced steak, damaged five of my vans and stolen stock right from under my bloody nose. And youz are doing sweet eff all about it. So don't you come around here threatening me. You want to speak to me, go through Dougie, here. He will arrange for my lawyer to be present. Now piss off and leave me to ma breakfast."

The big scotsman was puffing like a steam engine and his face was crimson. Dougie Murdoch unfolded his arms, laying a calming hand on McKaig's forearm. A quick shared glance and McKaig reluctantly dragged back his chair and sat down heavily.

"Gentlemen," insisted Murdoch, proffering a hand towards the door. Kramer remained seated, eyes locked with McKaig, while Daley rose, separately trying to suppress the urge to punch the senior officer or McKaig, or both. To Daley's mind, people rise to the level of their incompetence. Kramer, it seems, had yet to reach knee-height.

The air outside the cafe was fresh on Daley's face and the sweat beneath his shirt clammed to his skin. Beside him,

Kramer stood motionless, staring along the street to his car and the promise of escape it presented. He had waded in well out of his depth. Even at this first meeting, Daley had decided Paisley John McKaig was a king not a boss. In the old days that may have sufficed. He spoke and people agreed or suffered the consequences. Arbitrary decisions borne mainly out of rage. Rule by fear. But times had changed. The power behind the throne lay elsewhere, with educated men, decision makers, bean counters. People like Murdoch.

And Ray Kramer did not understand how to deal with them.

Was that what Allenby intended by persuading him to drag Kramer along? That the DCI would reveal his utter ineptitude and give MOPAC ammunition to side-line him? Maybe Allenby just needed enough to shove him sideways in the investigation? Either way, Daley had learned nothing of any importance.

"Inspector?"

Daley turned to find Dougie Murdoch, hovering outside the door.

"May I give you a lift?" The wiry scotsman pointed to the SUV. Clearly, transport was the last thing he was offering.

Kramer cocked his head. "We have a car..."

"Thanks. That would be great." In a moment of decisiveness which might yet prove to be foolhardy, Daley nodded at Murdoch and then tossed the keys to Kramer. "Sir, you take the car. I'll meet you back at base."

Now piss off out of my investigation.

Chapter 38

Lorry Park, Saw Lane Cement Works

The SUV pulled sharply off the road and bounced over the pock-marked ground, shaking Daley's organs inside his body and throwing up a rooster-tail of dust. He recognised the cement works, the tall storage silos towering against the clouds, shadowed tendrils across the dusty empty lorry park. Vast, empty, unnerving.

As the pair alighted, Murdoch produced a tin of *Davidoff Primeros* panatelas and offered one to Daley, who refused politely, despite knowing how expensive they were. In his teens had had gained a liking for cigars but the price had deterred him. There must be a tipping point where life expectancy outweighs the risk to health. Looking around the open space, no cameras, McKaig's enormous associates dragging their knuckles, he felt that point might be close right now.

"I have to apologise for the behaviour of my friend, Paisley John. He is highly strung at the best of times but at the moment he is easily excited."

Daley wanted to say *I am not apologising for Kramer. He's a twat.* Instead, he nodded graciously as Murdoch flicked the lighter, a yellow flame illuminating his eyes, a puff of sweet smoke evoking in Daley a nostalgia for his youth.

"I am not sure we have been properly introduced." Daley looked about as a slight breeze sent sand devils across the open ground. The sun was round, barely shaded by cloud and the sweat dampened his back. The hundred yards around the car was utterly deserted.

Murdoch smiled through the cigar smoke. "You can relax, Inspector. I have long since ceased to rip new arseholes. This is business." Turning to the rear of the SUV, he opened a cool box and threw Daley a bottle of water.

"And what business would that be?" The icy condensation burnt the palm of his hand.

Murdoch ignored the question.

"I am not Paisley John. My name is Murdoch, Dougie Murdoch. I am John's right-hand man. I provide the brains of the organisation whilst John provides the brawn. I head the management arm of the organisation and if I keep the money coming in, John is happy. As you can see from that tawdry pantomime at the Sonata, there is an uneasy relationship between Mr Kramer and Paisley John. Every few weeks, something happens and your people come around to put manners on him. John ignores them and stuffs them back in their box. The Drugs Squad feel they have done their bit and John makes a few changes. Life carries on as normal. It's a natural order to things. A *status quo*."

"So, Kramer lets McKaig get away with murder and everyone is happy?" The admission astonished Daley but it did not entirely surprise him.

Murdoch paused and surveyed the empty yard. After a long moment he turned back to Daley.

"There is a highway in Tunisia, the P19, which runs southwards across the Northern Sahara towards Libya. Along its length, men and boys sit under shades with containers full of petrol, smuggled across the border. When a car pulls up, they climb a stepladder and exchange a few gallons for a few dinars, or dollars—preferably dollars. Now and then, the Tunisian Police will confiscate some fuel and all the takings. But they never take the hoses and the ladders."

"Tunisia is a poor country, and the government realises it cannot afford to keep its people. The trade in contraband fuel keeps them fed and out of the welfare system so everybody wins. Shut it down, people will starve, the state will expend vast amounts in the attempt and be criticised for not spending it on the people. No-one wins. So, they show their faces, make a token gesture and leave the hoses and ladders."

Daley frowned. "So you believe the law is discretionary? That you can either choose to obey or not when it suits you?

You believe it is acceptable to exploit the most vulnerable in our society, for lives to be blighted by drugs?"

Murdoch cracked a wry smile. "What I believe, what you believe, is unimportant. It's a system and you can't buck the system. My father once advised me that if I swam against the tide, eventually my arms would become tired. Sure enough, they did. Fortunately, I met up with Paisley John and the tide turned. Now I swim with it. I let the system take care of itself and reap the benefits.

"Look, Inspector. This is just a game. If we didn't play it, then someone else would. Addicts will get their fix. Drugs gangs will continue regardless of the efforts of the police. The *status quo* will always prevail whether McKaig runs the district or Danilo Bašić. Like I say, it's a natural order."

"It might be a game to you but you try explaining that to Joe Gordon's wife and child, to Dean Hewell's fiancée."

"Lie down with dogs, you get up with fleas."

Gulping a mouthful of water, Daley could feel the blood rising but this was neither the time nor place. Murdoch could be a useful ally. Squinting against the sun, he wished he had accepted the cigar.

"What? We turn a blind eye and let you carry on?"

"Not blind, no. Maybe partially sighted." Murdoch smirked at a joke which, on another day, Daley may have found funny. "You play the same game. You make a few token arrests now and again. We keep our heads down and get on with what we know best. If Kramer wanted it, he could shut us down in days." Murdoch snapped fingers. "But what will happen then? There would be a vacuum so strong the whole of West London would implode. Every runt, street corner dealer, every immigrant overlord would descend, looking to make a quick buck. Every other John McKaig and Danilo Bašić would crawl from under their rocks to claim the territory. And it wouldn't just be drugs. It would be extortion, prostitution, money laundering, terrorism, everything nasty in the world would crawl around the borough. If you think it's violent now, you can't even imagine how it would be then."

"And it's not already like that?"

"No, Inspector. It's a *status quo*. They don't need step ladders and hoses to sell their contraband. They just ply their trade discreetly and quietly. The public at large sleep soundly and your people make token arrests, just to reassure them."

"But now two Drugs Unit officers are dead. That goes into a different in-tray—mine."

Murdoch smiled, arrogant and condescending. "From atop the moral high-ground, it's easy to slip and a long way to fall. I am not saying we are angels, given the business we are in, but I am telling you now, we did not kill Alex Jordan. Every now and again we fed him some bogus information, sometimes we fed him the right stuff. But we didn't kill him. Nor the other guy."

"Colin Standish. He was with the Cjevovod."

Murdoch shook his head. "Don't know him Inspector but if he were with the Cjevovod, then that's not a surprise."

"And Mick Bullard?"

Picking a fragment of tobacco from his tongue, Murdoch again chose to ignore the question. Daley felt it was time to move on.

"What do you know about Urdin Azeri?"

A flick of interest crossed Murdoch's face and once again a smile, this time tinged with respect.

"Nothing, Inspector, and everything."

Daley perched on the bumper, in the shade of the SUV.

"Tell me."

***

"About three years ago, there were reports of trouble with our people down the line. Intimidation, extortion. Street corner dealers being mugged." Murdoch leaned against the SUV and coaxed another panatela into life. "John and I had seen it all before. Some reprobate with ideas above his station fancies a piece of the action. It was small time. We put the feelers out, called in a few favours intending to give them a gentle slap."

"And?"

"And nothing. The feelers went out and nothing came back. Of course, John is convinced that this is all down to Danilo Bašić and the Cjevovod, some crude attempt to extend his territory."

"And Bašić swears that it is McKaig and the Westsiders," countered Daley. "He believes that you are attacking your own vans as an attempt to deflect attention elsewhere. *Plausible deniability* was the phrase he used."

"If the Cjevovod wanted to extend their reach across London, they could do it anytime. Quickly and decisively. We are easy pickings. On the other hand, if we wanted to extinguish the Cjevovod, we would be on a hiding to nothing. Bašić knows there are thousands in his homeland who would pour into London and annihilate us. The Westsiders are small. We have nothing to gain. Everything to lose."

"So what's changed?"

"Urdin Azeri. The Encubierto. The names started popping up in connection with the attacks. John was having no truck with it nor were the Drugs Squad. With no firm information, no name, no face, I must say I agreed."

"But?"

"Over time, I found out more. Rumours that Azeri came from Spain or Portugal, a Basque freedom fighter turned drug supremo, that he had men across London, awaiting his opportunity. Together they call themselves the *Encubierto*."

"Then around three months ago, the violence escalated. They began picking off our vans, taking anything they could, wrecking anything they couldn't. We varied the routes, not disclosing them until the last minute but still they found us. How was a mystery. John took his usual approach and broke a few limbs. But still we found nothing."

"And why are you telling me all of this? Surely this is DCI Kramer's territory?"

"You have seen how much use he is, Inspector. McKaig and I will sort out any trouble we have with Bašić but it's the death of your two undercover policemen. I feel sure neither

Danilo Bašić nor Paisley John would welcome that kind of attention. It was not a management decision made by us to kill Alex Jordan."

"And why should I believe you?"

Murdoch shrugged. "Because as clever as we are, as the Cjevovod is, nothing ties either firm to the violence, except as victims of it. Surely over the year since it started, the three months since it escalated, one of us would have slipped up? Either that or Bašić would have planted something to implicate us... or vice versa."

"So why this?" Daley swept a hand over the desolate car park. "Why this theatre, now?"

Murdoch sighed. "I needed to speak with you in private. Paisley John and Danilo Bašić are at each other's throats. This whole affair is escalating out of control and something needs to be done to stop them before one or other launches a full-scale attack and we see a bloodbath. The Drugs Squad are incapable. Neither John nor Bašić are interested in looking for a third party. I think you are."

"How do I know you're not spinning me a yarn?"

Murdoch smiled. "You don't, Inspector."

"I'm warning you now. The Drugs Unit have stepped up their activities. The Westsiders, and the Cjevovod are being watched. You both need to cut your losses now before it all goes tits up for both of you. In the meantime, all I am interested in is the cold-blooded murder of the two officers. If I find anything that links back to you, if you do anything to hamper my enquiries, then I will bring the full weight of the law down on you. The Westsiders and the Cjevovod, will go the way of the Krays. I can guarantee you that."

***

As the SUV slewed back onto the road, Daley stared aimlessly out of the window, enjoying the welcome chill of the air conditioning. Murdoch had said little to change his view that Danilo Bašić and the Cjevovod were most likely to be linked to the murders of Gordon and Hewell.

And Azeri? Man or myth. He still could not be sure.

Chapter 39

Hillingdon, 12:00pm

The desks that DCI Kramer had allocated were in the naughty corner. It was the only explanation Whetstone could find for the enmity which the Drugs Unit showed her. Daley had yet to rock up, so she picked the best of the two which was not saying much. Someone had hastily cleared them of crap and she feared she may catch something from the keyboards. Anyway, if she had her way, she would not be staying long. Apart from Phil Dodds hunched over his PC, the office was a desert. It was as if she had come to work on a bank holiday.

Today, that's how she preferred it.

Earlier, a uniform had recovered Parrish's vest and equipment a few streets from his wrecked patrol car, There was no sign of Parrish. With the Lexus gone, it was clear that the bird had flown. The question was why. Logging in to the PC, she checked the serials. Still nothing.

Taking the copies of Keith Parrish's bank statements from her bag, she brought up a map of the area around the ATM on the computer screen. Greenford? What was Parrish doing there? Always the same ATM, always the same time, give or take. Flicking over, searching her email, she found police rosters that DC Corby had requested. On each occasion Parrish had used the ATM, he was on duty. On every occasion he was meant to be miles away on a different patch.

Just what was he up to?

Glancing up, she watched Dodds fingers clicking on the keyboard furiously. "Where is everyone, sir?"

Dodds turned. "Uh? Out in the field. We've stepped up *obs* for a while. The factory fire has got Bašić excited so the guys are making their presence felt. We don't drive desks at Hillingdon."

Whetstone returned a sardonic smile. There was a cardboard cut-out copper, arms folded, standing in her local supermarket. A deterrent for casual thieves. That didn't work either.

On a whim, she brought up the footage from the Mercedes ambush on the North Circular, a traffic camera on the footbridge above. She watched the Mercedes race through the frame. Then behind, two cars following. Flicking to a second video clip, a mile further on as they crossed the railway. By now, one of the pursuing cars was alongside the Mercedes. What happened next was out of shot. Replaying the clips, isolating the pursuing cars, she enlarged the frame. Grainy and sepia. Maybe they were black or brown but they were certainly BMWs.

She ran the footage from Hanover Road. Hovering over the petrol garage, as a white van pulled in, parking off the pumps, headlights appearing in shot. She saw the coffees dropped and the hats raised, then the cars silently sped from view as bodies writhed in the road.

BMWs. What were the odds?

Seeking out the video from the Hewell murder, she scanned the footage from the camera facing the Range Rover. A black figure, Potter falling, the search for shell casings and the fire taking hold. Then, headlights streaking across the tarmac in front of the Range Rover, slowing for the gunman to board. BMW, maybe a 5 series, possibly dark blue.

Pulling out her phone, she called DC Taylor.

"The getaway vehicle recovered last night in the police chase. The one Keith Parrish took off after? What make was it?"

"Dark blue BMW 520i. Late model. Stolen in Winchester three days ago."

Sending the images to the printer, Whetstone raised her head above the monitors.

"Sir, can I ask you something?"

Dodds, laboriously wheeled round in his chair, sighing. "Why not? Fire away."

"What do you make of the cars? They all seem to be late model dark blue BMWs, stolen and replated. They were used in both murders and they appear on every piece of CCTV footage we have. One was recovered from the chase after the factory fire and another was outside PC Parrish's flat yesterday."

"So? Fast, fairly common. Those things are keyless. Anyone with a bit of nous and a piece of kit from *eBay* can nick one."

"Yes, but doesn't it seem odd they are at *every* van ambush, both on the Cjevovod and on the Westsiders?"

"Not particularly, sergeant. Perhaps Bašić likes BMWs."

"Bašić's car was a classic Mercedes 500E Sportline, sir. Why not boost Mercedes rather than BMWs?"

"I have no bloody idea," retorted Dodds, irritably. "Look, I have a lot to get through..."

As Dodds returned to his typing, Scott Daley appeared and scanned the room, taken aback as he spotted Whetstone in the gloom of the naughty corner.

"Is this us? Thanks for bloody nothing." Arriving back at Hillingdon, he was dismayed to find Kramer had abandoned his car askew across two spaces. There was a storm brewing.

"Any news, Deb?"

"No, gov. Nothing. Come and look at this, though, gov." She had arranged the blurred printouts on the desk.

"Same car?"

"Same model. Three separate BMWs, judging by the index plates. Four including the one burned out after the raid."

"Get DS Monaghan to speak to Traffic. See if we can trace their movements, and find where they are stored." Whether it was Bašić or McKaig, they needed to find the garage.

Dodds raised his head. "DCI wants to see you as soon as. Not in the best of moods. Oh, we've cleared a desk for you." Dodds dismissively waved a hand at the naughty corner and smirked. "Might have to clear another one when Allenby hears where you've been."

"Piss off, Phil," snapped Daley. In the gloom, Deborah Whetstone raised her eyebrows.

The smirk on Dodd's face was just begging to be wiped off but annoying another member of the Drugs Unit would not be great PR. However now, appeasing Kramer was his first challenge. Knocking on the office door, he took a deep breath and strode in.

Chapter 40

"Sir?"

"Inspector." Kramer's eyes stayed on his computer screen. There was still a layer of permafrost from Daley and Whetstone's previous visit. It seemed to have deepened.

"So tell me, the *senior* officer, what did Murdoch want?"

"Took me out to Saw Lane. The concrete works. To be fair, I was shit-scared most of the time. Thought he might be sizing me up for a support act on the Gyratory. Or new boots."

Kramer turned and faced Daley. His eyes were blazing. "What? You think this is some kind of joke? You're a bloody idiot, Daley. You dismiss me, the senior officer, with a wave of your bloody hand. *In public.* Then disappear off with a known criminal for forty minutes. There is no record of where you went or what you were up to. If we find Murdoch was in any way involved with Gordon or Hewell's murder, their brief will piss all over us. Bloody hell. I thought you were more savvy than that!"

"It wasn't like that. Gordon and Hewell were a distraction to them. He is adamant he had nothing to do with their deaths and I am inclined to believe him. The Westsiders and the Cjevovod are at each other's throats and Murdoch can see his whole organisation turning to crap. It worried him you—we—didn't seem to be doing anything to stop it. Personally, I think he saw me as a fresh pair of eyes and ears. Someone who might listen."

"Bollocks. He saw a new kid on the block and wanted to mark your card. Take it from me, one day, you will regret getting into that car on your own. And did he get it? A new perspective?"

Daley pursed his lips and shook his head.

Kramer puffed and ran a hand through what little hair he had left. "Paisley John—armed robbery, grievous bodily harm, murder, albeit unproven. He's a bloody psychopath. Dougie Murdoch—armed robbery, murder—proven, money laundering. All of them up to their necks in drugs and prostitution. Your maverick tactics might keep you out of trouble over at Lambourne Road but there is no *I* in team here, Inspector."

"So if they are that dangerous, why were Joe Gordon and Dean Hewell on their own the night they died, *sir*?"

"Because they're bloody idiots as well! They are a bloody case in point. You take too many liberties with these people and they will have you. If they think you are in any way a threat, you will go the way of Gordon and Hewell. Jesus Christ, man. The whole point of us going together was to offer you some kind of security."

"Seriously? With all due, sir, I wouldn't rely on you to protect me from a randy poodle." Any respect that Daley held for Kramer had disappeared long ago but he immediately regretted his flippancy as Kramer's face turned an unpleasant shade of red, a simmering pot, struggling not to pop its lid.

"Enough of this!" Kramer's palm slammed on the table. The permafrost turned arctic. "I *am* the senior officer. I *will* have respect for the rank!"

Daley kept his eyes firmly on Kramer as the air prickled between them. A thousand thoughts careened around his head. Why respect the rank when it doesn't respect you? Rank doesn't make a good copper. Seniority doesn't guarantee common sense. Come the MOPAC revolution... Instead he replied "Point taken, sir."

Kramer tossed the Audi keys across the room. "Well, you better make sure it has been. Now bugger off."

Chapter 41

"Come on. We're off." Daley charged past Whetstone, a face like thunder and clattered through the doors. Locking the computer and grabbing her bag, she scampered on after him.

"Where are we going?"

"Timbuktu, Casablanca, Mars. Anywhere away from that bloody waste of skin." Daley bulldozed through the glass door and darted the key fob towards the Audi.

"In that case, I'll need to pop home for my passport."

Daley stopped and half turned. "What?"

"Timbuktu... Mali. Might even need a visa and shots."

"What the hell are you on about?"

"If you think I am getting into a car with you in this bloody mood..."

"So, I have to stand there and take it from—him?"

"Yes, sir, you do. God knows I take enough shit from you. Pull yourself together and stop acting like a child. There are more important things in life than your childish squabble. Two police officers are dead and countless others injured. We can't allow it to get in the way."

"But..."

Whetstone sighed and rounded on him. Three days into an enquiry and Daley was already getting a carpeting from a senior officer.

"But nothing, sir. DCI Kramer will get his in due course. We will see to that as soon as we prove what a shower of shit the Drugs Unit are. The investigation into Joe Gordon's death was thoroughly incompetent. You can drive a fleet of Routemasters through the holes in their reports."

"So how come no-one else can see that?"

"Because Ray Kramer is good at protecting himself. Because the best form of defence is attack. You know that.

He plays politics. He schmoozes the right people but most of all he keeps a ring of steel around his department. You've seen how difficult it has been even talking to them. If we can see the holes, then so will he and he will do anything to protect his team. Just like you would. I bet, right now, he is on the blower bitching to some high-up about your attitude."

Daley puffed his cheeks resignedly. "So I will have another rollicking from Bilko Bob later. Fantastic."

"Isn't the first, won't be the last. What are you always telling me? Focus. Eye on the prize."

"But, you weren't in there just now..."

"Oh, grow up!" After a night stressing about Keith, about her own world tumbling in around her, she was in no mood for Scott Daley throwing his toys out of his pram over a dick-waving spat. Daley rounded the car muttering to himself in a way that constantly infuriated her and, not for the first time, she wondered how Terri managed without putting a hatchet through his skull. She wondered if he had listened to a single word she had said.

"Now...where are we really going?"

"Loughton Street. I need to talk to Harry Ramesh."

Chapter 42

Standing under the shower, feeling the rivulets of warm water massaging her body, Diane Browning forced herself to relax. To switch off just for a moment. Her Saturday gym session was an opportunity to destress and, boy, did she need it. Yet after half an hour where she nearly melted the exercise bike, she still felt tense. Even after taking out her wrath on the punchbag, she had failed to dissipate all her pent-up frustration. Now, even the shower was annoying.

After a week of MOPAC negotiations, she felt under siege from all directions. Slowly but surely, her command was being hung out to dry and half her buildings closed to satisfy the Commissioner and the Mayor. The Chief Constable had reminded her they were not *her* officers or *her* buildings and then patronisingly advised her not to take things personally.

Which had gone down like a shit sandwich.

Of course, she took it personally! A female entrant in the mid-Nineties, her path to promotion had been relatively painless, as the Met advanced its gender equality programme. Working hard, choosing her allies carefully, she had languished in the lower ranks for less than a decade. However, all this had come at a personal cost. Her strength of character and dogged career aspirations frightened off most men; the rest were either married or equally ruthless. Single, childless, the job was everything. It was her identity, her life. With gender equality now *de rigueur*, she had lost even that advantage. She had devoted too many years to the machine for it to fall derelict to political entropy. Her own command had been subjected to what was euphemistically termed restructuring before. In the ensuing bun-fight, she only barely survived and now it was happening again.

Outside the cubicle, she checked her phone and exhaled deeply. Ray Kramer. Now what was he bleating about on a Saturday? Wrapping a towel around herself, checking the clock, she thought of ignoring it but DCI Kramer was persistent at the best of times. He would only ring again... and again. Clicking the text, she dialled the number.

"DCI Kramer, it's ACC Browning. What is it?" She flicked automatically into her business voice, terse and clipped. "I haven't much time."

"Ma'am, sorry for intruding on your weekend but there's something I think you should know."

Inwardly, Browning collapsed. She had junior officers so they could handle operational matters rather than push them up to her. Obviously, Kramer had not read that memo as he always needed approbation or approval for his actions. Or was he passing the buck? Spreading the culpability around. "Which is?"

"Myself and DI Daley went around to see John McKaig, the Westsiders' boss this morning. I am afraid that the Inspector rather let himself down..."

***

Closing the call, Browning mused over Kramer's specific choice of words - *let himself down, covert meetings, known organised criminal.* The DCI would be cleaning blood off that particular knife for some time to come if he managed to remove it from Scott Daley's back. She still had half an hour but these unplanned interruptions tended to consume her time. This was a job for Bob Allenby. Hopefully she could wreck his weekend as Kramer was intent on wrecking hers.

Finding the other number, the one marked *VIP* she dialled.

"Hi, it's me. Looks like I might be a little later than planned. I have some calls to make."

"I'll keep the champagne cool and the bed warm." The voice on the phone sent a frisson of excitement through her.

"I'll come as quickly as I can."

"Not too quickly, I hope." She heard a chuckle at the other end.

"I've never disappointed you before."

Closing the call, she imagined the bed, the warmth of his chest, the lost hours being someone other than Assistant Chief Constable Browning. Was this all worth it?

A long while ago, at some dinner or other, Professor Patrick Gascoigne had shared his cynical view on policing with her. At the time she had taken it with a pinch of salt but increasingly she had understood how much sense it made.

"Diane, my dear," he had slurred over a particularly fine postprandial brandy, "There is a balance to the natural order of things. For every *yin* there is a *yang*. For every action there is a reaction, every *Morecambe,* a *Wise,* well you get the picture. Consider a small island inhabited only by foxes and rabbits. As the rabbit population increases, the foxes feed on them, then the fox population increases to the point where there aren't enough rabbits and they die off. Then the surfeit of foxes dies off allowing the rabbit population to increase again until it is too great to support itself. The fox population recovers and so it goes on."

"And your point, Patrick?"

"Crime and policing inhabit an island. The Metropolitan police could not exist without criminals just as foxes need rabbits and, indeed, rabbits need foxes. The island is always full. Sometimes there are more foxes, others more rabbits. It's like Poe's pendulum axe, swinging from side to side, slicing as it goes."

In hindsight, she understood. With crime rates falling, police numbers needed to increase to keep the rabbit population down. So MOPAC was counter intuitive, reducing police numbers in line with the reduction in crime. When the rabbit population flourished again, there would be no foxes. Within her own command, the staggering increase in violent crime, two officers dead and God knows what to follow, maintaining numbers should be her priority.

She dialled Bob Allenby's number. He needed to speak to Daley and his team. They all had to stick to the agenda—her agenda—whether they knew it or not.

Chapter 43

Loughton Street Forensic Laboratory

Prior to the arrival of Harry Ramesh, the Loughton Street Forensic Lab was very much a Dickensian institution. Wood panelling, marble corridors and a blanket of sober, respectful silence. Professor Patrick Gascoigne had been one of the *Old School*, content to follow tried and trusted methods, eschewing all but the most necessary advances. *If it ain't broke, don't fix it,* he used to say, but he said it with the luxury of the state-of-the-art facility one floor above and Ramesh to cover his back as time marched on. Little had changed in the ten years since Scott Daley had vented his stomach at the sight of his first dissected corpse and disappeared to the basement for a mop.

Professor Harbinder *Harry* Ramesh was archetypal Millennial. Tech savvy, switched on to the digital world, pragmatic and results-oriented. Since his arrival, they had upgraded the computers and ordered new photographic equipment, not to mention something called a mass spectrometer. His goal was to make the laboratory a one-stop shop for forensics to attract more funding in a world where purse strings were garrottes.

He had also installed a new audio system and as Daley and Whetstone pushed through the door, they were assaulted by the cacophonous thumping of Hard House. Once more Whetstone felt a pang of nostalgia for the days of Patrick Gascoigne and the respectable air of the library he preferred. She could hear the dulcet tones of Len Ganlow echoing across the Examination Room as he practised his art. The air was a heady mix of disinfectant and the undertones of an abattoir.

"Ah, Inspector, Sergeant. Thanks for coming over. This may or may not be important but I will let you decide." Reaching over the desk, Ramesh handed Whetstone a plastic evidence bag. "I recovered this from the factory fire."

The mobile phone was charred and blackened. The screen was crazed and a dusting of greasy soot covered the shell. She peered at it curiously and handed it to Daley, who shrugged.

"I thought we had accounted for all the employees' phones?" They had carried an inventory of the dead workers' possessions, and those who had fled the fire through a rear door. Of course, some may have escaped and just kept running.

"Indeed. I bagged and tagged this phone at 6:15am on the day of the fire. Simon has been matching SIM cards to people. This is the odd one out."

Removing other evidence bags, the rest of the phones were twisted and gnarled, the damage clearly far greater than the first.

"Any fingerprints?" asked Daley.

"Just one partial on the edge of the SIM card when it was inserted. Not enough for an identification but in my experience, it's probably some spotty oik at Carphone Warehouse." Ramesh handed him a second bag. The tiny card was similarly blackened and grimy, this time with fingerprint dust.

"The unidentified phone appears to have escaped the hottest part of the fire, which got me wondering why."

"And?" Still frustrated by the debacle at Hillingdon, Daley wanted Ramesh to draw a conclusion.

"I believe this phone was not in the factory fire."

"You mean someone threw it in afterwards?"

"Whoa. There you go again. Me forensics, you wild theories. There could be a million explanations."

"Theorise, Ramesh." Whetstone preferred it when he took the easy option and agreed with her.

"I would say, it was dropped as the perpetrators fled, or thrown in after the fire had subsided."

"Like I said…," remarked Whetstone, somewhat injured.

"Almost…"

"Which would suggest that it was planted to implicate someone?" surmised Daley. "Can we keep this between ourselves, Ramesh."

Ramesh put his hand to his mouth and chuckled theatrically. "You Homicide detectives and your secrets. Scout's honour."

"Can you trace the IMEA number, see who the phone belongs to?" Daley turned to Whetstone. "Take the SIM card back to Lambourne Road. Let's see what Steve Taylor can make of it. I'll catch you up."

"OK. No fighting. Remember what I said, sir."

As the door squealed shut behind Whetstone, Daley removed Gascoigne's key from his trouser pocket. "Somewhere there is a lock for this key. Do you recognise it?"

Ramesh squinted at the key as a small boy would a captured beetle. "Where did you get it?"

"It's one of Patrick's. Judith Gascoigne couldn't identify a lock to fit it," he lied.

"There are some old lockers in the basement. Six feet tall and covered in spiders." Ramesh shuddered, his Achilles heel all too apparent. "Do you want me to show you?"

"Don't worry, I'll find my way."

Daley had been down to the basement once before many years ago to find a mop and bucket having left his breakfast over the pathology labs linoleum floor. Even now, as he descended the bare stone steps, it evoked the rancid smell of primary decomposition. Acclimatising to the blinking white neon, he saw several banks of lockers and wondered where to start. One could be systematic, start at the far left and work one's way forward but those at the far left were deep in shadow. Daley heeded his primeval instincts and started in the light.

Finally, on his umpteenth attempt, he pushed on the head of the key and one of the locks yielded with a metallic clunk that would have woken the dead above. He breathed deeply and exhaled slowly. For a moment, he wondered whether he wanted to open it, given Gascoigne's profession. Yet as he drew the door wide, he felt suddenly relieved and exhilarated in equal measure as he saw the envelope.

There is still hope for a vintage Aston Martin, Scott.

Using his phone as a torch, he examined every crevice of the locker but it was otherwise empty. Removing the envelope, locking the cabinet, he retreated to the steps and sat beneath a weak strip light. There was a string of numerals - 1,3,8,21,55,144 - again handwritten, on the envelope. A mixture of odd and even numbers, in ascending order, like those on the key ring but different. Opening the envelope, he raised an eyebrow as a small computer memory card fell into his palm.

Chapter 44

Major Incident Room A, Lambourne Road

Allenby checked his watch impatiently as Scott Daley entered and raised a hand in apology. It was still early. The Golf Club Dinner started with drinks at 8:00pm and given the price of the new frock his wife had bought, there would be repercussions if he were late for her grand entrance.

"It's Saturday, 8th June at—5:15pm. This is the daily briefing for Operation Nightjar. Sergeant Whetstone. Have we found anything from the records you brought back from Hillingdon?"

For most of Friday, Whetstone had read and reread the details. A diversion from the situation with Keith, with her mother, with every bloody thing. Of the two dead officers, Joe Gordon had been the most prolific and the most vocal. Dates and times of meetings, names, locations, records of expenses, occasional prose adding detail. A hastily drawn chart mapped out what she took to be McKaig's organisation, sketched street-maps, augmented details of collections and drop-offs. Reports of fights, of punishments, of raids and of killings. He bemoaned every hour of his time under cover to the point where Whetstone wondered about his career choice. Dean Hewell had shared almost nothing. Again the ubiquitous expense forms. and transcripts of calls but this time neat and tidy. Lists of dates and times with events and names, an organisational chart with Bašić at the head. Clinical.

"Nothing more than we already know, sir."

"What about discussions they had with each other?" asked Daley. "Dodds said they had a secure mailbox to exchange information?"

"There is nothing in the files." Whetstone had already taken a disliking to Phil Dodds. She suspected that Kramer had ordered him to make life as difficult for Daley as he legitimately could and, by definition, that extended to her.

"Get onto DI Dodds again please. We need to know what they discussed and when they discussed it. If Kramer and Dodds are not sharing their toys nicely, we will need to put pressure on them. Taylor's good with IT. Ask him to help."

In Whetstone's experience, secrets will out sooner or later.

"So, sergeant," continued Allenby, fidgeting and flexing his elbow. "You think someone is orchestrating the raids?"

Whetstone made herself comfortable, a little space for her brain to regroup. Maybe she was reading too much into the CCTV evidence? She hoped she was reading too much into Keith Parrish's disappearance.

"Sir. We've examined the reports in detail and they are practically identical. The approach, the execution, the cars they drive, even down to the weapons used. Assailants similarly dressed and wearing black ski masks. The only raid that was in any way different was the one on the Mercedes but then that could be down to opportunity."

"And DCI Kramer?" asked Allenby. "What's his take?"

Whetstone shared a look with Daley. "He and DI Dodds are adamant this is a local argument between two opposing firms. That one of them is fomenting violence to oust the other."

For a long moment, Daley wondered whether he should add Urdin Azeri and the Encubierto to the mix. With no substantive proof of his existence, for now he would keep Azeri to himself.

Allenby sighed. He was hearing the same old bollocks regurgitated again. The Drugs Unit at Hillingdon was a black hole. Dodds and his team seemed to run around like blue-arsed flies and achieving little while Kramer's shoulders had a slope on them steeper than the Cresta Run.

"So, in the final analysis, what do you suspect is going on here?" He fixed his eyes on Daley, who swerved the curve ball and deferred to Whetstone.

"Sir, our best guess is that the Cjevovod, a Bosnian firm led by Danilo Bašić, is responsible. The ambushes on his own people and property divert attention away from him and towards The Westsiders, led by Paisley John McKaig. McKaig is turning over about fifteen million a year in drugs alone. That all seems a tasty motive for the Cjevovod to oust him. Of course, the same could apply to Paisley John. He can muster the manpower, perhaps even torch one of his own establishments but he hasn't."

"So Bašić decided on a war of attrition? Would it not be simpler to have a *night of the long knives*, march in and take over?"

Daley shrugged. "I spoke to Ray Kramer's counterpart in West Mercia. In the UK, the violence is shorter, sharper and final. In his view, it would have been over in a weekend if Bašić wanted it."

"Gordon and Hewell both professed to making a breakthrough. Perhaps, they had categorically identified the ringleader?" offered Whetstone.

"OK. Let's start by finding the garage where those cars are being stored." As Monaghan leant forwards and opened his mouth, Allenby held up a hand. "Yes, I know! I have spoken to the ACC. We are getting a few more bums on seats but for now, you'll have to manage."

Then Allenby turned to Daley. "Oh, Inspector? A word?"

***

"Shut the door behind you, Scott."

As the latch clicked with a telling finality, Daley checked the *throne of doom*, expecting to see leather wrist straps and a flex disappearing into the wall. There was the smell of a lynching in the air.

"I hear you and DCI Kramer had words earlier?"

Straight for the jugular. Daley sighed. "Him more than me, sir."

"I find that hard to believe. Tell me?"

"He took me along to see John McKaig, the leader of the Westsiders. I was hoping to discover a little more about Gordon's involvement with the gang, as Kramer's reports basically say nothing.'

"And did you?"

Daley pursed his lips and shook his head. "No. McKaig knew Gordon was an undercover officer and had been playing Kramer and Dodds all along. Kramer spent twenty minutes winding McKaig up, hoping that he would let something slip. Of course, he didn't. It was a complete waste of time. He fed McKaig every answer. All the guy had to do was say yes. Everybody knows what his empire is all about. Basically, he can say what he likes but without evidence no-one can touch him."

"Come on Scott, you've worked drugs, albeit for only ten months, so you know it's not as straightforward as evidence. It's a tactical battle. It's not about arresting ringleaders; it's about frustrating their operations, slowing them down."

"Maybe so sir, but there is little chance of that happening over at Hillingdon with DCI Kramer in charge."

Allenby threw his hands in the air. "What is it with you and Ray Kramer? And don't tell me he hit on your wife. That was centuries ago. You haven't even got the wife anymore. Can't you let bygones be bygones?"

"Kramer's a fuckwit, sir. You know it and I know it. I don't understand why no-one else can see how incompetent he is. Even Deb Whetstone was sticking up for him earlier."

"Fuckwit maybe, *Inspector*, but he's still a DCI and commands the respect of lower ranks—whether you like it or not."

Daley could feel a familiar sensation. His heart rate increasing, his breathing faster. Words flowing unchecked. "I don't see how someone who is so blatantly out of his depth is still in command of a team like the Drugs Unit. You were there yesterday. He was all over the place at the press conference."

"And it was noticed, but it's not your affair. If Kramer has slipped up, then sooner or later, his incompetence will be seen. People much cleverer than us are planning a root-and-branch reform of the Met. Nobody's jobs safe—and that includes Kramer, Dodds, me, you and even Whetstone and

Monaghan. We could all be working in Timbuktu this time next month."

Timbuktu?

"Is this Deb Whetstone? Has she been speaking to you?"

"For God's sake Scott." Allenby sighed resignedly. "Yes, Sergeant Whetstone had a word, earlier. She is concerned your relationship with Ray Kramer is impairing your judgement."

Daley puffed his cheeks.

"Now don't you go all petulant on me. She's a good officer. I wonder sometimes if you see that, or you're too busy wondering who is trying to stab you in the back. Take it from me, the only person who will wreck your career is in that chair right now."

"Sir?"

"This morning. Disappearing off with McKaig's oppo. What were you thinking?"

"I've had this lecture from DCI Kramer already, sir."

"Well, now you're having it from me! McKaig and his type don't stand on ceremony. They could have taken you out to God knows where and put a bullet in your head—just like Gordon and Hewell. You've put yourself in the firing line and left the door open for the whole enquiry to be compromised. I know you don't hold DCI Kramer in high regard but when push comes to shove, better to have him in your corner than not."

Allenby fell silent. The twinge in his shoulder and biceps caught again. He felt slightly faint.

"Look, sir. There is something funny going on, here. Something I cannot put my finger on. This recent spate of trouble is too organised, too sudden. The cars, the MO. Everything pointing to a single gang. The Drugs Unit can't see it—or they choose not to, but McKaig's oppo, Dougie Murdoch, smells a rat too. That's what he wanted to tell me."

"And you believe him?"

"Sir, frankly I do. Put yourself in his shoes. You're making squillions a year. Why would you jeopardise that in a prolonged feud? The Cjevovod have much more firepower than the Westsiders. Your *night of the long knives*. But it hasn't happened. Instead, just slowly escalating pointless violence. Both Bašić and McKaig are seeing the takings going down."

"So what do you think is going on?"

"I don't know, sir." Daley hesitated. Given the lambasting that Allenby had just handed out, did he really want to relate the fairy story of Urdin Azeri and the *Encubierto*? Better to keep his counsel and be thought a fool than open his mouth and remove all doubt. "Murdoch thinks someone else, another firm is stirring up trouble. As yet we have no evidence to back that up. Whatever it is, I feel sure that's what Gordon and Hewell found out. That's what got them killed."

"Well, get that evidence. Find those cars. Find that garage. If it means treading on Ray Kramer's toes, at least wear slippers. And please, make your peace with him for all our sakes."

Chapter 45

Team Room, Lambourne Road

Leaving Allenby's office, Daley felt he had, all things considered, got away lightly. Only six months previously, his principles had almost brought him to blows with his senior and his career a perpendicular course downwards. At least this time he had the sense to take the bollocking and live to fight another day. The focus on the drugs feud was drawing him further away from Gordon and Hewell rather than closer. Accusations and counter-accusations were crisscrossing West London like curare-tipped darts yet he was no nearer to discovering the real perpetrator or the reasons behind it. Maybe Allenby was right? Maybe the deaths of Gordon and Hewell were linked to the inter-gang violence? Daley, though, couldn't help believing the whole drugs feud was a distraction but by whom and why?

Frustrated and irritable, Daley decided he needed a diversion. Something to take him mind away from the search for the BMWs and the incompetence of Kramer and Dodds. He owed Terri some time. He owed himself some time. As Sophie Jennings, his trauma counsellor had advised, he needed to learn how to work to live rather than live to work. Tomorrow was Sunday, traditionally a day of rest, maybe he could go offline for an hour or two? Pick wallpaper, admire ornaments?

Out of the blue, he remembered the memory card in his pocket. He had heard of multi-part encryption, a password created from two separate parts. He suspected that was the reason for two strings of numbers but did not understand how to resolve them into a password. But he knew a man who could. Steve Taylor's PC could remotely control a mission to Mars.

"Steve. Would you see what you make of these?"

"Sir?"

Scratching his head, Taylor studied the numbers. "Fibonacci sequence, sir. Each number is the sum of the two before it."

Perplexed, and alarmed at the speed of the response, Daley took back the sheet and stared hard. "What? Both? How come there are two if it's a sequence? 1,2,5,13,34,89. I know you're the clever one here but one and two don't add up to five. Same with the other list - 1,3,8,21,55,144 - one and three don't add up to eight. In fact, none of them add up."

Taylor cocked a pitying smile which Daley felt a little too condescending. Yet when it came to grey matter, the junior probably had the upper hand. "OK, Steve. So I know I am slow on the uptake. Show me." He waved a hand at the whiteboard.

Taylor drew a deep breath and grabbed a pen. "Fibonacci, or Leonardo of Pisa, to give him his proper name, invented the sequence in the 13th century to describe the pattern of growth of rabbit populations. Basically, each number is the sum of the previous two. Originally, the sequence began with 1,1,2, although in modern maths we add a zero, 0, 1, 1, 2. That way, nought plus one can equal one, one plus one can equal two, etcetera. Keeps it neat."

"These two sequences are the full Fibonacci sequence taken to 12 places - 1, 1, 2, 3, 5, 8, 13, 21, 34, 55, 89, 144 - except that someone has separated alternate numbers out into different lists. Interestingly, the Fibonacci sequence also conforms to the Golden Ratio, although..."

But Daley's mind was already elsewhere.

Chapter 46

As Saturday drew to a close, Whetstone promised herself a lie-in the next morning. The lost souls in the North West London Homicide Unit had gradually called time and drifted back to their families, and Lambourne Road was a graveyard. She continued to sift through phone records from twelve separate handsets recovered from the factory fire until the numbers were bouncing like commuters on the New York subway. Still even that was preferable to the echoing void of her house in Ealing.

When finally she had had enough, she strolled down to the comms room and asked them to check with the PC outside Parrish's door but there was still no sign. Nothing. Her phone remained stubbornly silent, despite her checking it every five minutes to ensure the battery was OK. It was typical of Keith. Self-centred, arrogant, never a thought for anyone else. What had gotten into him?

Outside, the warm afternoon had given way to a blustery chill which howled through the now deserted underground car park. Pulling her inadequate summer jacket about her, Whetstone headed for her Golf, forlorn in acres of space, like a Labrador waiting patiently outside the bookies for its owner. She really had to sort her life out.

Since his dressing down from Bilko Bob, Scott Daley had been remarkably upbeat. Usually, she would have to endure hours of self-pity as he carped on about the injustices of life and the failure of senior officers to understand real policing, throwing in several hackneyed examples of how hard done by he was. But today, whatever pre-occupied him had transcended all of that. At one point, he had even made her coffee without being asked. Pondering this as she waited at the Golden Carp for her Special Chow Mein, she resolved that there was something going on to which she was not a party. The random comments about other cases, staying behind at Loughton Street after she had left. That key. Daley was up to something.

Of course, she knew better than to come right out and ask. She might just discover something she wouldn't like, especially with redundancies, redeployments and transfers the order of the day. Maybe Daley was getting the heave-ho, or at least being shifted upwards, sideways, anyways? That would leave a little elbow room for her once the Inspector's exam was out of the way. Then again, maybe he had heard she was being moved? A transfer to some hick town might just be what she needed. Away from Lambourne Road, away from Keith, or out of the force completely. Ten years would yield a handy severance package.

But what else would she do?

"Deb!"

Alarmed at the sound of rhododendrons whispering, Whetstone started, almost dropping the takeout on her doorstep. Below the bay window, a head appeared.

"For God's sake, Keith!" she spat, at once annoyed and relieved in equal measure. "What the hell do you think you're playing at? I have been worried sick. You could have been killed for all I knew."

"Not here, please." Parrish scanned the street. It was quiet.

"What? All these months, you don't visit? You never come to my house and now you're in trouble...?"

"Please, Deb." It was the whimper of a hungry cat, plaintive and feeble, disguising self-interest.

Looking over her shoulder, she too checked the empty street. Then, against all her better instincts, she ushered him through the door.

Chapter 47

Winding through the evening traffic, it took Daley an extra half hour to reach Alperton, during which his mind had been elsewhere. Somewhat flippantly, he was dismayed that the key had not been to a garage containing a vintage car, or a strongbox packed with used notes. However, now he was just as intrigued by what the card might contain. What was so important that Gascoigne would need to entrust it to him?

Opening the front door, a rich blend of spices assaulted his senses. Somewhere a radio or TV played, and he heard Terri's voice singing unselfconsciously and it reminded him of something she had told him during the darker days:

You've gotta dance like there's nobody watching, sing like there's nobody listening, and live like its heaven on earth.

The voice stopped singing and shouted through. "You are supposed to shout 'Hi honey I'm home' so I can rush out to the door to greet you, all perfectly made up, carrying your pipe and slippers. Now it's all ruined."

"You want me to go out and come back in?"

"Hmm, you'll probably brain yourself on those boxes."

Daley caught the look of scorn. "The weekend, I promise."

"And I believe you. Just not sure which weekend but it better be soon. The solicitor says Friday 28th and they are not coming in the van with us."

Even when she was being serious, her cheeks dimpled and the smile never wavered.

After supper, after the dishes had been cleared away, Terri turned on the television and promptly fell asleep. For a while he watched her chest rise and fall and tried to remember the time before, when the sofa was empty and out of favour. When he used the armchair and often slept there, fighting off the spectres of the night, the booming diesel engine which bore down as he screamed himself awake. Now, they were a memory. Thanks to his therapist, to Terri's unfathomable devotion, the spectres played harmlessly, and the locomotive veered off at the points.

Muting the television, Daley inserted the memory card into his laptop. It held only one folder and as expected, Gascoigne had used a password. He typed in each string of numbers then every combination he could think of, becoming increasingly irritated as the computer just beeped. Then he smiled, pleased that he had been listening to Taylor. He googled the word to check the spelling before typing it in.

Fibonacci.

The folder opened to show a cascade of pictures and a single text document entitled *Alicia Sheldon*. The name rang a distant bell. DS Monaghan would know. Daley displayed the pictures as a slideshow, stalling on each one, taking in the full picture.

In the first image he saw two silver grey planes, the magnified view of metal, scarred with deep blackened grooves. Close-up images of the rifling striations on bullets. The upper image bore the caption *Alicia Sheldon*, the lower *Joe Gordon*. The striations were practically identical.

Gascoigne had identified the gun that killed Joe Gordon.

The second image, slightly blurred and yellow brown from internal lighting, showed a handgun, a semi-automatic strapped by cable ties into an evidence box.

Clicking to the next, Daley saw a page he recognised as from the evidence log at the Cheveley Hill Storage facility. A single line entry for the 8th of April, and a name and warrant number he recognised immediately:

103XD - Constable Keith Parrish.

Confused, Daley finished the rest of his wine. Why would Keith, a Traffic Officer, visit Cheveley Hill? Usually he would hand evidence over to the desk sergeant or detectives on the case.

Feeling a sense of unease, Daley turned his attention to the document file.

14th April 2013
Scott,
*Excuse the melodrama but if you are reading this, then something
has happened. I have become involved in things which, on reflection,
I should have left to you.*
*Joe Gordon of the Hillingdon CDIU, approached me on the QT on
8th April. He was working undercover and his position was
precarious. There had been an upsurge in gang violence which had
been blamed on tensions between the various West London Drugs
Firms. When he was killed, I spent some time examining his
findings and there appears to be truth in them. It did not take me
long to link Gordon's death with that of Alicia Sheldon though the
killers are different. He had discovered the name of the ringleader, or
as he described him, the agent provocateur.*
*Alas, whilst I am certain Gordon is right, I cannot fully prove it,
hence the cloak and dagger...less of the dagger I hope.*
*Start with Alicia Sheldon, make the comparisons, find the
omissions, look for the inconsistencies. You can hide an awful lot in
plain sight if you know how to go about it.*
*You are a good detective so chew on this. It tells you everything:
The blue fox jumps over the lazy wolf, the bear and the boar to
please the ambitious vixen.*
All the time the rabbit was watching
Now the blue fox has pounced on the rabbit and he is no more.
Azeri = the blue fox
Oh, and sometimes a rabbit looks like a rat so look carefully.
*Please Scott. Proceed with caution. Trust no-one and watch your
back.*

Dr Patrick Gascoigne FRCPA

Two bullets; one for Alicia Sheldon and one for Joe Gordon. A gun stored in Cheveley Hill. Keith's name in the register. What was Gascoigne implying? Did he think Keith Parrish was involved in the murder of Alicia Sheldon? Could Keith Parrish have murdered Joe Gordon?

Gascoigne's short verse told a story. It was a fairy story of sorts but Gascoigne believed the blue fox was Azeri. Daley could feel the pain behind his eyes as he struggled to untangle the threads woven in the verse's fabric. His mind would need time to assimilate the meaning.

Closing the laptop, he flicked the TV onto standby. Beside him, Terri stirred. Daley crooked an arm and felt her soft hair on his skin, as the warmth of her face settled against his chest. Her light perfume invaded his senses and he felt his eyelids grow heavier.

Chapter 48

"So, am I going to get an explanation?"

Whetstone propped herself against the kitchen counter and watched Keith Parrish as he demolished her special chow mein. Behind her, kitchen knives were keen and ready in their block, an arms length away. All at once her emotions went into free-fall. He was both the first and last person she wanted to see.

"As if you bloody care. *I've had enough Keith. We both know it's over. I need to move on.* What's that supposed to mean?"

"Oh, come on, Keith! Don't play the innocent with me. Until Wednesday morning, I hadn't seen you in weeks. I don't know what your definition of in a relationship is," she gestured speech marks in the air, "but mine involves at least a degree of physical contact, the odd visit, maybe even a *card* on my birthday?"

Parrish closed his eyes, shamefaced. "Birthday? Shit. Look, I'm sorry, all right? I've been, well, you know, busy."

"Sorry? Is that the best you've got? My God, you're priceless! Like I said, I've had enough. You can crawl back to Jane Morris if she is fool enough to take you back because I am not."

"Jane?"

"I am a bloody detective, Keith. Not that I need to be, with the bush telegraph at Lambourne Road."

"Well, you're a bloody shit one then because I am not seeing Jane Morris."

"Oh, yeah, and I am supposed to believe that? I've seen the comms reports. All those times when you were on duty and didn't report in. I suppose you were too busy balls deep in *her* to reach over and give a status update - *Hang on a sec, sarge, while I get my pants back on.*"

Parrish cast down the fork and pushed away the foil container. His appetite had deserted him.

"What? So because I don't report in, me and Jane Morris are at it like rabbits? Grow up, Deb, for Christ's sake. Anyway, you're a fine one to talk, pulling extra shifts, always out on some case or other. Even if I wanted to arrange time together, I would have to get permission from Scott *bloody* Daley or even Mike Corby."

"So it's OK for you to play around but not for me? Even if I were seeing someone, it's none of your business. You have made that abundantly clear."

Parrish rose and his chair squealed on the tiles. All at once Whetstone felt a wave of fear as he towered over her. For the first time she saw genuine hostility in his eyes.

"Deb. OK, it's over! We'll go our separate ways. I'll walk out that door and you will never see me again. Is that what you want?" A finger jabbed towards her face. "But don't you come whining to me about your sad, pathetic, lonely existence because I will have moved on too."

She thought of all the times she had sat with her mother in the screaming silence, all the phone calls picked up by voicemail, all the nights in her bed staring at the Artex, hoping he would call. All the times she yearned for someone to notice her existence. Out there somewhere, Corby was cosying up to one in a long string of girlfriends, Scott and Terri were sharing a bed, yet she was having a slanging match as the man she once cared for was disappearing before her eyes. Enraged, her arm swung, the flat of her palm inches from his face as his hand clamped her wrist.

For a moment, she wanted him to pull her close, to swear it was all a mistake, that he would change. For a moment, she wondered if she could turn a blind eye to his indiscretions. Then she pulled herself away and turned towards the door.

"Damn you, Keith."

Chapter 49

Ealing Downs Golf Club

Just for a second, Superintendent Bob Allenby had the sensation of being watched. Maybe a deer or fox; he saw them regularly on the fairways. Well, they *were* here before the Golf Club. Unexpectedly unnerved, he hastened to the boot where he had left the presentation shield, conscious that Philippa, his wife, was at the mercy of the club secretary who was probably already into his second bottle of claret. He loved the ancient Georgian pile the Golf Club had bought. It imbued a cachet to an otherwise anonymous fairway. However, the way the grounds had been landscaped into an eighteen-hole obstacle course would have Capability *Whatshisname* rotating in his grave.

Reaching up to close the boot lid, his arm jarred. Now, it felt as if he had torn his whole shoulder. Maybe, a swift brandy in the clubhouse would ease the discomfort? No more excuses. Phone the doctor in the morning. If it needed a sling for a week or two, so be it. Suddenly feeling short of breath, he rested against his Volvo, as beside him, a car door opened and a tall, slim woman rose from behind it. She was dressed in blue jeans and a Barbour hacking jacket.

"Hi, Bob. You and I need a little chat and as you're hardly at the office these days..." Diane Browning motioned towards the clubhouse. Her face was set and emotionless; a business call. Sighing, Allenby invited her into his car.

"I thought you and I had an understanding here, Bob." Her tone was soft yet barbed.

"Ma'am?"

Oh, come now, Diane please. I think we have known each other long enough to skip the formalities."

"Diane." Allenby wasn't so sure. However long one owned a pet cobra, one still wore thick gloves to feed it.

"OK, I'll come right to the point. Scott Daley."

"Haven't we been through this, ma'am?"

"Maybe we have but I think I need to press the point home. You and your team need to concentrate on the police killings and not stray into territory that does not concern you."

"And we are, but inevitably there will be cross-overs." Beads of sweat cold against his forehead, Allenby's chest was now tightening. Reaching down, he found some antacids, tasting the mint on his tongue. "It's Daley's belief that someone is orchestrating the attacks to destabilise the relationship between the Cjevovod and the Westsiders. He also believes that Gordon and Hewell uncovered the identity of the ringleader and were dealt with accordingly. Increasingly, it appears that this group is not connected to the two firms but separate."

"And what evidence does he have?"

"Nothing concrete, yet."

"Meanwhile, he's stomping his huge *size nines* through the Drugs Unit's investigations with little or nothing to show for it. Look, they are at full capacity just keeping the Wembley and Neasden firms apart without Daley's interference and now I find out he's cosying up with the enemy."

"Hardly cosying..."

"He took off with Murdoch. Forty-five minutes off-grid with a known drug dealer. God alone knows what damage that has done. Is he that naïve that he doesn't understand the repercussions of appearing to take sides?"

"Ma'am... Diane. Scott Daley is an experienced officer. I trust him to exercise the appropriate..."

"You assured me you had your people under control. What sort of bloody show are you running here, Bob?"

"I have already had this conversation with Inspector Daley. I am confident he knows what he's doing." The tendons in Allenby's neck were tightening. He could barely hear Browning over the booming in his ears.

"Jesus Christ Bob. When this hits the papers we will have Professional Standards crawling all over us. Even without MOPAC, we will be lucky if any of us keep our jobs."

Through the arrows of pain coursing through his shoulder and left elbow, Allenby grew more and more angry at the less than veiled threats. "Is that all that concerns you? Three men have died here. God knows how many more in that fire. Wives have lost husbands, Gordon's two kids have lost their father. This isn't about jobs. It's about lives." Allenby paused for breath. "Frankly, I don't care what these drugs gangs do to each other, how they run their sordid, tawdry businesses. What is important to me is the sanctity of law and above all, the sanctity of life."

"Yes, *Bob*. It is *all* I am concerned with too. The sanctity of law is all very well but if there is no-one around to police it? Frankly, I couldn't give a toss what Scott Daley has gotten himself mixed up in. I need to concentrate on the bigger picture and that means protecting our resources and protecting order in our society. I will fight anything that threatens my ability to do that. *Anything*."

"I assure you, Ma'am, you have my full support."

"You always have been one for loyalty, Bob. You make sure that when he goes down, he doesn't take you with him. For Christ's sake sort out your team."

***

The pain in Allenby's chest had subsided to be replaced by a tightening band of steel which crushed the air from his lungs. His fingers prickled on the steering wheel as the numbness crawled up his arm. It felt as if his ribs were clamped in a vice. Now he knew it was no golfing injury. He barely heard the car door slam and the small sports car kicking up gravel. Fumbling about in his pocket, he found his phone but his eyes could not focus on the screen. His hands shook too much to press the buttons. Through the windscreen, through the mist of white and red polka dots the car park was still and he could feel panic setting in.

What if nobody found him?

Chapter 50

An eternity later, Keith appeared through the living room door, his face strobed by the light from the TV. The chair smelt of her mother, the gin tasted bitter.

"So what's happening, Keith?"

"I don't know what you mean." She could sense the deceit in his voice."

"Does it never stop with you? Thursday night, your squad car is torched, then you are AWOL for a full forty-eight hours. No-one knows where the hell you are and all you can say is *I don't know what you mean?*"

"Look, that's my business. OK? Just leave it."

"Leave it? How can I leave it? Your flat has been trashed. There's no sign of you anywhere. And then that car pulls up before driving off like a scalded cat as soon as we spot it. I know you went back there. Mike found your car keys in a drawer when we searched your apartment. When the uniform arrived, they were gone."

"Bloody Hell! Searching my gaffe, putting a uniform outside the door? What am I, public enemy number one? So I go out for a while. I'm a grown-up, Deb. I can look after myself."

"What about the money you've been taking out? Two hundred pounds every Sunday. Same time, same machine. And what are you doing in Greenford anyway?"

"Jesus Christ. It gets bloody worse. Not content with searching my flat, you're nosing around my bloody bank accounts." Keith edged around the living room curtain, keeping an eye on the road.

"What did you expect me to do? Bloody shit detective and all. I was trying to find out what happened to you."

"Nothing happened."

"Don't lie to me. What's that cut on your face. Scotch *bloody* mist?"

Instinctively, Keith's hand moved to his cheekbone, the congealed blood and an angry bruise. "I dunno. I bumped into a door or something. Just leave it, all right?"

Killing the TV, she swallowed the sour remnants of her drink. A sixth sense told her there was something wrong. "No Keith, I won't. Tell me. What's happened?"

"I am telling you, for your own good. Leave it!" Suddenly afraid, he pulled back into the room. "Shit! I've got to go."

Then she heard the engine, little more than a low rumble above the humdrum noises of a city that never rested. Peeking through the curtains her blood froze. Outside, in the warm sultry evening, the dark BMW 520i purred gently, round halo eyes casting an eerie white over the hedges and pavements. Quickly she dodged back behind the curtains, racing around to the front door and down the path towards the gate. At once, with a throaty roar, the front of the car rose and the lights burned her eyes. Pressing against a parked vehicle, she felt the draught as the car sped off down the road, instantly turning and sprinting after it. Through the orange and red fireworks, Whetstone squinted against the darkness but the car was gone.

Racing inside, she dashed into the living room, then out into the hall, and up the stairs. Finally, catching her breath, she returned to the kitchen where the back door gaped wide. Keith had gone.

Reaching for her phone, she found Daley's number.

Chapter 51

St Anns Shopping Centre, Harrow, Sunday 9th June

In days of yore, Scott Daley loved the weekend. Turning up at Lambourne Road after a leisurely, and usually unhealthy breakfast he could spend the morning chewing the fat with Dave Monaghan, who never seemed to have a home to go to. He could also catch up on the reams of paperwork and keep Bilko Bob off his back. Recently, however, all that had changed. Monaghan's eldest had procreated and the curmudgeonly Irishman preferred the company of a screaming, reeking, dribbling infant. For the life of him, Daley could not understand why, though he felt sure he would soon. Life had changed beyond measure. Rather than a focal point to his life, work had become a distraction from it.

Even now, as he gazed over at Terri Somerville in the bay window of the coffee shop, he was preoccupied with Gascoigne's cryptic message, on Alicia Sheldon, on foxes, wolves and rabbits. Outside, meandering souls peppered the High Street. Nothing more important on their minds than a lazy Sunday, each one wrapped up in their own world. He wondered how many of them could bring down the steel shutters on their problems for the weekend.

Taking his change, he returned the young barista's smile and lifted the tray.

"Did you remember my banana bread?" The lilt in Terri's voice was from another world; one not scarred by death and deceit. Over the months it had helped him reach a place inside his soul he had not visited for a long time.

"Naturally."

"And the sugar?"

"And the sugar."

"Seems that it's only boxes in hallways that slip your mind these days."

"Oh, come on now. Play fair. I have whittled them down and anyway the new house has a bigger loft."

"I suppose. But have you seen the junk in my spare room at Harrow? There'll be no room for boxes."

Frowning, Daley stirred his coffee, watching the flecks of cocoa powder explode and swirl into a hundred brown constellations. "So it's all right to clutter the new house with your junk but not with mine?"

"I have taken a sneaky peek inside your boxes, Scott Daley. Shoes and clothes are far more important than antique games consoles and vinyl records."

For a second, Daley wanted to disagree, to cling onto the flotsam and jetsam of his past but there was something comforting in the subtle way that Terri was separating him from it. It was a world he had yearned so often to rediscover yet been disappointed each time he tried. With Terri, things seemed different. She might be dragging him away but it was a direction he wanted to go.

"Some of those records are classics. And vinyl. It has a warmth, a tonal quality you don't get with CDs."

"Enough of the infantile whining!" Terri resembled a hamster, cheeks pouched with banana bread. "You can keep the records but the consoles have to go."

"Oh, the art of compromise. Why do I feel you have just picked my pockets?"

"You wait until we hit the shops." There was a vicious gleam in her eyes.

Daley scalded his lips on his coffee. "What's the point of new clothes? Give it a month and they won't fit."

"Do I detect a man trying to understand the psyche of a woman? Oh, you have so much to learn." Smiling, she reached over and patted his arm. "If you are a good boy, I will let you read the magazines in the newsagents, or slope off to the pub, or whatever men like doing."

"Actually, I'm thinking of renewing my season ticket at Craven Cottage."

"Don't see why not. You quite enjoy sleeping through the football at home. Why not pay to do it?"

"Harsh! No, I was mounting a charm offensive on the Hillingdon mob the other day. Me and Phil Dodds got talking. Seems he's into football so we might both go along. You know, like bonding. Blokey stuff."

Terri considered. "It can't hurt. You are different sides of the same coin. Maybe it would help to get to know each other a little better. You could even invite Ray Kramer along to your *blokey stuff*."

"Not sure that's such a good idea. Enough violence on the terraces already."

Picking up her coffee with both hands, Terri seemed distracted. Briefly, Daley saw the smile fall from her face.

"What's up?"

"I don't know. This stuff with Ray Kramer and Phil Dodds. You always seem to be picking an argument with someone."

"Takes two to tango." Daley felt a little hurt that she placed the blame squarely on him.

"Yes, but while you're doing the tango, everyone else is dancing a foxtrot."

Daley frowned and recalled Murdoch's words, the previous morning. *My father once advised me that if I swam against the tide, eventually my arms would become tired.* Perhaps Kramer and Dodds, Browning and Allenby were all in step and he was dancing to a different beat?

Terri squeezed his hand. "Look, Scott. I know all this—the baby, the house move—has all happened very quickly but now your life has changed and so must you. You have to think about your responsibilities."

"I said I will sort out the boxes and I will."

"It's not about boxes. It's about drug gangs and dead policemen, about MOPAC and redundancies. It's about rubbing people up the wrong way. It's about me, you and the baby."

Sipping his coffee, Daley stared out at the meandering Sunday streets, couples and families, ambling about, filling time as the sun warmed their faces. Deep inside, there was a part of him that thrilled to the danger, the edge that his work provided but every day, it seemed to shrink a little more.

Chapter 52

With a night spent trying to come to terms with some uncomfortable truths, the lie-in Whetstone had promised herself didn't materialise. Instead, she sat in the upstairs bay window, staring out at the street, her mind a confusion of difficult questions and unpalatable answers.

Not for the first time, she reflected on the path her life was taking, trampling over the same well-trodden ground. Her mother was gone. Louise was gone and now Keith too. The only thing that remained was the hideous wallpaper in the hallway and she could remedy that.

One question, though, remained stubbornly unanswered. Why did Keith abandon his squad car?

The logs showed that he started his shift at 4:00pm, despatched to Gunnersbury Park and North Chiswick. What was he doing in Greenford, several miles away? Then he was incommunicado until 11:17pm when he had radioed in that he was in pursuit of the fleeing car. Why did he not report in once the chase was over?

Then there was the money withdrawn from the ATM in Greenford at 5:53pm as he had done many times before. Was he in debt to a loan shark? Or was he being blackmailed?

It was clear, he was afraid of someone, some*thing*. Hiding in bushes, keeping an eye on the road, fleeing as the car had appeared the previous night.

Had he gotten in over his head?

That was the only answer. Why else would he go into hiding? Why else would he refuse to tell her anything? It was Keith they were after. Whoever they were.

As dawn crept over the rooftops opposite, utterly exhausted she had fallen into a restless doze.

Chapter 53

As Sophie Jennings, Daley's trauma counsellor had advised, he needed to learn how to work to live rather than live to work. However, a boutique stuffed with twenty-something women gushing over clothes which, to his unpractised eye, were virtually identical, was not his idea of living. He had yet to perfect the art of appearing blasé whilst leaning on a metal rack of indecently scanty underwear without looking somewhat predatory. Terri had been in the changing room forever and his legs were aching. He could not help feeling slightly relieved as his phone buzzed in his pocket. The relief however was short-lived as he sighed at the name on the screen.

"Ma'am?"

"Inspector. Where are you?" ACC Browning's voice was purposeful and clipped.

"Marks & Spencer. Is there a problem?"

"Bob Allenby is in Northwick Park. Heart attack. Happened last night apparently. At the golf club."

"Bloody hell. Is it serious?" Around Daley, the hubbub of the shop faded to a background murmur as he recalled an image; his father's face, agonised and purple, green-suited paramedics and tubes. The rhythmic beat on a motionless chest and his mother's tears as he held her.

"I've spoken to his wife, and she is with him now. He is in an induced coma to reduce any further damage but I am afraid they are not hopeful. Apparently, he was there some time before they found him."

"What about his kids? Has someone informed them?"

"All in hand, Inspector. One daughter is already there, the other is flying back from France. I hope she makes it in time."

"I must visit..."

"That might be a good move. Meanwhile, I want you to move back to Lambourne Road. I am relying on you to step into his shoes and run the show while we source a replacement."

Daley frowned, concerned at how quickly Browning had written off Allenby. He was on a ventilator not in a casket. "Very good, ma'am. Is there anything specific you need me to pick up?"

"Nothing that can't wait until tomorrow. Shall we say 9:30 at Lambourne Road? Oh, and speak to Sergeant Whetstone for me."

Chapter 54

Parrish gazed at the ceiling of the squalid room. Over-painted Edwardian mouldings, nicotined and indistinct, viciously sliced by the partition wall. A single unshaded lightbulb cast a yellow pall across the beige walls. There was an odour of sex and sweat and hopelessness etched into the space. He had not been able to recover many things from his apartment before escaping but with foresight he had taken a sleeping bag as the sheets were second-hand and soiled. You lie down with dogs...

It had been a close call.

Two days ago, waking with a start as dawn edged a blade of opal across the horizon, he was faced with a dilemma. Whether to stay or run.

He could claim they overpowered him but what if they had intercepted his assailant? Who knows what he would say to save his skin? Or he could lie low until he had figured out what to do next. The face. Recognition. A single second. Once seen, it could not be unseen. *This'll be our little secret, eh?*

So he had run.

Finding his squad car, ablaze, surrounded by coppers, he had ducked back behind a wall and regrouped. Then, stowing his stab vest and police radio in a nearby bin, he had headed back to the main road for a taxi. The flat was now toxic, so he had followed his nose to the nearest anonymous B&B. And with only a black-and-white TV for company, he had hunkered down pondering his next move.

Then there was the face. The instant tacit realisation he had already reached the point of no return. The mess room had been buzzing for weeks with reports of the drugs raids, Bašić and McKaig, of Urdin Azeri. The deaths of Joe Gordon and Dean Hewell had left everyone jumpy.

The face. Once seen cannot be unseen.

Perhaps, he should just get the hell out of Dodge. Maybe he could find somewhere to stay, away from the City? Spend a day or two with his parents. Maybe Azeri would be less concerned if he left the country? He could find a route across the channel then head off for the Costas. Well, perhaps not the Costas. Azeri may have contacts. Perhaps the Greek Islands.

It was then he discovered his phone was missing.

In his mind he retraced his movements. Perhaps it was dislodged in the tussle in the allotments? Then there was the standoff at the dead end. How long had he been out? Plenty of time to lift his phone. In a panic, he had driven to the refuse bin where he had stashed his vest and radio but there was no sign of his phone. Maybe he had left it in Irina's room? He pictured himself dressing after his liaison with her. He had piled his keys and wallet onto the dresser...

He would need to retrieve it before anyone else did.

Chapter 55

The news of Bilko Bob's heart attack did not surprise Whetstone. Like everyone else, she had noticed the shortness of breath, the aches and pains he always seemed to explain away. It disturbed her she had said nothing. But then, with Keith there were signs too.

More disturbing was the news that Hillingdon would take control of Operation Nightjar. They had achieved nothing concrete to date. Why would that change? Hopefully, Daley could come up with a persuasive reason to keep the enquiry before his meeting with Browning in the morning.

Unable to settle, agonising over the situation with Keith, she had set about the house with renewed vigour and a plethora of cleaning products. By mid-afternoon, she had moved her things into her mother's old room. Then, she shifted Louise's things into her old room. Having managed for twenty years in a box room no better than a large cupboard, Deb thought it the least she owed her. Finally, she filled the box room with the entirety of her mother's existence and closed the door.

Then she sat on the top step of the stairs and wept until the tears ran dry.

There had to be a line in the sand. A metaphorical boundary between the past and the future. Unlike her mother, she would not deny the truth and drink herself slowly into oblivion. Whetstone resolved that her fate would be different. For one thing, she would need to stop worrying and start living. With her Inspector's exam less than a month away, this could not go on. She thought of Diane Browning. How driven she was, how many obstacles she must have vaulted to reach the rank of Assistant Chief Constable. Childless, unmarried. Was that the price to pay?

Washing her face, repairing her make-up, she would write a new future and it would start with the wallpaper in the hallway.

Chapter 56

Wembley, 12:00pm

Fat Leon regretted not paying attention to Mr Anderson at the Comprehensive all those years ago. Balding and spindly, the fifth-form teacher had stared up at Leon's gargantuan bulk and prophesied a wasted life if he did not apply himself. Of course, the chubby teenager ignored him. He was already making a monkey a week dealing. In the evening, he was staring at his homework, watching the numbers and letters dance a polka around the page, desperately trying to corral them into something meaningful so he wouldn't be the subject of the class's ridicule.

He left with no qualifications, taking a job cleaning toilets down the factory, bored and frustrated. Two years custodial for persistent *twocking* convinced him his life was over before it had begun. Then the pendulum swung his way. A chance encounter with Paisley John McKaig led to five years as the big man's driver. Cash suddenly rained on him and his mum now owned the council house in Brent where three years earlier he had murdered his step-father for beating on her. At least she owned the back garden too, along with its raised flower bed.

Now though, once more, the pendulum had swung.

He stared deferentially into space as Paisley John McKaig noisily hefted his frame from the leather seats.

"Make sure you can reach that piece, Leon. I don't trust these bastards as far as I can spit a dead rat—and that's not very far."

Fat Leon nodded confidently and smirked. Inside he was shitting himself. Under the high sun, the scrub grass of the overgrown landfill site shimmered in the haze, making it difficult to judge how many Cjevovod there were. Leon counted twelve. Whether by agreement or serendipity, there were twelve of the Westsiders men behind McKaig's car too.

Apart from the screech of gulls and the background rumble of traffic, the atmosphere was muted and taut as elastic. Across fifteen feet of makeshift no-man's-land, Danilo *the Bear* Bašić was already standing by his vehicle, legs apart in a cowboy stance, hands clasped in front of him. Ivan Terzić stood to his right. To his left, a minder Fat Leon didn't recognise. Tall, wide, bald except for a goatee. Edging backward, he felt the door handle on his thigh. The sawn-off was across the passenger seat and the window was open. But a moment away.

The two leaders kept their eyes resolutely on each other and Fat Leon wondered who would be the first to blink. It was Dougie Murdoch and Ivan Terzić. With a nod, each took a few paces forwards until they stood face to face. Keeping his voice low, Murdoch reached out a hand, feeling the purposeful grip.

"Ivan. How are you?" Their smiles were genuine. An appreciation of an equal, even if an opposite.

"Tired, Dougie. I have spent three days persuading Bašić that he should not kill the lot of you. He loved that meat packing plant. Best Sudžuk this side of the Alps. And the Mercedes? That was an act of vandalism. That car was a classic."

Murdoch nodded noncommittally. "The Westsiders are not to blame. We did not burn the factory down or wreck the car." Hearing of the raid, McKaig had instantly thrown an almighty strop and promised every manner of unpleasant retribution on the person who had carried out the unsanctioned act. Then when the meat packing plant had been razed to the ground, they could have heard his rage in Brighton.

Terzić persisted "Four lives, Dougie. Six if you count the boys in the Mercedes who we executed. This *has* to stop. It is bad for business."

"We are suffering losses too. I am telling you, Ivan. This has *nothing* to do with us."

"Then who? Tell me? No-one knew of the Mercedes. *No-one.*" Murdoch could sense the fractiousness in Terzić's voice.

Did Bašić hold him partially responsible for not acting sooner?

"If no-one knew, how would we? We knew the van was going to Brent Cross, that was all. And that arrived safely."

"Because you also knew it was a decoy," countered Terzić.

Murdoch puffed irritably. "How could we know? As you say, you made a last-minute change." He turned briefly to McKaig, who was motionless next to Fat Leon, solid, immutable. "Look, Ivan, what makes you think any of this is in the Westsiders' best interests? Or the Cjevovod? Tit-for-tat attacks, losing stock, weapons, vehicles, not to mention the men, whilst all around us the other firms are pissing themselves laughing, biding their time, waiting for the opportunity to march in and take over. Why would I want that? Why would Paisley John?"

Terzić would not be deterred. "Or the Cjevovod are so weak that the Westsiders march in. *The Bear* came here today ready for a war. If you want a war, we can start one any time."

"So why hasn't he?" Murdoch was struggling with the first flush of anger. "You know as well as I do that the Cjevovod have more men than we do. If you wanted war, we would not stand a chance."

"Because he is thinking the same as Paisley John."

Murdoch surveyed the shimmering horizon behind Bašić. Twelve guards within fifty yards of the car. Each held a firearm pointed at his opposite number behind McKaig. Man-to-man marking. Terzić's eyes flicked left and right, assimilating the information. "So, if it was not the Westsiders then who? The Polish? The Chinese? The Jamaicans?"

It was Murdoch's turn to smirk. Scots, Polish, Chinese, Jamaicans and now a Mexican stand-off. All hail diversity. "All I know is that we are not to blame."

***

Above the pounding of his racing heart, Fat Leon could hear the voices but the words were indistinct. A trickle of sweat meandered down his spine and he rubbed a clammy palm on his trousers. Beside him, Paisley John was a rock, yet the tiny tick in the corner of his eye betrayed him. Leon loved Paisley John because he looked after him. A brother from another mother, even. It was comforting to know the *Big Man* was afraid too.

A low shuffling woke Leon from his daydream and he realised Murdoch was ambling back, his face expressionless, waiting for the shot to pierce his spine. It never came. Behind him, Ivan Terzić too was retreating.

"Paisley John McKaig!" Danilo Bašić's bellicose roar echoed around the man-made tundra. "Listen. This has gone on for too long. I am a patient man but you have stretched my patience to the limit. One more attack on the Cjevovod and I will wipe the Westsiders off the map."

McKaig lowered his eyes and smiled to himself. Then he whispered: "You got that piece, Leon?"

"Right here, boss." Over the sweat and the fear, Leon could almost smell the gun oil.

Fixing his eyes on Bašić, McKaig folded his arms. "No, Bašić. You listen. If you think you can waltz in from that East European shit-hole and take over West London, you have another thing coming. If you want a war, bring it on!"

McKaig took a pace forwards. Around him the cricket chirp of safety catches filled the air, and he felt the eyes of twelve shot guns staring at him. Fat Leon hung his arm through the open window of the SUV. But a moment away.

Bašić matched the pace. "No-one wants a war but if you want one, I will give it. Tell your men to lower their weapons and we will lower ours."

"When I need advice from you, Bašić, I will ask for it. Until then you need to get your own house in order." McKaig raised a hand and behind him, barrels tipped downwards but safety catches stayed off. "You are on notice. One more act of aggression and you will have your war. There are plenty of other firms who will be glad to see the back of you. And I will watch you die screaming for your mother as I cut off your bollocks."

Bašić smiled. "You're a very big man, standing there with your fat friend but if it came to a war, your allies will desert you. It will be you on your knees sobbing for your mother."

And with that, Bašić turned and disappeared through the open door of his car. Soon all that remained of the Cjevovod was a cloud of fine dust dancing on the wind.

"Get us the hell out of here, Leon."

As Leon revved the SUV, spraying dirt in rooster-tails behind, he could hear the two men talking in the back.

But he had learned not to listen too carefully. Soon, he would wish he had.

Chapter 57

Across from the Monarch View Hotel, Keith Parrish had a grandstand view of the front steps. The Astoria Lodge shared a similar salubrious reputation. Few people ventured this way unless they were after a trick or a fix or an uncomfortable conversation with a constable.

Or, like Parrish, they had a plan.

Having paid off the weasel man at the B&B, he loaded everything into his car and moved to Greenford, hiding it in the litter-strewn car park behind the Astoria. From the shadowed alley along the side the hotel, he could keep an eye on comings and goings and flash his badge if anyone got too nosey. But only as a last resort. If he could reach Irina's room, if he could persuade her to let him in, maybe he could find his phone.

Following that first meeting, in the kitchens behind the Monarch View, he had visited her once or twice a week. There was little talking but still he had found out some things about her. Sent by her parents to work in the hospitality industry, she had been pressed into hospitality of an entirely different kind. Her drug habit trapped her there. Drugs were not Parrish's thing. Irina was his addiction. Female, slender and beautiful.

And young.

She had a dream. A small cafe in Burgundy or The Dordogne. Somewhere neighbours said hello each morning, where she could wake up to the sunrise and time was endless. Free of addiction, free of men, pawing and grunting. The hotel manager had taken her passport as insurance, along with those of the other girls. Parrish was not without contacts. He could sort that; one with a slightly different date of birth. They could take the Eurostar, or a ferry. He could look after her, at least until she reached eighteen. Then it would not matter.

Parrish ducked into the shadows as Minolev, the manager, appeared in the alley alongside the Monarch View, propping open a fire door and hefting black sacks into a refuse skip before lighting a cigarette. Then, Minolev turned back into the hotel, kicking away the prop.

Maybe there was a way in without being seen? It was just a matter of time.

Pulling his light jacket about him, Parrish quivered at the drop in temperature. There was nothing to be gained by pontificating on a doorstep. Turning, he trotted back to his car and climbed in.

The dark Blue BMW 520i sat two hundred yards beyond the Monarch View. Holding station. Keeping watch.

Chapter 58

It was evening before Whetstone finally returned home. It felt like she had purchased the entire stock of her local DIY superstore and the Golf was groaning under the weight. Trotting up the path, sorting door keys, she recalled the assistant who had helped her load up. He was tall, handsome and very good-looking. He was also married. Then she stopped in her tracks. Through the fanlight above the door, a dull grey-white flickered across the ceiling. Reflexively, she looked back along the street.

The house was empty. It was always empty.

Pressing her head to the wood of the door, she could hear sounds. Muffled, weird, disembodied. Trying to stem her roaring breath in her ears, she unlocked the door and eased it open.

"Keith?" Should she phone the police? What happened if it turned out to be nothing?

Maybe her sister had returned from university? "Louise?" Her voice a gunshot through the house. "Louise? Is that you?"

There was no response, no movement in the house. Just the voices, the sounds, the dull flashing of lights. Silently latching the door, she listened intently. A voice—no two. A man and a woman, repeating like a jingle or an advert on loop. Through the open living room door, the lights ebbed and flowed, the sounds echoed off the walls. The TV was on.

"Keith? Keith. Stop messing about."

Twenty. Twenty pounds. No kissing, no penetration, just blowjob.

And for penetration?

Fifty for penetration but you use condom.

Then the sounds again. Desperate, eager moans. The rhythmic grunts and finally the gasp of release. Animal and visceral. The sounds of sex.

And the whole thing looped. Once, twice, mesmerising her, turning her stomach. Chilling her to the core.

Around her, the world turned suddenly hostile. In the street, she felt curtains twitch. She felt unclean, violated. But most of all she felt betrayed by the sounds. Closing her eyes, afraid to look into the living room, she longed for her mother, Louise, even Keith to be sitting there. How she hoped that this would all be some huge mistake. Her mistake. She had heard wrongly. How stupid was she?

Then she recognised the man's voice. Once it was the only voice she needed to hear; a voice she missed as soon as he left. Now, it was the last she needed to hear.

Sitting in her mother's chair, Whetstone stared at the screen. The TV played the clip over and over. Suddenly drained, staring at the treacherous images, her eyes filled with tears. On the floor, lay a note. Its message was crystal clear:

Give us Keith Parrish. Urdin Azeri will be watching. You need to choose your friends wisely.

Chapter 59

Northwick Park Hospital, 7:30pm

Detective Superintendent Bob Allenby was not a tall man. At five feet ten inches, he commanded his presence more by his demeanour than his stature. But now, through the motes of dust, Daley was moved by how small the prostrate shape beneath the bedclothes seemed. He squeezed Terri Somerville's hand, feeling her pull his arm closer. A sonorous incessant beep reminded him of a time, a year or so ago, when he flitted in and out of a coma himself, catching snatches of conversation, trapped in wild, hellish nightmares and a panic which ricocheted around his mind like a pinball. Deep inside, he wanted to flee.

Tentatively knocking, easing open the door, he smiled at the two women seated by the bed. He felt guilty for the intrusion, ashamed that he had never met Allenby's family, in all the years he had known him.

"Inspector Daley, er, Scott... We work together. This is Terri Somerville."

He caught the hand that was extended. It was devoid of feeling.

Philippa Allenby was an elegant woman in her early fifties, her hair was short and auburn. Though lined with worry, the smile was kind.

"This is Frances." Daley nodded to the slim girl in her late teens. A younger clone of her mother, the hair a tight ponytail.

"How is he?"

"He spent the night in Intensive Care but he's out of danger now. The doctors say the next twenty-four hours will tell. There is the prospect of some brain damage."

Behind her the monitor traces were regular and steady, a mountain range of peaks and troughs emerging from the right and disappearing to the left. Regular and steady. That described Bob Allenby to a T. Or should that be tee?

"The doctors said he must have been building up to this for some time. Days, maybe even weeks."

Daley thought back to the previous day, Allenby rubbing his arm, flexing his fingers and wondered whether things would have been different if he had picked up on the signs. "He said his arm and shoulder was playing him up. I thought nothing of it. He passed it off as a golfing injury."

"Yes, Scott. Men are very good at hiding things!" Daley caught a mischievous smile and wondered whether she knew of the boxes in the hallway.

"Is there anything you need, Mrs Allenby?" asked Terri.

Philippa Allenby laid a hand on Terri's arm. "No thank you, dear. They've been great. We have everything we need."

"He isn't far off retirement," remarked Daley "A couple of years, maybe." His father had died at sixty-three with no thoughts of retirement, wrapped up in the job, unable to conceive another way of life.

"Yes. Around that. We were making plans. What, with the Golf Club, the Rotary Club and the Metropolitan Police, sometimes, I think he sees more of you than he did of us. I don't begrudge him his career, his interests. It's just that we always thought our time would come. Now it may be too late."

After his father died, Daley's mother fell to pieces. It was a gradual corrosive process which left the once stoic and dependable woman forgetful and dependent. The small terraced house became a cavernous reminder of the jolly, quick-witted man who had evaporated in an instant on the living room carpet. Haunted by the memories, she eventually sold up and moved to an apartment block in Hastings to be near Daley's sister. He felt an overwhelming urge to drive down and visit.

"No. I know Bob. He'll pull through. I'll keep his seat warm until he is fit to return."

Philippa Allenby smiled again and motioned towards Terri. "Live your life, Inspector. Do what you need to but don't squander it over work. I am sure the Metropolitan Police Force is big enough and ugly enough to cope without you when you need to be with your family."

Daley returned the smile. Today was a day of advice and it all held the same message. "Do you mind if I pop in now and again? Just to sit and talk to him? I was in a coma last year and he did me that courtesy. I know he will hear us."

"I am sure he would like that." Philippa Allenby smiled, her face lined and pale. "I will let you know if anything changes."

Behind them, the door opened and the second daughter entered, a young child grasping her legs. Suddenly the room felt crowded, so saying their goodbyes, leaving best wishes, Daley and Somerville left the family to their vigil.

Retracing his steps down the soulless corridors towards the car park, Daley held Terri's hand as if his life depended upon it. Had he seen a premonition of his own future?

Chapter 60

I am outside now.

For twenty minutes, Whetstone had sat in the darkness, staring at the looping pictures until they were flat, devoid of meaning. Each rerun another gouge in the flesh of her soul.

The man's face, Keith's face, was etched on her mind, the sounds the voices long since dissolved into the dark fabric of the room. Still she watched the transaction, the sordid act of sex, the heartless act of betrayal, until it became meaningless. Now, her eyes prickled with tears, blurring the words as she texted back.

It's open. Living room.

"You shouldn't be here." Ramesh's voice was low, anxious but still more of a command than a statement. Raising her head, seeing the eyes, the images reflecting chiaroscuro flashes, she nodded.

***

"How could he do this to me?"

The teacup was burning her hands. The kitchen chair was hard. The house now still and silent. Ramesh was stirring sugar into his own cup.

"We men are thoughtless bastards at the best of times. We are lazy, we don't wash enough and we don't show enough respect to our partners. And we are selfish."

"Bastard!" The cup arced across the kitchen and exploded against a cupboard, a shower of steaming liquid raining down.

"Hey, Deb. A little extreme. So I don't make good tea."

Whetstone saw his eyes. They were soft and compassionate but most of all there was an implicit understanding. He understood entropy, that all good things eventually go bad. "What am I going to do, Ramesh?"

"Fetch a cloth, for one. Maybe boil the kettle again?" The boyish grin brought a smile, faint and fleeting. "You could scratch that nice Lexus he creams over. Go all bunny boiler and burn his clothes. You have unrestricted access to his flat at the moment. A good one is to stick a prawn in a hollow curtain pole. Stinks for weeks. He would never find it."

"Voice of experience?"

"That, as they say, would be telling. I think it's bedtime, don't you?"

"A little forward, Doctor Ramesh."

The reddening of Ramesh's face was visible despite his olive hue. "No, I didn't mean... I wasn't suggesting..."

"I know, Harry. You're one of the good guys, despite what you would like people to believe."

"Am I that transparent."

"Transparent no, but not as opaque as you think."

As Whetstone climbed the stairs, Ramesh sipped his tea. Then he set about cataloguing evidence, knowing he would find none. Below the geniality and good humour, the note troubled him. Whilst they sent it to Deb Whetstone, this was a message to Keith Parrish - *be sure your sins will find you out.*

Then he quietly climbed the stairs.

"You asleep?"

"Not really. I keep seeing those pictures over and over."

"Pardon my French and may my mother forgive me but Keith Parrish is a fucking idiot." Then he added: "You want me to stay?"

"On second thoughts, definitely transparent."

"Oh, no, no, no. I meant..."

"I know what you meant, Harry."

Ramesh took a blanket down to the living room and dialled Scott Daley's number.

Chapter 61

Monarch View Hotel 8:00pm

By night fall, impatience had finally got the better of Parrish. The car was claustrophobic and cramp was creeping up his thigh. As the sky darkened, moonless and grey, an automatic light switched on over the door of the Monarch View, casting sharp shadowed tendrils down the steps.

Irina Dąbrowska held a cigarette daintily between two fingers, ethereal through the smoke as she peered at her phone. She had an air of Audrey Hepburn, elfin and girlish. Her hair was cropped tight against her neck. A short pleated red skirt and a flimsy white strapped top revealed shapely porcelain legs and shoulders. The previous November, when he had first seen her shivering against the crisp air, she had been wearing something similar. But now it was warm, and he knew what it was like to have her. As if reading his thoughts, she aimlessly scanned the street then returned to her phone.

Maybe he could persuade her to leave right now?

Behind her, Minolev appeared, chugging smoke like a steam train and speaking loudly into his own phone, his cigarette a glowing arc in the air. Maybe the hotel manager was the key? Handled the right way, an audience with Bašić, both he and Minolev would be in *The Bear's* debt. But then, Bašić shot first and asked questions later. More haste less speed.

Across the road, Irina rubbed her naked arms and headed back into the hotel, followed by Minolev.

Should he even consider Irina, or Minolev for that matter? East Europeans were all the same—self-centred and treacherous. Why was he risking so much for this girl? The Mediterranean was full of girls. They threw themselves at men like him.

He pictured Irina in room twelve, naked to the waist, brushing her hair in the mirror. Every night the same. The lid firmly closed on her dreams as a procession of sad, degenerates came and went.

Parrish knew he could not leave her.

A thin shaft of amber lit the alley beside the Monarch View and Parrish watched as Minolev appeared, propping open the door. Two black sacks sailed into a skip, the door remained open and Parrish's heart leapt in his chest.

Nimbly, he crossed the road and up the alley towards the side door. Pausing as a car fired up, voices shouting and laughing, he pressed himself into the shadows until the street was again quiet and still. Inside, as his eyes accustomed to the dark hall, he glanced into the kitchen where all of this had begun. She was sitting at the reception, the skimpy top falling away. He recalled the bargain. Clandestine, illicit. *Fifty for penetration but you use condom.* Even now the thought of her youthful round breasts made him catch his breath.

Behind the seedy reception, gloomy and nicotine stained, a pug-faced woman flicked through a magazine, murmuring to herself. Holding his breath, assuming a nonchalant swagger, he rounded the corner and trotted up the stairs. Out of the corner of his eye, he sensed the pug-face rise, glance indifferently and return to the magazine.

Of course, he knew this was all wrong. Each time he saw her, he compounded the shame and guilt. If someone caught him it was game over. A stretch inside, a policeman branded a nonce, he would lose everything. More than that, he would lose Irina.

Focus, Keith. Focus.

Dropping his shoulders, cracking the stress from his neck, he edged along the corridor, locating the familiar mock teak door, the acrylic numerals.

What if she was not in her room? Or worse still, being pawed by some stinking low-life?

He was a copper. He would concoct a pretext. Drugs, yeah drugs. Or even her age. She was still officially a child. He was following a tip-off, uncovering a paedophile ring. Anything.

Paedophile? Was that what he had become?

Steeling himself, taking a deep breath, he grabbed the door handle and turned.

In the tiny office behind the reception, Minolev slouched in his chair and stared idly at the monitors. A succession of grunting, desperate men and bored naked women. Except in room twelve. Sitting up sharply in his chair, he watched the grainy figure moving furtively toward the room. He watched the door inch open and the figure disappear behind it. Then he reached for the phone.

"It's Dimitri... Minolev." There was brief irritation in his voice at not being recognised but it disappeared. "Yes, he is in there now. Yes, I am sure it's him. He has been here enough times!" Once more the irritation but Dimitri knew his place in the food chain so he let it go. There would be food aplenty after tonight.

Chapter 62

Monday 10ᵗʰ June

When Whetstone awoke, Ramesh was gone. A cup of tea steamed on the bedside table and her phone was buzzing like a demented wasp. A sheet of folded notepaper read:

First shout of the day. Meet you there when Inspector Daley finally gets round to calling you.

Through a long and fractious night, sleep once more eluded Whetstone. In that treacherous deceit of the troubled mind, she had been over and over everything. Looping like the DVD, raw and unresolved. The slow-motion car crash of her break-up with Keith, the pain of her mother's death. Eventually, there comes a point where so much is wrong, it can never again be right.

After a quick shower, she slapped on her daily disguise, before taking a deep breath and descending the stairs. In her hand, she sighed as her phone signalled the start of the day.

"Morning, sir."

"Oh, so you are alive? I walked into Hillingdon this morning, expecting to see your bright smiling face in the naughty corner but nothing. Had to make my own tea."

In contrast to the way she felt, there was an unfathomable cheeriness in Daley's voice which Whetstone could only attribute to Terri Somerville. "Yeah, gov. Life's a bitch then you die. Anyway, what is it?"

"It's—er—8:45am. Where the heck are you?"

"On my way in. Be there soon." she lied. The one time she sleeps over, Daley is in the office before her.

"Well, don't. I'm at the Monarch View in Greenford. Suspicious death—if you can spare the time."

"Piss off, *sir.*" The Monarch View in Greenford? What were the odds?

Parking outside the perimeter, she flashed her warrant card and was directed up the narrow flight of stairs. The door to number twelve was ajar, another uniform, another flash of the warrant card and a hand to her face against the overpowering stench of scent, blood and vented bowels.

"Gov?"

Daley swivelled on his heel. "Did he come back? Parrish?"

Rolling her eyes, Whetstone puffed, annoyed at another confidence betrayed. She shook her head "No."

"So what was all that about last night?"

"Look. It was nothing."

"Ramesh phoned me. Hardly nothing. What do you think they want?"

"Well, Keith, obviously." She didn't need this conversation.

"And?"

"And nothing. Keith's pissed off and I know nothing. They can post the severed head of Shergar through my letter box and I wouldn't be able to tell them where he was."

"Yet they sent a car round to mark your card."

"Well, yes, but they were after Keith."

"DC Corby can take care of this..." Daley gestured into the room.

Masking her irritation, Whetstone smiled her gratitude, "No, sir. I'm fine. Just a little tired."

"It's all right for you. Daley hmphed sarcastically. "I have cancelled a fun meeting with the ACC for this. Went down like a turd in a swimming pool."

The room was small and tired; magnolia anaglypta, peeled at the edges, water marked and discoloured above the ancient, over-painted sash window. The carpet bore the stains of many an encounter and a bed, a wardrobe, a TV and a chest of drawers were all that spared its blushes. A small en-suite led off through the back wall.

The girl was naked on the bed. She was slender. Alabaster skin unblemished by age, now purple and marbled, resembling pale salami. Lustrous blue eyes stared lifelessly upwards. Her head lay in what remained of her brains and the back of her skull, sheets crimson and sodden. The rest was a red scar on the wall. Like a Sikh *bindi*, the small dot was maroon against her forehead, the merest trickle into the socket of her open left eye.

Len Ganlow was crouching forwards, evidence bags and cotton buds, taking samples.

"Preliminary cause of death would appear to be a single gunshot to the head. I estimate between 9:00pm and 3:00am. I can't be more precise just yet. No evidence of any other trauma, although signs of sexual intercourse shortly before death. Lividity in the back, legs and arms suggest she died here and has not been moved."

"Do we know who she is?" Something disturbed Whetstone. A glimpse of recognition. *Fifty for penetration but you use condom.* Ramesh was scraping brain tissue from the wall into and evidence bag. He was avoiding her stare. He had seen the video. Was he thinking the same?

"Irina Dąbrowska." Daley handed Whetstone a passport, the Polish eagle, a sweet face holding back a girlish smile, round and formal. "Fifteen years old."

"Fifteen? Shit!" There was perspective to everything. Last night's video barely registered against the death of a child. Unless it was the same child. "A robbery?" Whetstone took in a room, empty except for a change of clothing, some toiletries in the bathroom and a bin full of tissues and used condoms.

"Doubt it." Daley indicated a handbag on the chest of drawers. "Nothing's been disturbed. Nothing to steal anyway."

Len Ganlow continued in his tired East Anglian drawl: "The lack of powder residue around the wound suggests that the bullet was fired from just inside the door rather than close up. Ramesh will retrieve it later."

"So, the gunman entered saw her standing by the bed and shot. Clinical."

Ganlow nodded.

There was a knock and DC Corby peered around the door. "Gov, sarge. You need to look at this."

The pair followed Corby back down the drab stairwell to the reception. The tiny office reeked of nicotine and sweat. A bank of CCTV monitors filled one wall, a kaleidoscope of rooms, uniformed officers and white overalled spectres drifting from one screen to the next. One screen was blank.

At the door, Corby hesitated, his eyes flitting nervously from Daley to Whetstone. "Sarge. You may not want to see this."

Whetstone was annoyed. She and Corby had trawled the depths of human degeneracy over the last year. "I'll make that decision please, *constable*." Inside a knot was tightening.

"You can watch all the first-floor rooms from here." Corby pointed to the blank screen. "That's room twelve. *That* recorder is switched off. No tape."

"Surprise, surprise," mumbled Daley, wryly.

"Where is that?" Something drew Whetstone's eye to another of the screens.

Corby peered down at the label below the screen. "*Kuchnia*, —er, kitchen." Once more, a chill ran through her as she saw the backdrop to her restless nightmares.

"So what have we got?" asked Daley.

Corby pressed play. "Ten-thirty last night. First-floor corridor." For a few seconds the shot displayed a seemingly still image. Then a shadow appeared across the floor closely followed by a tall, stocky figure, stooping periodically to check room numbers, before settling on room twelve. Hesitating briefly, the shape disappeared through the door. The knot in Whetstone's stomach became tighter.

"And this is thirty-four minutes later." Corby scrubbed forwards. The door opened and the same stocky figure bolted down the corridor. Suddenly the figure froze and turned, as if remembering something forgotten, then returned to the room and crouched.

"What's he doing?"

"Wiping prints off the door handle, I think."

Corby hit the pause button. The image was grainy and jerky but the face was unmistakable. Racked with panic, eyes filled with terror, Keith Parrish briefly glanced at the camera and straight into the soul of Deborah Whetstone.

She could feel her ribs pressing the air from her body, her head swimming. Dashing across the lobby, she made for the rear fire exit, stifled by the cloying, rancid stench of death and depravity. And then she was staring through the door into the kitchen. Her mind superimposed the images of Keith, of a short slender girl and the back of a head, now spread across a bedroom wall. Her gorge rose in an uncontrollable cascade.

Chapter 63

Major Incident Room A, Lambourne Road

One had to hand it to Bilko Bob. He was as good as his word. At 9:00am on the dot, five civilian support officers had reported for duty, even if the man himself could not do so. Now there was a buzz about the place as the disparate groups of people worked as a team.

There was still no clue why Gordon and Hewell had gone it alone but something convinced DS Monaghan their phone conversations held the clue. Simon Pearce, IT-savvy and curiously excited by numbers, was already knee-deep in mobile logs. He was assisting Steve Taylor in tracking numbers, identifying callers and highlighting connections. Miriam Dewar, an ex CID sergeant herself, had recently returned to work after illness. He had given her the task of sifting through the reams of drug-related incidents held in the database, looking for anything that might identify Danilo Bašić or Paisley John McKaig as ring leaders. She was also keeping an eye open for references, however oblique, to Urdin Azeri. Malcolm Botts had worked with Monaghan before. He was less keen on number crunching, so Monaghan had asked him to collate door-to-door and witness statements to discover any hitherto overlooked links.

That morning, Monaghan had reviewed the CCTV footage one more time, concentrating on the vehicles. Up to seven identical BMW 520is. Two at Hanover Road, Three outside the meat packing plant before the fire. Then another two intercepted Bašić's Mercedes on the North Circular; being significantly damaged. They had recovered one, burned out near PC Parrish's abandoned squad car. Even on the assumption he was seeing the same cars more than once that still meant between three and five separate vehicles.

Checking stolen vehicle records, cross-checking with the DVLA, he searched for thefts of BMW 520is matching the description. Whilst rare before, there had been a spike over the last six months, mainly clustered in and round London. Somewhere there was a garage where a small fleet of identical cars were being stored, serviced and repaired between raids.

Pinning a large laminated map onto the wall, Monaghan drew a rough two-mile perimeter around the location of Bašić's factory. Now, one of the civilian support officers, Elaine Wilson was busy phoning round dealerships, repair yards, parts retailers, chop-shops. She was looking for unusual patterns in the purchase of spares, cars being offered for scrap, anything that could link to the stolen BMWs. The other civilian support officer, Olivia Sprason, had the more convoluted task of locating where they were being stored. Now as Monaghan surveyed the sea of faces, he hoped for a breakthrough that would move them all forward. He was not to be disappointed.

Chapter 64

The Sonata Cafe, Wembley

Behind the checked tablecloth, Paisley John passed the wad of banknotes to Fat Leon who stuffed them into an innocuous hessian holdall. Then he clicked his fingers at the bottle blonde and demanded more tea. This whole situation with Bašić was grinding him down.

Then there was the matter of insubordination. He had not given authorisation to torch the meat packing plant. Someone was getting far too big for their boots. This was not some namby-pamby democracy he was running. It was a dictatorship. Either you played by the rules or you didn't play at all.

He should never have agreed to meet with Bašić. Handbags at bloody dawn and he, Paisley John, looking like a complete imbecile. Maybe that's was necessary to maintain Dougie Murdoch's precious status quo, but it stuck in his craw that these skirmishes still took place, that the police were aware and couldn't care less.

The occasional run-in with DCI Kramer, or his tame poodle Dodds, was part of the game. You scratch my back... This new copper was different. Practically silent for the whole of the meeting, he didn't seem to give a toss about the drugs and the prostitution. That concerned Paisley John. Like a graffiti artist being told his work is aesthetically pleasing, it lessens the joy of getting away with it.

No, this copper was interested in something else. Something he preferred to speak about only to Dougie Murdoch. Maybe the insubordination led all the way to the top?

As another grey face occupied the deal chair opposite, another envelope crossed the table, McKaig wondered if he should call time on the Westsiders. Fifty-eight was no age to retire but the lure of a Thai Beach and nubile women of indeterminate morals seemed more attractive every day. Liquidate the offshore dollars, buy an island and let someone else take the shit.

All at once, McKaig noticed a shadow cross the cafe window, and an explosion of sound briefly deafened him. One of the strong-arms shouted *what the fuck?* Instinctively, McKaig covered his eyes as shards of wood and glass flew through the air and the floor seemed to heave and yaw.

Blinking the dust from his eyes, he pushed away the table and struggled to sit against the wall. His ears rang like a herd of Swiss cows being chased by the bull. The sun shone through the hole which used to be the front of the cafe, fragments of the frame dangling like stray threads on a hem. Behind him the bottle-blonde was shaking and moaning.

At first, he assumed a bomb. Then, maybe a road accident. Until he saw the car. The round vulpine eyes, hazed by the dust, and the ominous, slow growl of the engine. The barrel of the shotgun bobbed through the open passenger window and he stifled a whimper.

Chapter 65

Lambourne Road

Spilling her guts, both actually and metaphorically, had left Whetstone drained. Daley had suggested she go off-grid for a while *to get her shit together* as he so eloquently put it. But she needed to be around when Parrish surfaced. She needed to hear the explanation. For now though, she would bury herself in the Gordon and Hewell investigations.

At least that was what she thought.

As soon as she entered the team room, Dave Monaghan rose to his feet. "You, Meeting Room 99. Now."

Whetstone's shoulders slumped even lower. Meeting Room 99 was the boiler room in the basement. The only place in the building where one could speak without being overheard.

Just how much of her personal life was common knowledge?

Glancing to her right, the blinds were shut on the Goldfish Bowl. "Browning?"

Monaghan nodded. "She's waiting for the DI. He can run but he can't hide."

Whetstone puffed her cheeks. "At least Daley's having a worse time than me." She followed Monaghan in silence down the stairs, across the ground floor and into the cramped basement room.

"Deb, you need to distance yourself from the investigation into this girl's death."

"Oh, come on, Dave!"

"Browning's orders."

"Browning? What's it got to do with her?"

It was Monaghan's turn to puff his cheeks. "Look, Deb. We have to play this by the book?" He paused, as if considering his words. "He is on tape entering and leaving her room, wiping his fingerprints off her door handle shortly after she died!"

"Or shortly before. Ganlow said any time between 9:00pm and 3:00am. If she was killed at 10:00pm, they may have been arguing or..." Whetstone lowered her head. She was all out of excuses for him.

"We have someone matching his description at the Gordon and Hewell shootings and the same gun was probably used for all three. And Harry Ramesh sent me a copy of the DVD from your house. The date puts it at 13th November 2012. Keith was stationed outside The Monarch View, keeping an eye on Connor Smith, a witness in *The Hand in the Van* enquiry. Both Ramesh and I are in no doubt it's Keith Parrish with the dead girl. After this morning, we have to consider Parrish may be armed and dangerous."

Whetstone was aghast. 'So he had sex with an underage prostitute. That's a far cry from murder." Did she just dismiss the act? "Seriously, Dave? You don't think...? A lying, two-timing shit certainly, and a pervert who prayed on teenage girls maybe, but dangerous?" The full ramifications of the morning were still sinking in. Keith Parrish entering and leaving the dead girl's room. The furtive look of panic as the frame froze.

"For your own good, Deb. Steer clear. If PC Parrish makes any attempt to contact you, should he wish to meet with you, make the appointment but let me know. Under no circumstances are you to meet him alone. Is that clear? The guy is a shit of the first order and we need to stop him."

Whetstone glared at Monaghan and hoped he could see the rage in her eyes as they glistened wet. "Well, if you thought that, why did you wait until now to tell me, Dave?"

"You know, Deb? You and Scott Daley are both the same. There is no helping you when you get a cob on." Monaghan was struggling to keep his own composure. These days, Daley or Whetstone, he always seemed to be babysitting one or the other. "Just keep your bloody head down until we have found Parrish. Then I will find a suitable room and you can kick ten shades of shite out of him. For now though, if you so much as hear his name in conversation, let me know."

Monaghan placed his hands on Whetstone's shoulders. "Look, Deb. You're tougher than this. You are not the first and you won't be the last. One day when this is all over, I will tell you about Maureen O'Donoghue. Now, dry your eyes, put on your game face. We have work to do."

Chapter 66

The Sonata Cafe

"Come on, boss. We got to go."

Fat Leon towered over Paisley John. There was blood in the big man's short coiled hair and his brown face had the grainy pallor of a pantomime dame.

Annoyed, Paisley John yanked away his arm. There was a message to deliver, otherwise those barrels would have blasted through his ribs already. Pushing the table away, he dragged himself defiantly to his feet and dusted off his sleeves.

"What the bloody hell do youz want?"

Herman and Eddie, McKaig's two strong-arms, had been by the door arms folded, watchful. Well, they didn't bloody see this. He could hear Herman coughing, harsh rasps, short, pained. If they ever got out of this he would do more than cough. Through the shattered tables, Eddie lay motionless, his bulky torso lifting the front of the BMW, his neck twisted. Maybe Leon had a point but McKaig's bravado was more powerful than his common sense.

Slowly, crunching away debris, the passenger door of the BMW opened and a masked head appear above it. The shotgun remained menacingly still. The engine of the car hummed seductively, like a cat on a warm cushion.

"Mr Azeri is very disappointed with the company you're keeping. He feels you should pick your friends more wisely." There was mockery in the voice and McKaig could feel the blood pumping harder, burning within his temples.

"What business is it of his who I see on my manor?"

Outside there was a siren, distant, blending with the buzz of traffic. The bottle blonde had ceased her moaning. Maybe she had scarpered through the back.

"Mr Azeri makes it his business to know what's going on. No-one likes a grass. Look at Mick Bullard. He grasses you up. Now he's dead. So when Mr Azeri hears you're speaking to the police, what is he to think? Double standards. That's what he thinks."

McKaig started forwards and Leon grabbed his arm. "Let it go, boss, please."

"No, I will not let it go, Leon." His eyes were wild, his voice spat through gritted teeth. "That prick has just call me a bloody grass. This wee streak of piss who thinks he's clever because he has a gun." McKaig's finger jabbed out towards the black mask, sensing the arrogance of the smile beneath. "I will hunt you down to the ends of the bloody Earth and you will eat that gun with your bloody arse, I promise you."

"Shit, John. Just leave it." Fat Leon tugged harder, seeing a breach in the window, sensing the escape but the bulk of McKaig would not budge and he kept shouting obscenities.

"There is nowhere you can hide. You will watch your wife and your babies die before I am finished with you." McKaig raged. There was nothing now that could stop him.

Almost nothing.

Through the driver's window, there was a crash of glass, a flash of orange and a wave of heat pushed McKaig back across Leon. Suddenly all he could see was a wall of flickering flame. Through it, he heard the two men leave the vehicle. Outside, an engine roared, and the sound faded as sirens echoed ever closer.

Then he was being hauled backwards. He felt the sharpness of broken wood against his back before an almighty ball of orange engulfed the cafe and singed his face.

Chapter 67

The Goldfish Bowl, Lambourne Road

ACC Diane Browning placed her cap and gloves on the desk and made herself comfortable in the *throne of doom*, a feat which Scott Daley had never managed. News from the hospital had been positive. Allenby was responding well to treatment. He was to be eased out of his coma in a day or two and would probably be allowed out a week or so later. Unfortunately, that turned out to be the highlight of Daley's morning.

"Sorry for the delay, ma'am. Murder in Greenford."

"So my PA told me. Not to worry. These things happen." She flicked a short business-like smile. "I will get straight to the point. Operation Nightjar. I need your team to stand down immediately. I need you to pass the investigation to Ray Kramer. That will leave you free to deal with the ever-increasing workload of your own department."

Incensed, Daley clenched his fists below the desk and vented his frustration in a silent roar. Calmly he said, "Do you think that's wise, ma'am?"

"I hope you're not questioning my judgement, *Inspector*."

"No, ma'am." Of course he was. "With the best will in the world, it will take DCI Kramer's team time to get up to speed. We have made a great deal of headway. I am confident it will only be a matter of days before we make an arrest."

"Funnily enough, Bob Allenby told me much the same yet here we are. From what I have heard you have been spending more time focussing on the feud between the two organised crime gangs than you have in tracing the killer of our two police officers. And this other officer—Constable Parrish? The one who has gone AWOL? What's his part in all of this?"

"PC Parrish?" Daley was confused. "DI Dodds thinks he was the middleman between Gordon and Hewell. Someone used his phone to contact Gordon and Hewell before their deaths."

"And now he is implicated in the death of this prostitute?"

"Seems that way." News travelled far too quickly in the halls of Scotland Yard.

"So, we have two officers down, a gangland war on the streets of West London and we are still no nearer to finding the culprits."

"In my view though, ma'am, the feud is a smokescreen for other activities that Gordon and Hewell somehow became mixed up in. We know the same gun killed them. I am sure we are on the verge of a breakthrough."

"Can I remind you that both Joe Gordon and Dean Hewell professed to being on the verge of a breakthrough and that got them killed?"

"Indeed, ma'am" The fact had not escaped Daley.

"May I also remind you they were experienced officers, and it didn't save them? Get the Drugs Unit up to speed quickly, then I need you to focus on your own caseload." Browning paused. "I have been informed that you have held secret meetings with known criminals..."

"Hardly secret, ma'am..." Daley's temper was fraying once more. The Goldfish Bowl was becoming stiflingly hot.

"... with *known* criminals," she emphasised.

Daley was sick of explaining himself. The rebuke caught him off-guard. Maybe he was under closer scrutiny than he had previously thought? The exasperation began to show in his voice. "DCI Kramer and I had a pre-arranged visit with John McKaig of the Westsiders."

"Inspector, we both know you have strayed over a very dangerous line by meeting Dougie Murdoch alone. If Professional Standards become involved... Frankly, I am worried for the safety of you and your team."

"Seriously, ma'am? Everything I have done was necessary to discover the identity of the killer." Daley tried not to sound too annoyed. Why, suddenly, had the focus landed on him? "My meeting with Dougie Murdoch more or less confirmed that this is not a spat between rival gangs but an orchestrated move by a third party."

"Third party? Who?"

Daley huffed. Now that his foot was firmly in his mouth, he had no choice but to continue. "Gordon and Hewell both spoke about the Encubierto, a Spanish outfit fronted by an Urdin Azeri. Until now, they could not put a face to the name however, we are seeing a pattern to the attacks. I am convinced it is this group that is destabilising the West side of London and pitting these two firms against each other."

"For what purpose?"

"I don't know, ma'am. Not yet."

"This is DCI Kramer's territory. You and your team are not equipped to deal with these types of people."

"And DCI Kramer is?"

"Inspector. That is my problem not yours."

Browning checked her watch and collected her cap and gloves. As she rose, she paused.

"Scott. I am sure it has not escaped your notice that Superintendent Allenby's coronary may be a blessing in disguise. Inevitably, he will leave a gaping hole in the chain of command. When the Homicide Unit and Drugs Unit merge, they will be without a superintendent and short of at least one DCI. And that makes me nervous."

"Ma'am." Frankly, Daley's mind was on more prosaic matters. Browning continued:

"The streamlining of staff under MOPAC, whilst being unfortunate for some, could prove advantageous to others. There will be opportunities for the right individuals. Those who show themselves to have the right skills, the right *attitude*. Those whose loyalties are not—confused, shall we say?"

"Surely, it's a one-horse race, ma'am? Ray Kramer?"

Browning considered. "One would think. The combined command would be around thirty people. I will need a safe pair of hands in charge. Someone I can rely on to move the department forward in line with our expectations. I am not sure that Ray Kramer is up to the job."

Daley raised his eyebrows. "And I am?" He hoped he was not presuming too much.

She chuckled dismissively. "Inspector. You are a loose cannon, a maverick. Every time your name gets mentioned, it is because of some misdemeanour or because you have ruffled feathers. However, you possess one attribute which I prize highly. Loyalty. Both to your team and your superintendent. God alone knows why but he seems unerringly loyal to you.

"When the effects of the rationalisation bite, things will get messy, both politically and out there on the street. I need a team about me who can grab my metaphorical balls from the fire when things become too hot. In return, I will show loyalty to them.

"There's still time to prove yourself worthy, Inspector. Hand over Operation Nightjar to DCI Kramer."

Chapter 68

North West London CDIU, Hillingdon, 11:00am

Whetstone felt drained of all emotion, a leaf on the breeze, blown from one disaster to the next. But more, she felt utterly foolish that she could not see these things coming. She was obsessing about BMWs. Every car that passed, every voice outside had left her cowering, waiting for them to leave. Or worse, to stay.

With Daley heading back to Lambourne Road, she decided on Hillingdon. Against Scott Daley's advice, she had decided that work was infinitely better than daytime TV. The naughty corner would offer a quiet place, away from the pitying eyes of her colleagues. Once again, she was to be disappointed.

"Sergeant Whetstone?"

She stopped doodling and squinted across the room.

"Sir?"

Phil Dodds raised his head. "I've just been reading the serials. Last night. The Monarch View?"

"Can you not just give me a break, sir." Whetstone sighed. Once more tact had eluded Dodds. *I suppose you've heard your boyfriend has blown his underage prostitute's head off.* She let it go and turned back to the naughty corner, welcoming of the seclusion. Maybe she could curl up in a ball and hide under the desk. Not even the cleaners went there.

"You need to look at this." Dodds insisted.

Wearily, she trudged over and unenthusiastically scanned the screen in front of him.

"It's a list of the times and dates of the drugs van raids over the last six months and Keith Parrish's shift rota for the same period. We have had our eyes on him for a while now."

The number of matches stunned Whetstone. Though sometimes he was simply off-duty when trouble occurred, for most he had been on duty and had missed check-ins.

"The times and dates fit exactly. Hours when he was AWOL, raids taking place. We tapped his phone and were watching his apartment. We were so close to an arrest. One slip and we would have had him."

"You can't really think Keith...?" But there were too many coincidences. Suddenly she felt as if she hardly knew him at all.

"We know he has been visiting the Monarch View during his shift for almost six months now. You saw the CCTV. Bašić knows everything that happens there. Keith Parrish was a naughty boy and Bašić caught him out. We think he was providing the Cjevovod with details of the movement of stock, of the routes, of any changes. Maybe he was involved in the raids themselves. Face facts. Parrish was in this up to his neck."

"It's all circumstantial. There's no real proof of any of this." She wondered if Dodds had yet seen the footage from Irina Dąbrowska's room. "Do you have a single shred of real evidence that places him at the raids, or even at the Gordon and Hewell killings?"

"There is his phone."

"His phone?" Whetstone's mind was reeling, there was too much to take in. "What about his phone?"

"How did it end up in the burning factory?"

"His phone turned up at the factory?"

"Yes, that unidentified phone found in the rubble. Didn't you know? Look, I know you and he..."

Dodds was now revelling in her anguish. Her heart was beating out of her chest and she could feel the anger welling but something was not right and she struggled to put her finger on it. "And, knowing him and me were...? You didn't think it something I should know about?"

"With all due respect, sergeant, how do I know you are not involved? How can we be sure you were not also in Bašić's pocket?"

Sergeant? Her rank wielded like a stick.

"Seriously? I suppose you also had my phone tapped, *sir.*"

"Well, you trusted Parrish..."

"God, you're a bastard, Phil."

Suddenly, she felt uncomfortably hot and fetched herself a glass of water. Dodds hypocrisy sickened her. Two months since Joe Gordon's death, since the Drugs Unit had lost one of their own, and they had done nothing to find the killer. Now, he was raking through every minute patch of pond scum he could find to discredit Parrish.

"Just how is any of this your business, *sir*? Homicide falls under the purview of Lambourne Road. If there is any investigation to carry out, we will do it. You need to get your own bloody house in order before you point out our shortfalls. You and your team are never bloody here and half the manor is filling their boots while you look the other way. Just what kind of show are you and DCI Kramer running— *sir?*"

"Listen here, Whetstone. This is *my* team and *my* department." Dodds hand slammed on the desk, rocking the monitor and making Whetstone start. "I will run it however I feel fit and I don't need lessons from a bloody sergeant whose boyfriend is a nonce and a cop killer."

Whetstone froze. The team room had stilled. Heads ceased conversations and buried themselves in work. Suddenly, to Whetstone, daytime TV seemed appealing. Dodds locked his computer and exhaled.

"Just—come with me."

As he led her to the side room, Whetstone braced herself for the inevitable bollocking as Dodd exercised the full weight of his perceived authority. It didn't come. Instead, he closed the blinds and fired up the screen. Soon she saw the familiar images of the Gordon and Hewell shootings.

"Look at the gunman." Dodds gesticulated as the screen. "The way he walks. The way he stands. Familiar?"

The blood drained from Whetstone's cheeks and suddenly she felt lost in a world that seemed to know everything whilst she knew so little.

"But that could be anyone. There must be a hundred..."

"Really? He was on shift on each of these occasions. Each time, he was uncontactable. Check the records. Face facts, Deb. This has Parrish all over it, so before you lecture me about how I run my department, perhaps you ought to look at yourself."

Returning to her desk, Whetstone struggled to hold herself together. Eschewing the naughty corner, she took the lift to the canteen, ordered a coffee and sat staring out across the skyline of Hillingdon. Whatever trouble Keith was in, it was not hers. She did not need to defend herself against Phil Dodds' chauvinistic hatchet-job.

Still something was niggling at her. What if he were right? In her mind, she replayed the CCTV clips, removing the mask, imagining the face, the eyes, the arrogant grin. Yes, it could have been anyone but, given the evidence, the phone in the factory ruins, his subsequent disappearance, only to turn up when the prostitute he had been screwing was shot dead?

What were the odds?

Chapter 69

ACC Browning's instructions had been clear. Daley was to hand over Operation Nightjar immediately. Which meant, it would grind to a halt once more. However much it rankled, dragging his heels would only piss off ACC Browning more and with Bilko Bob in Intensive Care, no-one would fight his corner. He knew Browning would be having similar conversations with Ray Kramer. If there was to be a bun-fight for Allenby's role, Daley wanted to be throwing buns rather than covering his head as they fell. At least over at Hillingdon, he could keep an eye on the pair. *Keep your enemies closer still.* So he travelled to Hillingdon to get it over with.

He need not have bothered.

The corral of desks occupied by the Drugs Unit was deserted. Even Ray Kramer's office was unlit and quiet. Suddenly at a loose end, he made a brew and settled into the naughty corner. Then he pulled the case file on Alicia Sheldon, if for no other reason than to scratch a mental itch.

Alicia Sheldon was a fifty-three-year-old spinster who lived her life in Southall where she ran the local sub-post office. On the 23rd October 2002, she was closing up for the night, drawing down the shutters, bringing in the A-board. As per normal, her assistant, Helen Wright, had taken the till drawer through to the storeroom for reconciliation. She was counting out the next day's float when she heard a loud rap on the floor of the shop. She told the police it sounded like the A-board collapsing to the floor, so she carried on counting. After a few minutes, Mrs Wright returned to the shop to find Alicia Sheldon spread-eagled across the floor with a hole in her scalp and a sizeable portion of her face missing. A specialist search team found the gun in the wall cavity of a derelict building two miles away, following a tip-off. An extensive but ultimately fruitless investigation concluded that Miss Sheldon had been a victim of a raid gone wrong. They had apprehended no-one for the crime.

So why did Patrick Gascoigne consider it so important?

In the last log entry, dated 2004, the Investigating Officer effectively canned the case. There were the customary mortuary shots and photos of the scene, a few unidentified fingerprints and boot prints, pictures of the gun, a Heckler & Koch semi-automatic pistol and reams of witness statements.

He looked up as the door hinges to the Hillingdon team room squealed and Phil Dodds appeared. "Scott. Finally put in an appearance, I see?"

Daley sneered. "Bugger off, Phil. I hear there was more trouble this morning? Sonata cafe?"

Dodds nodded sombrely. "Bašić fire-bombed the place. Waitress says two cars came around the corner. One rams the front of the cafe. They point a shotgun through the window then lob a petrol bomb and kaboom. Then the two occupants of the first car fled in the second. Forensics are there now."

"Anyone hurt?"

"Two fatalities, as yet unidentified. The waitress reckons McKaig and his bodyguard escaped through a window."

Daley recalled Kramer's reprimand the previous day. Now, to some extent, he understood. They had arranged the meeting with McKaig at the last minute. Bašić, if it were he, had acted quickly and violently. Daley could almost hear the jungle drums relaying his every move.

"Alicia Sheldon?" Dodds craned over Daley's shoulder. "Now there's a name I haven't heard in a while. Post Office Raid. 2002? I thought that was dead and buried."

Daley nodded. "An old case Allenby asked me to review," he lied.

Dodds raised an eyebrow. "You get all the exciting stuff. All I get are drugs wars and car chases."

"Why the Sonata Cafe, Phil?"

"Your meeting with Dougie Murdoch pissed off Bašić. Those two behave like teenagers. If you had met with Terzić, then I dare say John would have retaliated similarly."

Then he recalled something Whetstone had told him. "What make were the cars?"

"BMWs, I think." Dodds pulled out his notebook.

"Same as the street ambushes and the factory fire."

"Yeah, your sergeant mentioned those."

"And?"

"Used to be black Audis. Maybe the vehicle of choice has changed? Maybe they both hired the same rent-a-mob to do their dirty work?"

The blue fox jumps over the Bear and the Boar... Dark blue BMWs. "Or Urdin Azeri likes his Beemers and is muscling in on them both."

"Fairy story, Scott." Phil Dodds smirked dismissively. "Now Bašić has *you* jumping at shadows. I told you not to trust him."

"I don't get it, Phil. Bašić and McKaig knew about your undercover officers. Why kill them? Then out of the blue, vans being ambushed and factories torched. Something must have changed the natural order of things. Then there is Patrick Gascoigne. Gordon revealed something to him before he died... It's as if someone wants these two gangs at war."

"Gascoigne?" Dodds looked puzzled. "What about Gascoigne?"

Suddenly, a notion flitted through Daley's mind, barely pausing long enough for him to fix it. Bizarre, incomprehensible. "Oh, nothing. I remember him speaking about Joe Gordon shortly before he died."

Daley grabbed his keys and headed down the car park. If he were right, there would be one more bullet comparison to do.

Chapter 70

Staff Canteen, Hillingdon

Whetstone knew the telephone log condemned Parrish as a liar, a philanderer. Now a paedophile and possibly even a murderer. How could she have read him so wrong? Or was it desperation? Her biological clock ticking loud enough to mask any reservations.

On the table her phone spun, a locust buzz as it vibrated. Jerking her arm, spilling coffee, eliciting a curse. If it was Scott Daley, he could take a running jump. Pressing a button, the locust fell silent. They could *all* take a running jump.

She recalled an occasion a few months ago. She had been angry with Scott Daley, some minor indiscretion. Arriving home, her mother, already half-cut had bemoaned her solitary, sad existence and Whetstone had returned a volley tenfold. Angry, ashamed, retreating to her room, huddling against her pillow, she had called and Keith had not answered.

Now, as so many times since, she knew why. Why she felt more like a friend than a lover whenever they were alone. Why he refused to move in after her mother had died.

Again, the locust droned, a halo of light on the table. Impatiently, she stared at the screen. Not Daley, nor Monaghan. Not even Ramesh. Bizarrely, it was a landline. Again, she silenced the buzz. She hoped whichever call-centre had chosen that moment to call, was aware how fortunate they had been.

But the locust persisted and after a long moment she thrust the phone to her ear.

"What?"

"Deb, It's me. I'm so sorry,"

The room stopped. Her heart faltered and the world collapsed into the voice on the phone. She could feel herself quaking, a tear forming. Torn between anger and immense sorrow, she moved the phone to her other ear. Away from the room. Away from eavesdroppers.

"You're sorry? You're disgusting. Jesus Christ, Keith. She was fourteen when you met her. And to think I left you alone with my sister. It makes me sick to think of—us."

"It wasn't like that. Honestly."

"So, tell me. What exactly went through your mind as you pulled her onto the kitchen counter and banged her brains out?"

"It was a spur-of-the-moment thing, Deb, I promise. I saw her outside, one thing led to another. That's all. Anyway, she came on to me."

"And did you ever think of me? How I might feel? Bloody Hell, Keith. She was fourteen years old."

"How was I to know? It's impossible to tell these days. Even if I'd have asked..."

"Bollocks. There is no way she would have passed off as sixteen, let alone eighteen or nineteen. She was practically in nappies. You must have known?"

"Honestly, no. Not until they arrested her in February and I saw the charge-sheet."

Whetstone ran her hands through her hair. "You knew she was a prostitute. *Twenty pounds, fifty for penetration?* You see people like her all the time. How could you not know?"

"I was weak. I saw an opportunity."

"For six months?"

Parrish lapsed into silence, broken only by short, exasperated gasps. "Deb, I know what you must be thinking. I have been trying to tell you it was over for weeks. To let you down gently but, well, you know... Look, if I could change it I would but I can't and right now none of this matters, really it doesn't."

"You are bloody priceless, Keith. My boyfriend is screwing a fourteen-year-old prostitute behind my back. Sleeping with me while still dirty from his underage whore, and it doesn't matter? You've had six months to call it off but instead you said nothing. Six months, Keith and it doesn't matter? My whole life is teetering on the edge of a cliff. I need you there to stop me falling, not to give me a shove in the back and then apologise." Puffing her cheeks, she turned and gazed out at the rooftops. Her life was in ruins and he was dismissing her. The smouldering anger inside her suddenly ignited. "So just when were you going to tell me you were trading me in for a newer model? When she was shitting out your bastard child? Or were you going to leave me to cotton on in my own time?"

"Deb!"

"Or did the newer model become a pain in the arse? What was it? Did she need her visa renewing? Perhaps you wouldn't buy her sweeties after school. So you thought, I'll just put a bullet in her head and stick with old *bloody* faithful?"

"What?"

"Don't come the innocent. We have you on CCTV entering and leaving her room. You looked at the camera for God's sake. You even wiped the bloody door handle."

"Yes, I was there. I went to her room, but I didn't kill her. She was lying on the bed. She was already..."

But the words were a soundtrack to the images in her head. His body on hers, hands running around her breasts, holding her arms. Those same hands touching the alabaster flesh, watching the explosion of red as she fell naked, onto the bed.

"Why should I listen to anything you have to say ever again?"

"OK, OK. I can't talk on the phone. Meet me, later. Just this once. Meet me and I can explain then I will come back with you. Hand myself in. They can lock me up and throw away the key. I promise. Just do me this one last thing. You remember that Saturday just after we met, when it rained and we took shelter? Meet me there. Six o'clock tonight. Please, Deb."

And then he was gone, the phone collapsing to black.

The road below teemed with life, prosaic and uneventful, the kitchen clattered as plates were collected and food laid out. Keith had made her life public property and soon this place would heave with people, scrutinising her, overflowing with mock concern, wheedling their way into her business.

Scalding her mouth as she drank the coffee, she wanted to scream and sod them all. To Hell with Daley, and Monaghan, Ramesh and Allenby. To Hell with Lambourne Road and the bloody, sodding, Metropolitan Police Service. She would bury herself in reports of dark blue BMWs and hide for a while.

In another part of the City, as the phone call ended, a recording stopped, and an earpiece was removed.

Chapter 71

By the time Daley arrived home, the nag in his sub-conscious was palpable but still incoherent.

The blue fox jumps over the lazy wolf, the bear and the boar to please the ambitious vixen.
All the time the rabbit was watching. Now the blue fox has pounced on the rabbit and he is no more.

Bears and boars and wolves and foxes. Then there was the rabbit. Gascoigne was not known for his flights of fancy. Behind the childish rhyme, there had to be a thread of truth, however obscure. Sat at the kitchen table, staring at his laptop, Daley tried to reconcile the names with what he knew.

The blue fox jumps over the lazy wolf, the bear and the boar...

Gascoigne firmly believed Urdin Azeri was the blue fox, yet Azeri was a ghost. In Phil Dodds view, he was a figment of Danilo Bašić's imagination, designed to cover his attacks on the Westsiders. Bašić was known as *The Bear* and McKaig fitted the description of a Boar admirably but who was the wolf? *Jumps over.* What did that imply? Was Bašić circumventing the Cjevovod line of command, overstepping his authority?

All the time the rabbit was watching.

That had to be a reference to Joe Gordon, working undercover passing back information. Whatever he confided to Gascoigne left him so scared he feared for his life.

The blue fox has pounced on the rabbit and he is no more.

Daley scratched the stubble on his chin and stretched wearily, the nag in his mind now annoying him. Joe Gordon confided in Patrick. Then he was killed. Patrick takes a look. Then he dies in a car accident - a damn convenient one. Maybe the blue fox caught up with him too?

But who was the vixen?

"Haven't we discussed bringing work home with you?"

Daley started and looked up at Terri. "How long have you been standing there?"

"Not long. I got bored waiting for you to bring through the pickles. Time, tide and my cravings wait for no man. What are you up to?"

"Just something Patrick was working on before he died." Daley closed the lid of the laptop self-consciously. "Some loose ends."

Terri eased herself into the chair opposite Daley and took his hands.

"Scott, this case you're working on. You will be careful, won't you?"

Daley's brow furrowed. "Operation Nightjar? What's brought this on?"

"You know, things I've heard through the grapevine. Meeting with the gang leaders, the raid on their headquarters. We are not totally isolated over at Harrow Central. This whole thing with the drugs gangs, it's frightening me."

"The Cjevovod and the Westsiders may be at each other's throats but they are not interested in me. When I was with Dougie Murdoch out at Saw Lane, I sensed that I was safe. He needs my help to find out who is attacking his men."

"Like he needed Joe Gordon's help...or Dean Hewell's? Look, it doesn't matter who is fighting who, or whose side you are on. All that matters is me and you. I am worried sick that one day you will walk out that door and never return."

His mind flashed back to a dusty rail siding and the man bound to the tracks by cable-ties as a train bore down. Then he had escaped with moments to spare. If the tide turned, would Bašić or McKaig afford him that courtesy? Still, he resented the implication he could not look after himself. That he did not consider her interests. Inside, Daley could feel the tiny smouldering embers becoming hotter and hotter.

"Look, Terri, I have had this lecture from Ray Kramer, Bob Allenby and now from you. Hell, even Phil Dodds was telling me to lay off. I am sick to death with people telling me how to do my job. Then, there is bloody Browning, fawning over her precious Drugs Unit so much, she completely ignores the progress I have made on Nightjar and wants me to hand it back to them. Why? So when they follow my leads, they can claim all the glory? Where will that leave me when the redundancies start? Sitting on my bloody hands with nothing to show."

"It's not about Operation Nightjar. You're not listening, Scott. It's..."

"I am bloody listening. It's just that police work is not like that. How am I supposed to do my job if all the time I have to look over my shoulder, weighing up the risks, the repercussions?"

"Are you serious? What would happen if every police officer in London has such a cavalier attitude to their own safety?"

"Look," puffed Daley, "Of course I have to consider you—and the baby but if that's all I thought about, I would do nothing. When you're in the thick of it you have to think quickly, not always safely."

"But Scott. It is not just you anymore. It is *us*. You, me and soon the baby. Do you want junior to grow up without a dad because you didn't think before diving in?"

After yet another onslaught, it left Daley exasperated. "OK, I will leave the dangerous stuff to Phil Dodds or Mike Corby. Is that what you want to hear? Maybe I should always make sure I remain one step behind Deborah Whetstone? Perhaps I should hide under her coat? What sort of man would that make me?"

Grabbing his laptop, snatching up the car keys, Daley made for the door. "I am going out. I may be late back." Then he turned, suddenly weighed down with guilt and shame. Terri was resting her chin on her hands. Her eyes were red and tears tracked across her cheeks. "Look, I promise I will be careful."

Some promises were made to be broken. Others were impossible to keep.

Chapter 72

Park Royal, 7:30pm

The Vue Cinema would never sweep a woman off her feet as a statement of undying affection. Stuffed onto the grandly named Royale Leisure Park, hemmed in by the Western Avenue and railways on three sides, it was not the most glamorous place a boy could take a girl.

Back on that Saturday evening, the rain stung like sewing needles flung from icy clouds, biting and raw as she ran to shelter beneath the arched white canopies. Whetstone recalled the prospect of his arrival, her body shuddering at the thought of his touch, the anticipation almost eating her alive. They had taken in a film, or at least some of it, before grabbing some Mexican food. With the rain hammering on the perplex canopies, he had pulled her behind the restaurant, pressed her to the wall and made love to her, breathless, eager and passionate.

Now, the mere thought of him brought bile to her throat.

Tonight, it was the openness she craved; the car park was exposed, unoccupied. She couldn't see Keith's car or any dark blue BMWs.

In her pocket her phone buzzed. Annoyed she checked the screen. It was Scott Daley, probably wanting to deliver the inevitable lecture, so she silenced the call. He could leave a voicemail. Opening the glove-box, she hurled the phone inside. Tonight, it would be Keith and her and an awful lot of explaining.

Taking one last look around, Whetstone locked the Golf and walked across the open tarmac, skirting the edge of the cinema. As she did, she looped her keyring over her middle finger, feeling the sharpness of her house keys. Everything seemed disconnected and bizarre since she had heard the odious sounds, seen the grotesque images looping over. Since Phil Dodds had convinced her that coincidences do not happen. She was jumping when her phone rang, when a car passed too close. The world had turned, and it had turned ugly.

Between the Mexican restaurant and the cinema, beyond the canned Mariachi music, an alleyway disappeared into darkness as her eyes adjusted from the starkness of the evening sun. Isolated and suddenly silent, a frisson of panic coursed through her. Bewilderment, incredulity. Why, after all he had done should she agree to meet here?

Peering down the alley, she could see the light at the end, the rear courtyard beyond. Against all her better instincts, she took a deep breath and stepped into the dark.

Chapter 73

B470, Iver Lane, 7:30pm

Full of remorse for his infantile behaviour, Daley had decided he needed to be out of the house. To let the atmosphere cool. He and Terri rarely argued and for a moment he had been transported back to the endless weeks of bickering between himself and Lynne, the red mist had descended and he had lost his temper. Was the honeymoon period over? Would his relationship with Terri take a similar downward spiral? A slow descent through confrontation and indifference to hate and loathing and the need to be somewhere else. An emptiness echoed inside his soul as he thought of Terri, as he thought of Deborah Whetstone and Keith Parrish. Were they both destined to a life of loneliness and exclusion? Perhaps that was the natural order of things; the lot of a copper.

Daley pulled up outside a row of Thirties Semis. One of those unaccounted-for juxtapositions of town houses and open countryside. Passing by on his commute, Professor Patrick Gascoigne probably never registered how out of place they were. For him they would be a staging post on his journey, marking the edge of the town and the last leg home; onto the Broadway, Radio 4 News, Uxbridge centre, *Just a Minute*, Cowley, countryside, *not far now*. There were around twenty houses, set back thirty feet from the road, a rural dereliction of woodpiles and braziers, rusting cars and bean canes. Each, as it happened, was occupied by deaf blind mutes who could tell the police nothing. The road, dead straight, ran South West from Cowley; ahead of Gascoigne there would be a mile of unobstructed vista as it rose over the M25 and fell into Iver.

A damn convenient accident. What was the truth behind it?

With the light rapidly fading, Daley jogged to the opposite side of the road and a tree, still scarred and raw, green already subsuming the patch of ashen earth, fragments of glass and plastic disappearing beneath the new growth. Gascoigne's Jaguar had left grooved tracks as it leapt a small gully. Any drivers who witnessed the crash had not stopped. Whatever took place, started on the road; this was where it finished.

Why would an experienced driver in a roadworthy vehicle swerve into a tree? Occam's razor—maybe Gascoigne had dozed at the wheel? Through the town, out into the countryside, warm car, nearly home. Maybe that was true? Maybe he swerved to avoid a deer or a badger? Yet there was no evidence of an animal impact.

Maybe he swerved to avoid a fox? A *blue* fox?

Then a thought occurred to Daley. A thought so bizarre he almost dismissed it.

Swivelling on his heel, he scanned the hedgerow. Beside the houses, the fence gave way to a path that ran along the edge of the first field, perhaps behind the rear gardens. Almost invisible amongst the hedges, at its head, a barrier protected pedestrians from the road. Then he looked back along the mile of open road in the direction that the professor's Jaguar had come. The black dot visible for almost a minute, becoming more distinct as it came nearer. Daley peered the other way, down the road towards Iver into the sun, orange over the horizon as it relinquished the skies to a grey dusk. A passing driver, face stark and amber in the harsh light, drew down the sun visor. Had the professor seen something?

Daley pulled out his phone and called Ramesh, asking him to check the reports on the car; to check the front and rear windscreens. Back along Gascoigne's route, a more or less solid line of trees and hedging bordered the kerb beyond the narrow gully. The setting sun left the ancient hedgerow lit orange, and he waited a moment for his eyes to adjust. A tangle of vicious thorns covered the ground but above waist height the hedge thinned to a few straggling fingers and the rough, barked trunks. Periodically checking back, checking height and range, checking direction, Daley scoured the bark of each trunk in turn. It was not long before he found what he was looking for.

Fetching a penknife from his pocket, he carefully prised out the bullet.

Chapter 74

Park Royal, 7:45pm

Away from the bustle of the car park, Whetstone suddenly felt afraid. Her breath echoed off the walls and something inside screamed for her to leave, to run to her car and go.

"Hello?" She called, but the voice was inside her head. "Hello?" This time, the echo betrayed her to the world. Inching deeper into the dark, she stopped, as a tall, stocky figure dimmed the bright space twenty yards away.

"Deb?" As Parrish took a step into the alley, Whetstone thrust out a palm. She noticed her hand was shaking.

"No. You stay right there. I want you nowhere near me."

Parrish reciprocated, his palms outstretched. "OK, OK. I'm not moving."

Whetstone recalled his lips pressing against hers, hands struggling with clothing. The deep intoxicating aroma of his skin. She felt his weight on her, him inside her. Then she saw the slim, writhing back, the staring eyes and the alabaster face. The blood. She felt defiled and unclean. Her throat burned as her stomach spasmed.

"Just tell me, Keith. What you want?"

"Things have changed. I know I have no right to ask, and you have every right to turn around and walk away but I need your help. There is a lot more at stake. You must believe me."

"I don't know what to believe anymore, Keith. You are AWOL from your shift so often they think you have changed jobs. Then someone puts a hole in your Lolita's head and you're seen entering and leaving her room with her brains still dripping off the walls. I might not be Sherlock Holmes but to my mind that's pretty slam-dunk."

"Of course, its *slam-dunk*. That's what they want you to believe. Yes, I admit I was seeing her but it was just sex. She was a tart. I know that doesn't justify it but it's the truth. I had nothing to do with that girl's death."

"Someone saw you, Keith!"

"Yes...but...I didn't kill her! I needed to see her that's all. And when I got there... I took one look. Jesus God. She was only fifteen." In front of Whetstone, the silhouette leaned on the wall, the black merging, Parrish seemed to diminish in size. "Look, I am telling you. When I saw her... lying there, I freaked out. I turned and ran."

"Stopping long enough to wipe the door handle. Presence of mind, considering how freaked out you were."

"Because I knew everyone would think it was me."

"What's happened to the gun, Keith? Where is it?"

"The gun? I don't know. I never had the gun."

"And what about Gordon and Hewell? Did they find out about Irina?" Whetstone spat the name. "Or did they cotton on to you and Danilo Bašić? Found you out for the treacherous bastard you are? I have seen the CCTV. I suppose if you can blow two police officers' brains out, a teenager is easy—*child's play.*" She laughed at her own pun, a hollow, derisive laugh.

"You don't seriously believe I had anything to do with Joe Gordon and Dean Hewell?"

"Come to think of it no, Keith. I don't think I have met a single guilty villain in my life. It is always some other guy screwing their tart and spraying brains on the duvet. Nobody is ever guilty."

Parrish sighed and thumped a fist off the wall. "You must listen, Deb. I am in trouble."

"Too right you are."

"No, really! You need to speak to Scott Daley. You need to offer me protection." Parrish took a step into the alley. "Just listen. I know who is behind the van ambushes, the factory fire, the attack on the Sonata Cafe, even Dean Hewell and Joe Gordon. I know who they are and why all this is happening."

"What, so now you want to bargain?"

The crack in the yard behind the gym barely registered. The brief escape of gas from a *Coke* bottle. Only after, did she know she had heard it. A brief red mist billowed behind Parrish's silhouetted head. He fell against the wall, knees buckling as he knelt then pitched forward onto his face. Curiously, her first thought was the heat, the stress. He had fainted. No water, maybe no food. Then she caught the glistening crimson pool as it spread around his head. Her vision filled with yellow and green spots, she felt her own knees buckle and her stomach pulsed.

Then she sensed a darkening. A shadow against the light beyond Parrish's body, kneeling. The head rose, and she felt eyes burning into her. On rubber legs, her instinct was to turn and run for the light. Beside her ear, a bee buzz and chips of brickwork, behind another small pop and then she was blinking away tears in the evening sunshine as smiling faces, chattering voices milled about. Without slowing, she made for her car, forcing her leaden legs to run. Closing the door to the world, she frantically jammed the key into the lock and careered out onto the thinning rush-hour roads. Around her, streets blurred, horns echoed. Somehow the need for security, a bolt-hole, carried her through the traffic.

Then she remembered the BMWs. Had they followed her from Park Royal? Were they waiting? Leaving the car in an adjacent street, she made for the alley and her back gate and fell against the back door, replaying images of the crimson halo, the jerking corpse as the blood spread. The barrel of a gun as she sat in her own vomit. Then, consumed by terror, she realised she had felt the dust before she heard the sound.

Suddenly she froze as a shape stepped from the shadow of the house.

"Hello Deb."

Chapter 75

Alperton, 6:30am, 11th June

Terri was not answering her phone. The previous night, he had lain awake mulling over the juvenile spat and now, as consciousness swept away the last gossamer threads of sleep, she was his first thought. Then the experiences of the last twenty-four hours flooded into his mind and instantly, he was awake.

The BMWs.

Of course, there was every chance they were followed. If someone was watching Whetstone, it was logical they were also watching him. Thankfully, up and down, the street was quiet. Daley turned away from the window and padded quietly down the landing to the spare room. Thankfully, Whetstone had finally succumbed to sleep, so he went down to an empty kitchen to make breakfast.

Len Ganlow confirmed a bullet to the head had killed Parrish instantly. Probably a 9mm from behind. There were no signs of a struggle. Like Gordon and Hewell, it was an assassination. The graze further up the alleyway; a second bullet fired from roughly the same place as the first, ricocheting out into the car park. Instinctively, Daley knew Whetstone had been there. Parrish had gone from on-off lover, to paedophile, to a murderer. Now he himself was a victim. All in the space of a few days.

Leaving DC Corby to tidy up, he raced around to Whetstone's house in Ealing. Shocked and barely coherent, he could not leave her alone. A cursory glance had confirmed a dark blue BMW sitting in wait, patrolling the street. Packing her an overnight bag, they decamped through the back to Alperton. As the night grew colder, the BMWs could watch in vain.

Azeri and the Encubierto were real. The stalking BMWs, the attempts at intimidation. No-one was out of his reach.

Whether it was Bašić, McKaig or another of the local bosses did not matter. While the Drugs Unit chased their tails, he was on to them and he had free rein. He knew their every move practically before they did themselves.

As toast browned, Daley tried Terri's number again, but she had switched off her phone. At least it spared her his pathetic and clichéd apology. Of course, she was right about priorities. Right about what really mattered. If his future lay with Terri Somerville and the baby, maybe it lay away from the Force? Maybe the seismic shift was yet to come? But inside, there was still a part of him that resented the intrusion into his life, that resented the changes hurtling towards him like a Class 90 diesel locomotive. Inside, he was still a copper. Inside he knew soon the mist would clear and Azeri would be his. Ray Kramer had yet to call regarding Operation Nightjar. Hopefully, he could hang on for a few more days. He was buggered if he would let him screw it up now.

****

After a while, Whetstone appeared through the door, dishevelled and drawn. Her hands were still quivering and her eyes stared into her own deep abyss. Pouring coffee, he pushed it across the table. He wondered how much more she could take, yet still he would need more. She would have to work through the pain, at least for a while longer. There would be time enough for grieving, for self-pity and recriminations, once the threat of Urdin Azeri had disappeared.

"Deb, there are things you need to know."

Opening his laptop, he located the documents and photos left to him by Patrick Gascoigne. Then, as she sat squinting at the screen, he told her of the late professor's suspicions, and how close they were to discovering the secret of Urdin Azeri.

****

Whetstone watched through the nets as Scott Daley's Audi disappeared around the corner. Frankly, she was relieved to see the back of him. She needed her own space, at least for a while.

She held the business card Daley had given her. Sophie Jennings, Daley's shrink. With a decade in the force, two years in Homicide, her mind was a warehouse full of unspeakable horrors. Each day, as she waded through the morass of human depravity, she forced more memories through the cracks in the bulging doors. How long before the hinges split?

Earlier, her mind still numb, she had listened as Daley explained Patrick Gascoigne's fanciful story, of foxes, wolves and rabbits, that it somehow linked them to Gordon's death. She had listened but had taken little in. So with an hour to kill before Daley returned, she picked up the printouts and reread the details on Alice Sheldon, puzzling over the photos of the gun, of the log, of the damning evidence against Parrish.

Clearly, Parrish had become embroiled in something which had eaten him alive. The times when he was away from his post, the illicit visits to the Monarch View. The video of him with that girl. They all pointed to a secret uncovered. A scandal that would have destroyed his reputation, his career and probably put him in prison. Maybe Bašić himself *had* seen the video? Maybe he had seen a way to use Parrish in his war on the Westsiders?

Then, was Irina blackmailing him? He was a police officer. She was a whore, dependent and trapped. Maybe she too was looking for a way out?

So it had played out. Parrish, compromised, had fed details of the Westsiders movements, maybe even police operations to Danilo Bašić and the Cjevovod. In return his indiscretions remained secret until somehow, Joe Gordon found out. Then he stole the gun and shot Gordon in Holborn. Weeks later, Dean Hewell also cottoned on, meeting the same fate to protect the secret.

But what had happened when the factory burnt down? They found his phone in the embers. Was the car chase, the pursuit on foot just a sham? Either he was there aiding the Cjevovod, or they planted the device to increase their hold over him. How else could it have gotten there?

And what of the girl? Had he let something slip, some inconsequential pillow-talk giving him away? With Irina draining his bank account, becoming a problem, had she gone the way of Gordon and Hewell?

Whetstone had to admit that the evidence against Parrish was both overwhelming and compelling, but was she really to believe Parrish had stolen a weapon from police storage and used it to murder four people?

Chapter 76

Loughton Street Forensic Laboratory

In one of life's—or death's—cruel paradoxes, when Daley glanced through the window, the dead girl and Keith Parrish were lying under sheets on adjacent tables in the Examination Room. Harry Ramesh was in one of the forensic labs, hunched over a microscope.

"Take a look."

Daley followed a crooked finger to the eyepiece of the microscope. "What am I looking at?"

"Left is the bullet from Joe Gordon. Right is the bullet from the hotel room this morning. As you can see, they are the same. Striations show they were fired from the same gun." Ramesh spread a stack of printouts across the table. "Joe Gordon, Dean Hewell, Danny Potter, Irina Dąbrowska and now PC Parrish. Five bullets and I would bet my modest civil service pension they came from the same gun."

"And Alicia Sheldon?"

Ramesh cast down another photo. "Yep. Same gun."

It was no surprise that the same weapon had killed Gordon and Hewell. Potter was an incidental casualty. Irina Dąbrowska, even Keith Parrish, were puzzling. Seemingly unconnected, how did they fit into the equation?

Daley handed Ramesh the bullet from the tree near Iver and watched as he rolled it around in his hand.

"Where did you get this?"

"Is it the same?"

Ramesh placed it in the microscope, scanned it carefully and nodded sombrely. "Patrick's Jaguar is downstairs in storage. It was to be scrapped at the end of the month."

The pair left the laboratory and descended the stairs, taking a door into a cavernous corrugated steel garage. Humid and sweltering, Daley felt the sweat bead on his face. In the corner, a hulk, blackened by the fire, a bloom of bright orange rust, lay forlornly under a blanket of green PVC. Daley felt a lump in his throat, recalling an aroma of leather and cigars, Radio 4 and warm conversations with a good friend.

"I think we missed something," reflected Ramesh as he pulled back the sheet.

Daley recalled the night of the accident. The ethereal blackened shape through the billowing steam, the glistening, hunched mannequin, raw and burned, the acid bite in his throat. Now standing in front of the crumpled wreck, bonnet folded and scarred, he could feel nothing but anger.

"It is here. There is no way we would have even considered it if you had not specifically asked. Just here." Through the rear window, the parcel shelf was sequined with fragments of glass. Ramesh pointed to a kink in the roof, at the edge of the rear screen. Small, semi-circular, insignificant. The exit point for a bullet which Daley surmised would be around 9mm in diameter.

"You, Ramesh, are a genius." Pulling out his phone, Daley called Whetstone.

Chapter 77

Stuck at Daley's house in Alperton with her car in Ealing, Whetstone had little choice but endure the silence and her own thoughts. She vacuumed round, probably the first time in a year the carpets had seen the light. She washed the dishes, made the bed in the spare room, switched on the TV and then went slowly out of her mind. Even wallpapering held more appeal.

It didn't help that she kept going over that inane poem of Patrick Gascoigne's. Like an ear-worm, it bored into her consciousness, mocking her. Feeling suddenly ravenous, she found a toaster and some bread, leaving it slowly to cremate while she hoped for divine intervention.

Now the blue fox has pounced on the rabbit and he is no more.

She recalled Gascoigne's accident. Gordon was already dead; Hewell was alive. If Parrish had killed Gordon to protect his secret, maybe Hewell didn't know of his involvement until later?

The blue fox killed the rabbit. Gascoigne was sure that the blue fox was Azeri. So by definition, he was pointing the finger at Parrish.

So why had he not stopped him?

Maybe Gascoigne thought Bašić, not Parrish, was the blue fox? That would make sense if Danilo Bašić had a hold over Parrish, coercing him into finding the weapon and handing it over for Bašić to pull the trigger? Regardless, Parrish would be implicated up to his neck.

And then she realised. That night when she and Parrish argued. He was keeping an eye on the road, hiding behind the drapes, fleeing when the BMW prowled the street. Bašić knew he was there, that he had spoken to her. That the secret of Azeri was under threat. Had he killed Irina then set Parrish up to keep his mouth shut?

Had he then gone one step further when Parrish had met her at Park Royal?

Chapter 78

Cheveley Hill Storage Facility was an anonymous secure warehouse near the airport at Heathrow. When the North West London Homicide Unit was formed following the Police Reform Act of 2002, it was designated the *go to* place for evidence related to crimes in the West of London. Every piece of evidence connected to the Alicia Sheldon case languished somewhere within its anonymous, heavily fortified walls. Jim Pearson had been the custodian of Cheveley Hill for as long as Daley could remember. An ex-copper, well beyond his sell-by date, he had taken the civilian role to supplement an already generous pension. Grey-haired and lined, the face peered out from behind the mesh screen.

"Well, well, well. Scott Daley. I was only thinking about you the other day." A hand reached through the grille and Daley felt its undiminished firmness.

"Jim, Good to see you. You've met Sergeant Whetstone?"

Dutifully, Whetstone proffered her hand. Dutifully, it was taken. She was in no mood to socialise.

"So, Alicia Sheldon." Pearson turned and retrieved a logbook, opening it at a bookmark. "After you phoned this morning, I dug out the log entries on the system, as well as the original books from the basement. It's lay undisturbed until 8th April. A PC Keith Parrish badge number 103XD. This is the log entry. I have checked and computer records tally."

Whetstone pulled out a photo of the log entry. There could be no doubt.

Pearson continued: "Then on 15th, I get a call from Professor Gascoigne. At the time I thought it odd that he should be interested in such an old case but assumed that PC Parrish had found something of interest. This is the other entry. Again, it matches the computer."

"So what were they looking for? Did they give you any idea?"

Pearson shrugged. "Not my concern, I'm afraid. Nothing was removed or added so apart from the records of their visits..."

"Can we see the evidence boxes?" asked Daley.

After signing the pair in, Pearson led them through a claustrophobic maze of corridors formed by packed Dexion shelves to a small enclave amongst the racking. A single neon strip cast a stark white light across an empty table.

"I brought Professor Gascoigne round here, pulled the boxes out and stood out of his way. He took photos, made some notes and then I checked the contents, resealed the boxes and dated the seals. After you called, I checked and the seals are intact and dated 15th April, just as I left them."

Daley wondered what Gascoigne had seen beyond the things he had photographed? "Can we see the gun, Jim?"

Removing the boxes, placing them on the table, Pearson checked the short inventory attached to their lids. Returning one, he slit the seals on the remaining box. Then he stepped back, allowing Daley and Whetstone to rummage through.

White cable ties held the gun into a brown corrugated cardboard box. It was instantly recognisable as a Heckler and Koch USP 9mm semi-automatic.

"Is there any way at all that someone could have removed or replaced this gun?"

Pearson shook his head. "Nope. There is a consistent chain of custody. For someone to take a firearm out of evidence, even for five minutes, we would need authorisation from a senior officer and paperwork to file. This firearm has been in that box since they brought it here in early 2003."

Whetstone was bemused. The gun, the log entries all screamed Parrish. Yet here it was. How could he spirit it away to kill Gordon and Hewell? More to the point, how could he return it without being discovered after Irina's death? "Were you on shift when PC Parrish turned up?" she asked.

Pearson detached a walkie-talkie from his belt. "Sally. It's Jim. Can you come over to Aisle 85, Row 7 for a mo."

In time, a small blonde woman rounded the stacked shelves. She scanned the three, a look of concern across her face, smiling nervously. Daley explained the conundrum; an item of evidence both in and out of storage at the same time.

"Yes, I remember it as a matter of fact. Kicked up a fuss because of the lighting. That's why I asked maintenance to replace the bulb. He was looking for a particular item of clothing. A cardigan, if I remember. I had to fetch a standard lamp and plug it in to stop him moaning."

"And this was on the 8th April - PC Parrish?"

"Yes. Tall, man. Bit like you, sir." Sally nodded at Daley, who was undecided whether it was a compliment.

"Me?" He reached into his pocket, withdrew his phone and scrolled through the reams of photos he had meant to delete, finding one from the Lambourne Road Christmas do. "This is PC Parrish." He pointed to a tall, stocky man, smiling and holding a glass.

Sally grimaced and shook her head. "Possibly. It was a few weeks ago. I examined the warrant card as he checked in." Sally felt the need to defend herself.

Above the aisle, a camera stared down at Daley. "Would the CCTV still be available?"

Pearson shook his head. "After four weeks, no. Sorry."

"Bit academic at this point to be honest, sir." Whetstone was holding the evidence box up to the light, intently scrutinising the Heckler and Koch. "Someone has replaced these cable ties. You can see the indentations in the holes. Oh, and anyway it's a replica."

Chapter 79

With the Sonata Cafe in ruins, Dougie Murdoch knew the game had changed. Attacking people on the street, vans on the road, was one thing. Attacking McKaig's property, the heart of his organisation, was a whole new ball game. Clearly, Bašić wanted a war, upping the ante to start one.

He lurched sideways as the SUV entered the gated driveway of John McKaig's ostentatious mock-Georgian new build out towards Barnet Gate. Crunching to a halt, two minders jumped out and made a quick scan of the drive. With a private road to the front and a sprawling cemetery to the rear, unexpected visitors were kept to a minimum. Anxiously Murdoch climbed down from the SUV and, flanked by the two minders, hastened up the brick steps, under the grand portico and into a spacious air-conditioned hall. Across the oak parquet, the lower floor rose to a balustraded mezzanine which ran the width of the property, pouring down to the hall in a sweeping, grandiose staircase. Ahead, a set of panelled double doors led through the sitting room. The two minders peeled off as Murdoch entered, screwing up his eyes as the morning sun scoured the room.

Not that *ostentatious* was necessarily a bad thing. It impressed clients. It bestowed a degree of prestige and importance on the coarse Glaswegian.

Thankfully, the sitting room was empty. Seeking fortification before the big man appeared, Murdoch poured two fingers of malt before reclining into a sumptuous leather sofa. Outside, the rear lawns were scorched to the colour of straw. A gentle breeze carried an intoxicating scent through the open French doors. Inside though, Murdoch was in turmoil.

It was noon before McKaig finally appeared. Murdoch watched as the big man, wearing nothing more than shorts and a vest, sidled across the room, snatched up the TV remote and tumbled onto a second sofa, next to Murdoch. His face bore the rosy glow of flash burns.

"I have decided. We have tried it your way and it didn't work. I cannot allow him to get away with this any longer." McKaig's tone was measured and calm as he flicked the channels for snooker. Time to reflect had cooled his ire but not his determination.

"For once, John, I agree. So what do you want to happen here?"

"I want that bastard on his knees pleading for his life as I spray his brains all over the carpet."

Murdoch sighed. "There are a hundred more where he came from. You can't fight them all."

"I can bloody well try. I am not going to pussy out and let that Polack bastard screw me over anymore."

"Bosnian." Murdoch's punctiliousness overflowed into petulance. "Bašić and his men are *Bosnian*."

McKaig looked lazily away from the television. "I don't care whether they are Bosnian, Polack, Spic or even bloody Martian. I want them in this room to explain themselves before they die."

"Come on, John. Don't be so melodramatic. Situations like this call for a reasoned, measured approach." Murdoch rose and crossed to the window.

"I don't do reasoned and measured. That's what I have you for." Then he turned his head and hollered: "Who do I have to shag around here to get some bloody breakfast?"

Returning his gaze to the TV, McKaig pointed the remote at Murdoch "I won't allow that Polack scum to piss on my ground. You know that. I want to rain all manner of hell onto him and his organisation."

Beyond the window, a light breeze skimmed the borders. A cat rolled on the grass. The window was warm beneath Murdoch's palm. A woman, around thirty, appeared with a tray, deposited it on a table and wafted away expediently.

The Westsiders could not sustain the current level of losses. Men were defecting, takings were down and there had been murmurings that suppliers were considering alternative ways to move their merchandise.

"OK, John. This is how it's going to be."

"Tell me. I am all ears." Masticating bacon, a white slug of gut showing below the vest suggested differently. But he was calm and sober.

"We will gather the men and hit Bašić hard."

McKaig smiled, pointing a skewered sausage. "Now you're talking my language. I knew you would come around, eventually. What do you propose?"

"You leave that to me, John."

"Then we attack Bašić?"

"Then we attack Bašić. We will end this once and for all."

Chapter 80

"I don't get it, sir. There must be thousands of unmarked guns in circulation." Whetstone closed the passenger door of the Audi and reached over to fasten the safety belt. "Why would Keith risk stealing a gun from evidence?"

"I don't know, Deb, but the logs, the replica gun. They all point to the fact he did."

"It's all circumstantial, though, without CCTV of him lifting the gun. And anyway, if Keith is feeding intelligence to the Cjevovod, then surely that would be more valuable to Bašić than the risk of his snout being caught tampering with evidence."

"You're assuming that Bašić asked him to get the gun. Think about it like this. Joe Gordon discovers that Parrish is working for Bašić, feeding him information, compromising the Drugs Units operations. He speaks to Gascoigne about it. Maybe he lets something slip and Parrish finds out. It's *Parrish* who is under threat, not Bašić."

"So Keith steals the gun from evidence and uses it to kill Gordon?" After everything that had happened, after all the lies, the deceit, Whetstone still could not reconcile this man with the Keith Parrish she had known.

"Why not? Bašić has him over a barrel. He can't reveal that his cover has been blown without risking his own neck. He can't source a hooky firearm because Bašić would find out, or worse still, it would get back to the Drugs Unit."

However, as he pulled the Audi out into the street, Daley had reservations of his own. Ramesh had confirmed they were talking about a single gun. Used in a killing in 2002, stored as evidence, removed in early April, replaced with an authentic yet useless replica to fool the casual observer and balance the books. Who knew of the gun's whereabouts? More importantly, who could engineer its removal from secure police storage, under the noses of the stewards? That narrowed the field incredibly.

Could it be Keith Parrish?

When the factory fire had been called in, Parrish had been incommunicado, yet suddenly surfaced to pursue one of the getaway cars. Then again, he disappeared. Was this a smoke screen to cover his involvement? Now he was implicated in the elaborate theft of a firearm, the assassination of two police officers, a drug addict and a prostitute.

Then there was the bullet fired at Patrick Gascoigne. If Gordon had confided in Gascoigne and the professor had let something slip...

Having silenced everyone who could reveal his secret, Parrish was in the clear. So why kill him? Perhaps he had served his purpose?

"Sir. I think we're being followed." Daley's mind snapped back to the rear-view mirror.

"Seriously? You watch too much telly."

"One car back, are those BMWs?"

Daley eased off the throttle and stared intently at the thin row of traffic behind. Edging towards the middle of the road, two halo eyes stared back at him.

"Let's see, shall we?" Thinking on his feet Daley decided that if they were being tailed, remaining in traffic would be safer. As he was claiming expenses a few extra miles wouldn't hurt. Turning south, he took the Heathrow perimeter road towards Staines Reservoir and joined a caterpillar queue of traffic. Behind, the halo eyes turned too, now immediately behind.

Daley reached out a hand as Whetstone pulled her phone from her pocket. "No, Deb. Not yet." The trip to Cheveley Hill was unplanned; nobody should have known their whereabouts, yet still somebody did. In the mirror, the halo eyes blinked, the car edging closer. In front, the traffic crawled agonisingly slowly as lights changed to red.

Come on, come on. Change, damn you.

Whetstone turned, a look of panic in her eyes. "Definitely dark blue. Two people. I can't see their faces."

"Hold on, Deb."

Before she turned back, she was pressed into her seat as the Audi squealed through a gap and across the carriageway and into the oncoming traffic. In front, horns blared and lights flashed as startled motorist dived this way and that. Behind, the BMW kept pace.

Daley's knowledge of the road wasn't good. It seemed to go on forever, and he prayed for a turning. Free of the congestion at the lights, he gunned the Audi, but he knew it was no match for a 5 series. Soon the BMW was back on his tail. Then with a roar, it accelerated and came alongside. Glancing sideways, Daley saw the window glide down, the gloved fingers stretched, pistol-like. Then, as the mock trigger pulled, Daley floored the throttle but once more the BMW easily matched his speed.

Soon, the car was alongside again. The driver jerked at the wheel and Daley flinched as a blue wing impacted with the driver's door, showering him with crystals of glass, blasting his face with wind and noise.

"Sir!" There was terror in Whetstone's eyes. Her hand urgently darted forward. In the distance, a truck filled the horizon.

Gripped with a mixture of terror and anger, Daley reciprocated, hearing the sickening fold of metal, feeling the steering shudder. The BMW drifted away to his right then came in for another attack. As a front tyre gave way and Daley's Audi yawed violently, he hung on to the wheel. To his right, the BMW screeched backwards in a cloud of tyre smoke. In front, a horn whined and he could hear Whetstone scream. The oncoming truck jack-knifed, a broad sheet of navy-blue tarpaulin filled his vision. Daley wrenched helplessly at the wheel. Then, there was an impact, and the world was spinning. Pain sliced through his back as the Audi slewed off the road, the suspension grounded with a thud and the windscreen shattered.

Suddenly the earth twisted and trees loomed ever larger. His ears filled with a scream and his mind with thoughts of Terri and of the baby that may never know its father.

Chapter 81

Beyond the trees, the sky is verdigris, and the wind ebbs and flows like syrup, underneath the ivory clouds. Scott Daley's ears are ringing with the discordant chimes of a million bells as he stares helplessly across the vast panorama of scrubland. In the distance, he sees his father's estate car, smells the leather and the carpets. Behind it, a caravan door is open, the warm orange glow of the gas mantle flooding out, the promise of cocoa and pikelets. Terri is on the step, silhouetted against the glow. He senses her voice, words indistinct, but he hears the pain and yearning in them. Her lap carries a small child, reaching its arms towards him. An unfathomable sorrow grips his heart as he races across the endless pasture. His legs are pumping like pistons as the trees blur but the caravan grows no nearer, and a tormented howl fills the air.

Suddenly, he is aware of the eyes, sharp and challenging. The two foxes block his path, teeth bared, ears back, low and snarling. Behind them, the pasture fills with a wild commotion, tens of thousands of hens, darting this way and that, squawking in terror as the pack chases through the billowing cloud of feathers. Streaks of vermillion spray like geysers as the jaws snap at the birds and their heads flop incongruously sideways.

Daley screams for it to stop. The twitching carcasses and clucking heads hamper his steps. His feet slip on the gore. He needs to reach Terri, to hold the baby, to escape the horror. The pain of separation overwhelms him. A voice is calling for her, and he realises it is his own, but the caravan, the warmth, the security seems further away with each laboured step.

And then he knows. The fox and the vixen are not snarling. They are cackling. Ecstatic, rapturous and derisive, as his feet slide and the caravan dips beyond the horizon.

Now it is Cup Final day. Around him the pasture rises into towering stands, vast swathes of orange and blue as the crowd leans down from the stands, every voice roaring, every face close and claustrophobic, filled with expectation. The ball fades and blurs on the penalty spot and he knows he needs to score. In front he sees the foxes, staring eyes and white teeth, the goalmouth shrinking behind them.

Slowly the foxes are advancing, hackles raised, evil halo eyes, as they snarl and slaver. More and more of the pack massing behind them as Daley retreats from the snapping teeth. A wolf, tired and fat, rouses briefly behind Daley and cocks a disinterested eye as it sleeps in the sun. It goads him to stand and fight as all the time the jaws grow ever closer. And now he is screaming, backing up against his own goal, feeling his arms ensnared in the writhing serpentine mesh of the net. Desperately he struggles as the threads draw tighter and still the wolf sleeps. He screams at it to save him, to save Terri and the baby, to slay the fox. But the wolf just lies, its face a contemptuous grin, unaware of the cacophony.

Startled, the bloody carcasses of the chickens spring up and flee the foxes pouring past Daley and the sleeping wolf, into the yawning abyss of the goal, tumbling in their multitudes, dragging at Daley until his heels slide over and he is teetering on the edge of the black oblivion.

Suddenly, there is a stench of burning and finally he understands.

Chapter 82

As he blinked against the burning sky, a face filled Daley's vision, distorted, inverted. Where had the foxes gone, the chickens? Where was Terri? He felt disoriented and disconnected. There was a hiss and an aroma of oil and earth, The air tasted of bracken and burnt metal.

"Don't move, son."

Rolling onto his side, he saw the grey underbelly of the Audi sat against the tall trees, cracking and popping. Struggling, he dragged his mind back. Before the pantomime of foxes and chickens, and before the lazy wolf. Before Terri and the baby. Images flitted through his mind, wisps of smoke on a breeze.

"That was close, if you ask me." The man small and portly, around fifty, dressed in a T-shirt and jeans. His arms were a compendium of tattoos and he had a ponytail. He smelt of sugar and coffee.

Then Daley caught his breath recalling the truck, the screech of tyres, the sea of tarpaulin. Hauling himself up, performing a rapid reconnoitre, Daley established that all his parts were where they should have been and roughly working according to spec. The tightness in his chest was easing as he took deep breaths. His trousers, damp with blood, stuck to his shin.

Deb? Where was she?

The huge trailer was on the opposite side of the road, precariously tilted against the raised bank of the reservoir. It had gouged a wide trough of earth behind it. A spiked steel fence lay twisted and bent. Whetstone was sitting on the verge holding a rag or a towel against her knee.

"You OK, sir? You were out for a moment or two. The driver helped me unbuckle your seatbelt without breaking your neck. I smelt diesel. I thought it might—you know, like Patrick."

Daley raised a hand in acknowledgment. "I'm fine, thanks. You?" He watched her nod back, but he knew she wasn't.

"It's always the bloody same down here. Just 'cos it's a long, straight road, you think you can race your bloody cars." The trucker was wide-eyed, arms waving like windmills. "Do you know why they put a yellow background behind the road signs? *Do you*? It's because some poor bastard died here. You want to think yourself bloody lucky it wasn't you or your mate."

But Daley wasn't listening. "The other car? What happened to the other car?"

"They watched you somersault. Pulled over, took one look and then buggered off. If you ask me, you need to pick your friends more carefully 'cos they don't give a shit about you."

"They're not my bloody friends," snapped Daley, yanking out his warrant card, watching the man's face blanch. "Detective Inspector Scott Daley, Metropolitan Police. And you are?"

"Vic Thomas." Then he added urgently, "I wasn't driving. Rod was. Rod Thomas, my brother." Across the road another trucker was leaning against the cab, ankles crossed, smoking.

"I need you to stay here. Someone will be along soon to take a statement. I am sure of it." Daley glanced cautiously up the road, then waving a hand impatiently at the trucker. "Can I borrow your mobile?"

As he and Whetstone weaved through a stream of rubberneckers, Daley punched DS Monaghan's number into the borrowed phone and switched his own off.

"Monaghan?"

"Dave? It's Daley."

"Nearly missed me, sir. Packing up for the evening. This isn't your number. Is everything all right?"

"Call this phone back from another number, a landline. Not in the office. As quickly as you can." Then he killed the call and paused for a breath. Down the shallow slope, the Audi lay wrecked. Daley sighed. Too many things were changing, he could barely keep up. A new house, a new child and now a new car. Maybe even a new sergeant if Whetstone made Inspector. Or if she quit. Then there was the force. If Hillingdon and Ealing combined, would there be a surfeit of Inspectors? He hoped not, given the upsurge in drug-related crime. Maybe they were the exception that proved the rule?

Daley took Whetstone away, out of earshot. Her cheek was glistening red - airbag rash. Daley felt the sting in his own cheeks, a pain in the bridge of his nose and supposed he must look ten times worse.

"Deb, Switch off your mobile. I think that is how they knew where we were."

"That's how *who* knew where we were?" Whetstone's brow furrowed, but she relented.

Daley's hand shot out to the brow of the hill, at the vanishing point between the rows of traffic, two tiny sparks of flashing blue. A distant siren howled. "Them!

"This is all about keeping the secret. Gordon, Hewell, Gascoigne, Parrish. Now us. We have all gotten too close."

The sirens were growing louder, two marked units briefly disappearing in a trough in the road before re-appearing larger. Vic Thomas's phone bawled an AC/DC song.

"Scott. It's Dave. I'm at the newsagents on their phone."

"Deb and I have just been ambushed by those bloody BMWs. Hunting in packs. They took us off the road coming back from Cheveley Hill. Fortunately, no-one is seriously hurt, but they killed my Audi. I will hitch a lift in one of the traffic cars that are just arriving. For now though, we all need to keep a low profile.

"Scott? You OK?"

"Dave, not now. Just listen. Someone is monitoring our phones and our lives may be in danger. Get a lift home in a squad car. If they have come after me, they might come after any of us. And look after yourself. Trust no-one."

Dialling off, erasing the recent calls list from the phone, Daley walked across to the traffic cars as they pulled onto the verge and tossed the phone back to a wide-eyed Vic Thomas. The first traffic cop opened the boot of his vehicle and removed a pile of cones while the other flipped open a notebook and approached the shocked driver's mate.

"Did you see what happened here?"

As Thomas made to speak, Daley flashed his warrant card. "A rabbit, maybe a fox, officer. I swerved. The truck swerved. How the driver missed killing us all... It was fantastic reactions. Isn't that right, Mr Thomas? Your brother is a bloody hero."

But all the time, Daley was wondering how the traffic cars reached the scene of the accident so fast.

Chapter 83

By the time Terri Somerville arrived at Hillingdon Hospital, the Accident and Emergency waiting room had filled with clumsy drunks and homeless strays looking for a warm bed. In the view of the young registrar and a series of X-rays, a sub-arachnoid haemorrhage or a pleural haematoma would have done away with Daley and Whetstone by now so there was nothing too serious. Still, a slow bleed could take hours to manifest itself. Daley had thanked her for her optimism and, when he had plucked up the courage, called Terri. As she rounded the corner, her expression told him he was in for a rough few minutes.

"Look at the state of you two. What on Earth?"

"Looks worse than it is, honestly." Whetstone visibly shrunk under the glare from Terri.

"Just some idiot hogging the road, that's all," Daley lied.

"Hmmm. By all accounts, that was you. I spoke to Control. What about the car?"

Daley shrugged. Once the breakdown truck had righted the twisted wreck, he knew how lucky he and Whetstone had been. The trees behind were less fortunate.

The ride back to Ealing was tense, and awkward. Whetstone stared aimlessly out of the rear windows, willing the miles away as Daley sat silently in the front. Terri kept her eyes firmly on the road, keeping her ammunition dry. As they pulled up outside her house, it relieved Whetstone to see a traffic car parked behind her Golf. There were no dark blue BMWs. Gathering her things, she puffed awkwardly. "Right, I'll see you in the morning, sir." She had enough problems of her own without being drawn into a domestic. Terri's Insignia was off before her hand had left the door handle.

"So, tell me what happened, and make it good. You are not the only detective in this car."

Daley face was stinging, and he was tired beyond belief. So much had happened in the last forty-eight hours he was struggling to process it. Allenby's heart attack, Parrish's death, even the murdered prostitute, were clouding his thinking, drawing him away from the ideas coalescing in his mind.

"I made a mistake. I got impatient, pulled off at the lights."

"You don't think I called Dave Monaghan on the way over? It took some coaxing, but he gave me chapter and verse, so don't lie to me, Scott Daley. Why were they chasing you?"

Daley puffed. "Operation Nightjar. Whoever killed Gordon and Hewell, whoever is setting the Cjevovod and the Westsiders against each other, they're rattled. They're watching our movements, bugging our phones. We're getting close."

"And it's worth dying for? Did you not listen to a word I said the other night? You could have both been killed. How would you feel if Deborah Whetstone had died?"

Daley struggled to maintain an even tone, the illusion that everything was fine. "Terri. No-one has been killed. It was just a car accident. These things happen." Who was he trying to convince - Terri or himself? The speed with which the BMW found them was frightening.

"You might be Homicide, Scott, but it's not your job to chase down drugs gangs. That's a job for the Drugs Unit or Traffic. Leave it to them, please."

"I am a homicide detective, Terri. Comes with the territory. Honestly, it's not that serious. I was unlucky."

"Unlucky? You selfish bastard! Did you ever give a single thought for me?"

Slowly but surely Daley's temper again frayed. "Come on, Terri. Give me a break!"

"Maybe you think you need to prove yourself? That you have to justify stepping into Bob Allenby's shoes, taking over his office, becoming the big *I am*?"

"Of course not. I just didn't think that..."

"Too right, you didn't think," she snapped. "When do you ever think?"

"Bloody Hell, Terri!" Daley was at a loss for words because he knew she was right. He did put himself into the line of fire. He acted first and thought later. And yes, he felt he had to prove himself to the team.

"Look, I'm sorry. OK, so I screwed up. I should have thought it out more." Looking over, her face catching the yellow amber of the street-lights, for the first time he noticed she had been crying. There was absolutely nothing he could do to put things right. Any attempt would seem trite and pathetic. Hopefully, in the morning when tempers had cooled he could try again. As the car pulled up outside the house in Alperton, he was awash with conflicting emotions. The case, Terri, the job, all colliding and leaving him lost and confused.

"So are you staying here tonight?"

"No. I will go back to Harrow." Terri's eyes remained firmly on the road.

"Look, it's late. Stay over."

"It's only fifteen minutes back and anyway the way I feel at the moment I want to kill you myself."

"Terri!"

Daley leaned over and kissed her cheek but she made no attempt to reciprocate.

"I am serious, Scott. I am not having my baby grow up without a father. You need to decide where your priorities lie or you'll be living in the new house in Harrow alone. We have to meet half-way here. I will not sit by the telephone, dreading every call. I have to know when you go out in the morning, there is half a chance you will come back. In my opinion, the sooner you buy that bloody season ticket the better. I would far rather be a football widow than a real one."

Daley left the car and leaned in through the open door. "Please Terri. Just come in. We can talk inside."

"No, Scott. I am through with talking. Now, it's your turn. And get those damn boxes sorted out."

"For Christ's sake, Lynne!"

Even before the echoes died away, Scott Daley was praying for a hole to open and swallow him whole.

"Terri! Terri! Look, I'm sorry..."

But the Insignia was gone, and the street collapsed into a guilty silence.

Chapter 84

Alperton, 7:00am, 12ᵗʰJune

As dawn broke, Scott Daley reached a hand across the bed into cold sheets and felt bereft. The air smelt of dust and his aftershave, and he took a moment to realise he was at his own house, alone. Slowly pain crawled up his spine and his face stung. The hollow ache behind his eyes betrayed the alcohol. Just to take away the pain, to take away his thoughtlessness, to help him sleep. Now the half empty bottle betrayed his weakness.

Endless replays had filled a restless night. The bogus pistol, the acres of blue tarpaulin as the truck slewed sideways.

Blue foxes watching headless chickens.

Wincing from the pain in his lower back as he descended the stairs, Daley found some ibuprofen in a kitchen drawer. Since his tramadol addiction, they were the only pills in the house. He craved the buzzing numbness, but that episode was behind him. He hoped. Terri's phone went straight to voicemail. It was early; maybe she wasn't up, on her way to work, or a million other reasons she was ignoring him. He left another trite apology for the abyss he had plunged them both into.

Through the curtains, his eyes found the silver Mondeo parked twenty yards away. The driver peered up through the windscreen - *Good morning, Inspector. All quiet.*

Was the crash a warning or something more serious?

The previous evening, he had checked on Whetstone and stationed a babysitter outside her house. Then, he had called Dave Monaghan and set a morning briefing for 11:30am.

Blue and Orange. Now why did that resonate?

Gradually, pieces were falling into place. Bašić and McKaig, *the Bear and the Boar*, caught in a devil's stranglehold of attack and counter-attack, neither admitting responsibility nor understanding what was going on. The war was not between Bašić and McKaig. They were pawns in a deadly game.

Chickens without heads.

Violence between gangs was inevitable but usually sporadic and low key. Why, six months ago, had it suddenly escalated? Then why had it gone on so long? It was because Azeri wanted the war. He was the *agent provocateur* attacking Bašić's factory and McKaig's cafe, and more besides, turning the Cjevovod and Westsiders from uneasy neighbours to hostile enemies. Which meant that Gordon and Hewell—*the rabbits*—were incidental casualties. Tolerated until they discovered the truth. Then the blue fox pounced. Was that also what happened to Gascoigne and Parrish? Was it now happening to himself and Whetstone?

Checking his watch, fixing breakfast, Daley dragged one of the boxes into the living room and disgorged its content. A wave of nostalgia hit him as he thumbed through dog-eared album covers and ancient mix tapes. They filled his mind with memories of a single life, before Lynne and Terri. Late nights, early mornings, endless pizza. Soon he would have a new house in Harrow. A wife, two point two children and a Labrador called Sam. Briefly he yearned for that simpler life. Then he was gripped by an intense longing for Terri. He could not have both.

Dragging in a second box, opening the lid, Daley picked out the old Xbox console. Now dated and dusty, it had languished in the box as long as he could remember. In his twenties, in the section house, there had been a championship of sorts. Football Manager. Rummaging around through the games cases he found the notebook he had used to mark up his scores, musing he had not been half bad. Football Manager 2007 practically guaranteed Fulham a win under his stewardship.

Suddenly, an idea leapt into his head. Several strands, disconnected notions that had left him unnerved for several days, knitted into a pattern. A sudden increase in violence, two drugs gangs at each other's throats. A third party acting as an *agent provocateur*. Always using the same vehicles.

Racing downstairs, he grabbed his laptop and fired up a language translation website. Then he typed in 'fox'.

Azeri, the Encubierto. Blue and orange. Foxes and wolves. Was it really so simple?

Suddenly energised, he dialled Whetstone. The boxes would have to wait. If his theory was right, the only way to end the war was to find Azeri.

To flush out a fox, he would need some hounds.

Chapter 85

CDIU office, Hillingdon Road, 09:00am

"Game face," whispered Daley. "Just for a few more days. Remember, Azeri has eyes everywhere. Trust no-one. OK?"

Whetstone smiled weakly. Closing a door on the last two days would require more than a change of expression. Taking a deep breath, she limped up the steps behind Scott Daley. As seemed to be the norm these days, the corral of desks occupied by the Drugs Unit was once more stubbornly empty, except for Dodds, hunched over the desk, poring over data on his monitor.

"Philip. Uncharacteristically early for you? What's the matter? Couldn't you sleep?"

Dodds raised his head and peered into the gloom of the naughty corner. "Some of us have work to do. One could say the same... Jeez. State of your face!"

Automatically, Daley touched the bridge of his nose, immediately regretting it. "It's nothing. Some guy with more ambition than driving skills. Buggered my Audi though."

"Still, some say a few war wounds make you more attractive to the women. A little danger. Might even make you more attractive to Ray Kramer if you're lucky."

Daley frowned "You need to watch that razor sharp wit or you could end up like me." Terri was still not answering her phone.

Daley dragged a seat to Dodds' workstation, lowered his voice. "Look, Phil. I heard about Monday, You and Whetstone. Go easy on her. She's had a lot to deal with lately. What with her mother dying, and she was close to Patrick Gascoigne and now this thing with Keith Parrish."

"I'm sorry. You know me. In with both feet." Dodds smiled awkwardly, logging out of his computer. "How is she?"

"Not doing too well. The crash yesterday didn't help."

"Still, she's not doing herself any favours at the moment. What was she doing there—at Park Royal? I thought she was smarter than that. That second shot could have killed her."

"Sorry?"

"Come on, Scott. That was a hit, Surely. With the prostitute and the factory fire, Parrish had become a liability. Azeri had finally had enough. Well, for Azeri, read Bašić..."

"Makes sense. A man scorned and all that. So, you think Parrish was involved with the factory fire too?"

"How else could his phone have ended up there? Look, Scott, like I said to Whetstone, we have been monitoring him for weeks."

Daley pondered. "I hope none of this reflects back on Whetstone. She's running for inspector."

"Then she needs to be more circumspect about the company she keeps." Dodds turned from his screen. "I'm afraid it's not over yet, Scott. The word is that McKaig has gone ballistic about the attack on the Sonata Cafe. Rumour is that the Westsiders are planning to attack the Cjevovod on Sunday. My boys are out now trying to get a measure of it, to see if he is serious."

"And if he is?"

"Some might say the more damage they do to themselves the better. The DCI is inclined to let them get on with it, then drive in with a dustpan and brush afterwards. Make our lives easier if they reduced their own numbers."

"Seriously? So he is prepared to accept an all-out war to make his own life easier?"

"Of course not but it must be clear to everyone now Bašić means business. In the light of what happened to Gordon, Hewell and now Parrish, he's loathe to risk deploying any more officers into what might be a life-threatening confrontation."

"What about you? What do you think, Phil?"

"You know Kramer. It's not my place to think, but I had a word with the ACC on the quiet. She is also for a *laissez-faire* approach. If we pre-empt a war, then we might just start a bigger one. As far as she's concerned, this trouble between the Cjevovod and the Westsiders just highlights the danger of reducing the number of front-line officers. Who knows? A war might just get the Mayor's office to sit up and consider whether the MOPAC rationalisations are really worth it."

Daley frowned, recalling the phone call with Browning earlier in the week. Politics was never his strong point. If Dodds wanted to pally up with Browning, he could carry on. "I suppose she may be right. I just can't see it. Whatever the outcome of the war, the drugs trade, the crime will still go on, leaving whoever remains to expand and fill the territory available."

"Ah, well. It all makes work for the working man to do. Anyway, we have enough to do entangling the mess that Parrish has left for us."

Daley rose. "We have to get back to Lambourne Road." Then turning back, he added, "I'm serious, Phil. Be nice to Deb, please? For me?"

Chapter 86

Major Incident Room A, Lambourne Road

"It's Wednesday 12ᵗʰ at—11:30pm. This is the daily briefing for Operation Nightjar." Daley flicked a short paternal smile but there were no takers so he ploughed on. "Before we start, as some of you are aware, PC Keith *the Uniform* Parrish was gunned down on Monday. Over the next few weeks we will have to rake through all his dirty linen and probably uncover some unpalatable truths about him. Keith was a dedicated police officer, with a hitherto unblemished record of service. I am sure you will do him the honour of being discreet and treating the evidence that comes to light sensitively. He is still one of our own, whatever may have happened."

Behind a monitor, Whetstone lowered her head self-consciously. A liberal plastering of foundation had masked the airbag rash but no amount of make-up could hide the despair.

Daley checked the microphones, ensuring the gimballed video camera was parked. Then he began.

"On Monday, Sergeant Whetstone met PC Parrish in Park Royal. Only they knew the arrangements. Then yesterday, myself and Sergeant Whetstone were involved in an RTA after an unplanned trip to Cheveley Hill. When we factor in other apparent coincidences the raid at Hanover Road where the van made an impromptu stop, the attack on Danilo Bašić's Mercedes, swapped out at the last minute, the factory fire, the attack on the Sonata café—it's clear that someone is getting their news hot off the press and acting on it quickly."

Whetstone was finding it hard to concentrate. Her knee was giving her hell and her head ached. "So how did they know where we were?"

DC Taylor played with the keyboard, cueing up a video clip. "Look at this. It's the incident in Hanover Road." They watched as the grainy images showed baseball bats raised and dropped, bones splintered. Masked figures transferred the load from the van. Then Taylor paused the playback and pointed his laser pen. Daley saw a single image, a hand reaching under the wheel arch of the van. "What's that all about?"

Taylor cut to the video of the crash on the North Circular. Bašić's Mercedes on its roof. Instinctively, Daley touched the bridge of his nose and felt the pain as they dragged the man from the car. Again the baseball bat. "And there..."

One of the masked men removed something from the offside rear wheel arch.

"The vehicles were being tracked," Taylor added unnecessarily. "Also, I have located bugging software on several of our phones. Details of calls and texts are being sent to a third party. Unfortunately, the destination is scrambled, but I am still working on it."

"And how many phones are affected?"

Taylor shrugged. "Impossible to tell without the phones, sir. We have quarantined the ones we know of and left them switched on."

"What about Gordon and Hewell?" asked Whetstone.

Taylor pulled up a list and magnified it. "The bugging software is on both their Met mobiles and unregistered mobiles. Two weeks before Gordon died, he speaks to Hewell for ten minutes and forty seconds. Over the next two weeks, he calls Hewell increasingly more frequently. Hewell never contacts Gordon until the nights leading up to Gordon's death when there are three calls."

"Do we have transcripts, Steve?"

"No, sir. The CDIU didn't request them so they were erased after a month."

Daley frowned "So, Gordon was telling Hewell something repeatedly, hoping Hewell would get the message. When he finally twigs, it is too late?"

"Then there is this other number. Another unregistered mobile which appears on Gordons burner phone three days before he is killed. Three calls to Gordon and two returned, the last an hour before he was killed."

"The killer arranging to meet?"

Monaghan nodded. "There's a similar pattern on Hewell's phone."

"We may be able to recover transcripts for those calls," suggested Daley. "I'm preparing a court order."

"Then," continued Taylor, "there is the SIM card recovered from PC Parrish's phone found in the factory fire." Taylor glanced nervously at Whetstone. "Whilst the phone is definitely his, the SIM is unregistered. Check out the number."

Taylor displayed a call log. A table highlighted pink and fluorescent yellow. "This is the operators log for the SIM found in the phone. As you can see, this correlates with calls made to Gordon and Hewell's burner phones."

"What about Parrish's own SIM?"

"The SIM corresponding to his subscriber account is missing. Also, the action of inserting a new SIM card resets the call logs on the phone."

Daley's brow furrowed. He marvelled at the sophistication of the operation. Phone taps, vehicle tracking. The ingenuity and organisation needed to put it all together hinted at a big operation. Would Bašić, or even McKaig, have those resources? Keith Parrish had access to the technology but could he implement such a complex operation without arousing suspicion? Then there was the SIM used to trap Gordon and Hewell and now to implicate Parrish. Who had access to Parrish's phone to swap the SIM and make the calls?

Now, though, the tide was turning. The knowledge they were all being tracked, once an obstacle, was now an advantage.

"For now, think before you phone - landline or mobile - assume someone is listening. If you need to make a call unconnected with the investigation, use your infected phone. Keep up the pretence we haven't found the bugs. Sergeant Monaghan will distribute some unregistered mobiles in case we need to speak in private. Also, we need to review the CCTV, again. If we missed the trackers the first time, what else did we miss? And we need to find the location of those vehicles when they are not on the road."

***

Certain now that the phones were bugged, Monaghan limited the team to those he could trust. What happened in this room had to stay in this room. Now as he surveyed the sea of faces, he hoped for a breakthrough that would move them all forward. He was not to be disappointed.

"Dave, you need to look at this." Olivia Sprason handed him a piece of paper.

"Elaine has been ringing around motor factors and suppliers, asking about unusual trends in purchasing. This name keeps popping up across multiple suppliers. Orders for body panels, suspension parts, all for 5 Series BMWs. Look at the amount of paint this garage has ordered in the last three months."

"Sure, I could bath in that and still have enough to spray-paint the house."

"It's all the same shade of Deep Sea Blue metallic." She pointed at a chart on her screen. "Standard on 5 Series BMWs."

"What do we know about this garage?"

"It's a repair shop in Neasden. Kenning Autos. There is not a lot of information on the Internet but as far as I can tell they are not a BMW specialist. I've checked with Companies House, and it's a legitimate business owned by Arthur Kenning. No criminal record. Under the pretext of having work done on my car, I called Mr Kenning but he says he hasn't owned the garage now for around a year. Said someone made him an offer and, coming up to retirement, didn't want to look a gift horse in the mouth, so he accepted. He kept it quiet as it was £150,000, in cash, no VAT."

"Naughty boy. And since then?"

"Business has been operating as if he were still running it. They have filed accounts, paid VAT. I've checked with VOSA and they are still registered to perform MOT inspections though they have carried out only a dozen in the past three months."

"Good work. See if you can get a list of their current employees, maybe even details of the owners."

As she hurried off, Monaghan dialled Deborah Whetstone's number.

Chapter 87

Murdoch's House, Bushey, 12:30pm

Dougie Murdoch closed the call and tapped the handset against his chin, thoughtfully. Suddenly, he felt incredibly isolated.

On an easy chair, one of McKaig's knuckleheads was flicking the channels for a funny programme. In the kitchen, another was intently following the lines of newsprint with an index finger. Murdoch resented having muscle in the house but deemed it necessary given the upsurge in violence. Puffing loudly, he gazed out at the more palatable sight of the garden beyond the panoramic windows. A young man, bare backed and glistening, was raking lawn cuttings.

Since the Sonata Cafe had been razed to the ground, Paisley John McKaig had been baying for blood. The coarse Glaswegian had called a meeting and set about a cabinet reshuffle. They reorganised the street bosses and removed some permanently. That was the only downside to his association with Paisley John McKaig; the man's tendency for sudden stratospheric tantrums and uncontrollable violence. That and the fact that he had no conscience. They shipped the remaining bosses out to one of McKaig's knocking shops to show that for every stick there was a carrot.

Murdoch, on the other hand, preferred a more strategic, measured approach. Life was about ponds. The little fish either keep out of trouble or they are eaten by the bigger ones. Or they fight the big fish hoping to usurp their position. Yet, however high one made it up the food chain, there was always a bigger pond and bigger fish. The clever ones, struck up alliances. Remoras forging a symbiotic relationship with sharks, keeping them clean and problem-free and receiving protection in return.

Growing up in the Easterhouse tenements of the Seventies and Eighties had been tough but nothing had prepared him for the Bar-L. Apart from a select few, most of the inmates' intellects stretched to the ends of their fists. They measured their tolerance for those of Murdoch's own particular sexual persuasion in beatings. By the time he met McKaig, Murdoch had already realised the benefits of brain over brawn to succeed in life. Paradoxically, McKaig had realised the fallibility of his own minuscule intelligence, bellicose and deeply tactical, with no appreciation of the bigger picture. To fight fire with fire. Together, the two had ascended the food chain using symbiosis to form a powerful alliance.

Now that same symbiosis left Murdoch with a dilemma. Yesterday, he had promised McKaig a war. Today he wished he had not. Still, there seemed no choice but to fight fire with fire—so to speak. To execute a sudden prolonged and violent attack across the Cjevovod estate. Hit them hard and hit them quickly, but after a restless night Murdoch was already having misgivings. The uncomfortable truth was that the Westsiders could muster less than one hundred men. The Cjevovod's resources were practically infinite. Yet there seemed no option than to start a war otherwise the senseless tit-for-tat skirmishes could carry on indefinitely. Damaging for business maybe but at least the Westsiders would still be in business.

Although Danilo Bašić and Paisley John McKaig were set on a collision course, Ivan Terzić and Murdoch himself had other ideas. It was the eternal dilemma. Choosing what was right or what was easy. Now perhaps there was a third option. It would require tact, diplomacy and, above all, trust. Commodities that were in short supply at the moment.

Walking through to the bedroom, Murdoch opened a drawer and powered up a mobile phone, watching the start-up screens, wondering even now whether he should yank out the battery or smash the phone. Within a minute it rang. Taking the call, he pressed the handset to his ear and listened.

"OK. I'm in."

Chapter 88

Kenning Autos, Neasden

When DC Mike Corby pulled up outside the Hillingdon offices, Whetstone was already standing on the front steps. She had a face as long as a rainy Bank Holiday.

"You all right, gov?"

"What do you bloody think? Just drive, OK?"

Corby had never been a fan of Keith *the Uniform* Parrish. The tall, stocky, good-looking constable had been brash, opinionated and disagreeable. He was popular and self-assured. Everything that Corby wished he could be. Parrish had treated Whetstone like shit and now, even after his death, he was putting her through hell. Since joining the team eighteen months ago, the torch he carried for Deborah Whetstone had dimmed but never totally cooled. Briefly, awkwardly, he expressed his condolences. The look she returned told him he should not have bothered.

"Where are we going?"

"Kenning Autos, Neasden. Changed hands last year, No registered owner. Since then has started ordering a shit-load of dark blue BMW paint and BMW spares."

"That'll do."

"Going to have to."

***

Kenning Autos in Neasden, was to all intents in someone's backyard. Flanked either side by town houses and crenelated stone walls behind the ubiquitous ranks of parked cars, Corby almost missed the driveway with its overgrown yellow sign. *All makes and models. MOT free retest. Free quotes.* Parking up, the pair retraced the hundred yards to the entrance and then a further hundred along the pitted gravel drive with its mohawk sprout of weeds along the centre. Ahead, behind rusted mesh gates, the drive widened out into a yard. A padlock and chain hung loose beneath a sign declared *Lunch 12-2*.

"What a shit-hole. I couldn't imagine spending my life working in a place like this."

"And Lambourne Road is any better?"

Squealing open the gate, Corby saw a yard around the size of a tennis court, with a carpet of feeble weeds and sun-burned grass muscling through the cracked tarmac. The edges were littered with a motley assortment of stripped and rusting wrecks, a few tarpaulined vehicles and a yellow skip, made higher with plywood boards and overflowing with used car parts. Along one side, a row of damaged vehicles awaited their fate, whilst another few optimistically offered themselves for sale. The garage itself, no more than a large corrugated steel shed, spanned the width of the yard. Behind assorted oil drums and tyres, steel concertina doors were closed. This time, the padlock was secure, the space inside dark. Above an extraction unit lazily clunked into life.

"Look around the back, Mike. Be careful and try not to look too much like a copper."

Above Whetstone, the sun struggled to shimmy through the dense overhanging foliage and she wrinkled her nose at the odour of damp rot and used engine oil. Half-heartedly, she extended a reluctant finger towards the first tarpaulin, green with algae and coated with leaf litter and insects. Edging along until she found paintwork, it was mucky and beige, not blue. Further down, an opaque plastic sheet sheathed another vehicle. Altogether cleaner, Whetstone took the line of least resistance. At least she could take a cursory glance. Making her way around the back, she lifted a corner of the sheet. Beneath was a stripped shell, definitely dark blue, but she could not determine the make or model. With no-one around, they would need to visit again, so what did it matter?

Today, her mind was not on the job. Instead, it replayed a gunshot, a halo of crimson and a buzz which showered her in brick dust. Her mind was exploding, a domino effect of catastrophe after catastrophe. She felt every thread of her life was unravelling and she was powerless to stop it.

Was there any way things could get worse?

Then they did.

Across the yard, along the drive, a low grumble turned into a growl. Despite the wrecks as cover, Whetstone was utterly exposed as soon as the gates swung open. Hastily, she edged around the plastic-sheeted hulk and shrank down, gritting her teeth at the pain in her injured knee. Slowly, insidious and searching an unctuous, chill oozed through her shoes. A brackish, muddy oil pool, iridescent and reeking was soaking into the hem of her coat and she screamed a silent oath. She regretted the white blouse, bright and damning, now streaked with grime and there was the definite smell of cat poo. Edging along the wreck, peering down the line, she looked for Corby, hoping to catch his eye.

"Mike! Mike!" Her voice a hoarse whisper, there was no way he would hear. "Mike!" Shit! He would need to fend for himself.

Ducking down, she watched as the dark blue BMW pulled into the yard. The driver alighted and trotted smartly to the folding doors, unlocked and peeled them back. Dressed in a leather jacket and jeans, short and stocky, shaved and bald, his eyes were everywhere. The driver of the second BMW pulled his vehicle up behind the first. With the engine still running, he alighted, lit a cigarette and sent plumes of smoke through the damp, foetid air. He too was short and stocky. The pair could have been twins—or at least brothers.

Inside, the workshop was cavernous. In front of the ramps and tools, three identical cars sat—each dark blue, each a 520i. Their halo eyes, dimmed and still, stared out over the yard. On the far side, two more sat forlornly stripped and skeletal. Whetstone watched the driver as he resumed his seat, turned the vehicle and reversed it alongside the others.

Then with a squeal of metal, the concertina doors were closed and the driver set off back towards the second car. She could hear their voices but the words didn't carry. Crouching still further, a dog rose snagged her trousers and her thighs had cramped. She was sure a spider had crawled into her hair.

"Hang on a sec."

Whetstone froze as the first driver turned towards her. Ducking down, dragging her bag through the puddle, her heart exploding in her chest. Eyes tight, she heard the footsteps crunch across the yard and between the wrecks.

"Come on! We haven't got all day, y'know. We've got forty minutes then it will be too late."

"When you gotta go, you gotta go."

A spark of familiarity fired in Whetstone's mind; the voice forming a face, hazy and indistinct. She saw the factory fire, hoses writhing across the car park, lines of blackened, dishevelled workers. But the face wouldn't come.

The footsteps were within inches of her now. The air seemed to twist and press with the presence of the man. Then she heard the zipper, the trickle of urine, the sigh of relief before the footsteps retreated and she allowed herself the merest of breaths. With a metallic whine of gears and the sonorous clank of the gates, the second BMW reversed down the drive and the yard fell silent. Whetstone chanced a movement, gritting her teeth as blood flowed to her lower legs.

"Sarge?" It was Corby.

"Down here." Then a face appeared, a smirk that just begged to be wiped off. Corby, by contrast, had found a more comfortable hiding place. "Now that's what I call dedication to duty, *ma'am*."

But all she could do was scowl as her feet squelched in her shoes and a sodden hem of her coat adhered uncomfortably to her legs.

"Did you get a look, Mike? BMWs, dark blue. There are six in there. Then the one they left in."

"I texted Sergeant Monaghan the index numbers. Plates are false. There's another skip around the back, full of broken parts and body panels. I would guess they are from our BMWs. What about the men?"

"One of them was familiar. The driver of the first car. I know him from somewhere. I was thinking about it all the while he was pissing up my coat but it wouldn't come, unsurprisingly."

Corby checked his watch. "Quarter to two. We better skedaddle before anyone else turns up."

As the warmth of the sun caked the mud on her legs, Whetstone picked pollen and cobwebs from her hair before reaching for her phone. "I have had enough of this palaver for today."

Chapter 89

Lambourne Road. 3:00pm

Closing the blinds to the Goldfish Bowl, blinking as the strip lights clicked into action, Daley cast his eyes around a life interrupted. Allenby's personal assistant, Pat, had cleared away any papers from the surface of the desk and found a separate in-tray for Daley's correspondence but it still felt a sacrilege to sit in Bilko Bob's chair, to use his phone, play with his stapler. Before the daily brief, he had called the hospital for news of Allenby's condition. Stable but recovering. Back at any time, Daley hoped, huffing at the teeming townscape of manilla folders. Cases to review, courtesy of ACC Browning; to keep him quiet.

Much to his dismay, Kramer had called to wrest back Operation Nightjar. He would not let that happen without a struggle. Unlike Bob Allenby, tact often eluded Daley. However, in an effort to turn over a new leaf, as acting Detective Superintendent—a fact he reminded DCI Kramer of frequently during the call he would transfer the files by the end of the week. With Kramer's protestations still ringing in his ears, he had put down the phone and promptly let the fact slip his mind.

If they didn't make a breakthrough quickly, though, he would have no option.

He still could not reach Terri. At 3:00pm, he guessed that she would still be at her desk so he dialled her office phone. It took him by surprise when she picked up.

"Scott?" Her voice was subdued. Behind her, the sounds of an office bled through.

"I've been calling all day."

"And I have been ignoring all day."

Daley puffed. Now she answered, the rehearsed speech had drifted away leaving him tongue-tied.

"Look, Terri, I'm really sorry about last night. You're absolutely right. I wasn't thinking."

"Too right, you weren't. How dare you compare me to *that* woman?"

"I wasn't comparing you. It was a slip of the tongue."

"So who was chasing you?"

Daley closed his eyes and sighed. Once more the Metropolitan police bush telegraph had performed beyond expectations. "I can't talk too much about the case, not on the phone. Not right now but you know the other night? Urdin Azeri? The Encubierto? I think we were right. Gordon and Hewell got too close. I think Deb and I got closer than we thought."

"They could have killed you."

"I know that but that was not the intention. I think they are trying to scare us off."

"Watching your houses, ambushing your car, they're doing a good job. Have they succeeded, do you think?"

"The ACC has ordered me to hand the investigation back to the Drugs Intelligence Unit."

"Thank the Lord that someone has seen sense. And have you?"

"All in hand," he lied. Then he added. "Anyway, with the logs showing that Keith Parrish stole the gun from Cheveley Hill, Browning will most likely accept my view he killed Gordon and Hewell."

"Why, though? He's nobody. Just an ordinary plod. Why would he take that kind of risk?"

"Phil Dodds believes he was in Bašić's pocket. We found his phone in the ashes of the factory which places him there."

"So Bašić must have thought he was a threat and killed him?"

"That's Phil's reasoning." Daley, shifted the receiver to the other ear. "To be fair, I'm not sure I want any part, anyway. There's a war coming between the Cjevovod and the Westsiders and I have no intention of being in the middle.

I've heard the Westsiders are shifting operations tomorrow just in case. Kramer and Dodds can deal with that. I have done what they asked me to do. I have found the killer of Gordon and Hewell so now I am going to quit while I am ahead."

"Wow. What's brought this change of heart?"

"Last night, this morning. It hammered home to me what I am risking. You, the baby, a new life. I can't go on being *Suicide Scott Daley*. I owe you more than that."

"Are you in Allenby's office?"

"Uh-huh. Feels kind of disrespectful, him lying in a hospital bed and all."

"You know it could be yours if you played your cards right?"

"So ACC Browning tells me."

"Diane Browning?"

"Yeah. She called me on Monday, whipped my ass about meeting with the Westsiders on my own..."

"I can see her point."

"...then, before Allenby's chair had cooled, she was bartering his job with me."

"Bartering? Browning rarely barters. What was in it for her?"

"She wants to replace Bilko Bob with a tame poodle. Make her life easier."

"Not being rude but you are no-one's tame poodle, Scott."

"I wouldn't worry. I reckon she has had the same conversation with both Kramer and Dodds—and probably half the Met."

"Still, you would look pretty special in a Superintendent's uniform. I quite like uniforms, especially the peaked cap."

"Does that mean I am forgiven?"

"Hold your horses, cowboy. You have a significant amount of grovelling before I even consider forgiving you. Chocolate's, flowers, the list is endless."

"What about if I sort out the boxes in the hall? I already made a start this morning."

"And here's me thinking they were attached to the floor. Wonders will never cease!"

"How about I pick you up Friday, after work and you can show me how much you appreciate the extent of my grovelling?" Inside his pocket, Daley felt the buzz of his other mobile. "Catch you Friday. Got to go."

***

"Sir."

"Deb? Did you ring that number?"

"Not yet."

"Promise me you will."

"I will, honest. I have to get everything straight first."

"Anyway...?"

"I think we've found the garage."

"Get Corby outside. I need to know comings and goings but tell him to keep his head down. On no account is he to broadcast it. Radio silence. And on no account should he challenge them. We've seen what they are capable of."

***

Changing her mud encrusted clothes in a supermarket toilet, Whetstone surveyed the wholly inappropriate logo on her T-shirt and frowned. In her current mood, that was the least of her worries. Anyway, the leather jacket hid most of it.

Making her way back to Hillingdon, she resolved to review the evidence against Keith again.

Keith Parrish, working for the Cjevovod, stealing a gun from storage, killing Gordon and Hewell. The records showed him incommunicado when the murders happened, off the radar when the gang's ambushes took place.

So why did he blow his cover on the night of the factory fire?

The phone. That was his first mistake. Once he discovered his phone missing, once he realised he had left the wrong SIM inside it, he knew the game was up. Unsure of where he had lost the device, torching his own patrol car would make sense - destroy as much evidence as possible, including the phone if it had slid under a seat. But even so, he couldn't be sure and had absconded.

His second mistake was surfacing again.

Why had he gone to the Monarch View on Monday night? Surely, given the trouble he was in, he could keep his thoughts out of his pants? The girl was inconsequential. If he had not visited Irina on Sunday night, even given the two of them together on the video, they would have nothing to connect him with her death.

But no matter how hard she tried, everything seemed circumstantial. She needed something solid. Something that put his hand on the trigger. Otherwise this all suggested a set-up, or did she want that to be the case?

The team room at Hillingdon was unusually busy. In contrast, screens on the corral of desks occupied by the Drugs Unit displayed the Met logo to no-one. Even Dodds was absent. Behind the blinds, a light in DCI Kramer's office suggested he was in residence, though who knew these days? She dumped her bag on a desk in the naughty corner, sighing as the strip light above her hummed and flickered. After making a brew, she powered up the PC and set about enjoying the solitude. Inside her bag, her new phone buzzed and she frowned. So much for solitude.

"Mike?" She had left Corby outside Kenning Autos.

"Sarge. Just had a visitor at the garage. He squeezed through the gate and looked around. Then he left."

"What was he looking for?"

"No idea. He tried the doors, found they were locked and buggered off."

"Did you get a photo?"

"Yes. I emailed a couple over. There are automatic lights so I couldn't get too close. They're a bit grainy..."

Bringing up her email window, Whetstone paged backward and forwards through the photos. "I am sure I know this guy."

"Oh, yeah? Was he the one who pissed up you earlier? Pay a lot for that in Soho."

Smirking, Whetstone did her best to ignore the comment. Mike's boyish sense of humour helped her forget her own trials for a moment or two. "No, seriously. I have seen him recently." She racked her brain but it would not come. In her mind's eye, the man walked past her, flicked a brief smiled then continued, instantly forgetting her. Had he been in the crowd at Park Royal or an onlooker at the factory fire? Then, in a flash of recognition, the synapses aligned.

Was that what Daley meant by its not safe talking too much?

"Look, I'll call you back. Keep your eyes open and your head down." Cancelling the call, she found Steve Taylor's number.

"Steve, I need you to pull some photos and email them across. Quick as you like and between us, OK? Yes, I know what time it is."

For a frustrating fifteen minutes, she willed the email to arrive. Phoning Daley half-cocked would make her seem foolish. She had to be sure. When finally it did, the air turned cold, the hairs prickled on the nape of her neck. It would make sense. Parrish *would* need help. Or maybe he was the help, just another part of Azeri's team? As the mugshot stared out from the screen, she remembered the smell, the tarpaulin, the hard, filthy oil, the blind panic as the short one urinated against a wheel. Her mind in turmoil, she tried to reconcile what she saw with the inescapable conclusion that it drew. Azeri's men. The Encubierto.

Suddenly, all that concerned her was escape.

Chapter 90

200 Carrs Lane, Greenford, 9:30pm.

Four miles from the Hillingdon offices, Urdin Azeri slouched in a weary leather armchair resting his chin on his fingertips. The terraced house that served as his base in West London was a maze of corridors and shabby student lets. Now though, the students had left and only the top floor was occupied. At the front, overlooking the street, despite the hour the curtains on the upstairs bay-windowed bedroom remained shut. Stripped of furniture, an array of screens covered one wall, shining day and night. The computer furthest from the window pulsed as lines of text scrolled up the screen; its operator, listening intently to voices through his headphones, scribbled snippets from the screen. Bašić and the Cjevovod were continually exchanging information, much of it trivia.

The second and third screens remained stubbornly blank.

Yesterday, all three terminals had been buzzing in the aftermath of the raids on the two buildings. Daley and his team were running around chasing their tails, still under the illusion that Danilo Bašić was their main target, running in ever-decreasing circles as they tried to pin it all on Keith Parrish. Ivan Terzić and Dougie Murdoch had exchanged several heated conversations imploring the other to cease before things escalated any further. Both Bašić and McKaig were promising retribution against their counterpart to anyone who would listen, and a few that pretended to. The reckoning between the Cjevovod and the Westsiders was imminent.

Then last night, it all stopped.

The intense radio silence on the second and third screens had unnerved Azeri. Had Daley and his team discovered the tracking software? Despite the warning shots fired across their bows, the North West London Homicide Unit was becoming a thorn in his side. He had changed the encrypted phone number. Maybe that would keep them busy for a while.

The killing of Keith Parrish was unfortunate but unavoidable. Azeri and the Encubierto could only operate beneath the radar. Once Parrish had seen his assailant after the factory job, the consequences were inescapable. Like Gordon and Hewell, he would connect the dots. As with Gordon and Hewell, Azeri himself took care of him. He had missed the police sergeant with the second bullet. He could rectify that mistake.

Then there was the gun. Had Daley worked it out? Had *he* connected the dots?

The accident was a mistake too. Whilst, with Professor Gascoigne, luck had been on Azeri's side; a petrol vehicle, it had ignited on impact. Daley's Audi had a diesel engine, less combustible. Azeri could not help a wry smile. *Vorsprung durch Technik.*

There would always be a next time.

"Boss?" It was the operator on screen 3. "Daley is using his phone."

"Who's he talking to?"

"His girlfriend."

Grabbing a second set of headphones, Azeri listened. He would need to bring things to a head. Finally, forcibly.

Chapter 91

Drayton Green, West London, 5:30am, 13th June

Paisley John McKaig was in an unusually foul temper. Not only had he missed breakfast, but the sun was yet to make an appearance. He paid people to work unsocial hours, and he paid people to supervise them. The anonymous lockup on a tired industrial estate in Drayton Green was empty except for a neglected glass-windowed office in one corner. With no daylight and a grimy smell of machine oil and cement filling his nostrils, McKaig felt isolated. Yet today was important. Breakfast or not, he needed to be there.

Today, the war would start. Or at least the preparations.

At less than two thousand square feet, with no signage above the door, the lockup was one of five across the end of a cul-de-sac, each interconnected. This was the Westsiders' bolthole. In a crisis, they could move men, stock and weapons into the space, transferring them from one unit to another. With no access from behind, they could easily be defended.

And Bašić knew nothing about them.

Of course, he would prefer to be at the centre of the action, leading from the front, but Dougie Murdoch advised otherwise. Much as it infuriated McKaig, Murdoch was usually right. Staring out at the expanse of concrete, lit by dim neon tubes, he watched as Fat Leon reversed the SUV into the space, closed the steel shutters and began scraping bugs off the windscreen with a stolen credit card. Even through the glass partition, his whistling jangled every synapse in McKaig's frayed mind.

Murdoch planned to finish Bašić once and for all, hitting each of his bases in Neasden, Dollis Green and Monks Park in a multi-pronged attack. They would torch the Monarch View and two other knocking shops. That meant seven simultaneous assaults, extensive manpower, intricate planning and sub-second timing. It would overwhelm the emergency services, with the potential for maximum damage. According to McKaig's spies, Bašić was already under intense scrutiny from his lords and masters in the old country. They would replace him if he did not up his game. Notwithstanding, McKaig did not underestimate the Cjevovod. They also had spies. At the moment, three of them were engaged on a false errand out at Tilbury on the pretext of a shipment arriving from China; several others were on more creative wild goose chases. Misinformation was bouncing like a pinball across the territory.

Planning an operation of this magnitude was not McKaig's strong suit, so he had been forced to leave arrangements to his second in command. For the previous two days, cloistered in the house in Barnet Gate, under hermetic security, he had watched impatiently as Murdoch gathered together all the intelligence they had and calculated the optimum time to attack. First, however, the Westsiders needed to get their own house in order. So, much to McKaig's dismay, Murdoch decided to delay until they could move the Westsiders' operations to these anonymous lockups, out of the Cjevovod's inquisitive gaze.

McKaig trusted Murdoch. Right now, he had little choice but still the weevils of anxiety were eating away his insides. Contemplating the hundred yards to the burger van, with the full-scale assault on the Cjevovod in less than three days, McKaig could barely contain his frustration.

Chapter 92

The street in Neasden, where Kenning Autos did its best to be discreet, was quiet. Yet still Deb Whetstone was watching for the face as she turned the corner.

Last night, she had sent Daley the grainy image and the mugshot, sure they were on to something at last. However, he had been unconvinced. A punter, a deliveryman; there could be a hundred reasons he was there. They needed something more tangible. Irritated, she had slammed down the phone.

For days, Azeri and the Encubierto had been whispers on the breeze. Now, when there was a sniff of something concrete—more than a sniff, an actual sighting—he was not prepared to act. All he could suggest was that she and Corby keep a close eye on the garage and report any movements to him.

What concerned her more was the note of defeat in his voice. Finally, bowing to the inevitable, he was preparing to hand over the investigation to DCI Kramer. Despite her protestations, despite the progress they had made, he had made up his mind. Maybe when she made the leap from Sergeant to Inspector, she would be less dismissive, more determined.

Thirty yards down from the garage, Mike Corby's Corsa was also doing its best to be discreet.

"Anything?"

Shaking his head, the young constable took the takeout coffee and a greasy paper bag which smelled of Sunday morning. He looked like shit. "Nah. All quiet since last night."

"So the garage is empty now?"

Corby twisted his wrist and pretended to check the time. "I should bloody hope so. Haven't even seen the paperboy yet."

"That guy who arrived last night. Seems Daley was right. Tony Wrighton - Detective Sergeant. Works for DCI Kramer in the Drugs Intelligence Unit. I checked their logs. They asked Wrighton to check it out. He reported all quiet and suggested that he would look again in the morning."

"Good job we didn't shout about it. We would look right pillocks later. Anyway, he didn't look very hard. He only rattled the locks then buggered off. If he had looked round the back..."

"Yeah, typical of Kramer's team." Something puzzled Whetstone. How had they found out about the garage? With no solid evidence apart from a few car parts and a shed load of paint, Daley had kept the details within the team, pending a warrant. Apart from Wrighton, there had been no other visitors. Had Daley briefed Kramer and Dodds?

"Can we get any closer? I want to be there when Wrighton turns up. Put our marker on it."

"Yes, as long as no one sees us." Corby suddenly lost interest in the bacon sandwich. "What are you looking for?"

"Dunno yet," she lied. She needed evidence that would conclusively implicate Keith Parrish or exonerate him.

Defeating the lock on the yard gate proved straightforward. The chain was loose and Corby had wrenched the lower quarters of the gates sufficiently apart for them both to crawl through. Then she squinted as piercing halogen lights illuminated the yard.

"We need to find cover pretty quickly." She scoured the yard, running an eye down the lines of cars, settling on the monolithic rusting yellow skip which cut a deep shadow, relieved as the automatic light extinguished and red spots dappled across the gloom. Soon, their breathing had stilled and the yard again fell into silence.

Chapter 93

Carrs Lane, Greenford

"Boss. You need to look at this."

Azeri turned as a printer whirred into life and spat out a few pages, the second operator sitting up and scanning the sudden tsunami of data which filled his screen.

"The Westsiders are up to something. This is the tracker on McKaig's SUV. This is the location of his phone." The dots on the map were almost on top of each other.

"Where is this?"

"Drayton Green."

Azeri ran a hand through his hair, surprised. "What's he doing there? Bit out of his patch. Especially at..." he cocked his wrist, "...5:30am. Where's Murdoch?"

"The warehouse in Wembley. He's just sent a text to eleven numbers."

"What did it say?"

"*6:00.* Just that. The numbers belong to McKaig's firm spread out across his patch."

Opening a fridge, Azeri took out a bottle of water, feeling the condensation wet his fingers. "Anything else?"

The operator shook his head. "McKaig's driver is with him. He is on Spotify."

Azeri turned to the first operator. "What about the Cjevovod?"

"Nothing beyond a few deals being done and a few calls home. It's early yet. Hang on, though." The operator pointed as a series of lines scrolled up the screen, pairs of numbers and a message—*6:00.* "Someone has just relayed the message on. This last number belongs to Ivan Terzić."

Then another message. It was a post code.

"So the Westsiders are up to something in... half an hour?" Azeri recalled the phone traffic the previous evening. Murdoch and coded messages to his troops "So where is the postcode?"

Opening a new window, the operator copied the postcode and hit enter. "It's an industrial park in Drayton Green. That's the location of McKaig's SUV."

"Boss? Someone just sent the same message to Danilo Bašić." The operator opened a new window and pasted the telephone number and pressed search. "It's a burger van owner on the estate in Drayton Green. He has just told the Cjevovod where McKaig is."

"Really?" Azeri paced across to a massive map of West London, peppered with dots and *Post-it* notes, records of deliveries, ambushes, attacks and deaths. His finger hovered and landed on Drayton Green.

"What about the police?"

The third operator shook his head. "No, boss. All quiet."

Azeri took a deep refreshing draft from the bottle and offered it to the others. Ten numbers, ten locations, one time and McKaig where he shouldn't be. Just as expected, the Westsiders were on the move.

Chapter 94

Five miles from Drayton Green, Murdoch was suddenly racked with indecision. The hands of the wall clock were creeping relentlessly towards the hour. 6:00am. Could he call it off at this late stage, or was the die inexorably cast? More than in a long time, Murdoch felt the burden of responsibility. The moment he had hit send, every rational fibre within him screamed that it was a mistake but a war with the Cjevovod was an even worse prospect.

Had he made the right move?

The Westsiders controlled several properties throughout their patch; some they owned, some they didn't. They had seized most of them to cover a debt or settle a score but McKaig's empire also stretched to legitimate businesses— drinks warehouses, a light engineering factory, fancy goods, motor repairs. Even a plant that made sweeties, acquired when McKaig had been in a good mood. Others were a front. Their managers knew how to turn a blind eye along with a steady profit.

Normally, spreading risk across such a diverse portfolio would satisfy Murdoch. Normally, the firms had no intention of fighting each other. Normally sleeping dogs could lie uneasily together. Lately, however, the dogs had caught fleas, each suspecting the other of bringing them in. The destruction of the meat plant and the Sonata had underlined that nothing, nowhere was safe. Once a war started, all bets were off.

With five empty units at Drayton Green, Murdoch proposed that McKaig's personal guard make it their temporary base, then transfer the narcotics and ordnance there. Today, thirty men in ten anonymous rented vans were to set out, each from a different Westsiders' location and taking a different route. Some were empty, others full; some genuine, some decoys, with men deployed to ride shotgun in each of the vans. No two routes were the same; departure times and arrival times varied. They would converge on the small industrial park in dribs and drabs. Then they would park behind the roller shutters of the lockups. All the eggs in a single basket. A stockade they could defend.

Beside Murdoch, his driver was fidgeting, eager to be off. Of late, driving a Transit around London had become a dangerous, even fatal, occupation. What troubled him more was that, as a decoy, it was a fool's errand. The rear of the van contained nothing illegal, and they were completely unarmed.

Through the passenger window, Murdoch watched the hands of the clock in the warehouse align until they were exactly vertical. It was time to piss or get off the pot. He found the text to the ten drivers on his phone and added a reply.

Go

With a deep sigh, he pressed send.

***

In a van, in a different warehouse across the manor, Andy Groves almost missed the text. He too was fidgeting and eager to be off.

Go

Pulling an all-nighter had left everyone weary and fractious. Murdoch had called him in at 2:00am and told him the route. No deviation, no stopping and no opening the back. Then, as Groves watched, he had personally supervised loading. Whatever was in the back was important to the Westsiders. They left Groves and his passenger, Errol, to play cards until the text had arrived with the time - *6:00*.

The shutters opened and Groves watched as the sliver of grey morning grew larger. His mind was replaying the memorised route he should take. Down through White City and Hammersmith, across to Chiswick, then up through Ealing to Drayton Green. Errol, was staring out of the window, a million thoughts ricocheting through his head. Riding shotgun - with no shotgun, mused Andy. Would the Cjevovod be more lenient if they were unarmed?

Reaching into an inside pocket, pulling out his other phone, he located a number and relayed on the single word message. Then, with a sigh, he selected a gear and pulled up the ramp and into the early morning traffic.

Chapter 95

Kenning Autos, Neasden

Crouching in the shadows, Whetstone and Corby squinted against the dazzle of the halogen security lamps. With the gates unlocked, three cars drove into the garage yard, disgorging eight men who made their way towards the concertina doors. There was no conversation, just the crunch of boots on the concrete.

"It's him." Peering round the edge of the skip, Whetstone spotted Tony Wrighton glancing furtively around the yard. "Shit. I think that's the whole of DI Dodds bloody team."

"You mean I have spent twelve hours in my car for them to steal our thunder? Not bloody likely!" Corby made to rise. Even in the dimness of dawn, Whetstone could see the rage building and she understood. Once more, Daley's inability to trust her judgement would see the investigation drifting away from them as it seemed set to yield results. Then, suddenly, she felt uneasy and grabbed Corby's arm as the thought synthesised. An indefinable feeling that something was wrong. Very wrong. She turned her head cautiously around the side of the skip and eyed the team for a second as they assembled by the doors.

"If Azeri's men are meant to be armed, would you really turn up at one of his properties without tactical support?"

"Well, we did."

"Yeah but we are not intending to break down the doors—and we didn't bring keys." The men had opened the gates not forced them. Now the team gathered around the shutters. Whetstone was baffled. There was no sense of urgency as they unlocked the doors and dragged them back. Quietly she pulled out her phone and began taking photos.

Inside the garage, she could see the five dark blue shapes awaken from their slumber as strip lights flickered and buzzed and their halo headlamps caught the reflection. She watched as Dodds team disappeared into a room at the rear of the garage.

"Look, sarge, with the greatest of respect, I am not hanging around here to look like a prat."

Whetstone redoubled the grip on his arm. "Just give it a moment or two."

Then, as the team of men re-emerged, she almost felt her heart stop. Beside her, she felt Corby start, then crouch lower. He was shaking. On the screen of her phone, she tracked the men as they skirted the cars and opened the doors. Each man was dressed head to toe in black, ski masks over their faces, the long barrel of a shotgun in their hands.

In a split second, Whetstone knew what she had to do.

"When these guys have gone, I need you to go back to Lambourne Road. Phone Taylor and Monaghan and get them to meet you there. We need to find out where they are heading. I am going into the garage to see what I can find."

"Sarge? You can't go in there. Not on your own."

She knew he was right. Had Joe Gordon or Dean Hewell hidden behind this same skip, watched the cars fire up and the Encubierto set out on another raid?

"Just do it, Mike!"

One by one, Corby watched as the BMWs drove out, pulling up line astern by the open gates. The ominous rumble of the four turbo engines sent a shudder through him. He recalled the video footage of the attacks, the silent approach of the cars, the deadly swing of baseball bats. This time they carried firearms. "This is much more serious than before, gov."

But Whetstone was already gone.

***

"Are you sure, Ivan? There can be no mistakes."

With the phone to his ear, Danilo Bašić cast a glance at the brunette as she dressed. Since the text from Ivan Terzić twenty minutes before, he could not concentrate on anything so prosaic as sex. The Westsiders were on the move and he knew where they were going.

"Sure, boss. Our man just told me they are setting out."

"And are we ready?"

"Yes, boss. Everyone is ready for you to give the word."

Rumours of a mobilisation had been circulating for twenty-four hours. Insiders had reported a restlessness in the Westsiders' camp. McKaig and Murdoch had simultaneously broken their normal routines and decamped to the house in Barnet Gate. Much to his chagrin, Bašić had never successfully placed a mole inside McKaig's home. Initially, both Bašić and Terzić were sceptical; like Grand Prix teams, scurrying into the pit lane with tyres to force their opponents to react. Then the movements had started. Rental vans arrived at properties, they gathered weapons and they cancelled leave. The Westsiders were preparing for action. With several of the drivers feeding back the same story, this shit was actually going down.

So Bašić had prepared his response. Twenty men, six cars with weapons in the boots. Today, with a time and destination, the Cjevovod too would mobilise. They would deliver a lethal blow to Paisley John McKaig and the Westsiders. There would be no rerun; this would be short, sharp and final. And tomorrow, their people would belong to the Cjevovod. Most of all, his bosses in the old country will have renewed faith in him.

"If he thinks moving to Drayton Green will protect him, then he is a bigger imbecile than I thought. Surely, he must know we have our own spies?"

"I think he has proved how big an imbecile he is by taking us on at all." Bašić heard the rattle of Terzić's snigger down the phone.

"They say misfortune and arrogance are uncomfortable bed-fellows, Ivan. We can celebrate when this is over. Anyway, I give the word. You know what to do. And remember, radio silence. No one must know we are there."

Chapter 96

Palmerston Road, Drayton Green

Ivan Terzić glanced again at the clock on the dash, then testily turned to the driver, Emil Jankowski, who was tapping nervously on the stock of his shotgun.

"Enough with the percussion, will you?"

Jankowski, shrugged and turned to the window. The clock stubbornly refused to move. In the rear-view mirror, he watched as Bašić stared at the burner phone. Screen blank, it was being equally stubborn. Patience was not something one usually needed to exercise with a boss like Danilo Bašić. He made most of his decisions at lightning speed and expected them to be actioned immediately. That suited Terzić, who was, by nature impatient but today there was a need for calmness. At the moment, the street was as still as the grave. Terzić smiled to himself at the grim metaphor which might yet turn real.

The three Cjevovod cars had their pick of spaces along the road. Ahead was the entrance to the Industrial Park. One way in, one way out. So far, they had seen three vans enter the park, the burger van owner confirming that each had reversed into a lockup. With ten vans being despatched, Terzić knew the Westsiders would be canny enough to throw in a few decoys. Originally, Bašić had considered disabling each van at its point of origin but Terzić, perhaps unwisely, had talked him out of it. Attacking ten vans would spread the Cjevovod too thinly. With one destination, better to concentrate resources there. Once the vans were in the cul-de-sac they would be like rats in a trap. Even if there were decoys.

But that meant waiting for all the vans to arrive. As 9:00am approached, Terzić sensed that Bašić too was getting a little antsy, and that could only mean trouble.

"Bear, do you think McKaig has sold us a dummy?"

"What? So you don't trust our spies?"

"Well, no... I mean yes, of course I trust them but Paisley John is a devious bastard."

"Rush hour traffic is manic at this time of day. You know that, Ivan. Maybe roadworks have held them up before we do." Bašić grunted at his own joke and received a snicker of sycophantic applause from Emil.

"Soon the roads will be less busy, boss. We can't wait much longer. We stick out like a prick in a nudist camp as it is."

"You need to calm down, Ivan," said Bašić, leaning forward and patting Terzić on the shoulder rather too forcibly. "High blood pressure can be a killer at your age."

"Thirty-two. I don't think so. I am fit as a fiddle."

"I was talking about my blood pressure. What with Emil and his constant tapping and your fidgeting..." Bašić flicked the safety catch on his automatic. "Just relax. Put on the radio, break Emil's fingers."

Terzić smiled and slumped in his seat. Perhaps waiting was not so bad. It was clear Bašić's patience was also being stretched. Terzić found some Abba on the radio. Emil retuned to a sports station. The clock clicked over another drawn-out, painful minute.

Too soon and the vans would not be there. Too late and McKaig would be ready for them.

"Boss. You're not going to like this."

Bašić pulled himself up in the seat and stared at the screen of his burner phone. It was still blank.

"What is it, Emil?"

"A car went across the crossroads in front. Dark blue. BMW."

As one, Terzić and Bašić craned their heads around and scanned the street. It was quiet.

"You sure, Emil?" But Terzić knew he was. With Bašić in the car, everything was serious. "Keep your eyes open."

The three slumped down in their seats. Bašić kept one eye on the phone, the other scanned the street. He had stationed six cars around the entrance to the industrial park. Primed and ready. Each had a phone; each waited for the command from Danilo Bašić. In turn, he waited for the man in the burger van to report that all ten vans had arrived.

Behind, a box van entered the street, driving agonisingly slowly. In front, another turned into the gates of the park. That made five. Was this enough? Would McKaig expect him to jump early? Would the first vans be decoys only?

Then the screen of the phone lit bright. One word:

'drušina' - *company*

Not now, surely? Bašić cursed and slammed a fist into the seat in front, eliciting a yelp from Terzić.

"What is it, boss?"

"I don't know, Ivan. Something does not smell right." Bašić replied to the text:

'Reci mi' - *tell me*

'Dva automobile plavo BMW' - *Two cars blue BMW*

"Emil. Are you sure you saw the BMW just now?"

"Absolutely, boss. These days I would recognise one in my sleep."

"Pauli says two just passed him." Bašić watched as the phone screen dimmed. For months he had suspected a mole; someone working to subvert the Cjevovod. Now he was sure.

Unless McKaig was playing another of his games? He had used those BMWs before when he attacked the shipments, when he killed the Mercedes. Why not now? Why not feign a move out to Drayton Green and set up a raid on his own people? A few casualties, a minor skirmish to throw suspicion onto the Cjevovod again. Like before, he could blame the Encubierto. Like before, his enemies would make up their own minds, as would his superiors. But then again, maybe this was also an opportunity for the Cjevovod?

With both the vans and the BMWs converging on the Drayton Green lockups, the Westsiders were concentrating many resources in one place. Staging a mock attack from the Cjevovod would concentrate them even more.

The timing would need to be right but if he bided his time and allowed the situation to play out, this war could yet be over before it started.

Chapter 97

Fat Leon threw the cloth onto the bonnet of the SUV. In places he was sure he could see bare metal, he had polished so hard. Paisley John McKaig was gone. When the vans started to arrive, he had slunk off through the back door of the unit on the pretext of making a call. Not that Leon was too concerned. Secretly, he was proud that McKaig and Murdoch had seen fit to let him run the show. They had even provided a clipboard and pencil which inflated his ego to bursting point. As each van arrived, he ticked it off on his list, pointed to their allocated unit and supervised as they disappeared behind the roller door. He then sent the drivers and their mates off for a well-earned brew and burger on the house. Mr Murdoch's instructions were specific. Everything was under control.

But still he was concerned.

The short hairs on the fatty nape of his neck were prickling. Leon did not know this part of London. It felt alien. The indefinable feeling that made him feel outside, exposed and longing for the solidity of four walls he knew. Opening the side door, he peered into the gloom of the office. Mr McKaig was still not back.

His clipboard showed five vans. Fifteen men. Another five unchecked lines on his list.

What happened if the drivers lost their way... or they were hijacked by the Cjevovod? On his watch? How would he explain it to Paisley John? Would he get the chance? Time was ticking. He had expected the rest of the vans by now. Suddenly the burden of responsibility seemed to weigh heavier.

Ahead two more vans rounded the corner and headed towards him. Behind them the road was quiet. He tried to convince himself that he was jumping at shadows. After all, it was better to be on one's guard than to be taken by surprise.

With the vans safely stowed, Fat Leon decided he deserved a brew himself and strolled off towards the burger van.

But still his hackles were raised.

***

So far, Bašić had counted seven vans enter the park. Ahead, the last three turned the corner. Within two minutes they would be inside the five small units and ripe for the taking.

Then he found himself faced with a dilemma.

"Boss." It was Emil, his eyes on the side mirror.

Bašić turned and squinted down the line of parked cars. Fifty yards back, two BMWs had entered the street line astern. Blue metallic, engines purring and the halo eyes watching ominously.

Pulling out the burner phone, he texted the other cars: 'Da li vidite još BMW?' - *Do you see any more BMWs?*

If he gave the order now, the Cjevovod could launch their attack on the Westsiders. With the element of surprise, they would reach the units before the BMWs. McKaig would have no option but to defend himself. Once and for all, Bašić could expose the Encubierto for the fabrication they were. At the same time, he would have dealt the Westsiders a lethal blow. Win or lose, history would show he had taken the initiative. Maybe that would relieve the pressure from the old country. Maybe the next time Anatoly contacted him, the conversation would be less pithy.

But surely only a fool would bring his arsenal, his stock, his men to a location such as this? McKaig must know the Westsiders would be easy prey in the cul-de-sac, trapped like fish in a barrel. He may be many things but McKaig was no fool.

So what was going on?

Then it occurred to him. If McKaig knew that the Cjevovod were lying in wait, would it not make sense to continue with the mock raid? If the Cjevovod attacked first, then they would be fighting on two fronts when the BMWs arrived. If they waited until the mock raid was underway, then the raiders would turn around and join forces against Bašić's men.

A better strategy would be to wait. McKaig was expecting the Cjevovod to turn up. Bašić could call his bluff. If he followed the BMWs into the park and blocked off their exit, he could wait until they had played out their mock raid, wait until the BMWs attempted to leave. Then he could literally kill two birds with a single stone.

"Danilo. I don't like this." The three men crouched down in their seats as, behind them, the blue cars were inching forwards.

On the burner phone a text popped up - 'Dva ovde' - *Two here*, then another 'Vidimo jedan auto' - *We see one car.*

That made five BMWs. Whatever his decision, it would need to be quick.

Or he could live to fight another day?

But was it worth risking his men on a whim? There was a significant danger that the Cjevovod would be outnumbered. Rather than reporting a great victory, he would inevitably suffer a rout. His tenure as leader of the Cjevovod in London would be over, and possibly his life. Anatoly knew nothing of the operation. What he didn't know could not hurt him. Bailing now, he could wait a day or two, reorganise and properly execute an attack on the Drayton Green units. On his own terms, without those damn BMWs, he would have more chance of success. Something good to report back to Anatoly.

Suddenly, the BMWs roared past and made Bašić's decision for him.

Chapter 98

Kenning Autos, Neasden

What was she doing?

Behind the rack of tyres, Whetstone had watched the last of the cars leave the garage, relieved as the doors closed and darkness consumed her.

Eight people had arrived and left. That was the entirety of Phil Dodds team. She thought of the times when the corral of desks at Hillingdon had been empty, except for Dodds himself, bad tempered and irritable. All the time, behind his back, they were plotting the next attack.

That explained why the Encubierto were so hard to track down. Always one step ahead, feeding false information back to Kramer and Dodds, pursuing their own flawed leads? No wonder the team made so little progress in finding the killer of Gordon and Hewell.

Pulling out her phone, she texted Scott Daley. Then she sent the photos to him. Surely that must be enough to convince him that her suspicions had foundation?

Cautiously, she rose from behind the tyres. Aside from the stripped chassis, the garage was now empty, silent except for the rattle of the wind in the doors and the whirring of a roof fan. There was a bitter taste of exhaust fumes from the departing cars. Waiting for her eyes to acclimatise, she thought about the first visit to Kramer and Dodds, the heated exchange between Ray Kramer and Scott Daley - *We have to trust our operatives*. It seemed all along that trust was being betrayed.

At the far end, a small glass-partitioned office was a shambles. Opening the door, Whetstone screwed up her nose at a pungent odour of mildew. No-one had been in here in a long while. Dog-eared paperwork, grimy with oily fingerprints, thick with dust, covered every surface. An ancient computer sat at one end of the desk but it too had not seen use in a long while. Even the landline phone was dead.

Checking her mobile, concerned that Daley had yet to reply, Whetstone returned to the main workshop. As morning broke, it cast filmy mote-filled beams across the vast space. Expanding metal clicked and popped. She jumped as a pneumatic pump automatically started, filling its reservoir, then clicked off.

What was she expecting to find? If Parrish had been here, would he be foolish enough to leave evidence? Certainly not in the workshop or the parts store. One grubby fingerprint would look much like the next.

Now that the fumes had dissipated, Whetstone wrinkled her nose against the greasy smell of engine oil. She recalled a Sunday only four months ago but eons away when she had called on Keith. Dressed in overalls, grubby and sweating, she had found him craned over the engine of the Lexus. With the promise of a brew, she had dragged him up to his flat, and they had made love, consuming and frantic. Even now, she felt horny at the thought. Then she saw Parrish fall forwards and the blood pool spreading in the shadows.

Would she ever feel that way about anyone again?

Above the workshop, along the back wall, a mezzanine supported racks of tyres and exhausts gathering dust. Like the office, she doubted any of the Encubierto had set foot up there. Beneath the mezzanine, a second room occupied the space below the stairs, and boasted nothing but racks of unidentifiable car parts. She looked along the wall, past the two car ramps, to the mess room where the men had changed. A padlock and hasp fastened the door securely. Grabbing a tyre iron, she thrust it behind the hasp then paused.

Exhaling deeply, she had a silent word with herself. She had seen the cars leaving, watched as the Hillingdon Drugs Unit changed into the Encubierto and left in convoy. Wherever they were going, they would not be back for a while.

Chapter 99

Dougie Murdoch's van was the last to leave. Passing through Harrow-on-the-Hill, he would also be last to arrive at the lockups. His driver, a small rodent of a man, had been quiet throughout the trip. Eyes on stalks, the man checked every junction twice and drove slower than was strictly necessary. However, Murdoch understood his reticence. Driving a van for McKaig had become a risky occupation, but not as risky as refusing to drive.

Behind the penultimate van, they entered the business park and followed the road round to the cul-de-sac. Murdoch was relieved to see the immense bulk of Fat Leon waving his arms like ground crew marshalling an aircraft.

"Leon. Everything OK?"

"Boss." Leon nodded, watching the vans disappear behind the shutters.

"Where's Mr McKaig?"

"Dunno, Mr Murdoch. He went to make a call an hour ago. Haven't seen him since."

Murdoch clapped a hand on the enormous expanse of Leon's shoulder. "He knows he can trust you. I'll find him. Ten minutes and I want all the guys inside for a debrief, OK?"

Leon was unsure that he needed that level of trust. It made the fall longer and harder. "Right boss."

Inside the lockup, Murdoch's eyes adjusted against the gloom. An odour of diesel filled the space as the red box van beside the SUV cooled. At the back of the lockup, the office was empty. For once, John McKaig had done what he was told and made himself scarce. Now he had to do the same. Leaning on the horizontal bar, he pushed open the fire door. Checking his watch, he estimated he had less than five minutes.

His watch was slow.

Out front, a low growl resonated in the air. Suddenly, men were dropping drinks and burgers and racing back to the lockups, shaking the shutters as fists pummelled and urgent voices shouted. Running back into the unit, Murdoch hit the switch to raise the shutters a foot or two, watching as bodies teemed through the sliver of light. Fanned out across the road, engines purring, were five blue BMWs, halo eyes wide and piercing. Dressed head to toe in black the men stood, their shotguns levelled towards him. For a long moment, there was a deathly silence, broken only by the tinny grind of a transistor radio, and the grumbling impatience of five engines.

Then all hell broke loose.

"Move! Now! Hands on your head and don't try anything." There was a metallic click, a safety catch. One of the masked men jerked the barrel of his gun towards Murdoch. "Open them up. All of them."

As Murdoch felt his guts tighten, he took a deep breath and made his way onto the apron outside the lockup. Fat Leon's mouth was agape. His clipboard had fallen to the floor, his drink splashed over the concrete. In contrast, the owner of the burger van was drinking tea, watching the drama, seemingly unconcerned. Maybe Murdoch had found his mole. Now he turned his attention to the gunman with the loudest voice.

"These doors stay shut." Murdoch folded his arms. Inside he was in turmoil. Anger and panic vied for his attention but his face remained expressionless. Almost thirty Westsiders huddled at the back of the unit, none of them armed. Only he stood between them and a belly full of shot. The price of leadership.

For a moment there was an impasse. The gunman stood motionless for a long moment. Then he shouldered the gun. "Don't be a prick. Just open the bloody doors."

Fat Leon's eyes were darting between Murdoch and the gunman. The switch to the doors was inside, a lifetime away.

Murdoch stretched out his arm. "Hold it, Leon. You answer to me."

"I am not known for my patience, Murdoch. Get those bloody doors open—now!" The gunman took a pace forwards. The shotgun had been sawn off, the damage would be extensive.

"I don't take orders from the likes of you, you Sassenach gobshite. I want to see the organ grinder not the pissy-little monkey."

Slowly, the gunman turned the barrel until the rough-sawn ends stared at Fat Leon. The big man's eyes were closed, his lips trembling as he mumbled to himself. Behind them, a glass door pane exploded and Murdoch's ears rang.

"Next one won't miss. So open the sodding doors."

Murdoch scoffed, bravado masking the terror that was eating away at his insides. "You know that by tomorrow night, you will be dead. All of you. Paisley John McKaig does not take kindly to wee bairns with ideas above their station."

"Oh, yeah? And where is the cowardly Scotch bastard now? Probably tucked up in bed with some tart while you take all the heat. Some boss." The gunman briefly glanced back at his compatriots. Murdoch could sense the derisory snickering behind the masks. Every dog has its day...

"More to the point, gobshite, do *you* know where *he* is?" Murdoch nodded down the cul-de-sac. "One way in, one way out. Do you really think we would commit all our men to *this*? What have you got? Ten guns? No matter what happens here, the Westsiders will hunt you down. You will cease to exist."

"So where is he, then?" The gunman cupped a hand to his ear. "Wait... I can hear him coming. Oh, no I can't. Looks like you're all on your own. Now get the bloody doors open."

Nervously, Murdoch glanced past the BMWs. Beyond, the road was deserted, other yards were empty, onlookers preferring the sanctuary of their offices. He willed the cavalry to appear. This was taking too long.

"I could say same of your boss." He was now playing for time. "I don't see him here. Bašić! Danilo Bašić. Show yourself."

"Bašić? Is that who you think we are? The Cjevovod? You're even more stupid than I thought, Jockie. No, we're not the Cjevovod. They're all out there somewhere. They had planned some kind of raid themselves but they crapped their pants and ran away as soon as they saw us coming."

Behind the gunman, a car door opened and a tall figure paced purposefully forwards until he was within five feet of Murdoch. Like the others, he was swathed in black. A gloved hand held a semi-automatic pistol.

"No, Dougie. We are the Encubierto, I am Urdin Azeri and this is over."

***

"Ach, away wi' you. You're no more Urdin Azeri than I am."

"That, Dougie, is a matter of opinion. The other day in the Sonata cafe I believe it was Danilo Bašić; then at the factory, it was John McKaig, so Azeri could be me, it could be you. Maybe it's Fat Leon?" Azeri swung the pistol towards McKaig's driver, who elicited a whimper. A dark line ran down his trouser leg.

"Ok, perhaps not Fat Leon. Anyway, I don't think you are in any position to question me, do you?"

The pistol levelled at Murdoch's forehead and he could feel the sweat, clammy down his back. Every fibre of his body was screaming for him to run, to take his chances but his feet were rooted. How far would he get? Would he feel the bullets rip his abdomen to shreds? Risking a glance, he saw the Westsiders lined up facing the wall, their hands on their heads. The ultimate shame.

"Boss." It was one of the Encubierto. "None of these guys are armed."

Azeri's head briefly turned then snapped back to Murdoch. The Scotsman could sense a smile behind the mask. "Oh, so you thought we wouldn't notice your little trip? Jungle drums, Dougie, Chinese whispers, call it what you will but we know everything."

"What exactly are you after, Azeri? Don't you think you have taken enough from the Westsiders? From the Cjevovod?"

"Not nearly enough, Dougie, but you have to admit, it's been fun watching Bašić and McKaig at each other's throats. Adds a little entertainment to an otherwise boring day."

"What, you think this is a game? The beatings, the killings?"

"Who are you to preach? You peddle your shit to the ignorant and gullible, you enslave vulnerable women in your stinking bordellos. You steal, maim and kill. You leave lives in ruins, whilst you and McKaig hide behind a thin veil of respectability. No, this isn't a game. What the Encubierto does. It's a public service, ridding London of vermin like you."

Murdoch let out a gasp. Short, sharp. Azeri stood his ground, the barrel of the Heckler and Koch bobbing and weaving, as his eyes drifted down to the bright red blob on his chest.

***

"Armed police. Put down your weapons."

Behind him, Azeri heard many sharp intakes of breath.

"Drop your weapons! Now!" Behind him, the clatter of guns on tarmac.

"Down on the floor! Face down! Hands behind your backs! Move! Move!" Slowly, Murdoch raised his hands and linked them on top of his head. Fat Leon, through the tears, followed suit. Azeri sensed the shapes dashing about behind him, urgent shuffling, staccato shouts but he kept the pistol raised.

"You." The shout was insistent. "You with the pistol. Drop your weapon now!" Murdoch turned as, around the side of the lockup, he saw the muzzle of a rifle followed by an armed response officer. A second red blob appeared on Azeri's chest.

With his heart pounding through his ribs, Murdoch tried to think. Self-preservation. Would he be able to avoid Azeri's bullet before the marksmen cut him down? Around him, the yard hushed to the sound of distant traffic and a lazy wind through the trees, and the insistent rumble of five engines.

"So, Azeri. Just you and me. No Paisley John. No Danilo Bašić. No Encubierto. Just you and me. What do you want to happen here?" Behind the mask, Azeri's eyes were wide, but he held the gun raised, menacing and absolutely still.

"Drop the weapon...*now!*"

Murdoch smiled. "You're all out of options. I think probably we both are. If it were me—and it clearly isn't, I would do what he says. Cut your losses." Behind Murdoch, the rest of the gunmen lay on their faces, each with a rifle bearing down on them. Marksmen held their station. Murdoch held his ground and Azeri held the pistol outstretched. Stalemate.

Slowly, deliberately, Azeri took in the situation, then he spoke to Leon. "You. Walk towards me. Now."

Beside Murdoch, Leon moaned, his eyes pleading to Murdoch. "Do it, Leon. Slowly. Keep your hands where he can see them. It will be OK, I promise." His senses on overload, Leon's body shook with every petrified step, his lips mumbled incoherently. Murdoch wondered if he were praying. As he drew near, Azeri pinned the muzzle of the pistol to the nape of his neck. Murdoch heard the voice of the marksman, measured and low. "*Sitrep. Confirm hostage situation. One male hostage. Rescind critical shot.*"

"Right." Azeri's voice was a bark. Authoritative and clear, for all to hear. "Here is what's going to happen. Me and Leon are going for a drive. If you move, I will shoot. If you follow, I will shoot. Is that clear?"

"*Fall back. Mobile containment. No clean shot of subject, repeat no clean shot available.*"

Around him, Murdoch heard more shuffling. He imagined the armed officers dragging Azeri's men clear, hoping to hell it hurt. Leon was stumbling back towards the row of BMWs, Azeri's head bobbing left and right, appraising the situation. Behind the BMWs, a row of helmets, a row of rifles awaited their opportunity.

"Clear shot available. Request critical shot authorisation."

"Containment only. Repeat containment only."

All eyes focussed on Azeri and Leon. A sharp morning sun had risen over the factories and Murdoch squinted as the pair reached one of the cars.

Looking briefly behind him, Azeri shouted. "Clear a path. Now." He was standing between two of the cars, the gun buried in Leon's neck. The other hand was fumbling with a door handle. He stopped as a voice spoke, calm and measured.

"You're surrounded. Put down the gun. No-one needs to die today." The voice was familiar, catching Azeri off-guard. He spun round, the barrel of the Heckler and Koch USP 9mm semi-automatic darting between an armed response officer and a lanky Detective Inspector who was cowering behind a BMW.

***

In the rear of the marked car, Diane Browning twisted the earpiece. Out of the line of fire, she was helpless and frustrated.

"This is ACC Browning. Request Sitrep. SFO, tell me what the hell is going on."

"Mobile containment. Subject and one hostage. Subject armed. Small calibre handgun."

"Do you have a clear shot?"

"No clear shot of subject."

"Critical shot authorised. Repeat critical shot authorised."

Then she heard Daley's voice, barely a whisper. "Ma'am, we have the situation contained. I need time. No-one needs to die."

"Inspector, this is now in the hands of the firearms team. Stand down."

"Ma'am? This is under control, I assure you."

"This man has killed three police officers, Inspector. Can I remind you of that? Now stand down. SFO? Can you execute critical shot?"

"No, ma'am. No clear shot available."

Leaving the unmarked car, she sought a vantage point with a clear view of the situation, impatiently waving away the uniformed officer as he tried to stop her. Squinting against the harsh morning sun, two hundred yards ahead she saw the line of BMWs, wisps of vapour rising from the twin exhausts. Between two of the cars, the gunman dragged his hostage along. Behind another car, the crouched figures of Scott Daley and Ray Kramer awaited their opportunity.

When Daley had requested a firearms unit, she fully expected it to be a wild goose chase. None of her sources, not even the Drugs Unit, had reported the potential for activity of any kind. Still, she had given the Inspector enough rope to hang himself. Then, she was woken by a call telling her that all hell had broken loose. By the time she arrived, the firearms unit had deployed. The situation had flipped and now it was her head on the block.

With a stalemate developing, she assessed the possible outcomes and none of them were palatable. She could not allow Azeri to escape. Nor could she allow him to talk. Clicking the call button, she spoke clearly and slowly.

"Don't allow the subject to leave the scene. Is that clear? Take the shot when you can. Repeat critical shot authorised."

Chapter 100

Frustrated, Daley pulled out the earpiece, letting it dangle. Uniformed officers peered out of factory doorways. Two yellow and blue traffic cars formed a chevron across the exit. Beyond the row of BMWs, the sun was up and the cul-de-sac became oppressive and quiet. But where was Browning?

Fat Leon's eyes were as large and round as billiard balls. Behind him, an arm at right angles, a glint of light from the pistol. Cocked and ready. Fat Leon's chest heaved as red dots danced and weaved across it.

A year ago, Daley had saved a man from certain death beneath a train, then again before Christmas three more from a psychotic killer. *Suicide Scott Daley* may be his epithet but the deliberate killing of a gunman without efforts to disarm him? What would they call him then?

"How far do you think you will get? There are twelve firearms officers. Each has a Heckler & Koch MP5SF. Now there's a thing. They were probably built in the same German factory as the pistol you're holding. Yours is a lot newer, though..."

Azeri leaned back against the side of the car and pulled Leon close. Rising to his feet, Scott Daley adjusted the uncomfortable ballistics vest, releasing a pungent waft of sweat. The barrel of the pistol swung to within five feet of his face and he thought of Gordon and Hewell.

"Daley, don't be a prat!" Behind him, DCI Ray Kramer crouched even lower.

"You know I'm not afraid to use this." Azeri's eyes flicked around the cul-de-sac. Five rifles were trained on Fat Leon. Five bullets that would pass straight through. Leon was mumbling the Lord's Prayer, fast and breathy.

"Seriously, what are the odds? These guys are crack shots. Are you?"

"Not bad, as it happens. Ask Joe Gordon and Dean Hewell?"

"And Keith Parrish?"

"Hey, what's another dead paedo? Should've had your sergeant though. That was sloppy."

Daley smiled, bewildered by the utter lack of remorse. Inside, he wanted to vault the BMW and throttle the life out of the gunman. "And Patrick Gascoigne? Not such a good shot there."

"OK, I missed once. He was driving quickly. Typical Scott Daley. Always focussing on the negatives. Still it all worked out. Might comfort you to know, he was unconscious when the fire started. Wouldn't have felt a thing."

Daley saw the blackened mannequin, arms raised, pugilistic and stiff. On his chest, the earpiece chirruped wildly. "Why don't you let Leon go? With a hostage you're a dead man. Without, there's still a chance. You know what critical shot authorised means. I know you do."

Azeri sniggered behind the mask, "So what? You think these guys give a shit about Fat Leon? Look around you. This is a crime scene, two drugs gangs at each other's throats. What's a couple of dead bodies? I wouldn't be surprised if the IPCC don't congratulate you for keeping the fatalities down to him and me. You might even get a medal. Mind you, *Suicide Scott Daley up to his antics*, they probably don't much care about you, either. Get them to clear a path. Leon and I are driving out of here." Azeri's voice was urgent but Daley sensed the panic. Sirens echoed in the distance.

"And go where? You can hear them. Before long, this whole place will be swarming with coppers." Nervously, Daley took a pace forward, his hands open in front of him. "Look, Phil. Enough is enough. Give me the weapon now. I will guarantee to take you in myself."

Azeri started at the sound of the name. Reaching up, he dragged off the mask. Blushed and sweating, Dodds face broke out into a broad, defiant smile as he dragged Leon still closer.

Ray Kramer, tugged at Daley's trouser leg. "Leave it, Inspector. Leave it to the Firearms Team."

"Bloody Hell Ray. Rarely see you out of the office," shouted Dodds sarcastically.

Daley thrust a hand back. "Stay down, sir."

"Jesus, Phil! What are you doing?" From behind Daley, Kramer heaved himself to his feet. He was visibly shaking, his forehead glistening. What was it about senior officers that they couldn't take an order?

Kramer paced slowly forwards, utterly confused. "Christ, Phil. Just tell me why?"

"Come on, Ray. Get real. All we are doing is paying lip service to the problem. Containment rather than elimination. Me and my men are out there amongst the addicts and the tarts and all the filth and scum and for what? We are pissing in the wind. And now we are likely to be disbanded. When were you going to fight for us?"

"You know I am doing everything I can but it is out of my hands, Phil."

"Well, you weren't doing anything for us. You are more concerned with playing politics than looking out for your team. When was the last time you got your hands dirty, eh?"

"Ok, so I am not the best DCI but this?" Kramer's hand gestured pointlessly. Daley rolled his eyes and took a pace back as the pistol clicked in Dodds' hand.

"Do you know what my men have to look forward to, Ray? Broken marriages, kids on weekends—if they are not working. When the stress gets too much, most of them will leave and work in a DIY store or on nights patrolling a yard. The other half? They will end up in shop doorways with a needle in their arm. Drugs don't just kill the addicts. They kill everyone. Westsiders, Cjevovod, even us."

"So you thought you would get in on the action yourself." Daley had heard all the excuses why good coppers turn bad.

"Me? No, I can't take the credit for that. When we joined, Ray and I, the boys were already supplementing their wages. The odd kilo, chicken feed to McKaig and Bašić. Hustling dealers, passing on the gear, pocketing a few thousand here and there. I just ramped it up a little. If you can't beat 'em..."

"But why this whole charade with Urdin Azeri and the Westsiders?" asked Daley.

"Just a little fun, really—and it *was* fun, watching everyone chasing a ghost."

"And Joe and Dean?"

"They found out. I convinced them to turn a blind eye."

"So what changed?"

"MOPAC changed. If we were going to be disbanded, we needed to make hay while the sun shone. So we ramped things up. Unfortunately, Joe got arsey, so I got creative. Same with Dean. He and Joe were as thick as thieves."

"But Joe spoke to Professor Gascoigne?"

"Yeah. Ah, well." The smugness, the pride in his own cleverness was showing in Dodds voice. Daley could feel his dander rising.

"And how are you any better than the pushers and the pimps and the weirdos? I might not do everything by the book but deep down I believe in the system, however flawed, however cumbersome. If you don't like it, change it. Don't break it."

"Don't you preach to me, Daley. What has the Met ever done for you? Six months in therapy, off your face on tramadol and you have the nerve to criticise me?"

"Yes, Phil," barked Kramer. "He can criticise you and he isn't perfect. I am not perfect. Nobody is but this? To take a life. Six lives for God's sake. What have you become?"

"Fuck you, Ray. Fuck you Daley! Fuck the lot of you!"

Then there was a loud crack. A fist thumped at Daley's chest and the tarmac hit the back of his head. He heard another crack and Ray Kramer gasped. Suddenly Daley was suffocating as pain racked his ribs. In front of him, Fat Leon's head exploded. Then a dozen firecrackers sounded all around and the BMW reversed away, its engine screaming, spilling shimmering glass fragments onto the sunlit road.

Stars filled Daley's vision, and he gasped at the air. He felt the warm sticky stream of blood. He saw Kramer's expressionless eyes. He recalled the conversation with Terri. Some promises were made to be broken. Others were impossible to keep. Another time. Another place.

***

Diane Browning started as the sound of gunfire pricked the surrounding air. In her ear, someone barked commands, she heard the revving engine. She saw the BMW execute a textbook handbrake turn, avoiding the road block, leaping over a raised kerb and bursting through a fence onto the estate.

"Shots fired. Officers down. Two fatalities."

"Fuck, fuck, *fuck!*" Venting her frustration on the bonnet of the traffic car, she ignored the pain and waved at the driver. "Let's go. Now."

Through her ear she followed the chatter as the BMW disappeared deeper into the estate and its driver decamped. The bird had flown. In another tirade of expletives, she pulled out her earpiece and threw the radio into the footwell. In the rear-view mirror, eyes flicked anxiously over.

"Is everything all right, ma'am?"

"Just bloody drive will you."

Officers down. In her heart of hearts she hoped it was Scott Daley. He had always been too smart for his own good. Insolent and foolhardy, he deserved everything he got. In hindsight, involving Allenby's team had been a mistake. Far from bumbling along, they had actually stepped up to the plate. Even after they had warned off the sergeant, even after the attempt on his life, Daley just kept coming.

She had invested a great deal in Azeri and the Encubierto, covering their backs, helping them maintain their cover. In return, they had ensured that the violence escalated between the Westsiders and the Cjevovod. So, when she petitioned for more resources she got them, artificially bolstering her own command to stave off the dogs of MOPAC. Then, Dodds had stepped over the line. The two officers, Gordon and

Hewell, were needless casualties; he could easily have discredited them, had them kicked out of the force.

When Allenby finally succumbed to his heart attack, she felt rewarded for her persistence. Everybody knew it was coming yet these things are so unpredictable. All it needed was the right pressure exerted in the right place. With Daley and Dodds out of the way, Allenby certain to retire, that just left Ray Kramer to deal with. Now, Phil Dodds had seen to that himself. As for Dodds, he was on his own.

And so was she.

The way was now clear for Browning to set about her root-and-branch reform of the West London command. Yet in the cruelness of irony once again her trust in men had been betrayed. Once again, her future was in jeopardy.

Was thirty-eight too late to start again? To disappear off somewhere warm? Somewhere with no extradition treaty?

Finding her phone, she dialled her PA.

"I am afraid I won't be back in the office again today."

"You have an 11:30 with the Chief Constable."

"Call Roger. Tell him I am busy. He will have to wait, er, not in so many words...On second thoughts, Jean, rearrange all my appointments for the rest of the week." Then she leaned forward. "Constable, take me home. I will tell you the address."

With Dodds team in custody and Dodds himself on the run, there still may be a way out of this.

Chapter 101

With his chest aching, Phil Dodds paused and gasped at the air as his eyes adjusted to the blackness. The stench was putrid but at that moment he couldn't care less. With a helicopter overhead, he needed all the cover he could get. Five years ago, as a Detective Constable, he had found the body of a young girl in these sewers. Bound and gagged, her abductor had left her to die. Every cloud... Half a mile down the passage, the storm drain met the main rain water sewer. He had parked a car by a manhole, another hundred yards away. Dodds kept up an easy resounding canter, hearing the sibilant murmur of the underground stream growing closer. Then turning a corner, he made for the steel ladder fixed to the wall.

For close on twelve months, he had dreaded this day. The inevitable moment of discovery.

The affair with Diane Browning was a bad idea. Until then it had been a game. The CDIU could cover their tracks leaving the police one step behind. Until the MOPAC report, the inevitability of cut-backs, pillow talk and some rash promises made in the heat of the moment. Then, over a pizza and a pint, he had watched *The Usual Suspects*, the mysterious Keyser Söze, everywhere but invisible. Urdin Azeri and the Encubierto were born. Appearing out of nowhere, disappearing into the shadows. All the time, keeping one eye over their shoulders. By then the team had thought like a drugs firm. They ramped up activities. Properties bought, cars stolen, cash laundered and salted away.

When Gordon and Hewell got jumpy, Dodds had dealt with it. That's when it got serious.

Of course, he had hidden his tracks. Ray Kramer was as thick as pig shit and, even with a map and mountain guide, would have seen nothing. So he and his team had pressed on, watching the fun kick off between McKaig and Bašić. But still

Browning needed more. Not content with a feud, she needed a war. Something to guarantee her resources. Something to make them indispensable. Reluctantly, Dodds hit on the idea of torching the warehouse. As it turned out his fears were justified when Parrish recognised him. Like Gordon and Hewell, he had promised to keep his mouth shut then reneged.

It was the appointment of Daley to investigate the Gordon and Hewell murders that spelled the beginning of the end. Since then, he had waited for a knock at the door. Diane Browning, planning her exit. Duplicitous to the last. Reversing away from Fat Leon's body, he had caught sight of Daley and Kramer, the blood pool spreading. So, just how good a shot was he?

Easing open the manhole cover, Dodds peered out at the small car park. Five years earlier, a killer had escaped this way and never been caught. Now he would follow his example.

The car was cheap and inconspicuous, bought and never re-registered. Retrieving the keys from a magnetic box under the wheel arch, Dodds climbed inside, closed the door and exhaled heavily. It smelt of tobacco and sweat, an air-freshener dangling from the mirror had long since given up. In the glove-box, he rummaged around until he found the wallet— money, cards, all in a different name.

Now all he needed to do was reach the garage in Neasden. First, however, he needed to do a little tidying up.

Chapter 102

Kenning Autos, Neasden

Asking the traffic car to drop her off in an adjacent street, Diane Browning took an alley between two houses and found her way to the back of Kenning Autos. Pausing, she listened, hearing only the roaring of her breath, a rustle in the trees and her heart playing a heavy metal drum solo. Inside the pneumatic pump fired up automatically then went silent. Lifting a broken slab, recoiling as ants swarmed over the flattened damp soil, she gingerly reached for the muddy key.

Unlike Ray Kramer, Phil Dodds was a master tactician. He had known from the start that the Encubierto would have a limited lifespan. She knew he would make provision for the day when he needed to cut and run. Somewhere there was a stash of drugs and cash and her best hope was to find it before he did. But throughout the seduction, through the torrid nights and careless pillow talk, not once had he told her where it was.

The garage, vast, untidy and cluttered, was her best guess.

Opening the side door, the musty air in the small grubby office prickled her nose. Edging carefully through the confusion of paperwork, past the desk, she peered out through the glass partition into the workshop. There was no sign of life. Still and empty, it was the perfect place to hide something important.

A thud broke the silence and, turning her head, Browning watched a weak slit of light pulse through the messroom door. Had the boys left it ajar in their haste to leave? Quietly she made her way across the concrete, rolling her heels. Then her hackles rose as she saw the hasp on the floor and ran her fingers over the wood, torn and splintered.

***

Reaching the top floor of the terraced house in Carrs Lane, Dodds unlocked the bedroom that had served as the Encubierto base since Easter. A weak bulb cast a yellow glow over the room and the odour of last night's takeaway lingered. He imagined the bustle and noise. Data tumbling onto screens, Chris Morrison, Amil Kapour and Simon Ward chattering between themselves. The hive of activity as they tracked vans on the huge laminated map, red pins and blue pins, hurried calls to scramble, baseball bats and masks, the overdose of adrenaline.

Putting down the can of petrol, Dodds set about each of the computers, quickly unscrewing the cases and removing the hard drives. Then he doused the fuel liberally around. With wistful affection, he thought of the tattered leather chair, of evenings of camaraderie, bawdy, blokcy conversations. He would miss all that.

Watching as the yellow flames flicked and crackled, Dodds tossed in the can, pocketed the hard drives and left.

***

Something was not right.

Browning strained to hear through the messroom door but apart from the chirrup of a battery wall clock there was nothing.

Backtracking, she found a large heavy wrench. Forewarned is forearmed. Through the gap around the door, the space was squalid and anodyne. A melamine table, five plastic chairs and a bank of five tall lockers the only furniture. A saucy calendar the only decoration. A kitchenette screamed out for a rag and some bleach, upturned cups, probably dirtier than before they were washed. The same enduring odour of grease and grime, now mixed with rancid fat. Holding her breath, she pushed through the door but the room was empty.

So why was the lock broken?

Out in the main workshop, a loud metallic clank made her start. The roller shutters whirred into action, a horizon of sunlight swimming across the floor and she watched as a figure stood silhouetted against the mid-morning sunshine.

Chapter 103

Browning watched Phil Dodds enter. He carried a hold-all in his left hand. In his right, the Heckler & Koch USP. Taking a brief anxious look around, he headed towards the dark, cramped storeroom. Through the office, the external door gaped wide. Had he noticed? Did he know someone else was in there with him?

With his description being circulated across London, Browning knew there could be only one reason Dodds would risk coming to the garage. He had come for the Encubierto cache. Her best move was to let him find it.

Edging across the workshop, she heard the scraping of wood across the storeroom floor as Dodds heaved a shelving unit aside and removed a loose panel from the wall. Then under the dim yellow bulb, he removed neatly bundled piles of notes, stuffing them into the holdall. In front of her, next to the door, the gun lay on a Dexion shelf.

Presently, the holdall bulging, Dodds stood and carried it across the workshop. Then realising he had forgotten the gun, he turned back.

"Going somewhere, Phil?"

Dodds spun round and gasped as he saw the barrel of the Heckler & Koch. "Diane? Look, this has gone far enough. I want out. I'm just here to take my cut and then I'm gone."

"What about me? What about my cut or were you going to abandon me?"

"You can keep the coke. There are around thirty bricks in a cupboard over there." Dodds waved a dismissive finger toward the back wall. "I only want the cash."

"What the hell use is cocaine to me?" Browning cocked the trigger. "I am in this as much as you. I deserve my share."

Dodds puffed. "It's always the same with you, Diane, isn't it? Power. You need to have the upper hand. I have taken all the risks here. You can just lock yourself in your office at New Scotland Yard and keep a low profile until all of this goes away. What is there to connect you to the Encubierto? Nothing."

"Oh, come on Phil. You had your chance. You could have pulled out any time. Azeri and the Encubierto could have just vanished as quickly as they appeared. Nobody asked you to turn West London into a slaughterhouse."

"Seriously? *Critical shot authorised?* You were prepared to let them kill me out there."

"You were waving this bloody gun around. You left me no choice. As it was, three people ended up being shot, countless more in the attacks. Anyway, how did you expect this all to play out? With your team in custody, it will only be a matter of time before the trail leads back to me and I need to be long gone before that happens. Now, slide the bag over."

Eyes on the gun, Dodds lowered the bag, placed a foot against the side and pushed, smiling as the bag scudded weakly across the dirty concrete, making only half the distance.

"We'll take it from here, ma'am." As one, Browning and Dodds wheeled around. Unsteadily, Scott Daley held on to the office door. His face and clothes were matted with blood and he was wheezing heavily. Beside him, Corby was on his mobile.

"I thought you..." Dodds' eyes were wide, confused. Browning returned her attention to the gun.

Tapping the ballistics vest, Daley smiled. "Marvellous stuff this Kevlar, though I think it may have finished off a rib or two. Mind you, I can't say the same about Ray Kramer. You can add him to your tally."

Browning was stepping backwards, the gun still held high. "Thank God you're here, Inspector. I don't know how much longer I could keep him at bay."

Daley smiled and turned briefly to Corby, who nodded. "There's another unit on its way ma'am. Shouldn't be too long. I just want to get Inspector Dodds' take on a few things first."

"What are you going on about, Daley?" barked Browning. "Read him his rights and take him away."

But Daley quite enjoyed the *Poirot* moments and was not to be diverted.

"The thing that has always puzzled me was how Azeri and the Encubierto knew so much? How could they second guess the Westsiders and the Cjevovod? Well, they couldn't. When we checked the CCTV footage, when we saw the trackers being removed, it started to make sense. It had to be someone who was sufficiently well resourced that they could monitor phones and vehicles. So well connected that they could infiltrate the two gangs, plant trackers and learn their plans. Narrows the field, eh, Phil?"

Dodds stood impassive, calculating the distance between himself and the door. Whether he could grab the handle on the bag. Daley was incapacitated, no threat. Like all senior officers, Browning had received firearms training but how good a shot was she?

Daley continued: "You know Patrick Gascoigne had worked it out, don't you? He linked the bullet that killed Gordon to Alicia Sheldon but records showed that PC Parrish had taken the gun from Cheveley Hill. However, Phil, the log entries were in your handwriting. He must have discovered that *after* he had spoken to you. After he had revealed that he knew."

Dodds shrugged indifferently. "He should have kept his nose out."

"But did you have to kill him?" Daley's bruised ribs tightened as he felt the anger rise.

"I admit I fired the shot but the crash...? Like you the other day, I hoped he would take the warning, keep shtum. Instead, he swerved off the road."

"To avoid a fox." Daley smiled at the irony. The coroner had surmised that an animal had spooked Gascoigne. How close he had been!

"Even then Patrick Gascoigne was the key. Without him, I was floundering in the dark but he left me a cryptic message:

The blue fox jumps over the lazy wolf, the bear and the boar to please the ambitious vixen.

All the time the rabbit was watching.

Now the blue fox has pounced on the rabbit and he is no more.

"I got the Bear and the Boar straight away. Danilo Bašić and Paisley John McKaig. And the rabbit? Joe Gordon. He was the one watching. Funnily enough, it wasn't until that day we discussed football I knew for sure. Leicester City - *The Foxes*, Wolverhampton Wanderers - *The Wolves*. He was leading me directly to you and Ray. Then you mentioned Spain, Bilbao. I can't believe I took so long to work out that Azeri is the *Basque* for 'fox'. Encubierto is the Spanish for 'covert'. *The blue fox jumps over the lazy wolf.* Did Ray Kramer know anything about what you and your team were doing?"

Dodds sneered derisively. "Of course not. Kramer couldn't wipe his arse without help. We faked reports to cover our tracks."

"Bloody hell, Daley. Do we have to do this here?" Browning's arms were shaking, her fingers quivering on the trigger.

"Shouldn't be too long now, ma'am."

"Get your man to ask them to hurry." Diane Browning glanced nervously at Daley then back at Dodds. Her eyes betrayed her fear. She motioned at Dodds with the gun. "You, push the bag over. Slowly."

"Then there's the vixen. I spent ages on that one. '*To please the ambitious vixen*'. When exactly did you find out what the Drugs Unit were up to— ma'am? I'm guessing it was around the start of April when the gun was lifted from evidence. Before Joe Gordon was shot?"

Diane Browning was breathing heavily. "Push the bag to me. Now!"

"MOPAC was threatening all our jobs, so you hatched a plan to keep the crime levels artificially high. Just in your area." He reached out a hand towards Browning. "Ma'am. It's over. Give me the gun."

As Dodds reached for the hold-all, Daley shouted "Leave it, Phil!" Then, borrowing a phrase from Murdoch, he asked "So, Diane. What do you want to happen here?"

But Browning had not thought that far ahead. She motioned at Dodds. "Your car? Where are the keys?" Dodds tossed a set of keys across, disappointed that she caught them easily. "Ok," she continued. "You and I are going for little ride." Advancing, she spun Dodds around and rammed the gun into the small of his back. Then she grabbed the hold-all.

Daley scratched his head. "Well, it worked for you earlier, Phil, but it's not quite the same this time, eh?" Reaching out a lazy finger, he pointed. "Diane, the gun is empty."

"You think I am that stupid?" Dodds yelped as Browning pulled his arm tight across his back.

"You just have to count up the shots. The original bullet that killed Alicia Sheldon. There's Gordon, Gascoigne, Hewell, Parrish. Then there was Irina, the prostitute and the bullet that missed my sergeant. Add in the one that hit Ray and the one lodged in my vest and I think that's a full magazine. Mind you, I never was great at maths."

"You're bluffing."

Daley shrugged, painfully. "Check for yourself. Go ahead. Pull the trigger."

"Bloody Hell, Daley!" Dodds' eyes were wide as he tried in vain to free himself.

"Think about it, Phil. With you out of the way, I am just blowing so much hot air. Anything the Encubierto say can be refuted. Might be difficult for a month or two but the ACC could tough it out, I am sure. Might even be a gong for catching the elusive Urdin Azeri."

"Really, Inspector. This is your negotiation technique? Shoot the hostage?" Smiling, she swung the gun towards Daley. "There is more than enough cash for Dodds and I to disappear. Then neither of us will have a difficult couple of months."

"So shoot then. Come on." Behind Daley, Corby ducked further into the office. *Suicide Scott Daley* at his finest. Outside, a symphony of sirens began in the distance. The barrel of the gun scribed an arc in front of Daley's face.

"I will pull the trigger! I will." Behind Browning, the door to the mess room opened a little wider.

"Be my guest." Daley wondered, given the state of his rib cage, how quickly he could duck.

Then there was a click. Browning's eyes grew wide, and she pulled the trigger again and again. Frantically she checked the safety catch and tried again. Still nothing. With a guttural roar, she lobbed the gun at Daley. He ducked. Not quickly enough as it happened. With a loud crash, Whetstone launched herself through the messroom door and together she and Diane Browning tumbled to the floor. Phil Dodds fell backward with a groan, grabbing the handle on the hold-all. Then he made for the gaping mess room door.

Chapter 104

In the back of the ambulance, a paramedic attended to Daley's forehead, confused why so much blood should have resulted from so small a wound. As Deborah Whetstone held the evidence bag containing the Heckler & Koch USP and turned it over in her hands, she struggled to associate it with the death of Keith Parrish but couldn't. Unloaded, safety catch on, it was benign, almost pleasurable to hold.

"Bloody Hell, sir! What were you thinking? Did it not occur to you he might have reloaded it between raids?"

Daley smiled ruefully. "Had to hope that he hadn't. I had also forgotten the bullet he used on Fat Leon. Actually, I was counting on the ACC not to pull the trigger. Slight misjudgement there too. You won't tell Terri, will you?"

"You better hope she doesn't find out otherwise you'll wish there had been a bullet in the gun. Mind you, the way the grapevine works, I am sure she already knows."

Daley frowned, wincing as the paramedic dabbed something sharp onto his open wound. "Any sign of Dodds?"

"No, gov. Traffic found the car a few streets away. We are circulating a description. He won't get far."

But Daley wasn't so sure. "If he can mount an operation like this, in secret, under our noses for twelve months, I am sure he can evade a few plods. Anyway, It's a whole new ball-game for him now. With his face plastered over every airport, port and railway station from here to Australia, I am sure he won't be on the run for long."

EPILOGUE

Harrow, 5:30pm, 28th June 2013

Waving off the removals van, Daley sat on the front step of the new house in Harrow letting the coolness of the evening brush his face. Two weeks on from the raid in Drayton Green, his ribs had stopped hurting, unless he inadvertently rolled over in bed. The dinner plate sized bruise on his chest would be there for some time yet. Still, the removals men had been good enough to place what little furniture he had in the appropriate rooms in exchange for cash. They had unloaded the boxes along with the rest of Daley's meagre belongings into the front room. Without the contents of Terri's home, the new place looked spartan and empty.

The Force's quack had insisted that he took at least a month for his ribs to heal, which he had not. After three days kicking around an empty house in Alperton, waiting for Terri to call, he headed into Lambourne Road to bury himself in the pile of case reviews Browning had left him. They had also signed Deborah Whetstone off. Suffering only a few bumps and bruises, her psychological injuries were much deeper. After much persuasion, she called Sophie Jennings, Daley's shrink, before disappearing off for a fortnight in the Mediterranean. In contrast, Bob Allenby was unlikely to return. Out of danger, he was convalescing at home. The doctors had revised their prognosis and suggested that he could be on the greens before Christmas.

Back in April, the Mayor of London had demanded cuts to middle tiers of the Metropolitan Police Service, however Daley surmised that it was not his intention to have them all arrested or killed. Eight members of the Hillingdon Covert Drugs Intelligence Unit were in a secure unit awaiting trial. Diane Browning was also on remand and likely to be there for some time. The cruel irony, as Chief Constable Roger Summerhill had pointed out, was that it more or less confirmed Browning's fears. An even crueller twist was that the Mayor's Office decided to review MOPAC in the coming months and would likely water down their savage cuts. Awaiting an interim lead, Chief Constable Roger Summerhill had been forced to cancel his leave, which went down like a hippopotamus in an elevator. Daley had assumed the mantle of Acting Chief Inspector and tried his best to manage the newly combined Drugs and Homicide team.

After the raid in Drayton Green, Dougie Murdoch and the rest of the Westsiders spent only a few hours in police custody before being released without charge. A thorough search of the lockups, along with the vans and drivers, had yielded nothing. Not so much as a suspicious roll-up. Of the ten vans, five were empty. The remaining five carried fancy goods and cleaning products. No one was armed nor were any weapons found. As Murdoch had ruefully suggested during questioning, it was almost as if someone had tipped them off beforehand, though for the life of him, Daley could not think who could have set up such a sting.

Of course, Paisley John McKaig and Danilo Bašić had resumed their reluctant detente. With the Encubierto behind bars, Daley felt their businesses would return to normal, preferring to remain uncomfortable neighbours than mortal enemies. Daley laid down markers, promising them much closer scrutiny once everything had blown over but he knew that there was little he could practically do to eradicate them completely. That would fall to whomever they persuaded to take over the new Drugs Intelligence Unit.

Much to Daley's dismay, Phil Dodds was still at large. Despite his description being circulated widely, there was still no sign. It was a loose end which he felt sure would resolve itself one way or the other, given time. There were more important issues on Daley's mind right now.

Since the raid at Drayton Green, Daley had seen little of Terri Somerville. Hospitalised overnight, ashamed for once more putting himself in the way of danger, he had kept a low profile for much of the following week before venturing a call. Even then her phone went to voicemail. When they finally talked, it was an edgy, terse conversation. Naturally, she had heard about the foolhardy sting operation, about Daley stepping into the line of fire not once but twice in a single day. She was asking herself some serious questions about her relationship with him. There were choices to make, not just for herself but for her baby.

When they had met, become a couple, even in its loosest sense, Daley had agonised over whether it was fair to put her through the ordeal to which he had subjected Lynne. His ex-wife was now out of his life but she had always been a widow to his work, a neglected island in the busy sea-routes of Homicide and Serious Crime, eventually finding solace elsewhere. He had hoped the experience had taught him a lesson. But for change to complete, not only must one set the sails but the wind must hold a favourable direction. The mistakes were his to rectify. The ball was in his court.

So Daley threw himself into his work. Meetings with the Chief Constable kept him occupied and away from his phone. Afternoons with Bob Allenby, chewing the fat, learning the ropes, provided a diversion.

He looked up as a blue BMW drove into the Close, his heart skipping a beat until he realised it was a different model, watching as it parked on the drive opposite. The driver looked across and waved a hand. Harrow was a stark contrast to Alperton where he hardly knew his neighbours. Checking his watch, finishing his tea, Daley stood and stretched the cramp from his legs. Soon, Terri would arrive with the second removals van. He needed to order take-away.

***

Plentzia, Biscay, Spain. August

Despite the south-westerly scouring the parched hillside, the veranda held the relentless heat of summer, along with the flies and mosquitos. Phil Dodds emptied the remains of his mojito and ran a hand over his neck. Each time he came out here, the heat took him by surprise. His fair skin seemed to attract the insects and this year they had bitten him half to death. Inside, Anna-Maria was sewing a costume for the festival of Aste Nagusia, which was set to pack Bilbao in the coming days. Ordinarily, Dodds loved the carnival atmosphere, the long days and the general air of abandon. This year, he needed solitude. He needed thinking time.

"Anna-Maria. Voy a bajar al puerto para revisar el barco." *I am going down to the harbour to check out the boat.*

Throwing his arms around her, he kissed her neck. "Regresaré a las 5:00pm." *I'll be back for 5:00pm.*

"No olvides mis aceitunas y trae de vuelta una pizza." *Don't forget my olives and bring back a pizza.*

"Si, si, si, querida," and he kissed her once more.

With Anna-Maria already in Spain, he only had himself to consider after escaping through the fire door behind the garage. The EU guaranteed free movement of people and a few grand guaranteed a boatman who would ask no questions. The bogus passport guaranteed anonymity. Avoiding main roads, after ten days driving he had made it to Plentzia, to Anna-Maria and her family's finca.

Pulling the Seat off the Areatza Hiribidea, alongside an ice cream kiosk, Dodds flicked five fingers at the vendor - *five minutes*. The immense marina clicked to the tune of a hundred lines blown by the wind as the boats bobbed and slopped at their moorings. Beyond, the harbour gave way to the muddy estuary, shallow and winding, a danger to the unwary. Here the fresh ocean breeze cooled the sun; the salty air keeping the insects away. Dodds stood and breathed in the ozone.

Suddenly, apropos of nothing, he recalled Ray Kramer lying on the tarmac at Drayton Green as the side window of the BMW shattered inwards and he hammered the throttle. Some nights, he could still hear Fat Leon hurriedly whispering the Lord's Prayer. Sometimes, out of the corner of his eye, he thought he saw Scott Daley.

Soon he would need to find somewhere else.

The *Eliza B* was berthed on the furthest boardwalk. Anna-Maria's family were wealthy but not enough to afford a more sheltered spot. Dodds was looking forward to taking her for a spin once the festival was over, heading out into the bay, enjoying the calmer seas before the winter tides roared in from the Atlantic. Perhaps he would head North to La Rochelle, perhaps closer. Anna-Maria loved Biarritz.

Checking the moorings, tugging the ropes, Dodds hopped onto the deck and ran a hand along the furled mainsail before finding the key and disappearing into the cabin. He had secreted the holdall beneath a bunk, in the void where bedding was stowed. The money was all still there, apart from that used for his fare over. Until he moved on, he had no need of it.

Two hundred yards away, Dougie Murdoch started, even though he knew it was about to happen. The brightness of the flash, the instant blast of heat and air, and the mushroom cloud of orange and black. He had to hand it to Inspector Daley. He had been as good as his word. The sting was excellent. The last-minute change of plans, swapping the loads to innocuous goods from the warehouses. Ten vans, all unarmed and not a sniff of anything illegal between them. Of course, Murdoch had kept that fact from everyone, especially Paisley John.

As the clitter-clatter of shrapnel rained down, he raised his glass of gassy European beer. "This one's for you, Leon."

Beside him, Paisley John McKaig pocketed the small radio transmitter and also raised his glass.

"Fat Leon. Rest in peace, big man."

Dear Reader.

Thanks for taking the time to read this, the third in The Daley and Whetstone Crime Story series. I hope you enjoyed it.

If you would like to find out more about my other books then please visit my website for full details.

www.ryanstarkauthor.co.uk

If you enjoyed this book and would like to help, then maybe you could leave a review on Amazon?

Leave a Review

The most important part of how well a book sells is how many positive reviews it has. Some of the best books never see the light of day; some of the worst are bought in their millions. So, if you leave a review then you are directly helping me to continue on this journey as a full-time writer.

Hopefully I can continue to entertain you.

Thanks. It means a lot.

Ryan Stark

ABOUT THE AUTHOR

Austen Gower spent his working life as a Business and IT Consultant. He has been commissioned to write technical works on topics as diverse as programming, networking, communications, project management and anger management, for which he has several published articles.

Writing as Ryan Stark, *Unnatural Selection* is Austen Gower's third work of fiction.

Austen lives in Redditch, Worcestershire. He is married, with two grown-up children.

In a cruel twist, his current car is a deep sea metallic blue BMW. However, it is not a 520i.

www.ryanstarkauthor.co.uk

Made in the USA
Columbia, SC
11 February 2020